The Tsimbalist

a novel

The Tsimbalist

a novel

by

Sasha Margolis

Ode Ode Man Press

ISBN 978-0-9970601-0-2

Cover Art by Dunja Pelto
Cover design by Eli Rosenbloom
Interior design by David Moratto

Published by
Ode Ode Man Press
NY, NY

www.thetsimbalist.com

To my parents

Contents

Cast of Characters

≈

People of Balativke

Avrom, the tsimbalist
Koppel, his neighbor
Blume, Koppel's oldest daughter
Zlata, Koppel's second-oldest daughter
Yoysif, Koppel's son
Berl Melamed, Balativke's Hebrew school teacher
Rivke, a neighbor

People of Zavlivoya

Deacon Achilles, a priest at St. Vladimir's; full name, Akhilla
   Gerasimovich
Dovid Lipkin, Blume's betrothed
Moishe Shakhes, leader of the Klezmer band
Itskele, his youngest son
Kuz'ma, Russian bass player in the Klezmer band
Anton Antonovich Skorokhodov-Druganin, Zavlivoya's petty-
   governor
Doctor Artiukhov, a physician of Zavlivoya
Nikifor Kharitonovich Taktakov, Zavlivoya's police chief
Faddei Kazimirovich, "the Pole," a constable
Svistunov, a constable
Ukhovyortov, a constable

Father Innokenty, head priest at St. Vladimir's
Mirele, an orphan
Yudel Beck, a tavern-keeper
Parfyon Panteleyevich, a pensioner
Lev Grinberg, a wealthy merchant
Izrael Feldshteyn, a jeweler
Yasha, a horse trader
Khana Lipkin, Dovid's mother
Nison Vainberg, a tavern-keeper

People of the surrounding area

Agrafena Ivanovna Efimovskaya, a noblewoman
Oleg Olegovich Efimovski, or **Olezha,** her older son
Aglaya Olegovna, or **Aglayushka,** her daughter
Arkady Olegovich, or **Arkasha** or **Arkashenka,** her younger son
General Kondratin, a retired military man
Saveli Savelyevich, a wealthy merchant
Tatiana Savelyevna, his daughter
Marfa, the Efimovski housekeeper
Styopa, son of Marfa the housekeeper
Foka, an old servant of the Efimovskis
Shimmel Shenkman, tavern-keeper at the Efimovski village
Gitl-Golda, tavern-keeper in the north village
Andryushechka, a peasant of the Efimovski village, Styopa's
  cousin

Others

The Kelmer Maggid, a famous Jewish preacher
Vitaly Valentinovich Pugovitsin, a visitor
Lemel, Zusman, and **Selig,** three Lithuanian Jewish merchants
Anshel Pempik, a traveler

A Note on Tsimbls
and Tsimbalists

This novel is called *The Tsimbalist*. Since *tsimbalist* is not a word found in a great many dictionaries, it might be helpful to begin with a definition: a tsimbalist is someone who plays the tsimbl ...

Which leads to another definition: a tsimbl is a musical instrument, a member of the dulcimer family. It consists of a trapezoidal wooden box strung with metal strings, played on with sticks likewise made of wood. The tsimbl produces a haunting sound which, in these latter days, evokes a faraway time and place.

Among the Jews of nineteenth-century Russia, the tsimbl was an indispensable element of the klezmer band, a musical ensemble itself indispensable for weddings of the time. According to one Yiddish proverb, "a wedding without musicians is like a funeral without tears"; while according to another, "a wedding without musicians is worse than a bride without a dowry."

In those days, weddings were more than just simple, short ceremonies. They lasted days, and included all kinds of rituals, capped with hours upon hours of dancing. Not just the dancing, but the rituals too, were accompanied by the klezmer band.

It may thus be seen that the tsimbl was fundamental to Jewish life of the time — just as a certain tsimbl-playing protagonist is fundamental to the story that follows.

Chapter 1

What Was in the Lake

The day was hot, and exasperatingly slow. Inside the little house, the air was sweltering, every breath coming like a sigh, though it was only early June. The sun had refused for hours to drop any lower in the sky, and was casting a blinding light over the lake, while off to the left and right of the house, the dense thickets of birch were utterly motionless, the trees' slender trunks and delicate leaves unstirred by any hint of life or breath. As for the yard, which ordinarily was no better than a bog: it had managed to bake itself since just this morning into a fine yellow crust, broken only, here and there, by a few hopeless clumps of colorless grass.

Little Yoysif was squatting out there, poking holes in the ground with a rusty wheel-spoke he'd turned up from somewhere or other. If he'd had a mother, she would have scolded him: his legs were covered in mud. Meanwhile, his six sisters remained indoors, in the house's back room, where one tiny square window looked out past the yard onto the water. Through this they could see, not more than ten *arshins* from shore, but submerged nearly up to her great, terrified eyes, Masha, the family cow. She'd gotten stuck in the lake again.

It was hardly the first time. The poor, foolish thing had got herself unhitched and marooned at least three times before — the first when mother was still alive. Back then — it was a hot day, just like today — Masha had wandered into the water to cool off, and when she hadn't been able to get out, Mama had waded in. She'd put her slim arms around the cow's neck, and pulled and pulled. But it was no use. The lake bottom was too muddy, and Masha, too big and heavy.

Next, with Mama still out in the water, Blume, the oldest of the girls, had gone to fetch a rope (since Father was out working in the forest, as he used to do back then, before he had to take charge of milking the cow and making the butter and cheese, not to mention the many other duties more properly carried out by a mother than a father.) Mama managed to slip a loop of rope around Masha's neck. Then *all* of them pulled and pulled. But that was no use either.

The whole thing, in fact, had seemed nearly hopeless, until their neighbor, Avrom the Tsimbalist, happened to wander by. When he saw what was happening, he fixed things up in the blink of an eye — which was a relief, but not a surprise, because, even though the tsimbalist was a very quiet type, or at least quiet when he wasn't playing on his tsimbl, at the same time, when he put his mind to doing something, it was sure to get done.

And that was the case this time, too: good Avrom went around their entire village of Balativke (which was really not much more than a collection of ramshackle huts squeezed, lengthwise, between the forest and the lake.) Within half an hour, twenty fellow villagers showed up, all of them sinking to their boots in the boggy yard. Even Deacon Achilles the priest came, though he was no Jew and didn't, strictly speaking, belong to their village, but lived one *verst* to the south along the lake. On the other hand, Deacon Achilles, as much as anyone, was already well-acquainted with Masha and her troubles.

The deacon, who was practically a cossack, was very fond of horses, and always had one or two in a little corral next to his house. Not only that, he had a nice, grassy pasture for grazing them. For hours on end, he would sprawl on a post at one corner of his corral, admiring his latest pinto, chewing on a straw or whistling. And that's where he was sitting one day, about a year before the cow's first adventure into the lake, when who should trudge by but Mama and Masha?

The deacon had seen them going past every day for a while now, and somehow or other he knew just where they were headed: to a bit of pasture-land three whole *versts* away, which back then was the closest place the family could find to graze the cow. Now, as Mama went by, he called out in his booming low voice, without any preamble: "Off to the pasture then?"

Mama stopped in surprise, and, pulling away a flap of babushka that had fallen over her face, approached. Hesitantly at first — since not only was Achilles a Christian priest, but also a real giant, approaching three *arshins* in height, with legs like tree trunks and a long black braid going halfway down his back — she answered, "Y-yes." (The girls still laughed at the memory of Mama imitating the priest's deep voice and slow speech, but in the event, she was as shy as could be.)

"Hmm — " continued Achilles. "Hard, it must be ... taking the cow such a long way ... every day ..."

"Why ... well ..." replied Mama.

"Awful lot of time it must take ... going back and forth like that ..."

"No ... not ..."

Finally, Deacon Achilles got to the point: Mightn't she want to — if she'd like — mightn't she like to graze the cow here? On his land?

But ... "No." She couldn't.

And why not?

"Well ..."

For a good ten minutes, she hemmed, while the deacon hawed. But in the end (how could she say no?) she accepted his offer. Ever since, the family had taken Masha to graze at the deacon's.

Mama decided after the fact that this too, the deacon's generosity, must have been the work of Avrom the Tsimbalist. After all, he and the priest were friends, of a kind. Deacon Achilles was well-known for his singing voice, and liked to come, afternoons, here to Balativke, and belt out Russian songs, while Avrom accompanied him on his tsimbl. You could hear it all up and down the shore, just like if it was in your own yard — especially when the water was very, very still. It must have been on one of those afternoons that Avrom put it into the priest's ear to take pity on poor Mama.

Ah, how much did they have to thank the tsimbalist for! That first time that Masha got stuck, and all the subsequent times too ... thanks to Avrom, and with everyone lending a hand, the cow — praised be the Master of the Universe — just popped straight out of the water, and onto land.

If only Avrom could so easily help them out of their many troubles this time!

~

Meanwhile, the girls' father had been out of sight most of the day, closeted in the front room while they occupied the back. Now, they heard the whine of the outside door opening, and then closing. A moment later, their father appeared in the yard.

What a mess he looked! His shirt was untucked on one side and bunched up on the other, exposing his pale skin, his yarmulke had slipped nearly as far down as his left ear, while his black hair stuck straight up on top. At the same time, his forehead was burning red as paprika, his eyes had turned nearly the same shade, while an enormous hole was opening up in his bushy black beard as he shouted out with breaking voice, "Masha! Masha! Masha!" — each repetition coming out higher, and the last syllable crawling entirely down into his throat, so that he choked on it. He looked on the verge of breaking down altogether.

Until he caught sight of Yoysif. Then, very suddenly, his whole demeanor changed. His hunched-up shoulders fell. His closely clenched brows and nose and lips drew apart. His face took on a most tender expression indeed, as he joined the boy, bending gently beside him and talking in low tones.

The girls couldn't hear what he was saying. But they could guess without any words. First Tatte (that was what they called their father) pointed appreciatively at the holes the boy had made. Then he pinched his son's cheek. He pointed one thick finger at his muddy legs, wagged the same appendage in good-natured reproach. Finally, always with the same finger, he gestured toward the lake.

Yoysif turned toward the water, then shook his head and looked stubbornly down again, continuing to move the half-buried spoke in wide, uneven circles.

Next, with his enormous, clumsy hand, Tatte grasped the boy's other arm, the one not holding the wheel-spoke, and pulled him to a standing position — but very gently, mind you. Gesturing toward the lake again, he reached for the spoke. But this made Yoysif shake his head even more violently back and forth, and clasp the thing close to his ribs, sticking out his lip for good measure.

Tatte let out a deep sigh, but what else could he do? He picked the boy up in one brawny arm, spoke and all, and carried him over to the water, with Yoysif kicking his legs furiously and opening his mouth wide as could be, in a long, silent wail. Then Tatte did something unexpected: he walked into the water himself. Shoes, socks, trousers, no matter: he walked

right in and sat right down, and Yoysif in his lap. The wailing
stopped as suddenly as it had started. The boy grinned, slid off
his father's lap. A moment later, his toy forgotten, he was pad-
dling around in the water.

And while the boy paddled, Tatte — or Koppel, as we should
name him now, since that is what he was called by everyone but
his girls — Koppel crawled out of the lake, and collapsed on the
ground. He let out a groan, looked up at the sky, and as he lay,
he began to move his lips, inaudibly at first, and then with
sound giving voice to his words.

"*Lehko doidi likras kale,*" he was saying. "Come my beloved,
to meet the bride, to welcome the Sabbath." The words belonged to a prayer — but Koppel wasn't saying them in a prayer-
ful way. His voice came out like broken glass.

"There are all kinds of brides, aren't there?" he asked the
air. "For example, my Blume. She's supposed to be a bride, and
in less than a week, too. Or *was* supposed to be — may she live
and be well. But of course," he raised both hands in the air, in a
gesture of reasonableness, his voice dulling a little, "there's no
doubt about it. The Sabbath is also a bride. And, as the proverb
says, *a khisoren di kale iz tsu sheyn.* Only a fault-finder com-
plains that the bride is too beautiful."

He clasped his upraised hands to the sides of his head.

"Believe me, Merciful Father," Koppel's voice trembled
with sincerity, "I don't wish to be a fault-finder. On the other
hand, isn't it just possible that sometimes even the most beautiful bride begins to grow a little tiresome to her wedding guests?
For example, my neighbor Avrom told me last summer he
played at a wedding that went past eleven in the morning. The
band had already played "Walking Home the Bride and Groom"
twice, and the "Good Morning Song" three times, but that
didn't stop the bride from twisting the guests' arms to buy one
more dance, and then one more after that and one more after

that. A bride is a bride, but isn't it also true that a pig remains a pig? In other words, please tell me, and don't hold back, O You whose Name I am unworthy even of pronouncing: Am I a fault-finder? Or do I have a right, now and then, to find fault where fault really exists?"

If Koppel was hoping for a mighty voice out of the sky to answer him, he was disappointed. Instead, there came a light splash of water. He sat up quickly. His son had come to the water's edge to present a rock for his father's inspection.

Koppel took the rock in hand. "Very nice. How did you find such a nice rock? Now go and scrub your legs."

The boy shook his head, a look of mischief in his eyes, and, scraping off some of the mud that still clung to his leg, stuck it on his father's nose — then ran back into the water and paddled off. Koppel, rubbing away the mud with the back of his hand, turned his eyes heavenward.

"Now before you answer, *Gottenyu*, just consider: Is it not the case that, on every other Sabbath, I am the first to rejoice and to thank You for this world You have made us, and for the day of rest You have given us? Do I not refrain, on each and every Sabbath, from engaging in any work, any kneading, baking, sewing of stitches, kindling of fire, or any of the other thirty-nine categories of prohibited activities? For example" — and here a wily expression entered Koppel's eyes — "do I ever bring outside of the house any object?"

He said this last with an innocent air, as if not overly concerned with the answer. Then he pounced.

"For example, Master of the Universe, do I ever bring out of the house — a rope? A rope, such as I would need to pull this cursed cow out of the lake? My teeth should all fall out but one, and that one should ache, if ever I bring out from my house on the Sabbath so much as a thread, a piece of string, let alone a whole rope. And so what I'd like to ask You, *Gottenyu*, is this:

Was it absolutely necessary, today of all days, to send Masha into the lake, when You knew I couldn't get her out till day's end, till sundown?

He gestured toward the cow. "And her, sinking deeper and deeper all the time into the mud out there? And everyone sick with worry?"

Yoysif, seeing him look up, waved an arm. He had swum out almost as far as where Masha stood, and was looking very proud of himself for having gone so far. Koppel raised his arm to wave back, when, for one, brief second, the boy's little head ducked under the water.

Almost at once, he resurfaced. But in that second, the cold reason with which Koppel had hoped to sway his maker suddenly and without any warning abandoned him, overwhelmed by a tightness in his chest and his throat that made him feel as if he himself were being drowned. He returned Yoysif's wave with a brave smile at odds with the tears which had sprung to his eyes, and, returning his watery gaze heavenward once again, cried out, "And what about my boy? My boy, who has still never had one word pass his lips, not once, since his mother, my Sora Hinde, was taken away? Believe me, I don't know what I did to offend You, *Gottenyu*, but I beg You, if You'll only tell me — only, don't take it out on the boy!"

His voice dropped.

"And as for the cow, if for some reason I don't understand, because I am only an ant, a flea, a worm crawling in the earth, while You are all-powerful and all-knowing ... If for some reason You did have to choose a Sabbath-day on which to send her into the lake, then did it have to be this particular Sabbath-day? Because today a cow in the lake, which would usually be the beginning and end of my troubles, is nothing, compared with the sorrow I feel taking just one glance at my daughter Blume. What are we going to do with her now, Master of the

Universe, tell me please, after those thieves stole everything last night? And especially her dowry-money."

～

Inside the house, clustered around the window, the girls were asking each other the same thing (all except Blume, who seemed able to worry only about Masha and not a jot about herself): What were they going to do?

And whoever heard of such a thing — thieves on a Sabbath eve? How could it happen? All the money Tatte had been saving for Blume's dowry, gone. And more besides. An equal sum that had been put by for the other girls' dowries. A smaller amount meant for the added expense soon to be incurred when the bridegroom would come live with them on *kest* (that is, at the expense of the family, to allow him to pray and study, instead of working.) All these monies, stolen — and Mama's jewels, too!

How could such a thing happen — and now, of all times? Why, just yesterday, as they walked down the lake road, with the sun on its way to setting into the woods away to the right, the coming Sabbath had promised to be an especially wonderful one — indeed, the most wonderful and memorable of their young lives.

In the first place, it was to be the last Sabbath prior to Blume's wedding. Next Friday — in less than a week! — the oldest of the sisters was to be married to a young man named Dovid, who lived not in Balativke but down the lake in Zavlivoya. This much larger polis, of which Balativke was more or less a satellite, lay only a few *versts* away, at the lake's southern end, and the girls were more than familiar with it: Zavlivoya was the destination for most of the butter and cheese they made. Each Tuesday, market-day, they would set up shop in Zavlivoya's main square, selling to the peasants and fellow Jews and nobles' servants who all gathered that day to exchange goods. And they also went most Sabbath afternoons, taking a stroll down the lake road, and meeting acquaintances along the way.

Up till now, they'd barely laid eyes on Zavlivoya's main *shul*. It was Koppel's habit, each Sabbath eve, to go to worship at Balativke's tiny *shul*, and as for the girls, they stayed home, waiting for his return and the dinner to follow. But last night, they'd all gone to *shul* in Zavlivoya. Dovid — as befitted a bridegroom on the Sabbath before his wedding — had been called to the Torah. Naturally, they were all there to see it.

What was *especially* exciting about this Sabbath, though — and what drew every one of their neighbors from Balativke, not to mention all the Jews of Zavlivoya, to the *shul* that night — was something that had nothing to do with Blume's upcoming nuptials. It was the arrival in town, a few days earlier, of a very famous personage, who would be delivering a much-anticipated sermon: an itinerant preacher known as the Kelmer Maggid.

The Kelmer Maggid! What Jew in all of Russia hadn't heard of him? Who hadn't heard mention of his sermons, their high-flown rhetoric and their homespun wisdom? Who hadn't gotten wind of the extraordinary effect his visits had on those fortunate enough to receive them? Whole towns transformed, entire villages in spiritual ruin renewed overnight, merchants of the very worst repute casting aside their sharp practices and dishonest ways after hearing the holy man speak just once!

The Maggid, it was said, held that strictness in religious observance alone was far from sufficient for the living of a proper life. Days spent in the prayer house could not, according to him, make up for dishonesty in the market place. Therefore, he urged his coreligionists to be scrupulous *not only in observance*, but also in their dealings with others, Jew and Gentile alike. So righteous was the preacher that he was unafraid to speak plainly even to a wealthy man. And those who heard him listened.

A few of the Maggid's sermons had by now been published,

so that there were some among the Jews of Zavlivoya and envi-
rons already familiar with his words and thoughts — though he
had never before been to this part of the country. But he was
here now, giving the first of several scheduled sermons, right in
Zavlivoya.

It went without saying that the visit of such a famed preacher
was a once-in-a-lifetime event. Even if Dovid hadn't been called
to Torah, all of Koppel's daughters would have been there —
there wasn't a Jew around who wasn't. They went, and they were
spellbound. As Berl Melamed, Balativke's young Hebrew school
teacher, put it afterward, the preacher's words were as honey, and
of silver was his tongue. No end was there to the memorable turns
of phrase, the striking images, for them to hear, and to savor.

For example, the Throne of Justice. That was something
Reb Berl Melamed reminded them of more than once as they
returned home up the lake road: "The Throne of Justice — I
wouldn't mind seeing that! What about you, Zlata?"

And the angels, Michael and Gabriel, who stood by the
Throne: "Can you imagine, Zlata, standing right there with them?"

Zlata, it ought to be explained, was the second oldest of
Koppel's daughters, who Berl Melamed was walking extremely
close to as he said these things. In the past, the teacher had always walked close like that to Blume. But since her engagement,
he'd been keeping his distance, only occasionally looking over
at her with an aggrieved air, while he paid court to her sister.

"Now Zlata," he said, as they passed Deacon Achilles' house,
"when the Maggid said, Not only your food must be kosher, but
also your money? What he meant by that, you may not have
understood, was that spending money that hasn't been honestly
earned is as bad as choking down a whole plate of pork."

In between the teacher's enthusiastic recollections, the others wondered aloud whether the Maggid's words would have
any effect next market-day, with Zlata claiming that she could
name three or four merchants she knew for a fact would cheat

even their own mothers, though she wouldn't dream of naming them aloud — except for Yasha the Horse-trader, who everyone already knew about anyway, and who should be taken by the cholera!

Then, as they approached Balativke, Berl Melamed remarked that Reb Koppel's house looked very dark. And he was right. When they went in, they found that one of the candles they'd lit before sundown, the one in the back room, had been snuffed out. In the kitchen, right on the table, sat the bones of the very chicken Blume had baked for their supper, picked clean. And everywhere, there was dried mud, some of it bearing exactly the print of a man's boot-sole.

But it wasn't until Tatte looked under his mattress that they realized the extent of the tragedy.

~

Out in the water, there was another splash — a loud one, this time, and then another. It was Yoysif, madly thrashing his arms. Koppel jumped up, ready to swim to the rescue. But Yoysif wasn't drowning, he was swimming, as fast as he could, for the shore — and then, when he'd come in close enough, running, right out of the lake.

Koppel opened his arms wide, but the boy rushed past him, his voice silent but his eyes loud with terror. Up the yard he ran, and even further, into the road — where he bumped smack into something: the waiting legs of Avrom the Tsimbalist, who, just at that moment, was approaching the house.

A second hadn't passed before out of the house streamed Koppel's six daughters, led by Blume, to whom the young boy instantly ran, hiding in her skirts. An incredible chatter arose, with only Blume's voice rising clear as she asked "What is it, Yoysif? What's wrong?" And then their father sprinted up, mud all down his front — he must have slipped on the way. "Yossele,

Yossele," he put a muddy hand on his son's back, "nothing to be afraid of. It's only good old Masha out there." When this had no effect, Koppel mumbled, "just a moment," and ran back in the direction of the lake.

Blume, running her fingers through the boy's hair, looked up at the tsimbalist. "I'm sorry about this, Reb Avrom. You know, it's just that sometimes he ..."

"Of course."

"*Gut shabbes* to you."

"*Gut shabbes*, Blume."

Reb Avrom was looking as he always did: short grey beard well-trimmed, clothes spotless. He wore a black peaked cap with a high crown, and a short, German-style coat, which had incurred the disapproval of Balativke's more traditional-minded residents. It made him look, they whispered, like an *apikores*, a heretic, practically — which, in fact, according to them, he was anyway.

There was about him, in all, an air of preternatural calm. His lips wore a wistful smile, while his eyes, which were a transparent grey, brimmed over with warmth, managing, however, at the same time, to give the impression that their owner was a bit here and there, close at hand but also far away.

Those eyes now took in each of the seven siblings in turn, resting longest on little Yoysif, and then on Blume. She looked, thought the tsimbalist, as lovely as always — the darkest of the sisters, she had hair as black as her father's, but features as delicate as his were coarse. But there was something amiss today, something other than the cow in the lake (Avrom had spotted Masha out there several times in the course of the day) and the boy clinging to her skirts.

"My dear," he asked, "how is it with you?"

"Oh ..." answered Blume, shaking her head in denial that anything might be the matter. "Praise God, I'm — "

One of the other sisters broke in, "We were — "

But at the same instant, Koppel returned, all out of breath from running, and wheezed loudly over both of them: "Yossele! Here! Your toy!" In his hand, he held the wheel-spoke.

The boy peeked over. But the sight of the spoke, far from comforting him, made him even more distraught, and he hid himself still deeper in Blume' skirts. Koppel's face fell.

"Reb Koppel," said the tsimbalist. "*Gut shabbes.*"

Koppel looked dazed for a moment, then recollected himself. "Oh, Reb Avrom. *Gut shabbes.*"

"But I see you have troubles."

Koppel glanced at his daughters, then back at Reb Avrom. "The truth is — "

Zlata blurted it out: "We were robbed!"

And at once, the whole story came out, told in bits and pieces by one member of the family and then another: "Every last kopek!" "Last night, while we were away!" "Of course the whole village was deserted — " "Surprised they didn't rob your place, too — " "Mudprints, everywhere — " "Snuffed out the candle in the back room — "

"Now, that's odd," interjected the tsimbalist.

"Everything! Our supper!" "Blume's dowry-money!" "How's she to get married now?" "And the set-aside for *our* dowries!" "And Mama's jewels!" "And we can't even go to report it till to-morrow!" "Not tomorrow, that's Sunday — not till Monday!" "Or do anything about Masha — " "Till sunset — " "The whole village will be furious with us — " "They'll all be wanting to go hear the Maggid — " "Instead of pulling Masha out of the lake again!"

"Alas," the tsimbalist held up a hand to quiet them. "That's what I came to tell you. I'm very sorry. Young Oleg Efimovski," he named the scion of one of the area's leading families, "has decided to hold a ball this evening, and needs music for it. I won't be able to help out with the cow this time. I have to rush off as soon as the sun goes down."

~

Luckily, even if Reb Avrom was busy, shortly after the Sabbath ended, most of the rest of the village arrived to help (if with a little grumbling.) They were joined by Blume's betrothed, Dovid, who, wondering why he hadn't bumped into his intended amongst the Sabbath strollers on the lake road, had come to find out — even though, officially, the bride and groom weren't supposed to meet in the week before the wedding. This eagerness met with some opprobrium from the villagers, who, in truth, already had their doubts about the young man. Even though Dovid could often be found in the study house, as befit any good Jew ... physically, he looked altogether too robust, more robust than a real scholar ought (just as Blume was too slender to be considered truly beautiful.) Like Avrom the Tsimbalist, he trimmed his beard. And, besides these things, every one remembered the strange and even dangerous things the young fellow had been heard to say at the time of the last pogrom in Odessa, a few years back: that the Jews of that city — if it was to be believed — ought to have defended themselves when the Greeks and Russians set upon them!

However, in the present situation, Dovid proved himself most useful. He got a lasso around Masha's neck on the first try — earning the instant admiration of Deacon Achilles, who had shown up to help without being asked, saying he'd heard all the commotion from his house down the shore. Then, as always, it was pull-pull-pull, without falling over into the mud yourself.

With the deacon as their anchor, they gave it their all. And, after an initial struggle, they were rewarded by seeing the cow come unstuck and charge two steps forward.

After that, it should have been a simple matter of steady effort. Only, for some reason, after one or two more steps, the cow's progress suddenly halted. This had never happened before. What could be the matter? Nobody knew. Well, all they could do was go on pulling, harder than ever.

With the extra effort, Masha leaned promisingly forward. But then she went back again. And when they tried once more, the same thing: pull, forward, then back. It was as if there was something in the lake, in Masha's way, impeding her path. But what?

"Someone ought to go take a look," proposed Berl Melamed, taking charge of the situation. "Any volunteers?"

"I'll do it," the bold Dovid strode forward, and plunged in. A few strokes, and he'd reached the cow. Next second, he was underwater, where he stayed for a few seconds. Then, up for air, and straight back down again.

"Do you think he found something?" Blume turned to her father.

Koppel shrugged, straining his eyes in the failing light to see what Dovid might have discovered out there.

A few seconds later, the young hero emerged once more. This time, he shouted for help. He'd found something, all right — two things, in fact. A wagon wheel, and, tied tight to its underside, the body of a man.

Who he was, they couldn't tell at first, when they laid him on shore a few minutes later and held their lanterns close. His face was shrouded in a tangle of aquatic weeds, as was his bare, white chest. They could see only that his hair, which was as wet and limp as the weeds, was blonde, with perhaps a tinge of red, that he was clad in nothing but a pair of breeches — and that he hadn't been dead for long.

Chapter 2

≈

Another Engagement

The nasal bark rang out in French: *"Promenade à une paire!"* A shudder went through the drawing-room's gleaming wooden floor, as ten dancers came galloping across.

The five gentlemen and five ladies cut a boisterous and unpredictable swath: over the brilliant parquet, beneath an archway and through to the entrance hall, a sudden double-back over the entryway's red Smyrna rug — which slipped perilously underfoot — and on straight and fast toward the buffet, where a sprinkling of spectators stood.

The room held its breath. Would the dancers ram the buffet? No! At the last moment the couple at their head — a tall and dashing gentleman with reddish-blonde curls and an elegant little mustache, and a rosy-cheeked ingenue who looked everywhere but at her companion — reared up and executed a sharp maneuver to the right.

An ancient waiter in crisp dress-coat was standing there, just arrived to relieve them with cold, refreshing seltzer-water. Forced to dodge arthritically out of the way, this paragon of the serving class managed, miraculously, to spill not a single drop.

"Sorry, Foka!" shouted the dashing gentleman as he sped by.

A moment later, the five couples had regained their starting marks, and were looking expectantly at the man standing before them, a septuagenarian who awed them all with his resplendent, spade-shaped white beard and genuine military get-up, complete with Nevsky cross and ceremonial sword.

"*Grand-rond, balancez,*" barked out the general. The obedient dancers rearranged themselves into a circle, caught their breath, wiped their brows, and sprang back into action.

Overhead, the glittering chandelier trembled. In a far corner of the room, a second waiter, who had been sniggering at Foka's near-pratfall, could now be seen sampling from the tray of champagne flutes with which he had, perhaps unwisely, been entrusted. Enthusiastic clangings of fork against plate had resumed at the buffet, while from the parlor off to the left came the wooden knocks and abrupt exclamations of a billiards game. Together, these noises all but overwhelmed the dance music — a toneless scraping emanating from a solitary bass-fiddle, whose torturer, a sallow and balding Russian, was, aside from everything else, obviously drunk.

The dancers whirled. An unexpected tear in the fabric of sound was instantly patched over by a well-starched female voice from the buffet: "Ah, the salmon *coulibiac* — sublime!" The inebriated musician squeezed out the *Grand-rond's* final notes, the men bowed on bent knee to the ladies, and, while the rosy-cheeked ingenue scurried off the other way, the dashing gentleman fetched himself a glass of champagne and joined an older lady to whom he bore a striking resemblance.

"Well, *maman,*" he looked about the room. "What do you think?"

"Bravo!" exclaimed the lady, who wore a cream-colored organdy gown, and an adoring expression. "Bravo, Olezhka! No-one could take their eyes off of you!"

"And why should they?" A wild happiness lit the dashing

host's green eyes. "It's my evening — I'm not ashamed to say it. Though I do hope I didn't frighten old Foka too badly."

Olezhka — Oleg Olegovich Efimovski, to give him his full name — swiveled his head in search of the ancient waiter. Instead, he found the bass player. His happiness flickered into annoyance. "But where is our Jewish Orchestra?" he cried. "I'd expected them by now!"

Behind him, a peal of feminine laughter tickled the air, as another obvious relation appeared. "Impatient tonight, isn't he, *maman*?" The new arrival, gloriously appareled in ivory lace and voile, tapped her brother on the elbow with her fan. "*Chaque chose en son temps, mon frère.*"

A romantic sigh escaped the charming Oleg Olegovich. "But you know I can't bear to be separated from my Tanya a moment longer. And the announcement only requires the orchestra's arrival."

"And your brother's," put in his mother. "I won't have you engaged without Arkasha here. How would it look?"

"You mean to say he still hasn't returned?" Oleg Olegovich sighed again. "The devil take it, how long will I have to wait?"

"Ah, such strong and sudden passion!" his sister gave him an approving look. "*Mon cher*, you seem completely transformed."

"Nonsense," huffed their mother. "We've always known he'd marry the girl."

"We've always known her father wished it. But I never believed Olezhka did — until I saw his passionate eyes tonight. It's only a shame that the object of his affections can't yet bear to look at *him*."

"Aglayushka! Be nice to your brother."

"Oh, was I unkind?" Aglaya Olegovna bit her lip. "*Pardonnemoi*, Olezhka. I wish nothing but your happiness."

In reply, her brother performed a swift bow.

"Besides," continued their mother, "There's nothing unusual in the least about the way Tatiana Savelyevna is behaving. I was just the same at my own engagement party, so nervous I could barely breathe. If the two of you could only have seen how handsome your father was that night, may his memory be blest! And you are his spitting image, Olezhka. What girl wouldn't be thrilled to marry you? Especially a merchant's daughter. You'll quite elevate her."

"Not so loud, *maman*," her son scolded. "Don't ruin things. Saveli Savelyevich will hear!"

"He'll do no such thing, he's at the buffet stuffing himself in the most vulgar way."

"*Maman!*" tittered Aglaya Olegovna.

"And anyway, Saveli Savelyevich would be the first to agree." Their mother lunged suddenly forward between them: "Foka, offer the musician tea."

The ancient servant, who was just passing, nodded gravely in reply, before she continued. "No, as I say, Tatiana Savelyevna will be thrilled — just as soon as your brother Arkasha arrives."

Concern creased Aglaya Olegovna's elfin features. "I wonder where he could be. He said he'd be here without fail."

Oleg Olegovich clicked his tongue. "I wish he'd hurry then, the devil take him. And the musicians, too!"

～

It was dark now. A cool breeze was blowing up out of the forest, coming to greet the wagon as it rattled down the rough road — a whispered promise that the weather would soon break. High above, the moon was out. By its light, Avrom could see, rearing up on each side, the orchards on the outskirts of the Efimovski estate. Here, the cherries in full fruit ... now the plums ... off there in the distance, flickering light: peasants come for the harvest and camped around a bonfire. In a moment, the wagon carrying the Jewish Orchestra, as Zavlivoya's klezmer band was sometimes called, would rattle past the burgeoning apples, and soon after, reach the gate to the estate. Avrom knew the route well. Once upon a time, he used to give music lessons to Aglaya Olegovna, the Efimovski daughter.

To Avrom's left, a tall and emaciated Jew with flame-orange hair and beard, and a long curving nose, sat driving the wagon: Moishe Shakhes, the Jewish Orchestra's fiddler and leader. (When the band was called on to perform for weddings, Shakhes had another role, too: that of *badkhn*, a sort of combined master-of-ceremonies, rhymester, and jester-at-large.)

Moishe Shakhes didn't know the way as well as Avrom, and now asked, for the fourth time in the last half hour, "How much further?"

"Almost there," Avrom replied.

"Aha! Almost there, boys," Shakhes called out behind him. Three of the fiddler's sons rode in the wagon's rear, the flutist, second fiddle, and drummer of the band, each one an increasingly diminutive miniature of his father, like the dolls of a *matryoshka* set.

Shakhes turned back to Avrom with a self-satisfied air. "It was a fine idea of mine, having you borrow the wagon yesterday."

"Hmm," replied the tsimbalist.

"I tell you, it would have been an extra half-hour, easy, if we'd come to Balativke to fetch you, instead of you coming to Zavlivoya to fetch us."

"Perhaps," said Avrom with a faint smile. According to his no-doubt faulty memory, it had been he who had proposed the "fine idea," which, yesterday, had met with some little resistance.

"And by the way, in case you were in any doubt about whether it was worth all the fuss," the fiddler continued, slipping now into *klezmer-loshn*, the secret language employed by musicians of the time to speak behind their employers' backs, "let me tell you, I got an extra couple of *feivels* out of the gull for this gig."

"Slow down a little here," said Avrom, as they passed by the apple orchards.

"You're probably dying to know how I did it," Shakhes went on, paying no heed to the tsimbalist's advice. "Nu, how do you go about squeezing a gull like Oleg Efimovski for two slices extra?" He paused for effect. "Simple."

"There," Avrom interrupted, pointing at the rapidly-approaching turnoff to the estate. Shakhes pulled hard on the reins, but too late. They sped straight past the turnoff, and were only able to come to a stop some way down the road. "You should have said something sooner," said the fiddler.

Without a word, Avrom jumped lightly down from his seat, took the horse (whose name was Pasternak, that is, "parsnip") by the bridle, whispered a word in his ear, and then led him in a careful ellipse, turning the wagon around on the narrow road.

The fiddler went on talking all the while. "Listen to this," he said, "and I'll tell you what I said to the poretz. I said, Your Illustriousness, any Jew would be honored to perform at a ball you threw. Only how much of a Jew would a Jew be if he skipped the Kelmer Maggid for you? What's the Kelmer Maggid, he asks — and he didn't have to ask twice. The question, says I, isn't what but who. And the answer is, the Kelmer Maggid is only the biggest wheel ever to do little Zavlivoya the honor of rolling through. Speaking on our Sabbath, he is, and for two nights following. And anyone who misses out'll get a good hollering. In short, may the good Lord grant that you have the ball of the summer and the ball of the year. But duty calls, and who I am I to turn a deaf ear? Unless — "

Avrom, his job done, leapt nimbly back into the wagon.

" — Unless you happen to be ready and willin' ... to slip four senderls above the usual garnish into little Itskele's tefillin."

"And did Efimovski know what you meant when you said tefillin?" asked Avrom. It seemed unlikely to him that even a Jew would have understood Shakhes's words, let alone a Russian nobleman. To a Jew, of course, tefillin were those little leather boxes worn during prayer, containing scripture written upon parchment, and attached with straps to forehead and arm. When Shakhes talked about *tefillin*, however, he meant the band's money box, which hung by a strap from the drum played by his young son Itskele.

Before Shakhes had a chance to answer Avrom's question, this very Itskele piped up from the back of the wagon: "Four *senderls*, Tatte? I thought you said we was makin' two."

The fiddler replied to the tsimbalist rather than to his son: "Four *senderls* was what *I* proposed. But a Jew plans, and a Russian laughs. He proposed one. And we settled on two."

"Well done, Reb Moishe Shakhes," said Avrom. "And I see that your skills as a *badkhn* are in no danger of dulling. But let me ask you a question: Would you have turned down the job and gone to see the Kelmer Maggid if Efimovski hadn't agreed?"

Moishe Shakhes' eyes bulged out of their sockets, and he looked up at the sky. "Would I have turned down the job, he asks." He looked back at the tsimbalist. "Of course not, Reb Avrom. I just fed that to the gull."

"Ah," the tsimbalist nodded his head. "Then let me ask you another: do you think this is something the Maggid would approve of?"

"Huh? The Maggid?" Moishe Shakhes looked suddenly panicked. He peeked around to see if his sons were listening, and whispered, "Avrom, you're not saying I did wrong?"

Avrom let Shakhes wait a moment for his answer, during which time Shakhes graduated from panic to full-out terror. Finally, the tsimbalist said: "I leave it to you to arrange our fees. I come and play, whatever you've arranged. And I'm always happy for the extra money. In other words — "

"In other words?"

"In other words, it's not for me to say what you should have done."

"Then you're saying — "

Avrom smiled. "I'm saying it's not always easy to be a Jew,

Moishe ... But I'm not sure the Maggid would have approved."
The tsimbalist raised his voice in a perfect imitation of the visiting rabbi's sing-song oratorical style: "Your money must be as
kosher as your food."

"Well ... but," reasoned Moishe Shakhes, "I hadn't heard
him talk yet then, when I made the arrangements, had I? Had
I, Avrom? Let's see, I squawked with the gull on Wednesday,
and the Maggid only squawked to *us* last night. All right, I
stretched ... can you blame me, with so many mouths to feed?
After all, when was the last time we had a job?"

That was a point, Avrom reflected, as the lights of the Efimovski mansion rose up before them. It had been a full two
months since the members of the Jewish Orchestra had last
performed together, since before Passover. And even before
that, work had been scarce.

In the first place, most of the local gentry — the Efimovskis,
for example — lived elsewhere during the winter. For half a
year or more, there were few balls at which to entertain. More
problematic still was the forty-nine day period of mourning following Passover, during which weddings, the mainstays of a
klezmer's livelihood, were forbidden among the Jews, and along
with them, the very playing of instruments. Not to mention
that even at the best of times, the musician's profession was
hardly a lucrative pursuit.

Indeed, like klezmers everywhere, the members of Zavlivoya's Jewish Orchestra were forced to supplement or even
make up the bulk of their income by working at other jobs between their musical engagements. Avrom himself, in addition
to giving music lessons, plied the trade most common among
klezmers, barbering. (Owing to his steady hand, open ears,
and closed mouth, he was perhaps the most popular barber
in Zavlivoya, where he walked five days a week to shave his
customers.) Moishe Shakhes and sons labored at the klezmers'
second-most common trade: they were glaziers, manufacturers

of mirrors and windows (for which reason they owned the long wagon in which the band was now riding.) Meanwhile, Kuz'ma, the band's Russian bass-player, was a house-painter. Kuz'ma ... a little bit of a hopeless case, Avrom thought ruefully.

Shakhes was thinking about the bass player too. "I hope Kuz'ma is getting along all right by himself," he said, as the wagon pulled to a stop in front of the mansion.

"What do you mean?" asked Avrom.

"I told him to come early and start without us. So they wouldn't notice we were late."

"By himself?" exclaimed the tsimbalist. "Let's get inside. Fast."

~

With the arrival of the Jewish Orchestra, the Efimovski ball whirled upwards toward still greater heights. The band wasted no time launching into Oginski's famed "Farewell Polonaise," followed in short order by an elegant *pas d'espagne*, a rustic *vengerka* dance, and a complicated quadrille. The by now numerous dancers executed them all with near-military precision, aided by shouted instructions from their indefatigable choreographer-general.

When the musicians embarked upon their fifth consecutive selection, however, a charming *valse mignonne*, all but four of the dancers were forced to declare themselves *hors de combat*, retreating to the sidelines or to the buffet. The remaining quartet included Oleg Olegovich Efimovski, partnered again with the lovely if still uncongenial merchant's daughter; and his sister Aglaya Olegovna, gamely dancing with an ill-favored gentleman whom no-one seemed to know, and about whom everyone seemed to be asking whispered questions.

One of these whispers passed directly in front of Avrom the Tsimbalist, who had no difficulty in overhearing the answer:

Madame Efimovskaya, the lady of the house and mother of two of the dancers, by choosing to stand so close to the band, was forced to raise her voice above the music to be heard. "An acquaintance of Olezhka's from Kiev," she proclaimed. "What's that? His name? Oh, who can remember that sort of thing? Anyway, he's only some low-ranking bureaucrat — no more than a Collegiate Registrar."

At the waltz's conclusion, madame was joined by the quartet of dancers, who were replaced on the floor by several other couples attracted by the lilt of a second *pas d'espagne*. "Bravo, children!" she exclaimed above the din.

"Has Arkasha arrived yet?" her son eagerly demanded.

Madame Efimovskaya shook her head. "Not yet."

"*Maman* won't allow Olezhka to make the announcement till our brother arrives," Aglaya Olegovna explained to Tatiana Savelyevna, who was unable entirely to hide her delight at the news.

"Will we wait all night then?" Oleg Olegovich burst out.

Aglaya Olegovna took his hands in hers. "Olezhka, he's only late because he's doing a kindness for you."

"But — "

"I'm certain he'll be here soon," Madame Efimovskaya held firm. "Surely an hour can't make a difference."

"I suppose not," said Oleg Olegovich, and hung his head.

At just the same moment, Tatiana Savelyevna seemed to notice Avrom for the first time, and greeted him with a radiant smile. He returned it. Tatiana was another of his former music students.

"I suppose we're obliged to meet this gentleman," Madame Efimovskaya remarked, eyeing the unknown guest.

"Ah yes," replied Oleg Olegovich, "allow me to introduce my, er, friend, Collegiate Registrar Vitaly Valentinovich Pugovitsin."

"*Ravi de vous connaître*," Pugovitsin began to bow, then, halfway down, straightened up and instead grabbed Madame

Efimovskaya's hand, which he pulled unceremoniously toward himself before depositing a kiss there.

Her reply, as she retrieved her soiled appendage, was unenthusiastic: "*Enchantée.*"

"I happened to be visiting from Kiev," Pugovitsin hurriedly went on to explain, "and so when Oleg Olegovich and I ..." But after this promising beginning, he lapsed into silence. As did the others.

The moment was rescued by the appearance of a waiter carrying a tray of champagne flutes. Avrom was surprised when he saw who it was: a former serf of the Efimovskis named Styopa. The son of the housekeeper, Stopya had been a servant on the estate for a short time following the emancipation of the serfs. But — Avrom remembered this quite clearly from the time he had been Aglaya's music teacher — the housekeeper's son had been thrown out for thieving from the family. Avrom had always thought him an unpleasant sort, and the intervening years had done nothing to improve him: Styopa's teeth had turned a sickly yellow, and in addition, he now wore disreputably long mustaches. Avrom saw him loitering about town from time to time. He hadn't expected to see him at the Efimovskis' tonight.

"Your Illustriousness," the waiter approached Oleg Olegovich.

"What is it?"

"A word?"

Oleg Olegovich stared at the man with distaste, then walked a distance of three or four *arshins* away, with Styopa following. At the same instant, an older man with close-cropped grey hair strode up, dressed in an official uniform and riding boots with spurs attached: the petty-governor of Zavlivoya, Anton Antonovich Skorokhodov-Druganin.

"Spectacular affair!" Skorokhodov-Druganin greeted Madame Efimovskaya.

"So good to see you, Anton Antonovich."

The petty-governor kissed each of the ladies in greeting,

then looked inquiringly at the stranger from Kiev, who saluted in military fashion, and began again, "Collegiate Registrar Vitaly Valentinovich Pugovitsin. I happened to be visiting ..."

He was interrupted by Oleg Olegovich's return. "Styopa tells me all the ice is melting and the champagne will get warm. I'll have to go unlock the icehouse for him." He held up a key and, looking most put out, departed, followed by the waiter.

"Spectacular affair!" the petty-governor said again.

"Tell us," said Aglaya Olegovna, "what is new in town. We've been away so long."

"Ah," replied Skorokhodov-Druganin, rubbing his hands together. "Something quite interesting. Quite interesting indeed. You know that our three richest Yids are Grinberg, Feldshteyn, and Rosengauz."

When he uttered the word "Yids," Avrom noticed, Tatiana gave a start, then regarded the petty-governor with a critical stare.

"Well," Skorokhodov-Druganin went on, "last night, all three of them had their houses broken into. They were all robbed!"

"No!" exclaimed Madame Efimovskaya.

"*Mon dieu!*" cried Aglaya Olegovna. "Last night?"

"Have the culprits been caught?" asked Madame Efimovskaya.

"Great God, is the inn safe?" Pugovitsin turned pale.

"Not to worry, my dear Agrafena Ivanovna," the petty-governor replied to madame, ignoring the bureaucrat. "The circumstances were highly unusual. All three of the Yids, it seems, were away from home ..."

"Ah," interjected Madame Efimovskaya.

"... and for some reason, the whole Yid quarter was empty ... some something-or-other at their church ... that is, syna— ... their place where they pray ... so to say. So you see ..."

"Yes."

"Of course, Nikifor Kharitonovich"—he mentioned Zavlivoya's police chief—"will have to make a good show of looking into it." His forehead creased. "Not that you can ever tell for certain what our Nikifor Kharitonovich is going to do ..."

Avrom smiled to himself. Zavlivoya's police chief was indeed unpredictable, as he himself knew firsthand: he was Nikifor Kharitonovich's barber, and most weeks, saw the chief every weekday.

"Do you mean," Madame Efimovskaya asked the petty-governor, "that Nikifor Kharitonovich might ignore the robberies altogether?"

"On the contrary, Agrafena Ivanovna. What I mean is that he will sometimes take a little more interest in these Yid matters than seems entirely necessary, and ... Ah, *mademoiselle*," Skorokhodov-Druganin suddenly pirouetted to face Tatiana Savelyevna, the merchant's daughter. "It sounds as if this number is ending. Would you do me the honor of joining me for the next?"

The tsimbalist watched the rosy-cheeked ingenue blanch. But before he could hear her reply, and as the last notes of the *pas d'espagne* were vanishing into the air, a whisper came from his right: "Avrom!"

Reluctantly, Avrom turned his head. "What is it, Moishe?"

"Avrom, we left Pasternak hitched to the wagon. I'm worried about him."

"The other drivers — "

"They'll all be in the kitchen drinking up the vodka."

"Yes, you're right," Avrom nodded. "So, you'd like to take a break to go look after him."

"You do it, Avrom."

"What?"

"You have a way with Pasternak."

Avrom was at a loss. "Of course, if he were my horse — "

Suddenly, Moishe called out, at full voice, "*Eyns, tsvey, drai.*" The rest of the band lunged for their instruments, and before a second had passed, they'd struck up a Lancers' Dance.

"All right," said the tsimbalist to himself, setting his wooden sticks down on the tsimbl, while managing at the same time to shrug his shoulders. "Why don't I do it?"

~

Before going outside, Avrom visited the corner of the buffet where the neglected *samovar* stood — it was too hot that night for even Russians to drink tea — and pocketed a lump of sugar, then went to find Pasternak. He found him a short distance from where they'd left him, a little way from the house, still hitched to the wagon.

"Well, Pasternak," Avrom murmured, giving the nag's withers a good rub. "What do you think? Shall I unhitch you first, and then you can have the sugar afterward, or do you prefer it the other way around?"

He held out the sugar lump in his hand, and Pasternak gave it an enthusiastic lick.

"Ah, I thought so. Take your time. And so, what have you been hearing out here? Between you and me, it can't possibly be as interesting as what I've been hearing inside."

He chuckled. The horse's tongue was tickling his hand.

"Don't believe me? Listen to this: if I didn't know better, I would think Tatiana the merchant's daughter was secretly in love with some Jewish boy. What do you think about that?"

No reply came from the contented Pasternak.

"I see you're not convinced. I'll tell you my reasoning. In the first place, anyone can see she doesn't want to marry young Efimovski. And in the second ... well, you should have seen her face when the petty-governor said 'Yid.' Although I don't know why she should have been so surprised to hear him say it ..."

The horse continued to hold his peace.

"No? All right, what about this? Three thefts in one night. Three. Whoever heard of such a thing? And that isn't even including poor Koppel. The question is, why would a thief rob the three richest Jews in Zavlivoya, and then go eat a chicken in Balativke? Or, if it was two different thieves, which is, after all, possible, how does it come about that two different thieves are at work on one night? Or maybe there were even four thieves. Did every criminal in the county think, aha, the Kelmer Maggid is talking tonight, I'm going to go rob a Jew? And however many thieves there were, was one of them Styopa? I can't wait to ask Nikifor Kharitonovich about it when I trim his beard on Monday ... But what do you think, Pasternak, eh?"

Still Pasternak said nothing — but someone else did: voices, coming from around the corner of the house, along with lantern-light. Speak of the devil, it was the disgraced housekeeper's son, Styopa, carrying a large tub of ice in his arms, and beside him, Efimovski, carrying the lantern. The unpleasant waiter said something Avrom couldn't make out as they rounded the corner. Then the nobleman replied: "I can hardly leave the party to continue with you now. Come see me about it — "

Efimovski stopped short when he saw Avrom. After a moment's pause, he called out, "Friend, perhaps *you* have a job to give to this poor soul."

"I?" said Avrom.

Efimovski laughed. "I'm only joking, I — "

But here again, Efimovski stopped short, and this time his eyes squinted into the darkness beyond Avrom.

Avrom spun around. There was someone running toward them ... a Jew ... one of his neighbors, the woodcutter Hezkel. He looked like he'd sprinted all the way from Balativke.

"Your Illustriousness," the woodcutter panted. "Your Illustriousness ..."

"What is it?" asked Efimovski.

"Your — "

"Yes, yes, Your Illustriousness. Get on with it."

"Your ... brother ... they found him ... in the lake. He's ..."

The woodcutter lurched forward, embracing the nobleman to keep from falling. "Peace be upon him ..."

✎

Chapter 3

Fire at Night

"**M**y brother?" Efimovski cried out, staring at the wood-cutter, whose face was nearly touching his own. "Nonsense!"

He thrust Hezkel away, and the woodcutter tottered backward, then forward again, finally collapsing onto one knee. "Please, Your Illustriousness —"

"No!" Efimovski had already spun on his heel and taken a step toward the house. "I won't believe it! Not Arkasha!"

Styopa loped up behind him, and purred in an insinuating tone, "Your Illustriousness, you should know that you can't hide an awl in a sack."

Efimovski looked back over his shoulder in some confusion.

"That is to say," Styopa enlightened him, "sooner or later the truth always comes out ... so why not find out right away if the Yid is telling tales?"

Efimovski looked as if he would shout out another denial; but then wilting, said instead, "Well?"

"Just listen." The malignant waiter turned his attention to Hezkel. "Tell us, Yankel" — and then, without any warning, he swung his arms so that the tub of ice he was carrying struck the kneeling woodcutter hard on the shoulder, knocking him to the ground. A sorrowful groan escaped Hezkel, punctuated by the clattering of ice, as Styopa dropped the tub on the ground and then leaned down over the woodcutter, braying, "You found him in the lake, eh? What do you mean by that? Did you put your hands around his throat till he went belly up so you could sell his horse? Or did you slit his guts open before you tossed him in? You'd better hope nobody saw you do it, they'll take your thirty pieces in blackmail money."

Avrom took a step forward in outrage, before Efimovski rushed up and pulled the raving waiter away from the woodcutter, exclaiming: "Stop it, are you mad?"

"Begging pardon, Your Illustriousness." The repulsive waiter, who didn't sound sorry at all, looked at the nobleman, his eyes twinkling. "Sometimes, when truth is reluctant to come into the world, the midwife must cause a little pain pulling it out. But I should be more careful," he looked over at Avrom. "That's Nikifor Kharitonovich's Yid, that cuts his beard. Who knows what he might let slip to get a good Orthodox believer in trouble. They say the chief'll sometimes listen even to a Yid — I guess he'll listen to anyone!"

"Enough," Oleg Olegovich silenced him. "You," he turned to Hezkel. "Now — "

"Please, Your Illustriousness," Hezkel pleaded, "may I be buried in the earth if I haven't been saying true. I was sent, not for any virtue of my own but only on account of my quick legs, to say what every one of us saw. It wasn't anything like he said. We were pulling at the rope, and the cow wouldn't budge, and — "

"The cow?" asked Efimovski sharply.

Avrom, who was only now recovering from shock at the sudden violence that had erupted in front of him, hastened to explain. "A cow got stuck in the lake today, it's happened many times before. In Balativke. The whole village comes to pull her out, as they did this evening. It must have been close to where the cow was stuck that ... that your brother was found."

Efimovski was silent a moment. Then, in a voice devoid of all emotion, he said, "So it's true."

"Peace be upon him," whispered Hezkel once more.

A heartrending wail split the air. It was Styopa. "Woe is us," he howled. "O Rus, who dared touch one of your noblemen, who dared cut down one of the flowers of your ancient Slavic stock?"

Efimovski stared at him, and anger kindled in his eyes. He turned to the woodcutter. "Was he killed then?"

Hiding his face, Hezkel answered. "He was."

"You can bet it was the Yids," the repulsive waiter returned to his purring. "One of them or all of them, take your pick."

Ignoring him, the elegant nobleman closed his eyes for several seconds. When he reopened them, he appeared to have mastered himself. To Avrom, he said, "Your wagon is at the ready. Show me the place. You," he crisply commanded Styopa, "go inside and tell my mother I've gone to look for my brother —but say no more!"

He leapt lightly into the wagon, and took the reins. "Come," he urged Avrom, and in the next breath instructed Styopa: "When you've done with that, bring this man inside to rest." He indicated Hezkel. "And give him water."

The moment Avrom had one foot in the wagon, Efimovski pushed the lantern into his hands and snapped the whip. Avrom was thrown backward, into his seat, as the wagon sprang into motion.

~

Down the drive Pasternak raced, at a furious clip. Efimovski took the turn through the gate at full speed, blazed past the orchards, plunged ahead into the forest — all without saying a word. For his part, Avrom didn't so much as open his mouth. The breeze had whipped up by now, and was whistling shrilly past his ears. Branches snapped beneath the wagon's wheels, loud in the quiet night. With each bump in the road, the lantern shook, and shadows of trees careened up and down around them. Pushed on by the master driver, Pasternak's hooves beat a rapid tattoo into the ground, while the rickety wagon shuddered, one of its bent rear wheels hee-hawing like a mule. It was a night to trouble the soul — even without the news that Hezkel had brought, and the violence Styopa had done against the woodcutter. With last night's robberies, too, Avrom thought, the police chief would have his hands full — surely too full to do anything about Styopa, even if he saw fit to call what the repulsive waiter had done a crime. Avrom shivered, despite the hot night. Meanwhile, Efimovski stared straight ahead unblinking, his face white as powder.

Up above, the moon now hung half-hidden, swaddled in woolly clouds. As the woods fell away, its feeble light caught upon a collection of domes and crosses off to the right — the tops of Zavlivoya's churches, which towered higher than the town's other buildings. Only after dome and cross had been left behind did Efimovski finally speak, asking in a forlorn voice, like a little boy's, "Can it really be true?"

Taken aback, Avrom said nothing. He had no idea whether Efimovski, who hadn't moved a muscle, was asking the question of him, Avrom, or only of himself. But then the pale nobleman spoke again: "You know, he was very fond of your people."

This time, Avrom replied. "Your brother was held in high esteem among us, in turn."

It was nothing other than the truth. Arkasha, that is, Arkady Olegovich Efimovski, had, so far as Avrom could tell, been universally well-liked in the town of Zavlivoya, and no less so among its Jewish population than its Orthodox one.

Though he had only rarely conversed with him, Avrom had often observed the younger Efimovski when visiting the family mansion to give music lessons, and seen him any number of times around town. (Of late, he'd also frequently spotted Arkady Olegovich riding his horse along the lake road through Balativke, but this, unlike his other impressions, gave little idea of the young man's character.)

Arkady Olegovich Efimovski had been, according to Avrom's observations, a man of uniformly good-natured disposition, and more than that, a truly kind soul. In his dealings with the Jewish merchants in the marketplace, he'd been unfailingly polite — not something that could be said of every Russian nobleman — and lately, Avrom happened to know, he'd gone even further.

Avrom's informant in this regard was a very interesting young man by the name of Dovid Lipkin, who was betrothed to his neighbor Koppel's daughter. A few weeks ago, Dovid had told Avrom about his budding friendship and meeting of minds with the affable Efimovski, mentioning their shared passion for a certain important subject: the future of Russia. It was a future which, according to the two of them, would include contributions from Jew and peasant alike, working together — standing each one on his own dignity, but holding above all else the common good. The landowners would be a part of things too, of course — once they'd given away all their possessions.

Obviously, thought Avrom at the time, quite a sweet and naïve idea, and also an amusing one. The two youngsters were dreamers, no doubt about it, bound to be disappointed by the real future they would come to encounter one day — but very likable dreamers, and he'd take them over many whose feet were planted more firmly on the ground.

Avrom sighed. He would have liked, at least, for young Efimovski to have lived long enough to see his dreams shattered.

"I'm sorry for what has happened," he said aloud.

"He was a good man," Efimovski said, solemnly. "He loved all his fellow men. Do you know, he spent this winter with the peasants?"

Avrom did know it. Unlike in other years, when the Efimovskis were known to be absent from the area all through the long cold months, it had been common knowledge this winter that Arkady Olegovich was staying at his house, and making daily visits to the various peasant villages around the lake. These visits were much talked of, since country gossip always fastens on the surprising and the eccentric. How much more, then, did folk speak of the peasant shirt that he was now unfailingly seen wearing, and the breeches and woven bast-fiber shoes that went along with it.

Dovid Lipkin had explained to Avrom that, as singular as Arkady Olegovich's oddities appeared, he was in actuality only one of many young people throughout the empire behaving exactly the same way; that hundreds of these *narodniks*, as they were called, were spreading through the countryside, learning traditional customs from which they, the sons and daughters of the rich and middle class, had become tragically alienated, and, at the same time, urging the slumbering peasants to band together and rise up to improve their lot.

Avrom recalled the last time he'd seen Arkady Olegovich. The young nobleman had been riding on the lake road through Balativke, sitting straight and proud upon his white stallion, and clad, indeed, in his peasant shirt, white, with a blue skewed collar. With the sun shining down on his golden hair, he'd looked, that day, like a prince out of a fairy tale — a prince in peasant's clothes.

"I often saw him riding northward past my place," Avrom said aloud.

"Indeed?" said Oleg Olegovich, who drove along for a moment, looking thoughtful, then nodded. "Yes, yes. I remember now, he told me that the dearest to him of all the peasant villages was the one here on this side of the lake, up north past your town. He said the villagers there were the purest, the most unspoiled." He twisted in his seat to face Avrom. "But his was the purest soul of all, my Arkashka's." More quietly, he added, "Whatever will we do now?"

Oleg Olegovich's words hung in the air, unanswered, and he returned his gaze forward, while Avrom himself now twisted in his seat, searching for a comforting word.

"Peace be upon him," he whispered, and Oleg Olegovich pressed his lips solemnly together.

On the right, the lake now came into view, smooth as a marble, and black as birch pitch. Silence took hold once more of the morose nobleman, and of Avrom. Only Pasternak's hoofbeats could be heard, along with the insistent whine of the bent wagon-wheel.

It was not till they were passing by Deacon Achilles' house that Oleg Olegovich spoke again: "Which part of Balativke?"

But he needn't have asked. Just beyond the deacon's house was a point known as "Big Hand," where a piece of land jutted away from the road, in a form that really did resemble the shape of a hand. The hand's palm and all six fingers were covered in trees, which were thick with leaves at this time of year, and bent out over the water at more or less precipitate angles. As a result, they wholly impeded the view up the shoreline from the road.

Once the wagon had passed "Big Hand," however, the vista cleared, and, right away, an orange glow could be seen further upshore. As they approached closer, the riders in the wagon began to distinguish points of individual flame — flickering and real on the land side, trembling and reflected on the water side — coming from torches and lanterns. A few seconds more, and they saw wagons and horses on the road up ahead, blocking the way. Oleg Olegovich pulled Pasternak to a stop, snatched his own lantern from Avrom, leapt down from the wagon, and disappeared into the haze of orange and black below.

~

With no light of his own, Avrom made his way down from the road more slowly, stepping gingerly between the bushes that grew by the roadside before the land turned to marsh near the water. As he approached the light, the air grew smoky, and a hubbub arose from the assembled onlookers and the hissing of the torches. He saw Deacon Achilles, a head taller than the others, then made out the faces of several of his neighbors, and of others, too, residents of Zavlivoya, among them Dovid Lipkin. He could see Oleg Efimovski pushing through where the crowd was thickest, and then disappearing — he must have crouched down next to his brother's body. Next to where he had vanished stood one of Zavlivoya's constables, a thick-set, flaxen-haired man universally known as "the Pole."

Avrom had only been standing there a moment when, from behind him, someone shouted, "Make way!" It was the physician, Anton Pavlovich Artiukhov. As soon as Artiukhov reached the center of the crowd, he vanished, just as Oleg Efimovski had.

Avrom took a few steps closer to where the body lay, and saw another familiar face. "Reb Koppel," he whispered.

Koppel jumped in surprise. "Oh, Reb Avrom. You're here … Your ball must be all done with, then."

Avrom let out a grim laugh. "Under the circumstances … How's Masha?"

"Fine, all tied up, thanks to the Master of the Universe. But He blesses with one hand and punishes with the other — she's made a lot of trouble around here."

"I don't think it was her making the trouble, Reb Koppel — unless she had anything to do with putting poor Arkady

Efimovski in the water. But tell me just what happened, I haven't heard the whole story."

And Koppel told him about the cow, and Dovid, and the wheel, and all the rest.

"So without Masha getting stuck in the lake," said Avrom, "the poor young man might have stayed hidden there for a good long while, with no one having any idea about it. Which, I'm afraid, was somebody's intention."

"Avrom," said Koppel. "I think Yoysif — may he live and be well — I think he saw it."

"What?"

"You remember the way he ran up, so frightened, this after-noon? He'd just been swimming next to Masha."

Avrom looked around. "Where's the boy now?"

"Inside the house, with the girls." Koppel let out a great sigh.

Avrom heard a footstep crunch behind him, and swiveled his head. Nikifor Kharitonovich Taktakov, Zavlivoya's formi-dable police chief, was arriving, his Tatar features arranged into a tense scowl. (Avrom noticed that the chief's pointed silver beard and delicate, dragonfly-wing mustache, which he himself had trimmed yesterday morning, were still perfectly manicured.)

"Wait, if you please," Avrom called out, and the chief paused in his stride.

"What is it?" Nikifor Kharitonovich gruffly asked.

"There's something you should know about — "

"Now?"

" — in connection with what happened down there."

"Ah? Tell me."

And Avrom introduced the chief to Koppel, who proceeded to tell him about the robbery of his home while he and his fam-ily were away at the Kelmer Maggid's sermon.

"Another one?" exclaimed the chief as Koppel narrated the chain of events. "And right here, where ..." And then when Koppel had finished. "Well, well, we'll see what our Doctor Artiukhov has to say about when the poor man died. Quite interesting. And be sure to make a list of whatever was taken." Then, like the doctor and Oleg Olegovich, Nikifor Kharitonovich disappeared into the center of the crowd.

Avrom was astonished, and pained, to see who arrived next — so much for Styopa's discretion. Madame Efimovskaya hobbled down from the road, leaning weakly on the arm of the petty-governor, and was followed by Aglaya Olegovna, herself supported by old General Kondratin. Walking in front of them was Styopa, whistling under his breath as he carried a lantern to light their way.

Just as they arrived at the place where the body lay, Doctor Artiukhov stood back up, his luxuriant brown hair and beard and pince-nez spectacles appearing just next to Nikifor Kharitonovich. He opened his mouth, and a hush went through the crowd.

The doctor spoke in a sober tone, neither loudly nor quietly, and addressed himself solely to police chief, though, of course, everyone else could hear, too.

"I regret to say," he began, "that the deceased has been identified with certainty as Arkady Olegovich Efimovski."

A brief whispering followed this initial statement, but was cut off by the doctor's next words.

"Although his body was discovered in the lake" — Avrom heard a sob from either Madame Efimovskaya or Aglaya — "he did not die from drowning. Rather, he was already dead" — another sob — "when he entered the water. Arkady Olegovich died from hemorrhage, after being viciously struck on the side of the head." Now both women were crying. "The instrument of his death was blunt, but fairly narrow." The doctor held up his thumb and forefinger at a distance of no more than half a *vershok* (the width of the wheel-spoke, thought Avrom.) "He was killed some time around dawn — four-thirty this morning, give or take an hour or two."

"Dawn!" exclaimed Nikifor Kharitonovich. "Are you certain, Anton Pavlovich?"

The doctor removed his pince-nez and held them aloft like a lottery ticket. "Quite."

The moment he uttered the word, the dam of silence broke and a river of chatter swept over the lakeshore. And then several things happened, almost at the same instant. A howl, more animal than human, rose above all the other voices: "If it was dawn, then the Yids must have seen it! And if they're not saying anything, it's because they're the ones who did it! The Yids killed our young nobleman!" It was Styopa — who, as all heads turned his way, took a few bounding steps, straight toward where Avrom was standing.

Thinking of what had happened to Hezkel, Avrom was on his guard at once, and took a step backward. But it was not him who the malignant servant had in mind to attack this time. Bending low in mid-stride, almost to all fours, Styopa dashed his lantern against the ground, smashing the kerosene-filled glass globe within. Then, as he rose, his bounding steps carried him straight past Avrom and directly to Koppel. The next second, his hand darted out, snatched the yarmulke from Koppel's head, and promptly set it ablaze.

The constable known as the Pole, who was standing just behind Koppel, burst into laughter, while Styopa bared his yellow teeth in a merry grin. Koppel himself lunged forward to try to retrieve the burning skullcap, and Avrom, afraid of what Styopa would do next, took hold of Koppel's shoulder to pull him away. But he didn't pull him far enough. Quick as lightning, Styopa reached out to grasp hold of Koppel's beard, and yanked it toward the naked flame.

Koppel stumbled forward, with Avrom pulling still harder on his shoulder, but to no avail. The next thing anyone knew, the whole beard was aflame. Koppel let out a shriek and slapped at himself. Everyone else went silent with shock — until, from out of nowhere, Dovid Lipkin appeared, throwing himself at Styopa and raining blows down upon the miscreant's face with his fists. A second later, Deacon Achilles was there, picking Koppel up by his legs — Avrom had already been trying and failing to do the same — and carrying him over to the water to put out the flames. Meanwhile, the Pole jumped into the fray, delivering Dovid a well-placed punch on the back of the neck that felled him in one go. Instantly, a bloodcurdling scream came from above: it was the merchant's daughter, Tatiana Savelyevna — she must have just arrived — standing near the road and lit up by the light of her own lantern. And then Oleg Efimovski arrived too, knocking Styopa to the ground with an uppercut to his chin, and gazing over to see if Tatiana had seen him do it.

The repulsive waiter sprang right back up, his eyes blazing and blood dripping from above one eye down to his long mustaches. He shouted at Oleg Olegovich, "After what I did for your brother? You'll pay for that!" But he didn't shout anything else. Nikifor Kharitonovich, the police chief, had stepped up next to him, with an air of quiet menace.

"Take him," the police chief ordered his constable. "We'll arrest them both." Nikifor Kharitonovich bent down to pull up the unconscious Dovid, while the Pole just stood there, and Styopa hopped from one foot to the other. "Well?!" bawled Nikifor Kharitonovich. Looking most unhappy, the flaxen-haired Pole took a step toward Styopa. But before he could lay a hand on him, Styopa jumped back several steps, chirping, "Not me!" and took to his heels. As for the constable: he hesitated, saw the look on Nikifor Kharitonovich's face, and then broke into a lazy run, disappearing after the criminal into the darkness.

"He won't catch him," grumbled the police chief, to no-one in particular.

Meanwhile, the petty-governor had ambled up. "Really, my dear Nikifor Kharitonovich," he said, slapping the police chief on the back. "I don't see any need to arrest the man. It was only a bit of high spirits, wouldn't you agree?"

"I'm afraid I wouldn't, Anton Antonovich. If once we allow the fuse to burn, before long the whole keg will blow."

"The keg? I don't — " began Skorokhodov-Druganin, obviously confused.

But the chief was evidently in no mood to explain. "Now then," he said, more loudly. "I'll need to question everyone who lives around here — beginning at once." He looked down at the unconscious Dovid. "And I'll need to get this man into the house till my other constables arrive. Avrom Moisevich, you can help me get him inside."

Avrom had been gazing toward the lakeshore — a small crowd was gathered there by now, crouched around Koppel, amongst whom Avrom recognized Deacon Achilles and Doctor Artiukhov, along with what looked like all of Koppel's daughters. Now, he looked at Nikifor Kharitonovich in surprise.

"You're really arresting Dovid?"

"What's that?" the petty-governor spoke up. "What'd the Yid say? Lucky if you don't give him the birch for putting on airs."

But the police chief ignored Skorokhodov-Druganin, answering Avrom instead, in a voice as icy and clear as vodka: "I said I'd arrest him. Everyone knows I do what I say. Now, help me to get him inside."

Chapter 4

Villagers

The night was far from over; but the remaining hours passed without great event. As soon as Avrom had resigned himself to helping Nikifor Kharitonovich bring the prisoner inside, and grasped Dovid Lipkin's left arm (the chief already had a firm hold on the right) the young pugilist came to. He quickly looked all around, and when he saw Koppel down by the water, broke free and ran over. The chief, following close behind, permitted Dovid to stay long enough to observe his prospective father-in-law's condition: Koppel's face was burnt and bare, and Doctor Artiukhov was in the midst of applying a salve there. But, apart from being drenched (thanks to the deacon's good offices) Koppel was otherwise unharmed, and went so far as to instruct his daughters to thank the Almighty, since things hadn't turned out worse. Finding Koppel more whole than harmed, Dovid tried to speak to Blume. But at that, Nikifor Kharitonovich took hold of him again, and pulled him away.

The path up to the house took the chief and his prisoner close by the lifeless body of Arkady Olegovich, which the deceased's brother and the mayor were in the process of attempting to lift. Extracting a promise from Lipkin to wait for him inside, Nikifor Kharitonovich stayed to lend a hand, and was joined a second later by Deacon Achilles. Then the four of them carried the fallen nobleman up toward the road. A plangent cortège brought up the rear: Madame Efimovskaya and Aglaya Olegovna, General Kondratin, Saveli Savelyevich the merchant with his wife and daughter, and last of all, Doctor Artiukhov, who, however, done with his medical duties, was really only walking in the same direction to find his calèche and drive it home. A moment later, Avrom joined Koppel's daughters in walking their father back into his house. The neighbors drifted uncertainly away. And soon, the yard was left empty.

Inside, they didn't know what to speak of first. Tatte's ordeal, Efimovski's death, whether the reprehensible Styopa would be brought to ground — for ten minutes they pursued each of these subjects, with only Dovid Lipkin remaining strangely silent. Then the door flew open, and Nikifor Kharitonovich entered, followed by two of his three constables — thankfully not including the Pole. The police chief pointed informationally at Lipkin. Without a word, one of the constables approached the prisoner.

The prisoner, however, no longer appeared to be in quite so cooperative a mood: he stood stiffly where he was, his mouth set and his eyes upon the ceiling. The constable, his hand already halfway toward grasping Dovid's arm, hesitated and looked toward Nikifor Kharitonovich, who appeared, without having taken a step, to have moved nearer to Dovid. Ominous was the chief's air. Even his mustaches seemed held taut. Nor did anyone else in the room so much as breathe, for the space of what should have been three or four breaths.

But then, Dovid lowered his head. He allowed himself to be led away. And with Koppel and the girls and Avrom all looking at the door through which he'd just gone, the chief, as if nothing had happened, began questioning them concerning what they'd seen at dawn that morning.

All had the same answer — nothing.

"I was gazing out at the lake," said Avrom.

"I was talking to Masha," said Blume.

"I was searching once again," said Koppel, barely moving his lips so as not to cause himself pain from his burns, "for the dowry-money."

As to that — the robbery: What about it? Who knew you would be away from home?

Who knows who knew?

All right, then, the wheel: was it yours, the one that —

No.

Do you know whose it was?

The Lord alone knows.

And Arkady Olegovich Efimovski: Were you acquainted with him?

Yes, in a manner of speaking. But ... not to speak to. He was a nobleman, after all —

When was the last time you saw him?

The interview didn't last long. But Avrom's night still wasn't over. In order to question the other inhabitants of Balativke most efficiently, Nikifor Kharitonovich opted to commandeer the tsimbalist's house, and sent Svistunov, his remaining constable, to gather the rest of the village there.

Left alone with Avrom, the chief removed a slender cigar from one of the pockets of his green tunic, and busied himself for some time with lighting it. When the cigar was fully ablaze, and he'd savored several mouthfuls of its smoke, Nikifor Kharitonovich turned to Avrom, and said, as though they'd been arguing the point for a while: "Well — and what do you suppose would have happened to your young friend if I *hadn't* put him under arrest?"

Avrom, who had been tidying up, although the place was already immaculately clean, stopped, and slowly replied, "I suppose ... he would have gone off ... and then later, one of Styopa's lot would have waylaid him, for daring to lay his hands on a Russian."

The chief inclined his head respectfully. "It is a pleasure to deal with an intelligent man. And I note that Styopa did not attempt to set *your* beard on fire."

"Meaning?"

The chief glanced around the room. "I see you have no mirror. If you did you'd know what I mean without asking. Does *your* beard drag on the ground, Avrom Moisevich? No. And besides that, you roll your *r* like a good Russian, and you dress in a thoroughly modern fashion." Nikifor Kharitonovich sighed. "You are respected among your people, Avrom Moisevich, I've seen it. Listen, suppose you could convince them to be more like you — more like the rest of us. So much difficulty could be avoided — "

"So you believe it was Koppel's fault that he was burnt?" Avrom interrupted.

The chief's eyes narrowed. "Of course not. Styopa is scum. However — "

"And what about the Pole?"

The chief's eyes narrowed further. "What about him?"

Avrom hesitated. "It does not fill the Jews of Balativke with confidence, when one of your constables behaves that way."

Nikifor Kharitonovich's eyes were now reduced to two perfectly opaque slits. He sucked in a great mouthful of smoke, and let it out slowly, before replying, in his clearest, iciest voice: "My dear Avrom Moisevich. You go too far."

For a long minute, neither of them said anything. The chief sucked very faintly on his cigar, and a thin wisp of smoke rose straight up out of his mouth, fluttering his delicate mustache and swaying like a charmed serpent toward the ceiling; while Avrom debated whether he ought, solely in order to break the tension, to offer an insincere apology.

Finally, the chief spoke. "You'll come Monday morning, as usual?"

"Certainly."

"Good."

Immediately after, the door opened, and the constable led in the first of the neighbors, Pinkhus Khaikin, a laborer at the turpentine works located in the middle of the forest. Behind him came his wife and nine children. Avrom evacuated at once.

One of the few pieces of furniture the tsimbalist owned was a large wooden chair, which he kept outside, next to the shed where he stored his tsimbls (the smaller instrument, which was made to be hung by straps from the shoulders, was still in there, though he'd left his larger one behind at the Efimovski mansion.) For the next hours, while the residents of Balativke came in and out of his house to be asked the same series of fruitless questions, that was where Avrom sat, staring out at the smooth, black lake.

~

Avrom's neighbors were curious to see the inside of his house — even if it meant being questioned by the terrifying Nikifor Kharitonovich at the same time. None of them had ever been in, and they were dying to know, for example, whether the tsimbalist kept books — they'd definitely seen him outside his house, reading — and what sort of books they were, and what sort of a household he kept. Was he really an *apikores*, as his short jacket and trimmed beard suggested? When he came to worship at the *shul*, was it only for show, or did he mean it? Could a man so friendly with a Christian priest and the chief of police really be a good Jew?

It wasn't that they didn't respect Avrom. Despite practicing the disreputable profession of music, he himself was reputable.

Beyond doubt, he was a considerate neighbor, a man who went out of his way for others. And he radiated a certain undeniable personal propriety and rectitude, despite his unorthodox choice of beard and jacket. They respected him. They simply didn't know what to make of him.

There were so many rumors, too, concerning his biography, the life he had led before arriving in their little village. Was it true that he was born in St. Petersburg, to a wealthy merchant who was barely a Jew at all, but instead a follower of newfangled ideas that were even more newfangled at that time than they were now? No-one knew. And was it true that his mother had died when he was a baby? And that at about the time when he ought to have had a Bar Mitzvah, his father, who wasn't in favor of Bar Mitzvahs but *was* in favor of becoming extremely wealthy — as who wouldn't be? — went into his study after losing a fortune of millions, and blew his brains to smithereens with a pistol? Again, no-one knew.

Nor did the mysteries end there. Avrom *may* subsequently have been raised by a devout grandfather, may have then gone off to study with a famous rabbi, may have inexplicably transformed himself three short years later from a yeshiva *bokher* to a virtuoso performer upon the tsimbl, may even have toured Europe in that capacity.

No-one knew for certain whether any of these things *had* happened. But it all made for interesting talk and never-ending speculation.

What they found inside his little shack didn't make things much clearer. There were books, reassuring ones, in Hebrew and Yiddish. What looked to be three or four ethical treatises could be spotted among them, including one by the famed Rabbi Yisroel Salanter, the very same Rabbi Salanter who was rumored to have taught and inspired the Kelmer Maggid himself. But there were other books, too, strange books in strange languages; and even a novel in Russian, though upon closer examination, it was written by somebody named Osip Rabinovich, so maybe that was all right.

Aside from the books, the place was spotless, and, though no larger than their own tiny hovels, quite luxurious in size for one man living alone. Which led to another question — was it true that the tsimbalist had been married once, before coming to live in Balativke? Was it true, in fact, that one night, in a spa town in Prussia, while he was traveling as a virtuoso performer, he heard that his young wife in Russia had taken ill, and rushed home, but too late to see her still alive? And that thereafter, he renounced the role of virtuoso, and contented himself with playing in Jewish orchestras?

Even if that was all true, the question remained, why hadn't Avrom ever remarried? Or on the other hand, if it wasn't true that he'd once been married, well then, why not? How did he manage it, living alone so long?

Mysteries, one piled upon the other ... Although, as to the last question, there *was* an answer of sorts to be had, which although it resided in the same realm of uncertainty as the many rumors about Avrom's former life, had at least the advantage of dealing with matters of the present.

~

A few doors up the road from where Avrom lived, there stood a dwelling, upon which the generous villagers had bestowed no fewer than two epithets. Some called it the Goy's House, while to others it was known as the House of the Aguneh. In this dwelling there lived a woman named Rivke.

The house couldn't help but be noticed by travelers through the town. Or was it rather the garden in front that attracted their notice? Orange and blue with marigold and periwinkle in the springtime, and in the summer still more colorful with cornflowers, sunflowers and red poppies bursting forth from the ground. The house of a Christian, these travelers would think. Of course they would: for what Jew was known to grow flowers?

Nor was the garden the house's only remarkable feature, for upon lingering to sniff at those sweet scents, the traveler would undoubtedly be startled by a sharp noise emanating from behind the door: the yapping of a little dog, a spaniel. And here was final proof, if any were needed, that this was no Jew's dwelling. Flowers might be considered an eccentricity. Dogs were an impossibility. For these reasons was the place called, by the more malicious amongst the neighbors, the Goy's House. As for the house's other name — that owed its origins to an altogether sadder story.

Some fifteen years previously — this was before the tsimbalist had arrived in Balativke — the young Rivke had been married to a merchant named Tsemakh. One day — it was in the spring, but at that time she had not yet begun to grow her marigolds — Rivke received a goodbye from her husband, as he set out on a trip to Odessa. Tsemakh was carrying upon his person a large sum of money, some of it his own and some belonging to two business partners from Zavlivoya. With these pooled sums, he was to procure a large bundle of fine goods, which he would then bring back so that they could sell them to the locals, at no small profit.

It was expected that Tsemakh would return within a month. But the month went by, and a second too, without any sign of him. The two partners visited Rivke at her home, at first every few days and then daily, asking for and then demanding an explanation. But she had none to give. After a third month passed, they set out themselves, to retrace Tsemakh's steps. However, in all the country between Balativke and Odessa, they could find no sign of his passing.

It was by now clear that something serious had happened. But whether it was that Tsemakh had absconded with their money, or that he had instead been waylaid, even murdered, no one could tell. The authorities were turned to. But they declared themselves likewise unable to retrace the missing merchant's steps (this was in the days before Nikifor Kharitonovich arrived as police chief in Zavlivoya) and contented themselves instead with imprisoning Tsemakh's business partners for a week or two, on the suspicion that it was they themselves who had murdered him, for his share of the money. When these charges proved impossible to substantiate, the matter was dropped, with nothing at all having been proven.

The mystery surrounding Tsemakh's fate put Rivke, already distraught with worry and grief, in a difficult position. Had her husband been found to have been murdered, she would have been declared a widow, pure and simple. She would have mourned, and then, with a little time gone by, would in all probability have remarried. Instead, she was transformed over night into that chimerical creature known as an *aguneh*: neither fish nor fowl, neither married nor unmarried, a half-widow bound to a shadow. Unable to entertain offers of marriage from any new suitor who might come along, thanks to her still-binding contract with Tsemakh, she was forced to go on living alone. And to make matters worse, she was left with hardly a possession to her name. Tsemakh had sold all they owned before setting out. To support herself, she began to bake bread, which she sold at the Zavlivoya market.

Her neighbors felt all her grief — for a while. It wasn't long, however, before rumors began to attach themselves to her and to her dwelling place. The first whispers came at the same moment that the first flowers started to shoot up from the ground by her door. When a spaniel began to bark from behind that door, the whispers grew louder.

The loudest whispers, however, had nothing to do with these flora and fauna which, un-Jewish as they might be, were at least *of this world.*

To the certain knowledge of at least one village gossip, how-ever, when moonlight shone on the flowers, and the little span-iel fell asleep, when night came to the village by the lake, the *aguneh* Rivke would receive in her house spirits of the other world, unholy spirits, that is to say demons. Unless it was one demon only, a demon who would howl like the wind and shake the walls of Rivke's house on stormy nights while he carried on with the lonely woman, causing her little dog to whimper in its sleep.

The *aguneh* was not without her defenders, who steadfastly claimed that, dog and flowers aside, Rivke was an upstanding woman who would never have any truck with demons. In addi-tion, it was well known that she could be seen walking outside late at night. Why would she be walking outdoors if she had demons to entertain indoors?

"Oho! In that case, where does she walk?" — the others would rejoin. Why not to the house of a neighbor, a certain unmarried neighbor, who happened to be eccentric in his own right?

"Reb Avrom? Nonsense! Even if Rivke might carry on that way, Reb Avrom never could! Our tsimbalist may be eccentric, but when has he ever been improper? He never has even a crumb on his coat." An unassailable argument.

And yet, definitive as it was, this reply never seemed to pre-vent the same conversation from occurring again, a month or six months later. Nor did it prevent prying eyes on this night from looking for some evidence of a dalliance between the *aguneh* and the tsimbalist, some trace of her presence in his house.

No such evidence presented itself. And as it turned out, there was little time to look for it anyway, with so many difficult questions coming out of the terrifying Nikifor Kharitonovich's mouth. It had to be admitted, furthermore, that these were themselves highly interesting questions — especially the one the police chief didn't ask aloud: who killed Arkady Olegovich Efimovski?

⁓

When Avrom awoke, the sun had already poked its face up over the far side of the lake. He rose stiffly from his chair, lit the coals beneath the now-cold samovar, and ate what was left of an aging loaf of rye. He was famished.

Most days, he would have proceeded to greet the day playing on his tsimbl. But this morning, it seemed unseemly. Sound traveled so readily and eagerly across the lake's surface — from time to time, standing at the lake's edge, he'd even overheard conversations coming from Deacon Achilles' house, or from his neighbors'. On this morning after Arkady Olegovich had been found dead, it didn't seem right to regale his neighbors with music. A hole had been made in the world, and had not yet begun to close.

The tsimbalist's uncertainty over how to begin the new day was solved by a knock on the door. It was Itskele, Moishe Shakhes' youngest. As soon as Avrom opened the door, the scrawny young redhead sniffed at the air, then ducked under Avrom's arm through the doorway, without so much as a greeting. Once inside, he swiveled his head one way and then the other, before piping up, in his high-pitched voice, "It stinks in here, Reb Avrom. Since when've you been nibbling *megillahs?*"

The tsimbalist suppressed a laugh. The boy was very like his father. "It wasn't me, Itskele, but the chief of police, who was smoking cigars."

The youngster whistled. "You in the woods?"

"No, I'm not in trouble. But where is your father? I suppose you came for the wagon."

"Not exactly. Tatte says we've got a whole load of lookers to fire today. So it's on you to take the rattler back to the gull's nest, and make the gull bug over the garnish. And he told me if you made a fuss, to say the reason it's on you, is on account of we had to shank it all the way home, after you bolted with

Pasternak and the rattler last night. So ... what was the *koyen-godl* doing here anyways, if it's not 'cause you're in the woods?"

This time Avrom couldn't suppress a laugh at Itskele's mono-logue — the boy had learned his *klezmer-loshn* too well. But then he grew serious. "You must have heard that the gull's — I mean, Oleg Olegovich's brother was found in the lake last night. It was Oleg Olegovich himself who decided to take your wagon, to get here as quickly as possible."

The boy clicked his tongue. "Yeah, we did hear about that. I guess that don't make you any keen to collect on the garnish, if his brother just kicked. But look at it like this," the youngster suddenly adopted an avuncular air. "This way, you might get another chance to lay eyes on the gull's sis. Did you get a look at the milk-cans on her?" Itskele licked his lips. "Now *that's* a drink to only be drunk on *holidays*. Anyway," he said, throwing open the door, "you can just drop me back in Zav."

If Avrom hadn't already been well acquainted with the boy (and his father and brothers, for that matter) he would have been shocked. Itskele was only eleven.

~

Itskele was right that Avrom wasn't "any keen to collect on the garnish," that is, request the fee for the previous night's enter-tainment. But the tsimbalist did need to retrieve his tsimbl from the Efimovski mansion. So, a bit bemused, he followed the youngster out to the "rattler," and hitched up Pasternak. Itskele wasted no time in sprawling in the wagon's rear like a king.

"Are you sure you're comfortable?" Avrom asked, a twinkle in his eye.

"Couldn't be better," replied the lad.

"In that case ..." Avrom flicked the reins, and away they went, in the direction of Zav.

"Say Reb Av," Itskele spoke up after they'd been riding a

short time. "I've been meaning to ask you something. It's about you and that *aguneh* lady that's your neighbor."

"My neighbor Rivke, you mean?" Avrom sighed.

"That's the one. Well, they say you and her, that the two of you are — well, you know what I mean. And I wanted to know is it true, on account of they also say that she's got a demon that — "

"Itskele," Avrom pulled the wagon to a stop. "You mustn't engage in gossip. People say things all the time that aren't true. Have you ever been unhappy about anything?"

"Unhappy? Sure, like the other day my Tatte said I wasn't allowed to — "

"Then imagine what it must be like to be unhappy all the time."

"All the time? But — "

"Therefore, don't add to that poor woman's suffering by speaking ill of her."

"But my Tatte says — "

"On this subject," Avrom cut him off, "what your Tatte says is of no concern to me."

～

A little past Deacon Achilles' place, the wagon overtook another early riser.

"Good morning, Reb Berl Melamed," Avrom pulled Pasternak to a halt. "A ride?"

"Gladly!" The slight, bespectacled Hebrew school teacher placed the several books he was carrying carefully into the wagon, then lifted the skirts of his caftan and climbed in. "And a good morning and good year to you, Reb Avrom."

"I hope you slept," said the tsimbalist, who had last seen the teacher only a few hours earlier. Berl Melamed had spent all the previous day in Zavlivoya waiting to hear the Kelmer Maggid's sermon, and only returned to Balativke after the night's great events had already occurred. For that reason, he was among the last to be brought to Avrom's house for questioning.

"The less you sleep, the more you live," the teacher quoted a well-known proverb. "I don't regret a thing. You should have heard the Maggid last night, Reb Avrom!"

"Believe me," replied Avrom feelingly. "I wish I had. Especially with everything that happened."

"Yes, terrible, terrible!" Berl Melamed spat three times over the side of the wagon, nearly losing his spectacles in the process — they were far too big for his narrow nose.

"But where are you off to so early, Reb Berl?"

The teacher straightened up, and said, importantly, "I'm on my way to Reb Grinberg's house, in Zavlivoya."

"*Nu?*" called out Itskele from the back of the wagon. "Since when are *you* friends with a millionaire like Grinberg?"

"Itskele!" Avrom turned back to scold the boy. "Mind your manners."

"I wouldn't exactly say we're friends," admitted Berl Melamed, addressing himself solely to Avrom. "But the Maggid is staying at Grinberg's while he's in town, and I'm hoping to go learn with him."

"So why not wait till a decent hour," the unchastened youngster persisted from behind, "and find the Maggid at *shul*?"

Looking embarrassed, Berl Melamed again directed his answer to Avrom: "The truth is, I wanted to get a look at the inside of Grinberg's house — they say it's something to be seen! *Hoyn v'oysher baveyso*, as the psalm goes." He twisted around to face Itskele. "That means, wealth and riches shall be in his house."

"Is that so?" Itskele replied. "But Grinberg's — wasn't that one of the houses that got tossed night before last?"

"Terrible, terrible," Berl Melamed nodded. "Terrible."

"They oughtta change the psalm then," cackled Itskele. "Wealth and riches shall be taken *out* of his house, right under his nose."

"They took everything, then?" Avrom asked the teacher.

"In a manner of speaking. Grinberg keeps his money in a desk with seven locks on it, with seven — "

"With seven different keys, I've heard," said Avrom. "So the thieves left the money, and took — "

"They couldn't get into the desk?" Itskele piped up. "What kind of thieves are they?"

"Itskele, *Sha!*" shouted Avrom, and the boy jumped all the way to the back of the wagon. "What was it they took, Berl, my friend?"

"Only what was small and valuable — candlesticks, a menorah, one very small painting, snuffboxes, jewelry — "

"It sounds like you took the whole inventory."

"Reb Grinberg was telling everybody. He was beside himself."

"So tell me, was the thief a Jew or a Russian?"

"Reb Avrom! How would I know that?"

"Simple. You say the Maggid is staying at Grinberg's house. Well, did the thief steal from him too? If he did, he was a Russian. No Jew would dare rob the Kelmer Maggid."

"Ah! Very clever. In that case, I suppose it was either an illiterate Jew, or a strange Russian. The Maggid's trunks *were* broken into. But the only thing the thief took was the Maggid's best prayer shawl. He left all the books behind."

The tsimbalist furrowed his brow. "What Russian wants a prayer shawl to wear? But what Jew would leave behind a book?"

"It's a puzzle," Berl Melamed agreed.

"And what about Reb Grinberg?"

"What about him?"

"I suppose he regrets hosting the Maggid now."

"You know, I think he does — how did you know? He kept talking about how he's never been robbed before, and then looking at the Maggid, as though it was his fault for bringing bad luck on the house." Berl Melamed spat once again over the side of the wagon.

"The theft can't have helped, after the things the Maggid was saying the night before. I'm surprised a rich man would host the Maggid in the first place."

"I had the same thought, Reb Avrom! The Maggid's words were more likely to please the poor than the rich ... The Throne of Justice ... and kosher money ... and how it's not enough to be devout, if you don't treat your fellow man with the same devotion. But on the other hand, I've never heard anyone speak against Reb Grinberg's honesty. And he's a great support to the needy. After all, would the Master of the Universe have made Grinberg rich if he hadn't deserved it? ... Tell me, Reb Avrom, did *you* like what the Maggid had to say?"

The tsimbalist laughed. "Me? What does it matter what I thought? But he aroused my curiosity. I'd like to ask him a question or two."

"Ah yes?"

"It's nothing — I'm only curious to know whether he's really a disciple of the great Rabbi Salanter, as some say, or if it's just that some of their ideas coincide."

"Ah, I saw Salanter's *Letter* in your house! Are you a follower of his?"

Avrom paused to formulate his answer. "I think there is great merit in his thought."

"Perhaps you should come with me now."

"Alas, I can't. But maybe I'll see you later. At the very least, I'd like to see the Kelmer Maggid close up."

~

It was not yet eight o'clock when the wagon pulled into Zav, but there were already many people abroad, dressed in their Sunday finest. The main street was loud with the clanging of the town's "singing icons," as the Russians poetically name their church bells. The *kampans* of St. Vladimir's, the principal Orthodox church, were already ringing when they entered town, and by the time Itskele jumped out of the wagon, they'd been joined by their rivals at the smaller Il'inskaya and Jesuit churches. Moishe Shakhes, who lived along the bottom edge of a triangle formed by all three churches, often complained that his mirrors and windows, not to mention his eardrums, were sure to be broken any day now by the racket. Now Avrom could hear why.

Quieter was Zavlivoya's south end, the Jewish quarter, where Reb Lev Grinberg's spanking-new house sat up on a hill. As Avrom drove up, he saw several Jews congregated near Grinberg's door. Standing at their center was Svistunov, the constable who'd been assisting Nikifor Kharitonovich last night. Today, it seemed, he was charged with investigating the robberies here in Zavlivoya. Not wishing to be delayed further, Avrom deposited Berl Melamed a short way from the house, and then steered Pasternak southward.

The forest road was empty of travelers, and the wood on either side quiet. The weather, though cooler than yesterday's, was windless and still. Alone for the first time since Itskele's unexpected intrusion, Avrom left it to the horse to find the path. He himself was chewing over something which had begun to make an unpleasant taste in his mouth: this task he was on his way to undertake. Granted he wouldn't even consider trying to collect the fee from the mourning Efimovskis, his would still be an unwelcome presence, on this of all mornings.

On the road ahead, a cart appeared, traveling the opposite way. Its driver was swathed in black. A long white beard protruded from beneath his hawk-like face. It was Father Innokenty, the chief cleric at St. Vladimir's.

Strange, thought Avrom. Shouldn't Father Innokenty be at church by now? But no, he must have been summoned to the Efimovski estate, to bless the body and pray over it during the

wake — that, Avrom seemed to remember, was how the Orthodox went about things after a death. And with a family as illustri-
ous as the Efimovskis, it was only to be expected that Zavlivoya's
chief cleric would officiate. But in that case, why was he already
returning?

Avrom was pondering this question when, upon each side,
the forest began to thin. The Efimovski orchards came into view,
gold and green and red in the morning sun. Pasternak took a
curve to the right, and then, around the bend, a colorful crowd
of people came into view, filling the road and forcing Avrom to
pull the horse to a violent stop.

Thirty heads turned to see whose wagon had nearly run
them down. As they did, Avrom felt an unaccountable sensa-
tion, a prickly feeling of danger in his very skin. He saw hostile
eyes, whispering mouths, slowing steps, a gradual shift of bodies in his direction, and then heard a rising muttering.

There were many familiar faces in the crowd. Avrom had
exchanged a polite nod with more than a few of them, more
than a few times, at the Zavlivoya market. They were peasants,
former serfs of the Efimovskis, who inhabited what was known
as the "Efimovski estate village," a collection of huts only a *verst*
from here on one end of the noble family's estate. The road split
just here, one branch leading to the village, and the other onward
to the Efimovski mansion and beyond. Evidently, the peasants
were returning to their village from the mansion. Undoubtedly,
they'd gone to pay respects to the deceased.

Their occupation was a sorrowful one, and their clothing
pastoral, *sarafans* of purple and red for the women, white blous-
es and bast shoes for the men. But their mood appeared angry,
even vicious, as they stared at Avrom in his wagon.

Indeed, there now stepped forward from their midst a man
who, though slighter of build than the others, was undeniably
threatening in his manner. He bore, too, as Avrom saw when the
man raised his face, a striking resemblance to Styopa. Avrom

recalled that Styopa's mother Marfa had family in the Efimovski village. Styopa himself was said to have gone to live there, after his dismissal from his post at the house. Certainly, this was one of his relations.

The man lurched forward to put a rough hand on Pasternak's muzzle, causing the horse to rear, and then turned to face his fellows. He spoke — something that sounded like, "my friends" — when a sound of hoofbeats was heard, approaching from the little road that led from their village. Abandoning his sentence before it had begun, the man, Styopa's relative, took several long strides across the road, and passed into the woods on the other side. The others, taking fright, scuttled after him. A few seconds later, the horseman, Avrom's savior, came into view. It was the Pole.

Upon reaching the main road, the Pole turned in the direction from which Avrom had come, taking notice neither of the peasants, nor of Avrom himself. He appeared lost in his own thoughts; on his face was a broad grin. Soon, he had disappeared down the road to Zavlivoya. He'd barely passed when Avrom spurred Pasternak forward, and a minute later, they too were far away.

The turnoff to the mansion was almost upon them when Avrom heard another horseman come galloping up behind, closing the distance between them in a matter of seconds. As he drew level, the horseman and Avrom exchanged surprised glances. It was Nikifor Kharitonovich.

Chapter 5

A Lost Knight

t once, the police chief pulled up short. Avrom, following suit, reined in Pasternak, and Nikifor Kharitonovich trotted over, erect in his seat, and with an expressionless face beneath his green cap.

"Avrom Moisevich," he said. "I can't seem to escape you."

Quite a greeting, thought the tsimbalist, who, for a moment, had been happy and relieved to see the police chief, even contemplating telling him about his unsettling encounter with the peasants. Abandoning the idea, he sardonically replied, "I apologize ... for insisting on spending the night at my own house."

Nikifor Kharitonovich's eyes narrowed in their characteristic way; but only for a moment. Then he burst out laughing. "Very good, very good. *Touché.* But Avrom Moisevich, this is a house of sorrow. Why do you come to disturb the mourners' peace?"

"Alas," replied the tsimbalist, this time expressing honest regret. "I have little choice. Last night, we were forced to leave our instruments. I've come to get them out of the way."

"Ah," replied Nikifor Kharitonovich. "Well, try to be quiet about it, will you?" With which, grimacing, the chief spurred on his horse, while Avrom looked after him. It seemed that the chief himself did not relish disturbing the mourners' peace.

"Do you hear that, Pasternak?" Avrom said aloud, flicking the reins in his hands with a hint of irritation. "Try to be quiet, will you?" And he maneuvered horse and wagon, slowly and quietly indeed, around the turn the chief had just taken.

The vista that now greeted him was no less impressive for being familiar. Two rows of poplars formed a long avenue leading to the mansion; tall and dark, they cast narrow stripes of shadow across the lighter green of avenue and lawn. Away to the left stretched a field of weeds and wildflowers, bordered on its far side by a woods belonging to the neighboring estate of General Kondratin, and separated from the main house by several outbuildings. Ahead where the poplars ended could be glimpsed the mansion's elegant, elongated columns and yellow façade, along with the sea-green cap of its rotunda, protruding above.

Halfway along, the avenue took a slight leftward curve, and Avrom's eye was caught by a burst of purple off to the right: malva flowers, garlanding a bench which formerly had stood lone and unadorned — or so he seemed to recall. The recollection was reinforced by the sight of several lanterns, mounted behind the flowers on poles just higher than the bench — an arrangement undoubtedly made for last night's affair. A patch of white showed behind the purple of the flowers: the long-deserted and now dilapidated family chapel, surrounded by a scattering of well-bleached gravestones. Beyond stood several cottages, which Avrom knew to be designated for servants and also, at times, renters; and further off, the primitive huts, and church and tavern, of the estate village, surrounded by still-green fields of wheat and rye.

And then the last few poplars passed in front of Avrom's eyes, and Pasternak, of his own accord, came to a gentle stop.

"Thank you," said Avrom to the horse.

The next second, the crunch of a boot made him turn his

head. The police chief was walking toward him from the direction of the stables. Wishing to avoid a further encounter, Avrom
quickly bent over and pretended to rummage for something at
his feet. Not till he heard the door of the house open, and then
close behind the chief, did he sit back up. A suitable minute
later, he knocked at the door himself.

For some time, nothing happened. Avrom heard a buzzing
of insects, and, far off, the bark of a dog. He was about to knock
again, when the door slowly opened. Standing in the doorway
was Foka.

The ancient servant was pale, and his livery unbuttoned
and askew. He must have been deeply affected by the death in
the family. He seemed to have forgotten what he was doing while
doing it: his eyes rested on the hand that held the doorknob,
and it took him several seconds to remember to look up. Once
he did, he beckoned the new arrival to follow, and hobbled
along a corridor, which Avrom knew to lead to the ballroom.

It was clear at once that a misunderstanding had occurred.
As they approached the ballroom's threshold, Avrom could hear
chanting. He stopped short of entering the room behind the
servant, but could see all there was to see: the casket, in which
Arkady Olegovich's body was stretched out, and the priest, diminutive and bald, with what looked like a piece of sponge
glued to his chin in place of a beard. This was Father Zacharias,
second in rank at St. Vladimir's. Father Zacharias was chanting
psalms from a psalter, while nearby sat three mourners. One of
these was General Kondratin. Oddly, none of the family was to
be seen. But of course — they would be shut away with the police chief.

As Foka entered the room, Father Zacharias, without ceasing
his chanting, looked up from his psalter, took in the situation at
once, and stared pointedly at Foka. The three mourners turned
to give Avrom unwelcoming looks, and then Foka seemed to
catch on that something was amiss, and turned to study the

Jewish visitor. Discovering him to be no mourner come to pay respects, he let out a deep sigh, then set off back down the corridor they'd just come along. With an apologetic nod toward the mourners, Avrom followed.

Foka next led him to a door which, when opened, revealed a closet into which the instruments had been crammed. The old servant then appeared to lose all interest in the matter, and shuffled away, while Avrom turned his quiet attention to the instruments.

Two violins. Flute. Drum. They were all here. And even the bass. (How Kuz'ma had gotten his instrument here last night appeared to be a puzzle, since he'd obviously left without it.) It wouldn't do to take too many at once: they would certainly make noise bumping against each other, and he didn't wish to create more of a disturbance than he already had. It therefore took several minutes, and several trips, to get all but the tsimbl into the wagon. Especially awkward was the bass: he even knocked it against another door on the corridor on his way out.

The accident proved significant: returning to retrieve his tsimbl, which had been shoved into the closet's rear, he found the door he had bumped against open a crack. And through that crack, he could make out, most distinctly, the voice of Nikifor Kharitonovich, and even his words: "Of course you are right," the chief was saying. "Suspicion does most naturally fall on him, since it was just outside his house."

So. They were talking about Koppel.

The next voice Avrom heard was the exhausted alto of Madame Efimovskaya: "And so?" she said, making the words sound like both a groan and an accusation. "Why do you wait?"

"Ah, my dear Agrafena Ivanovna," the chief answered. "I know, I know, the more quickly an arrest is made, the sooner justice can be done, and the sooner your heart may find some comfort. However, I believe that false justice would be worse than no justice, would it not? The unhappy truth is that a number questions must be answered before it would be truly proper to act."

"Such as?"

"To begin with — but I pray you, madame, stop me at once if you find it too painful to go into the details — to begin with, there are the robberies. The fact remains that, even if Dr. Artiukhov is right, and it was at dawn that — well, even if the doctor is right, there is the fact that the house was robbed the previous evening."

"So the Jew claims," said Madame Efimovskaya.

"Indeed. And so then I balance against this the additional fact that three other houses were robbed as well. And I am left hesitant to believe that these are all — you know, coming on the same night — is it realistic to think they are all unconnected events? It is worth taking the time to consider the question. However, these are, if I may put it so, my problem. But you can help me, I believe, with certain other questions."

"Please," Avrom heard Oleg Olegovich say.

"For example, why was Arkady Olegovich there, in the Jewish village? It was quite widely known that he was spending time with the peasants, that he had become — this is what has been said, which you can perhaps confirm, or else deny — it was said that he had become one of these *narodniks* we hear about, trying to revive the true spirit of the land, and so on."

"A passing fancy," Madame Efimovskaya dismissively remarked.

"*Maman*, I think it was quite lovely of him," Avrom heard Aglaya Olegovna say. From the sound of it, she was on the verge of tears.

"Indeed," the police chief replied soothingly. "But I am left slightly confused. Does it not seem a bit, if I may put it so, incongruous, that he was also, as I have heard, friendly with the Jews? It has been my impression that these *narodniks* — "

"He was not friendly with *the Jews*, certainly," Madame

Efimovskaya interrupted again, "even if he may have been friendly with one or two of them. But Olezhka, you know more about it."

"Arkasha *was* friendly with at least several Jews," Oleg Olegovich replied in a considered tone. "Of course I'd seen little of him myself since he conceived this particular passion — I believe it really took hold of him in the fall, in Kiev, and he left to come back here before I'd heard much about it. For myself, *I* only arrived from Kiev on Spirit Monday, and Arkasha left two days later, on Wednesday, so you see ..."

"I understand perfectly."

"However, he did tell me the other day about a certain writer, he was quite passionate about his theories ... of course you know there are so *many* theories flying about these days, with one new group forming, and splitting immediately into several factions — or so at least it appears to me, from my provincial perch. So that you might have one group of *narodniks* who would probably like to run all the Jews out of the country, but then others who ..."

"Yes, I see," said Nikifor Kharitonovich.

There was a pause, during which Avrom heard the striking of a match, and then Oleg Olegovich, saying, "No thank you, I have my own," and after that, sounds from another part of the house — perhaps made by Foka, or else the housekeeper Marfa. A moment later, an odor of smoke — from cigar and cigarette both — wafted in from the drawing room. Finally, Avrom heard two voices begin to speak at once, before the police chief gave way to Oleg Olegovich.

"Nikifor Kharitonovich," the young nobleman said in a quiet, tentative tone, "I've heard it said ... regarding the *narodniks* ... I've heard it said that their activities have attracted the interest of the Third Section." (His quiet tone was well-justified, thought Avrom. The Third Section was the tsar's dreaded secret police branch, charged with the investigation of political crimes.)

"Yes, yes," the police chief replied with a sigh. "I'm afraid the thought cannot be avoided. There could have been some involvement from that quarter."

Here, Avrom heard crying, coming from Aglaya Olegovna.

"However," continued the chief, "on the whole, I am inclined to dismiss the idea. A trial and a stint in Siberia are more in their line, not — "

"But surely," interrupted Madame Efimovskaya, "they cannot have suspected Arkashenka. He can only have been playing at politics. He was" — here Agrafena Ivanovna's softened — "he was a dreamer. Dreaming, and talking, but never, Nikifor Kharitonovich, he would never have — Aglayushka, darling, who was it you would compare him to?"

"Oblomov," replied the young woman, whose next words were difficult to make out, interrupted as they were by little sobs and sniffs. "You know ... the character ... Goncharov's novel. I always teased ... just like Oblomov, never really getting around to ... anything. But I didn't ... anything bad ... honestly I didn't. He knew I only ..." Her last words were lost in sobbing, and she made a great effort to repeat them: "He knew I only said it to make him laugh."

"Of course, of course," said Nikifor Kharitonovich soothingly. "Of course. Of course."

This went on for some time, until the chief, evidently directing his words to Oleg Olegovich, asked: "Forgive me, but just so that I may draw a clear picture of events in my head — you say that Arkady Olegovich left here on Wednesday, four days ago now, and that you had only arrived two days earlier?"

"Yes."

"That was all of you?"

"No, I had spent the whole of the winter in Kiev, and — "

Madame Efimovskaya interrupted: "Aglaya Olegovna and I wintered in Biarritz. We arrived in Kiev Monday, to find Oleg Olegovich had just left, ahead of our plan, which was to all journey here together. Then on Wednesday he wired us that he was to be engaged, and so of course we came right away, because he'd even already announced the ball. You were in quite — "

"We've discussed that, *maman*," Oleg Olegovich cut her off, with some rancor in his voice.

"And so, Madame, you arrived — "

"Friday night, at the station in Bakhmatch. The ten-thirty train. Olyezhka came to fetch us. I suppose we can only have been home a few hours when ..." Her voice quivered.

"So," Nikifor Kharitonovich asked quietly, "you didn't see Arkady Olegovich at all."

"N-na-no."

"But *I* had a note from him," said Aglaya Olegovna. "He left it for me in my room."

"Did he? And you have it still?

"I have it here." Avrom heard a rustle of paper, and then Aglaya Olegovna began to read. "'Well, my dear,'" she started. But she could get no further. A renewed attack of sobbing forced her to desist.

A few seconds later, Oleg Olegovich read out: "'Well, my dear, as my brother has just told me he's engaged — I expect you knew even before I did to whom — I find that I have a piece of *rather* important business to attend to. I know you were expecting to see me when you arrived — I hope you'll forgive me for leaving this note in my place. Something tells me you'll understand, though, won't you?'"

By the time he had finished reading, both women were sobbing.

"He sounded ... quite happy," murmured Oleg Olegovich.

"May I see it?" asked Nikifor Kharitonovich. After a minute, he asked: "Again, so that I may be quite clear. You wired your mother and sister before you saw your brother?"

"Yes. I was in town to work things out with Saveli Savely-evich. As soon as I had, I wired Kiev. And then I came back here, and shared my good news with Arkasha."

"I see. And so then — if I understand correctly — as a result of learning you'd become engaged, Arkady Olegovich decided he had some business to attend to, which furthermore, he knew would keep him away for — what, two days? Three?"

"Well, no," said Oleg Olegovich, "he may have thought per-haps as little as one. At the time he left, we thought that *Maman* and Aglaya would be arriving on Thursday. But then they wired me later that it wouldn't be till Friday night."

"Because we needed new clothes for the ball," explained Agrafena Ivanovna. "We hadn't had any warning."

"And do you have any idea what Arkady Olegovich's busi-ness was, or where it may have taken him?"

There was a brief pause, and then Aglaya Olegovna said: "We know that it took him to Chernigov. And we have a guess what it was."

"Well?"

"Olezhka, you tell."

"All right," said Oleg Olegovich. "That day, Wednesday, when I told him about the engagement — first he congratulated me, of course — and then we began talking about one thing and another. I suppose I was describing the new life I imagined, and we were in here, and my eye fell on ... well, you see — "

"His eye fell on the chess set we always kept in here," Agla-ya Olegovna broke in. "You see, when we were children, Father went on a trip up north and came back with one of those sets of Kholmogory chessmen, you know, the ones made from walrus-ivory? And to match them he'd found a board of Karelian mar-ble, pink and white. It was so lovely."

Another sob escaped the young woman, but she went right on.

"Arkashenka and Olezhka loved to play with it, they would go at it for hours. You should have seen it. It was really quite miserable."

To Avrom's ear, Aglaya Olegovna's voice suddenly sounded unnaturally high, and her tone strangely merry.

"Arkashenka would stare at the board, and forget it was his turn," she went on, "and Olezhka — he was just as impetuous then as he is now, and would make his moves much too quickly. And then at the end, it would come out that Arkashenka had a brilliant strategy in mind the whole time."

She let out a noise that sounded as much like a shriek as it did a laugh.

"You know, Olezhka, you looked like twins, but you played like opposites. And at the end, you'd always be pouting when you lost."

She laughed again.

"Oh, and Olezhka would always want to bet money on the games, but *maman* wouldn't let them."

This last was punctuated by a whole volley of laughter, which, halfway through its flight, took a nosedive into out-and-out hysterics. It was a while before anyone spoke again.

At length, Oleg Olegovich good-naturedly admitted, over his sister's last, faint hiccups, "Yes, that's all quite true. But, returning to the matter at hand: I was telling Arkasha on Wednesday that I wanted to teach my Tanya to play chess, and he said that the last he'd checked, two of the pieces had disappeared ... a knight and an elephant, I think ... and he'd had to stick two stones in with the pieces — or no, not an elephant, it was a ship that was missing, a knight and a ship. Yes. Anyway, he said he had an idea where to get new pieces, in the same Kholmogory style."

"And you think — " began Nikifor Kharitonovich.

"Yes, well, at that point it seemed natural to actually have a game. We decided to play in the ballroom, because it's lighter in there, and he was carrying the board, and — he dropped it. It quite shattered. And a little after that, he left, saying only that there was something he had to do."

"But I'm certain," said Aglaya Olegovna, who had now recovered, "that he was going to find a new set of pieces and a new board. It would be just like him — so very sweet," she said mournfully. "So gentle and so sweet."

"And in any case," said Oleg Olegovich, "he certainly went to Chernigov, because on Thursday I had a telegram from him that came from there."

"Ah?"

"Yes. It says ... here it is: Search taking longer than expected. Return delayed. Absolutely back in time for ball."

"May I? ... And this was the last you heard from him?"

"I'm afraid so."

"Hmm ... The order of events, then, was this — please correct me if I've misunderstood any point: Arkady Olegovich learned that you were to become engaged ... as a result of which he felt he must take care of a piece of business, perhaps the purchase of Kholmogory-style chess pieces ... and perhaps a board of — what was it? Karelian marble?"

"Yes."

"He left you, Aglaya Olegovna, this note, departed on his horse, was in Chernigov the following day — a distance of about sixty *versts* from here. He was at least initially unsuccessful in his search, and so delayed in his return, sending a telegram to that effect. And after that ... Who knows? We lose all track. Until he arrived very early on Saturday morning in our own Balativke. Hmm, I wonder ..." Nikifor Kharitonovich trailed off.

"Yes?" asked Oleg Olegovich.

"A small thing, only ... but what do you think became of his horse?"

In response to this, there was silence.

"And," the chief asked one last question, "I don't wish to

keep you any longer from your vigil, but ... I don't suppose any of you knows when Arkady Olegovich was last in Chernigov, or with whom?"

～

The chief's final question, like the one that came before, went unanswered. The interview seemed to have reached its end. Not wishing to be caught eavesdropping by Nikifor Kharitonovich, or by the family returning to keep watch over their fallen son, Avrom retrieved his tsimbl, as quietly as he could, and carried it outside.

Not far from the wagon, standing near to one of the elegant columns, was Foka. The ancient servant was staring downward in unhappy reverie, a watering can in his hand; at his feet was a patch of bare earth, wet and dark against the surrounding purple. (Malvas, of the same sort planted by the bench, grew around all the other columns.)

For a few seconds, the ancient servant seemed not to notice the tsimbalist's arrival; even when Avrom said, in a most gentle tone: "Ah, Foka. It's a great loss, isn't it?"

Then, as if upon some invisible cue, the old man jerked his head upward, revealing two perfectly round, cataract-shrouded eyes. "God gave, God took away," he uttered, in a faraway voice. "They've already washed his body, and soon they'll place the crown upon his head ... Old Foka helped with the washing," he concluded, a bit more brightly.

"Arkady Olegovich was lucky to be cared for by a servant like you — all his life, if I'm not wrong."

"Thanks to God," the old man agreed, "I've served the family since I was a lad. The first Oleg Olegovich, and his father and grandfather too — all of them gone now, as God wished it. But I didn't guess that Marfa would be boiling the *koliva* again so soon." The old man made the sign of the Trinity.

"He was very young," Avrom nodded.

"Yes. Sometimes ... he would even still call me *dyadka*."

"This winter, too, I suppose, he depended on you quite a lot."

"I prepared his clothes and shaved him every day, the winter long, even that last day. Every morning, he went galloping," Foka moved two fingers up and down in imitation of a horse, "stayed out all day. But the next day he still needed Foka to take care of him."

"They say he rode off Wednesday, too, to Chernigov."

"I don't know to where, just that I saw him go. Marfa and I were over there," Foka pointed away toward the bench, garlanded with flowers, "taking the malvas from here, and planting them there — Oleg Olegovich wanted to make the young lady happy at the ball, he said he would take her there to the bench, once they were properly tied up — and we saw Arkady Olegovich go by in a terrible hurry. Only this time, as God wished it, he didn't come back."

Chapter 6

Emancipation

Moved by the poignance of the old man's words, Avrom remained silent; while Foka gazed over the grounds, his shrouded eyes passing from the flower-garlanded bench to the long avenue of poplars, and out over the woods. Then, recollecting himself, the ancient servant ducked his head in a humble bow to the tsimbalist, and began to hobble away, the water-can in his hand bumping lightly against his leg with each step.

As he went, he muttered something. It sounded like, "They oughtn't ever to have done it."

"What was that?" Avrom called out automatically.

The servant halted, then hunched his head down into his shoulders like a turtle as he turned around. "It was nothing," he protested. "Only ..." He looked downward, but then took courage, and said, "The emancipation." He straightened up. "It was against nature. They oughtn't ever to have done it."

"Ah." Avrom was intrigued, and puzzled. Why had the old man brought up such a thing now?

"I never agreed with it," Foka warmed to his subject. "Gave folk bad ideas — especially some folk."

That was interesting. "Which folk?"

"Well … folk. In the old days, a peasant kept his distance from his master, and a master kept a distance from his peasants. But now it's all *anyhow*."

"I suppose so," Avrom replied, still unsure why Foka had brought up the emancipation at all. However, the conversation seemed once again to have reached its end. Once more, Foka turned to hobble away. But as before, he mumbled something as he went. This time what Avrom heard was a derisive snort, followed by: "It was the *Yids* that did it."

"What was that?" he asked sharply.

Foka turned his head, and his round eyes widened as he looked Avrom up and down. "Begging your pardon," he hastened to say. "I was only thinking of what Marfa said this morning. But *I* don't think it's so. She said that Arkady Olegovich, may he rest in peace, was — well, as I said. But you can be sure it was somebody else, may God forgive him."

For a few seconds, Avrom remained silent. Then he drew closer to Foka, saying in a low tone, "You meant Styopa."

The old man blinked, then turned his gaze to the ground.

"You meant it was Styopa who got bad ideas after the emancipation," Avrom went on, drawing very close now.

Foka looked up with watery, unfocused eyes, but didn't reply.

"And that it was Styopa who killed Arkady Olegovich."

The old man chewed on his lips. "Old Foka doesn't sleep much anymore, at night."

Again, Avrom waited a few seconds to reply. "You saw something."

Foka hunched his head into his shoulders again, and looked back down at the ground, saying more to himself than to Avrom, "You can't blame her, bless her. She's always been a God-fearing woman. And a right good housekeeper."

"You mean Marfa. Did Marfa do something last night? Did she — did she have a visitor?"

"It's just that blood isn't water," Foka sighed.

"And you heard something."

The old man nodded, almost imperceptibly. He was now licking his lips very rapidly.

"I suppose," Avrom said, "that he told her to say it was the Jews. It was the same thing he said last night. And you think that it was him who — "

Foka looked sharply down at the ground.

"Is he still here?"

Foka looked up and shook his head.

"In the village then."

This time the old man looked longingly at the path.

"So he's in the village?" Avrom pressed him.

Foka rushed to change the subject: "Father Innokenty, he said the same thing." He seemed to regret this subject, too, as soon as the words were out of his mouth.

"Said what?"

"Nothing, that is ...that is, he was here for the wake. That's all I was meaning to — "

"Foka." The old man, perhaps thinking he had successfully avoided a question he didn't want to answer, was now taking a step down the path. "What did Father Innokenty say?"

"Oh ... begging your pardon. The serfs was all here, from the village ... the peasants that is. And so the father gave his sermon, and said ... well, about the money-lenders and the tavern-keepers, who cheat the poor Russian and keep him drunk. Begging your pardon."

"I see."

"But please don't upset yourself. It's only what any priest would say — even if he was wrong to bring it up now, may I be forgiven for saying it, since it was Styo — "

Here, Foka went silent, looking terrified.

"And was that all that Father Innokenty said?" asked Avrom.

"He said we must never forget who it was that killed Christ," Foka solemnly replied.

Avrom nodded once, deeply, and sighed.

"I'll fetch the water now," said Foka, tentatively.

But Avrom wasn't quite ready to let him go. "Foka, tell me. Who was Styopa's father?"

Avrom had wondered whether this question wouldn't torture the old man as much as the others. To his surprise, however, it seemed to come as a relief.

"Marfa's husband, of course," said Foka. "Grisha, we called him, God grant him rest."

"I see."

"I'll fetch the water now," Foka repeated. When Avrom said nothing, he took up his can, hobbling round the corner of the house and down the path that passed between icehouse and stable, till he reached the well.

Avrom was still standing in the same spot watching him when he heard boots behind him, and then a familiar voice: "Still here, Avrom Moisevich?"

Avrom turned to face Nikifor Kharitonovich. "I'd like to speak with you," he forthrightly replied.

The police chief looked at him in some surprise, then nodded. "In the orchards," he said. "In a few minutes." And he proceeded onward toward the stable.

~

Nikifor Kharitonovich was already perched on the cherry orchard's low stone wall, smoking, when Avrom pulled Pasternak to a stop and walked over to join him. Overhead, the leafy boughs were largely bereft of fruit, while underfoot, the ground was littered with squashed cherries. A light breeze had blown up. The smoke of Nikifor Kharitonovich's well-chewed cigar pursued Avrom as he paced in front of the police chief, telling him everything.

Nikifor Kharitonovich had no visible reaction either to

Avrom's description of his encounter with the peasants, or to his account of the various things Foka had revealed: the contents of Father Innokenty's sermon, Styopa's nighttime visit to his mother, the fact that the miscreant was now hiding out in the estate village.

"It certainly isn't helpful when Father Innokenty talks that way," the chief merely grumbled when Avrom had done. "It becomes more and more difficult to keep the peace around here."

"I worry," said Avrom, "about Shimmel Shenkman and his family."

The chief looked at him quizzically.

"The tavern-keeper in the estate village," Avrom explained — not mentioning that Shimmel Shenkman was also a relative of Koppel's, as he was married to Koppel's cousin. Avrom was acquainted with both husband and the wife, who lived behind their tavern in the village (they were the only Jews for *versts* around) but could often be seen in Zavlivoya. He liked the wife more than the husband, whom he found a bit coarse. The wife, however, was delightful, as was the couple's ever-expanding household of well-behaved children.

It was the welfare of these children that Avrom had become concerned about when he heard Foka describe Father Innokenty's sermon. The father had mentioned tavern-keepers "who keep the poor Russian drunk." The meaning of these words was not lost upon the tsimbalist. The good father was expressing a time-worn idea that had lately become fashionable once again, one which mixed up certain known facts with other more controversial opinions to reach a very sinister conclusion.

At the heart of the matter was the hard-earned reputation of Russians for being enthusiastic consumers of alcohol, especially vodka. Drinking, and drinking to excess, was well-recognized as a popular pastime, in the empire at large, in city and countryside, among nobles and among merchants. Indeed, every student of history was familiar with the famous declaration made by Vladimir the Great, Prince of Kiev, nine-hundred years earlier, that "drinking is the joy of all Rus'. We can not live without that pleasure."

However, no one loved to drink more than the peasants, or so it was said. According to general agreement, the peasant imbibed more than was either strictly productive, or entirely healthy. Furthermore, according to those who worried about such things, the peasants' hitting of the bottle had only grown more rampant since emancipation, as the former serfs now found themselves at liberty from the strict supervision under which they had formerly lived.

Naturally, inns and taverns servicing the thirst of the masses dotted the empire, most of them owned by nobles, who still held title to the majority of the empire's lands (though many, left poorer after the emancipation, had begun to sell off their holdings.) Nobles who owned inns and taverns rented out the privilege of running them. And most often, in those areas of the empire where Jewish populations had been permitted to grow up, they rented it out to Jews, who had a reputation for loving alcohol less than the Russians did, and were therefore thought to be more reliable and less likely to consume the merchandise.

Now, the fashionable and sinister idea to which Father Innokenty had alluded at the Efimovski mansion this morning was this: that the blame for the excessive drinking of the peasants, their chronic inebriation, and by extension their lack of productivity, endemic poverty, and general miserableness, lay not with the peasants themselves, but with those who supplied them their drink; in other words, that without the corrupting influence of the Jewish tavern-keepers, the peasants would be models of industriousness and righteous living.

An obvious crack lay at the foundation of this edifice of reason: the fact that, in the many corners of the empire where Jews were prohibited from residing, the incidence of excessive drinking among the peasants was no less well-chronicled, nor were its consequences any less deleterious, than was the case in the Pale of Settlement, where Jews *were* allowed to live. A good idealist, however, is too high-minded to be distracted from the grandeur of a towering theory by flaws at its footings. And this was the case, it seemed to Avrom, with Father Innokenty and his likeminded reformers.

Nevertheless, as familiar as he was with the idea that Jews were to blame for the plight of the peasant — he'd heard of it and read it a number of times — this was the first time Avrom had seen firsthand quite how dangerous an idea it could actually be. The folk of the Efimovski village, after being inspired by the heavenly fervor of the good father, had grown hostile upon spotting *him*, Avrom — a more or less random representative of the Jewish tribe. What might they not do the next time they saw Shimmel Shenkman? Not only was Shenkman the wicked cause of their drunkenness, as Father Innokenty had just reminded them. He had compounded his sin (Avrom happened to know) by extending them credit for their drink, so that they now all owed him money; or else by accepting items from them in pawn, so that some of their dearest possessions now lay just out of their reach in the back of Shenkman's tavern. Even if the peasants did not immediately set upon the man when they first laid eyes on him, they surely would once they'd gotten a bit of drink inside them, in his tavern, with him standing before them. And what if his wife, or one of the children, happened to be around?

Nikifor Kharitonovich seemed to be thinking along the same lines. "I suppose it's still the Efimovskis who own the tavern there in the village," he speculated.

"I suppose," replied Avrom.

"It seems to me it would be an excellent time to close the place down for a little while," the chief mused, "at least until this is all straightened out." He nodded sharply. "I'll suggest it to them."

"Thank you."

"Why thank me? I merely want to keep peace in the village."

"Ah." Avrom took a step backward, to avoid a persistent waft of smoke. "I wonder," he said. "Do you think that the peasants there in the village would try to hide Styopa, or protect him?"

"They could try to," the chief scoffed. "But he isn't there, anyway."

"How do you know that?" Avrom asked in surprise.

"Because I am the chief of police," Nikifor Kharitonovich arctically replied.

"I — "

"And because," he added, his tone thawing by a degree or two, "I saw Faddei Kazimirovich this morning."

Seeing Avrom's look of confusion, the chief impatiently explained, "the Pole, as you all call him. I met him on my way here. He'd already been in the Efimovski village looking for Styopa. He searched his house and everywhere else, but," Nikifor Kharitonovich threw up his hands, "no sign of him."

Avrom wondered whether the Pole could be trusted to bring Styopa in if he *did* find him. Judging it wiser, however, to keep his doubts to himself, he remained silent, until Nikifor Kharitonovich asked, "Was there anything else?"

Avrom hesitated, until the chief gruffly prompted him. "Well?"

"I had hoped," said Avrom, "that I might follow you as far as the fork in the road."

Nikifor Kharitonovich's eyes, contrary to custom, widened, and he let out a laugh, which ended in a little cough, right in his throat. "But of course, Avrom Moisevich." He shook his head, and laughed again. "With great pleasure. Come along."

He stubbed out his cigar underfoot and, laughing a third time, mounted his white horse — who, for his part, had been getting along quite famously with Pasternak, all through his owner's conversation with Avrom Moisevich.

⌒

After wishing Pasternak a fond farewell, Avrom, who did not wish to walk all the way home to Balativke carrying his tsimbl, asked Moishe Shakhes if he wouldn't mind keeping the instrument for him until Friday.

"Friday?" asked the fiddler-glazier. "Why Friday?"

"Our next job," Avrom explained the obvious.

"Blume and Dovid's wedding?"

"What else? Don't you remember? The preliminaries Friday day, and then the ceremony once Shabbes is over."

"I remember, I remember. But I wouldn't hold my breath waiting for them to go under the *khupa*."

"Why?" Avrom frowned. "Because they put Dovid in jail? He'll go before a jury tomorrow morning. I'm sure he'll be at liberty by afternoon."

"I'm sure you're right," agreed Shakhes. "But that's not what I'm talking about. Think, Reb Avrom: after that robbery, your little Blume hasn't got the garnish for a dowry, not so much as a kopek. Who's going to marry the girl now?"

"Ah," said Avrom. "I wonder."

"What's to wonder?"

"I wonder whether Blume and Dovid don't love each other."

Shakhes burst out laughing. "Love?"

Avrom gave him a withering look. "Love."

"Reb Avrom's talking about love," said Shakhes, in the direction of the sky. And then, to the tsimbalist: "Maybe they love each other now. But you know what they say — love and hunger don't take rooms together. What are they going to live on?"

"They also say," Avrom countered, "that the three things that can never be hidden are coughing, sneezing, and love. In other words, what does it matter what they're going to live on?"

"It matters, it matters. Why else would they say, love is like butter — it's best when you also have bread?"

"And yet they also say, when you lack butter for the bread, that is not yet poverty. And since Koppel is a dairyman, how much richer will Blume and Dovid be, since they'll have all the butter they need. Which is why I look forward to seeing you, Reb Moishe Shakhes, on Friday."

~

It was less than ten minutes after Avrom left the glass shop, as he was walking near the courthouse and jail on his way to the lake road, that he saw Blume herself. The girl was hurrying in the opposite direction, her face lit up with happiness.

"Blume," he greeted her, drinking in some of her happiness for himself. "What are you doing in Zavlivoya today?"

"I came to see Dovid at the jail."

"You are an extraordinary girl," said Avrom. To go and see her betrothed in the week before the wedding, to go to the jail to see him, no less, and to do it by herself — it really was extraordinary. "And how is Dovid managing?"

"He wasn't there. They let him go free."

"Did they?"

"The constable — that one who took Dovid away last night — he didn't want to tell me so at first, and just said the prisoners couldn't be seen. But then he took pity, and what he told me was that the police chief had just been there, and told him to let Dovid go, because it didn't make any sense to hold him, if the one with a complaint against him couldn't even be found. He left just before I came. I'm on my way to find him at his house."

"Well, well. So Nikifor Kharitonovich let him go."

"Yes," said Blume, looking impatient to be on her way.

"Well, I won't keep you — your father is no worse than last night?"

"Well ... no, no worse."

"I'll go see him when I get back."

"Oh yes, please do."

"And now, off with you. Tell Dovid I'm happy he's been let out."

"Yes, I will," said Blume. And she hurried away, south, toward Zavlivoya's Jewish quarter.

~

It was only a minute later, as Avrom was passing by the town's chief inn, that he heard a low, booming voice call his name. It was Deacon Achilles.

"Good day," he greeted the giant priest.

"Good day. What brings you to Zav today?"

"Many things," answered Avrom. "But now, I'm on my way home. And you — I believe you had an important day today, did you not?"

"Did I?"

"I saw your superior riding in the woods this morning after the bells had already rung at St. Vladimir's."

"Oh, did you see the father? He was down at the Efimovski mansion early, early."

"For the wake."

"Yes."

"I remember you once told me your nightmare: that both of your superiors would be away some Sunday, and you'd have to lead services and say a sermon. I know that Father Zacharias went with Father Innokenty. So, did your nightmare come to pass — did you lead the service?"

Deacon Achilles flushed a darker color. "I did, to start with."

"And I imagine it went very well, after all your worries. How was the sermon?"

"Well ... well you see, as for the sermon — we were only a little way in, you see, I'd gotten lost a little and gone back to the beginning, and then Father Innokenty arrived. So he could give

the sermon. It was his second in one morning, if you can believe it!"

"I can," Avrom drily replied. "I can even imagine what he
might have said."

"Oh yes?"

"Yes. Did he mention the money-lenders?"

"Why yes, he did," Deacon Achilles smiled, "how did you
know?"

"And the tavern-keepers?"

"Yes, them too."

"And the Christ-killers?"

"He said we must never forget that the Jews crucified our
Lord and shed His precious blood."

Avrom looked hard at Achilles. "And how did it all go over?"

"Oh, very well. Father Innokenty is a wonderful speaker."

"And how did it go over with you, Akhilla Gerasimovich?"

Deacon Achilles shrugged. "I always enjoy the father's sermons. But why do you ask?"

Avrom's eyes opened wide. "Must you ask me why I ask? I
had hoped you, at least, might approve less of the father's words
than some others."

"But Avrom Moisevich, it's true. A good Orthodox *mustn't*
ever forget who crucified Our Lord."

"You, of all people, say that?"

"Why not?" Achilles looked baffled.

"Because you helped Sora Hinde with the cow."

This explanation did not appear to enlighten the deacon.

"And you still help her family now that she's gone. And you
come to my house, and you sing with me. And last night you
carried Koppel over to the water."

"But what do any of those things have to do with it?"

"Ah, my friend, you may not have noticed it, but Sora Hinde
was a Jew, and so am I, and so is Koppel. Do you think we shed
his precious blood?"

"Well ..."

"Do you?"

"Well no. That is, it was a long time ago that — "

"And what do you think Father Innokenty was bringing it up for? Because it was a long time ago?"

"But what does it matter why he brought it up, if it was true? The father wouldn't do anything that was bad, Avrom Moisevich, he's a very holy man."

"And the money-lenders, and the tavern-keepers? Why do you think he brought them up?"

"But Avrom Moisevich, a fact is a fact. You shouldn't feel bad, though. You're not a moneylender or a tavern-keeper."

"Do you really mean it, Akhilla Gerasimovich?" Avrom sadly asked. "And what about Koppel's beard?"

"Terrible," said the deacon, bunching his enormous hands into fists. "I'd like to get ahold of that Styopa myself."

"But don't you see how it all goes together?"

Achilles looked puzzled, then answered, "No."

After a long silence, Avrom said, in a quiet voice, "Then I suggest you think about it."

"All right," said Achilles, and then asked, because Avrom had started to continue on his way, "Are you leaving?"

The tsimbalist turned. "Yes."

"Well, then ... would you like to go fishing at my house later?"

With a sad shake of the head, Avrom replied, "No."

"Then ... well ... what about doing some music?"

With a final shake of the head, Avrom again replied, "No," and then disappeared, to the deacon's surprise, through the doors of the inn.

Chapter 7

≈

Smoke and Mirrors

T he interior of the inn was as dark as Avrom's mood. Three small north-facing windows permitted a few weak rays of sunlight, which once inside, joined forces with the feeble flicker of the paraffin lamps and candles scattered here and there atop rough-hewn tables. Even in consort, sunlight, lamplight, and candlelight were no match for the thick haze of tobacco smoke holding sway over the room. Intent on oppressing throats as well as eyes, this noxious cloud extended its dominion into every corner, barely troubled by the waft or two of fresh air that managed to drift diffidently in through the windows.

Or was it only Avrom who found the haze oppressive, while others at the inn would have agreed with the famous writer Griboyedov, who wrote that "the smoke of the Motherland is sweet and pleasant for us"? Alas, it was an easy enough question to answer — and furthermore, anyone seeking to answer it would need have peered no further, through the thick cloud of smoke, than the other side of the room. There, at a small table, sat Khana Beck, the innkeeper's wife, selling tobacco, in all its forms.

Fat cigars for the gentlemen, slender *pakhitoskas* for the ladies, shag and paper for those wishing to roll their own cigarettes, all nudged each other for space atop the luxurious bed of notes and coins in *Froi* Beck's rectangular walnut box; while a second, square box of pear-wood held aromatic pipe tobacco, ready for stuffing (when need arose) into the clay chibouks, cherry-wood bowls, and meerschaums already billowing out little blue cloudlets around the room.

It was not tobacco alone that was to be had here, however. No! Any vice might find a home in this inn. At the first table Avrom came upon, a quintet of townsmen — amongst whom he recognized the postmaster, the inspector of schools, and the superintendent of charities — were tossing dice and drinking champagne. An enormous, half-eaten sturgeon lay on the tabletop between them. As Avrom passed, the fish stared at him with its white, pupil-less eye, while its needle-sharp snout nuzzled the ample pile of coins the superintendent had been clever enough to amass.

Nearby on the checkerboard floor sprawled a solitary Gypsy, puffing at a red Turkish chibouk, and listening to an old, beardless Ukrainian at the next table, who was singing a doleful tune:

The wind is blowing, blowing hard, see how the forest sways
My tears are pouring, pouring out, today, and all my days
My years are spent in sorrow cruel, I see no end ahead
My heart grows lighter only when a few sad tears I shed
For joyful tears no succor give, to hearts that woe has taught
Once joy, true joy, is truly lost, it cannot be forgot

After each slow line of song, the old man fortified himself with a gulp from his cup, while the Gypsy took another long draw on his pipe.

With the oldster sat several young women, misty-eyed and sniffling. Avrom could guess, from their scanty mode of dress, why they were there at the inn. Passing them by, Avrom suffered a pang of recognition and guilt: one of the girls was none other than Mirele, an orphan whose long-deceased parents Avrom had known well. After their death, he had vowed to keep an eye on the daughter, even trying to find her a husband when she first came of age, though without success. But that had been quite a while back. How long was it now, he wondered with shame, since he had spared a thought for her?

Resolving to speak with the girl immediately upon completion of his other business, the tsimbalist continued past the next table, occupied by as ecumenical a group of gamblers as one could wish for. Avrom recognized there, from the ball last night, the ill-favored bureaucrat who had been dancing with Aglaya Olegovna (Pugovitsin, if Avrom recalled his name correctly.) With the collegiate counselor sat a most unlikely quartet: Faddei Kazimirovich, that is, the Pole; and three short-bearded Jews who were strangers to Avrom, but appeared to be Litvaks, that is, from Lithuania. The improbable quintet looked to be playing the game of *shtoss*. Their table was littered with playing cards, chips, and paper money.

But Avrom did not tarry to watch, continuing instead to the back counter, domain of the man he'd come there to see: Yudel Beck, the tavern-keeper.

⌒

The tavern-keeper was an abrupt man with a sharp rodent's face, half-hidden behind a great brown beard. Before the tsimbalist had quite stepped up to the counter, the man was already greeting him: "Well-well, Reb Avrom. A rare honor seeing *you* here." His voice was like a rodent's too, high-pitched and squeaky.

"If only I were fortunate enough to be able to give more custom to taverns," Avrom replied, "I would surely visit yours as often as I could."

Yudel Beck bowed his head, slightly and briefly, then asked, "To drink?"

"I didn't come for a drink," said Avrom, "but for a little talk."

The innkeeper curled his lip and raised his eyebrows. "All right. Talk."

"You've heard, of course, about Arka — "

"Of course I have."

"In that case, I'll tell you what happened to me this morning. I was on my way to the Efimovski estate ..."

And Avrom proceeded to tell Yudel Beck about his encounter with the peasants, about Father Innokenty's sermon at the estate village, and then about the repeat of the same sermon, here in Zavlivoya.

"All of which," the tsimbalist concluded, "leads me to worry about Shimmel Shenkman, and about you and the other tavern-keepers here in Zav."

"And you came here just to tell me this?"

"I thought you ought to be on the lookout for trouble. And I hoped you might take it upon yourself to warn the others."

"Well," sniffed Yudel Beck, "I thank you, I suppose. But what exactly would you have me do? I can hardly close things up here." The innkeeper waved an arm in the general direction of all the customers.

"Perhaps not," said Avrom. "But — "

"I wouldn't have anything to live on," interrupted Beck. "You know, just because I take in money hand over fist, people think I make a good living. But do you know who owns this place?"

"Count Bestuzhev, I suppose," Avrom hazarded.

It was a logical guess. Count Bestuzhev owned most of the lands and forests surrounding the lake, including Balativke (he was Avrom's landlord, in a manner of speaking) and most of the town of Zavlivoya. For all that, the count was rarely seen in the area from one year to the next.

"Yes indeed, it's Count Bestuzhev," Yudel Beck barked out. "And since the Count, or rather his representative, knows very well that there are fifty Jews who would bust his door in for a chance to run this place, he can charge me whatever he wants for the privilege. And I'm left with barely enough to survive — with ten mouths to feed, too!"

There was at least some justice in what the innkeeper said. Avrom had heard Shimmel Shenkman make similar complaints about the exorbitant fees the Efimovskis charged him for running their tavern. And Yudel Beck did have a large household, which included, in addition to the innkeeper and his wife, two young sons, two unmarried daughters, two *married* daughters, and two sons-in-law living on *kest*.

"It's the Count the priest should be railing against," Yudel Beck continued, in a state of high agitation now, so that his whiskers shook. "And as for Shim — "

He broke off. Someone was calling for a bottle of vodka — it was the superintendent of charities.

"Certainly, with the greatest pleasure, Your High Nobleness," Yudel Beck called over, suddenly all obsequiousness.

Avrom watched the innkeeper walk, cringing, over to the table where the townsmen were throwing dice. He cut an odd figure, dressed in a short jacket, necktie and paper shirtfront, none too clean, with his long beard making his head look twice its size, and atop everything, a little yarmulke.

When he arrived at the townsmen's table, there appeared to be a bit of haggling. From Beck's sour face upon his return, it looked as if he had come out on the short end.

"And may you choke on it," he was muttering under his breath. "Trying to starve an honest Jew, and me with ten mouths to feed — "

"You were mentioning Shimmel Shenkman, I think," the tsimbalist reminded him.

"What? Oh ... yes. I was going to say that the fact is, Shimmel Shenkman is doing that entire village a favor. If it weren't for him, those peasants would spend the livelong day beating their wives and children, instead of only doing it after they get home from the tavern."

"But certainly you'd agree that the peasants drink too much?"

"Ah, they do," said a voice from behind Avrom. "But it's not their fault."

"Kuz'ma," the tsimbalist turned to greet the bass player from the Jewish Orchestra. "*Sholem aleikhem*." (It was a joke among the musicians that they spoke to their bass player as if he, too, were a Jew.)

"*Aleikhem sholem*, Reb Avrom."

Kuz'ma's reply put a confused look on Yudel Beck's rodent face.

"And so what is this you're saying?" the tsimbalist asked Kuz'ma. "It isn't the peasants' fault that they drink too much?"

"No, no more than it's my fault that I drink too much."

"Of course not," scoffed Yudel Beck.

"You see," the bass player went on, "I come from peasants myself, and for years, we had to buy vodka from our master, the Count, so much per year, by law. It was the same everywhere, all over the empire, and for hundreds of years, they say. If we didn't want to buy it, we still had to pay, and then they'd dump the vodka out right in front of our houses. So naturally, we bought it."

"You see!" exclaimed the innkeeper. "Always the fault of the nobles."

"Is it really true?" asked Avrom, though he seemed now to recall having heard something about the matter before.

"The Lord's honest truth. And then of course, we also always had to drink at weddings, and funerals and baptisms. And also on the Feast of the Assumption, and Elijah's Day, and Holy Cross Day, and the saints' days."

"Quite a burden," observed Avrom.

"Yes. And that's not to mention the twelve days of the *Sviatki,* and the three days of the Intercession, and the week after

Easter, and the days before and after Lent, and the days before and after *Maslenitsa* ... And then, too, the priests always commanded us to drink on the pagan holidays as well, so as to drive away the evil spirits. So that, as you'd expect, vodka became part of our blood, so to say. We can't help but drink, even as we know we shouldn't. Why, I grit my heart, every time I'm about to raise a cup to my lips. But what am I to do? Inn-keep?"

Kuz'ma handed the empty wood cup in his hand to Yudel Beck, who filled it with vodka and then exchanged it for a coin.

"*Nazdrovia*," the house-painter-bass-player said, before emptying the cup. He took a step away from the counter, whispered "privy" to Avrom, and walked off, out the inn's back door.

～

At the same moment Kuz'ma walked away, a series of increasingly loud shouts arose from the other side of the room, where a group of men and women, country folk, were sitting.

"Not another fight!" Yudel Beck looked alarmed, and hurried around the counter in order to make peace. Avrom watched his efforts for a moment, until something even more interesting close at hand — almost beneath his elbow — drew his attention.

During Avrom's conversation with Yudel Beck, the five card players — the three Litvak Jews, the Pole, and Pugovitsin — had continued to play. Their game was two-man *shtoss*, the rules of which are quite simple. Each player has a deck of fifty-two cards. The first player acts as "bank," and the second as "bettor." Action is initiated by the bettor, who turns up one card, the "bettor's card," and wagers on it. The bank then turns up two cards, one after the other: the "banker's card," followed by the "*carte anglaise*."

If the numerical value of the "banker's card" is the same as the value of the "bettor's card" — for example, a jack of spades to match a jack of hearts — the bank wins. But if the *carte anglaise* matches the "bettor's card," the bettor wins.

If all three cards are of the same value, the bank wins; while if none of the cards match, play continues, with a further two-card deal by the bank.

The thing that had drawn Avrom's attention — he couldn't have said why, only that something had suddenly made him look — was that one of the players was cheating. At the moment, two games were being played: the Pole was playing against one of the Litvaks, while in a separate game another Litvak played bank against Pugovitsin. This second Litvak was the cheat. Avrom saw him deal, quickly and deftly, not from the top of the deck but from its middle. The card was a seven of spades, which matched Pugovitsin's seven of diamonds, laid down a moment earlier.

"Lost again!" the bureaucrat shouted. "But my luck's bound to change soon."

Another hand began, as Avrom continued to watch. This time, Pugovitsin laid down a jack of clubs, and the Litvak, a three of hearts and an ace of spades — no match. But on the second deal, the "banker's card" was a jack of hearts.

The cheating was well done. If Avrom hadn't been watching for it, he would never have seen it. But he was watching, and he did see.

At that moment, Yudel Beck returned.

"All settled?" Avrom asked.

"A fight over a woman," said Beck. "I told her to leave. The men drink more."

"Ah." Avrom leaned closer to the innkeeper and dropped his voice. "This Pugovitsin. Is he staying at the inn?"

"All those punters are," sniffed the innkeeper, "except the Pole. The three Litvaks, too."

"An unlikely group, it seems."

"May be. But the four of them — that is, not including the Pole — have been at table together every day."

"Always playing *shtoss*?"

"Always. And the bureaucrat always loses." The innkeeper dropped his voice still further. "Something else I'll tell you — something about this *chinovnik* doesn't smell quite right. What he loses is more than a bureaucrat of the fourteenth rank ought to have in his pocket. Nothing unusual about that — except he always pays his debts in cash."

"Oh, yes?"

Yudel Beck nodded. "Cash, on the spot. The truth is, I can't work out why he's here in Zav — he's been here since Thursday ... doing what, I don't know. But a few folk have been whispering that he isn't what he seems."

"A government inspector of some sort?" suggested Avrom.

"Or worse," whispered the inn-keep. "Third Section."

"Secret police?" Avrom said doubtfully.

"Could be."

"I fear the Tsar's life is far from safe if this is the sort of agent they have in their secret police ... or perhaps he's merely playing the fool. But his opponents are certainly cheating him. Reb Innkeeper, tell me about these Litvaks."

"Merchants. Arrived Thursday as well — in early for Tuesday market, they said, since they'd heard the Maggid would be here, and always wanted to see him preach."

"Hmm. How odd."

"What now?"

"Because I've always heard that the Kelmer Maggid made his home in Slonim, practically in Lithuania itself. It ought to have been easy enough for them to see him there."

"I wouldn't be so sure, Reb Smartypants. If they travel, and he travels ..."

"And what line of business are they in?"

"Household items, they say, and personal articles. 'Secondhand,'" Yudel Beck squeaked, "'but first quality.'"

⁓

When Avrom stepped up to the gamblers' table, the Pole was holding forth in a loud tenor, addressing himself to Pugovitsin.

"But where you have one *narodnik*," the constable confidently declared, "naturally you'll find more. As they say, rot will always spread, on people as on bread."

"Quite," replied the bureaucrat. "Damn it. Lost again."

"Oh well, luck is fickle," said the Pole. "You're sure to win later. But as I was saying, where you find one of these mischief-makers there will always be more, and this Yid I was telling you about was one of 'em, without a doubt. Been heard plenty of times around town, plotting with the other one."

The Pole took a puff on a particularly malodorous cigar.

"And so, when I saw him punch Styopa—that's the one who's disappeared now, if you remember—I knew at once he was trying to stir things up, create an incident. You know, profit off the death of his cohort. Well, I decided to put and end to that, and I did, as fast as you like. Struck him down, so that he's in custody as we speak—as I'm sure anyone like yourself who's in, well, let us say, *government service,* will be pleased to know."

So, thought Avrom. The Pole was one of those who thought Pugovitsin was an agent of the Third Section. And, perhaps, wouldn't mind being an agent of the Third Section himself.

Aloud, he said: "Actually, Dovid is no longer in custody."

The Pole looked up, glaring. "What's that?"

"He was let out, a short time ago."

"Now who—" the Pole began, then looked back at Pugovitsin, and said: "The problem, as I was already explaining earlier, is that our Nikifor Kharitonovich doesn't agree these young trouble-makers are to be taken as a serious threat, though I try to tell him. Now, if it was me in charge of things ..."

Meanwhile, Avrom had managed to catch the attention of one of the merchants, the one who wasn't playing. "Pardon me," he said. "I'm told you deal in second-hand goods."

"*Sholem aleikhem*," said the merchant, looking Avrom up and down. "And have a sit. They call me Lemel, and this is my brother Selig." He indicated his neighbor at table, whom he strongly resembled — they were both rather fat, with blonde hair and beards, pink skin, and bright green eyes. "And Zusman, our partner," he pointed to Pugovitsin's opponent, who was long and thin, with oversized black eyes and hollow cheeks.

"I'm Avrom," said the tsimbalist.

"*Nu*, Reb Avrom, is it something particular you're looking for?"

"It was pointed out to me recently," replied the tsimbalist, "that I have no mirror in my home. I have a friend who makes them new, but I wondered ..."

"We do have a few mirrors at the moment, though they don't come cheap. Very finely made, very nicely put together. You could come upstairs to see them, if you like."

"They're very dear?" Avrom hesitated.

"Dear enough," Lemel inclined his head. "We'll have them at market on Tuesday, of course."

"Ah, you're here early for the market then?" asked Avrom.

"We heard that the Kelmer Maggid would be coming, and rushed down from Chernigov, straightaway the market was done there."

"Ah, yes, the Maggid. The Kelmer Maggid! You did well to come here to see him," Avrom enthused. "It's quite an honor for Zavlivoya that he's come. A marvelous speaker."

"My heart was lifted up," Lemel declared.

"So many memorable phrases ..."

"Yes."

"So many important thoughts."

"Yes."

"When he said, 'Your money must be as kosher as your food' ..."

"Ah, yes. Yes."

"Too often today," Avrom declared, "we believe that prayer alone is enough. Or that following the commandments is enough. But what good are those things, if we still cheat our neighbor? Even if ... well, say, even if we cheat him at cards."

At this, Pugovitsin's opponent, the merchant Zusman, looked up.

"Why, even if no one sees you cheat, well, that's no better than if you forget to say a prayer and no one else knows. *Someone* is always watching."

"Yes," replied Lemel, nervously putting a hand on Zusman's shoulder, just as Zusman was about to deal his cards.

"If our money is ill-gotten," Avrom continued, "why follow any of the commandments at all? Anyway ... that's what I understood the Maggid to be saying."

"Finally!" shouted Pugovitsin, who had just, at long last, won a hand.

"Yes, it's true indeed," Avrom said again. "Your money must be as kosher as your food."

"What does that mean," inquired Pugovitsin. "What is that word, *kosher*?"

A somewhat lengthy explanation followed, during which Avrom and the merchants interrupted each other several times, and in the course of which Pugovitsin won two more hands. The tsimbalist finished by saying, "in this case, it means that money must be clean, honestly earned."

"That is quite true!" declared Pugovitsin, with surprising passion. "In fact, this is exactly what is wrong with our Russia today. People don't earn their money cleanly, and — that is, it's understood that a small bribe here or there is to be expected, but ... what is really intolerable is that, on the other end of things, no one pays their debts cleanly either. It's as good as stealing." He looked fiercely all around the table, his brown bangs skipping across his pimpled forehead.

"Indeed," said Avrom when everyone else remained silent. "That is something I hadn't thought about. So you believe that not paying a debt is like stealing?"

Pugovitsin nodded enthusiastically. "Yes, yes. Not only must you earn your money honestly, but you must pay it over honestly when you owe it. But who does so? And so it's left to the hard-working and unappreciated debt collectors to do it. If not for them, the empire would grind to a halt. If only — well, if only they were better appreciated. I myself ... am quite grateful for them."

"You yourself, perhaps, have some experience in the matter?" asked Avrom.

Pugovitsin didn't answer right away, as at that moment, the merchant Zusman reminded him with a tap on the table that he was still in the midst of a game of *shtoss*. At once, Pugovitsin turned up his "bettor's card," the three of spades, and then, buoyed by his lucky streak, pushed all his money to the middle of the table.

Zusman, all slowness and deliberation, and holding his deck forward and up for all to see, dealt out a "banker's card" for himself. It, too, was a three of spades. Pugovitsin had lost.

Only then did the Collegiate Registrar answer Avrom's question. With his bangs suddenly plastered to his forehead by a cold sweat, and a tear in his eye, he said in a quavering voice: "I, have experience in the matter? No, I ... have never had the funds to loan out. So that no one has ever been in debt to me."

An awkwardness descended over the table. The Pole looked at the bureaucrat in confusion and disgust, while the merchants stared at their hands. Fortunately, after a moment, the awkwardness was broken by a loud noise from the side of the room where the country folk had been sitting. Avrom spun around, to see two bodies whirling about, a flash of peasant shirt, an upraised fist, the crash of a chair.

"I'll deal with this," announced the Pole. He jumped up, and threw himself into the fray.

Avrom himself got up too, and went over to speak with Mirele. But when he got to the table where she'd been sitting, Mirele was gone.

Chapter 8

A Woman Abandoned

Outside the tavern, the world was startlingly bright. For a few seconds, Avrom could see nothing at all. Then, slowly, the wide, dusty street and long, low buildings across the way came clear, while Avrom squinted to left and right, in hopes the orphan girl might still be near by.

There — across the street, and to the left, passing in and out of the shadows cast by a row of columns: a slim silhouette. He started after it, then leapt back. A droshky hurtling down the street had nearly run him down. Something pushed against him from behind — a smell of alcohol filled his nostrils — another tavern guest making his exit. A dog, yapping after the droshky, ran past his knees. By the time he started off again in pursuit, the silhouette had disappeared, swallowed up in the shadows of another long building.

Across the street, he had to crane his neck to look over the heads of three Jews strolling the opposite way, before he caught sight once again of the girl's slender outlines. A brief delay, occasioned by the necessity of exchanging pleasantries with the trio in his path — they were the brothers Nisson and Girsha

Balender, butchers, and Pesakh Ziske the *shokhet* — and he was off again, following the yet-again-invisible Mirele.

She must have been going quickly. He lengthened his strides, with the reward of spotting her for a third time, now walking in open sunlight. A little closer, and —

But this girl wasn't Mirele at all. The skirt hugging her churning legs was too long, too respectable. Come to think, her gait was a familiar one too — but not Mirele's. Of course. It was Blume.

But what was Blume doing here again already, instead of still being at Dovid's? Avrom called out, and the girl turned.

"Oh. Reb Avrom."

As soon as she spoke, he knew something was wrong. The girl's voice wilted as it traveled toward him, the words of her greeting falling to the street between the two of them.

"On your way home already?" Avrom cautiously asked, closing the distance that separated them.

"Yes. Back home," Blume sighed. She turned up the corners of her mouth in a weak smile, which only had the effect of making her eyes look unhappy. There was no doubt about it. The joy which had been streaming straight out of her only a little while ago, bright as sunshine, was nowhere to be seen, hidden behind some dark cloud.

"Perhaps you wish to walk alone?" suggested the tsimbalist.

"No," the girl quickly protested. "No ... You're on your way as well?"

"I am."

"Then ..." Lifting a foot, and her brow, in invitation, Blume started forward, and Avrom fell into step beside her.

Side by side, they walked toward the lake road. But it did not seem to Avrom as though the girl really did want any company. She was entirely silent, her pretty dark eyes cast down to the ground in front of her. Whatever she was thinking of seemed to consume her entirely. For minutes, they went without exchanging a word.

Avrom would have liked to have asked her what was the matter. But something held him back. He had known Blume since she was a little girl. Even if she was not quite a daughter to him, she was at least something like a niece. But she was also about to be a married woman, deserving of a certain respect. Furthermore — didn't it seem very much like whatever was wrong had something to do with Dovid? And didn't that make it none of his business? He remained silent.

It wasn't till they turned to go down the lake road that the silence was broken by Blume, in a most incomprehensible fashion. First, Avrom noticed the girl pause very briefly in her step and nod her head, in what seemed to him a resolute manner. Then, after another minute, she said, in a commonplace, everyday tone, "I hope the ointment doesn't run out too quickly."

Ointment? "What ointment?" asked Avrom.

"For Tatte's face. Doctor Artiukhov left a jar with us last night, but there was only a little in it. He told me to come get more at his house, and I tried earlier, but he wasn't there."

Avrom stared at Blume, then said, "You have the wrong name, my dear. You are much too strong to be named after a weak little thing like a flower. Now tell me what has happened."

The girl stopped walking, and then, to Avrom's surprise, smiled at him, a genuine smile this time, if subdued. "Nothing has happened. Only ... I wasn't able to give Dovid your message."

"Did I send him a message?" asked the tsimbalist.

"You asked me to tell Dov — " She hesitated, then smiled once more. "You asked me to tell Dovid you were happy he'd been let out of jail."

"Ah ... Yes, I recall now."

"But I couldn't."

Saying this, Blume began to walk forward again, at a quicker pace. Avrom scrambled to catch up.

"I suppose he wasn't at home," suggested the tsimbalist.

"No ..." She slowed again. "He was. I heard his voice."

"Oh?"

"Yes, when I knocked, they were arguing behind the door
— Dovid and his mother and his father. But when it opened, it
was only his father standing there. He said Dovid didn't believe
we ought to see each other in the week before the wedding. But,
Reb Avrom, Dovid's never believed that. He's always saying
these traditions are stupid — like when he said the bride shouldn't
go to her ritual bath before the wedding accompanied by musicians — no offense to you! He said the bath is something private, and shouldn't be turned into something public like that.
He said he wouldn't even think about living on *kest*, loafing
while everyone else was working. Why, Reb Avrom, he even
said he didn't want to be called to the Torah last Shabbes! Only
he knew it would make everyone unhappy if he didn't, but that
I shouldn't get to thinking that once we were married we would
be going about things in the traditional way ... And I'm sure he
said that it was stupid for us not to see each other before the
wedding, too."

Avrom hesitated, before saying, "How strange that he
should have changed his mind."

"Dovid's father didn't seem very happy to say it, either, as if
he knew what he was saying wasn't true. Then, when I didn't
reply — because I didn't know what to say, Reb Avrom — he
said that anyway, Dovid wasn't at home right now. Just after I
had heard them arguing! And then he just looked panicked, and
shut the door in a hurry."

"How truly strange."

"That was what I thought, too — only now, it doesn't seem
so very strange to me."

They walked ten paces more before Avrom reluctantly
asked, "How not?"

"Well, it's simple, isn't it?" Blume said, with a little laugh.
"I've lost my dowry. And now that I've thought about it, it seems
to me, it's really for the best. After all, what would Yoysif do,

and Tatte, and Zlata, and Tzippe and Khaya and Reizel and Rokhel — and Masha! — without me there to take care of them?"

~

What Avrom said next arose from a natural impulse to console the poor girl. He regretted his words at once. But how could he help it? If he couldn't find the orphan Mirele right now, at least he could give comfort to Blume. Poor thing! Exactly how many misfortunes could befall the girl and her family at one time?

But no — this *wasn't* a misfortune, that was the main thing. That was what he had to convince her of. It was laughable to think Dovid wasn't hers, heart and soul, or that he would care anything about a dowry. Granted, in the old days, back when it took a matchmaker to bring together a young man and a young woman, and two letter-writers, who would supply flowery missives for the youngsters to exchange — in only the finest handwriting, mind you — back then, when everything was done in a very certain way, people cared about the dowry more than they cared about a little thing like love. And, no doubt about it, some people still didn't care about love, still hired matchmakers and letter-writers and insisted on depositing the bride's dowry with the rabbi well ahead of the wedding, treating the whole thing like nothing more than a matter of business.

But with these two? Anyone who had seen them together could tell that Dovid loved Blume, and Blume loved Dovid.

Fine. They loved each other. So far so good. That being the case, was it not also the case that if anyone could be expected to object to the loss of the dowry, it was Dovid's parents? But it sounded as if, when Blume came to their door, they were the ones arguing Dovid should see her, instead of the other way around. The only possible conclusion was that the girl had completely misunderstood everything.

Which was why he went ahead and declared: "Blume, my

dear, that's all nonsense." And continued by immediately asking, "Do you know what will happen in a few days? I'll tell you.
In a few days, the sun will rise, and I'll rise with it. Before long,
I'll go outside, and walk all through Balativke, with my sticks in
my hands, my tsimbl hanging in front of me, and Moishe
Shakhes at my side, along with his sons, and our Kuz'ma. We'll
go to the houses of every one of your guests, and we'll play to
invite them to your wedding, one by one. And when we've finished, and everyone is invited, we'll walk out of the village,
down the lake road, and wait for Dovid to ride up in his carriage. Presently he'll come, handsome like a prince, in his finest
clothes, he'll step down from the carriage while we play a song
of welcome, everyone will shout, 'The bridegroom! The bridegroom!' And he'll walk with us to the house where he is to be
hosted. After that, while he stays there to prepare himself, we'll
come to the house where you are to be hosted. All the women
will already be there, and when we arrive, they'll place the veil
over your head, while Moishe Shakhes makes up such rhymes
to make you cry for leaving behind your girlhood. Then we'll
fetch Dovid to come place the kerchief over your face, each of
the guests will dance around you in a circle, one after the other,
they'll whirl you about — my dear, what a joyous day it will be!"

Almost as soon as he had begun this recital, Avrom knew
it was a terrible mistake. After all, who was he to be so certain?
There was a chance — wasn't there? — that he was the one who
was wrong about everything, and that Blume was right — that
even Moishe Shakhes was right.

In fact, on second thought, what other explanation was
there for what had just happened at Dovid's house? Blume was
the one who had been there, not him. And if he was wrong,
then — may all the suffering of her family be visited on him
instead — all his words of comfort would do nothing but raise
the girl's hopes, when it would have been better to let them lie.

Nonetheless, having started down the road, he plunged ahead toward his destination with all the enthusiasm he could manage, even repeating for a second time his last sentence — "What a joyous day!" — while looking out of the corner of his eye at Blume.

He needn't have worried. His words seemed to make no impression whatsoever on the girl. While he spoke, she kept shaking her head, and when he was done, she replied: "You're kind to say those things, Reb Avrom. But it isn't so. But please don't worry about me. I'll be fine."

This reply left Avrom so completely speechless that, as Blume seemed to have nothing further to say either, they walked for a long while afterward in silence.

~

It wasn't till they were nearing Deacon Achilles' house that Blume spoke up again.

"It was so good of the deacon," she said, "to come to Tatte's aid. He's always such a help."

"Indeed," mumbled Avrom, who decided there and then that the whole walk to Balativke was doomed to awkwardness.

When the deacon's pasture came into sight, they saw, grazing there, Masha the Cow, attended by Blume's sister Zlata.

"Oh Reb Avrom," Blume exclaimed at once, looking anxious. "I can't tell her. I'm not ready yet."

"All right," said Avrom, and quickly called out, "Good day, Zlata. How does your father?"

"The same, how else?" Zlata called back. "He's very anxious for the ointment. Hey Blume, you'll never guess who came to help take care of him!"

"Who?"

"The *aguneh*!"

"Zlata, can't you call her by her name?"

"Why should I, is she an *aguneh* or not? Anyway, she came just after you left."

"Then we'd best go to help, too," Avrom shouted, hurrying away before Zlata thought to question whether this made any sense — and before she could ask about Dovid. "Come Blume."

"Thank you, Reb Avrom," said Blume, hurrying behind him. After a moment, she added: "I suppose I'm not surprised that Rivke has come."

"And why shouldn't she?"

"Oh, no ... only that we haven't seen her for a while."

"I suppose I've noticed that," said Avrom.

"Perhaps it's wrong of us ... but by now things have become so complicated. To begin with, there's the matter of the bread."

"Bread?"

"Because Rivke sells her bread at the market in Zav. We used to buy from her, we would just run down the road for it. But lately, we've been getting our bread from Dovid's — " Her voice broke.

"From Dovid's mother."

"Yes. Because she sells bread at the market, too. And — you see, after Mama died, Rivke ... she was very good to us, always helping out."

"I remember."

"But after a while ... Reb Avrom, may I say something terrible?"

Avrom looked into her eyes. "Please do."

"Well, after a while, it seemed to me, because we were not quite so unhappy anymore ... of course Mama will always be gone, and we'll always feel it ... but especially once Dovid and I ... once we began to be a little bit happy again, it seemed to me that our being happy made Rivke feel *un*happy. Or at least, I wondered if that was true. I talked about it with ... Dovid, and he said of course, old-fashioned ideas had doomed her to be unhappy forever, and now she couldn't bear being around happy people. And he said we should pity her, because in a more just society, she'd be a different person. He's right of course ... Reb Avrom, only when we actually have to spend time with her ... Anyway, finally she stopped coming around. And I suppose we should have gone to see her, only it was the first time in so long that *I* felt any happiness, and the way she would always be sighing ... What happened with the bread, with buying bread from Dovid's mother, that really only happened afterward."

"Ah ..."

"I'm sorry, Reb Avrom," Blume looked intently at the tsimbalist. "I know ... we know, that is ... of course, you are also friendly with her ... that is, since she's a *neighbor* ..."

Avrom, looking away from Blume, replied with a piety: "We must all be as good as we can be to the unfortunate amongst us."

He was thinking: *Imagine, poor thing, how often Rivke will visit you now, if you've really been abandoned by Dovid.*

⁓

Blume was not done surprising Avrom that day. Only a moment later she said: "It was good of Dovid to defend Tatte. Do you know, I'm happy, really happy, that at least Dovid was let free."

"Why," Avrom stopped in his tracks, "... yes."

"But Reb Avrom? That man who attacked Tatte — "

"Styopa?" asked Avrom, taken still further aback.

"That's it, Styopa. I was wondering, won't he be in more trouble now than if he had let himself be taken?"

"Why ... yes. I'm certain that he will."

"Then why do you think he ran away? I was wondering earlier, because ... well, I was wondering what would have happened if Dovid had run away, too."

"If Dovid had run away, he too would have been in more trouble."

"I could see that it went against his grain to be taken in, when he thought what he did was right. Dovid believes we Jews should defend ourselves if we're attacked."

"He told you about that, did he?"

"Oh, over and over again. Always, on our walks on Shabbes. But that was the first time he had the chance to — well, to do anything about it."

"And what did your father say when Dovid told you all his opinions on the matter?"

"Oh, Tatte never said anything, he only listened. But," she sighed, "Tatte never says much about anything, for years now, except when he's talking to himself."

"And you? What do you think about the idea?"

"I hope that Arkady Olegovich Efimovski was right."

"Ah — did you know Arkady Olegovich?"

"Me? No. But Dovid would mention him all the time, they were great friends. He always told us everything they talked about."

"And what did Arkady Olegovich say that you hope he was right about?"

"He said that soon, Jewish self-defense would be unnecessary. I'm not sure I remember it all exactly, there were some French words, but the meaning of it was that once the landowner class stops hanging on to the wealth and land that could belong to everybody, then the peasants and the Jews — and the Greeks as well, because they were especially talking about the pogrom in Odessa — once the landowner class stops that, then we'll all live together in peace. Do you think it's true, Reb Avrom?"

The tsimbalist attempted an answer that was honest but kind. "I think it would have to begin," he said, "by having the land-owner class give up all that wealth and land. Then, we can see."

"But that's just what Arkady Olegovich Efimovski was trying to do. Dovid said he had just inherited a lot of money and land from his mother and father, and he immediately gave it all away to the peasants of the estate village, so that he'd have less and they'd have more."

"Arkady Olegovich had just inherited? But how, when his mother is still alive?"

"I don't know about that."

"And he gave the money and lands to the peasants of the estate village? Well, well. That must have made them hold him in high regard."

And made them more angry about the young nobleman's death, he thought. Then he remembered the other village, whose inhabitants Arkady Olegovich had held dearest of all, since they were, as his brother had said, the purest, and the most unspoiled.

He asked Blume: "What about the peasants in the north village? Any mention of them?"

"I don't know," Blume shook her head. "Not that I can remember."

"Hmm. Still," he mumbled, "perhaps another tavern-keeper to keep an eye on."

"What's that?"

"Nothing — just that it may be time to — do you know old Gitl-Golda?"

"The nice old woman who runs the inn in the north village? Yes."

"I'm thinking of paying her a visit."

"Ah ... Reb Avrom, I have a question now."

"Ask."

"If things are worse for that man because he ran away, then why do you think he did it? It doesn't seem to make any sense. Unless ..."

"Unless what, my dear?"

"Unless he had already done something else that he didn't want to be caught for."

Avrom turned to look at her more closely, raising his eyebrows. "And what something else do you have in mind?"

"Oh Reb Avrom, I wondered if he was the one who stole our things. And also, if he was the one who ... murdered ... Arkady Olegovich Efimovski. Or is that a foolish thought, when it could have been anyone?"

"It may be a foolish thought, but it was the same thought I had myself."

"Well ... if it *was* him, or at least, if he was the one who stole our things, then ... do you think it's possible if they find where he lives, that — "

"That they could retrieve the things he stole?"

"Yes."

"It could be. But, Blume, please don't allow yourself to hope for it too much. They've already searched the place where he lives, and he wasn't anywhere to be found."

"I see ... Well, anyway, who knows if it was really him? There are so many strange things about what happened. I couldn't stop wondering about it all night."

"Tell me."

"For example, why would ... Styopa ... have come back, after he'd already robbed us? And when he did come back, why was Arkady Olegovich Efimovski there? And then — why would he have ... killed him?"

"You ask very good questions — "

" — *and*, why did none of us hear anything?"

" — another good question, and I wish I could tell you the answers. I can't understand why none of you heard anything, nor do I have any idea why he might have killed Arkady Olegovich. Nor am I quite certain why Styopa would have come back. However, as to why Arkady Olegovich was there — with regard to that, I will say, it's possible he wasn't. "

"What?"

"That is, he may have died by your house, but it could just as well be that he was brought there, after he was already dead."

"Why would anyone have done that?"

"Who knows? To hide his body? If Masha hadn't gotten into the lake, Arkady Olegovich might have stayed where he was for quite some time. Or, perhaps his body was put there in the hope it would be found, and that someone — your father, for example — would be made to look guilty. Didn't Styopa suggest as much last night? He said it was the Jews. Doesn't that make you think it was really him?"

"Yes. But no one could think it was Tatte!"

"Of course not," Avrom lied, and quickly returned to the previous subject. "Another possibility is that Styopa killed him, and then, looking for a hiding place, simply thought of the last dark place he had been, a few hours earlier. Of course, it might have been easier for him to put the body in the water further down the lake — but I would say it's easier to see that part of the water from Zavlivoya, or from a fishing boat — there might have been someone fishing at that hour — or from Deacon Achilles' house. Wouldn't you say so?"

"I suppose. But Reb Avrom, you make me think no one could possibly decide which possibility is the right one."

"Indeed. And that isn't even the end of it. It still is possible that Arkady Olegovich was killed near your house. And if, on the other hand, he was brought there, there is the question of how — in a wagon, or by boat?"

"A boat?" said Blume. "That would have been quieter, wouldn't it?"

"It would, yes."

"Then I think it must have been a boat. A wagon would have woken us all up. It must have been a boat."

"Perhaps. One thing I'd like to know, though, now that I think of it — and this is a question that, unlike all our others, we have some hope of learning the answer to ..."

"What is it?"

"Only this: where do you think your brother found his little wheel-spoke?"

~

Reb Avrom was right. They were able to learn where Yoysif
found the wheel-spoke that very same afternoon. Arriving at
Koppel's house — following a close brush just outside of Balativke with a barouche speeding the opposite way, in which rode
the merchant Saveli Savelyevich and his wife and daughter
— they found the family huddled with the *aguneh* Rivke in the
front room. Koppel was laid out on a makeshift cot, with Rivke
hovering over him, her tall, thin frame nearly horizontal as she
applied a wet rag to his forehead. A strand of silvery hair had
escaped her red kerchief (Rivke was said to have gone completely grey in the months after her husband disappeared) and now,
as she looked up at the new arrivals, fell across her brow. As always, Avrom thought, the expression in her dark and deep set
eyes was disquieting. As she welcomed them, a contented smile
played upon her lips, which were notably sensuous. More than
once, in the next hour, she darted mysterious looks at the tsimbalist — something to which he had long grown accustomed
when in Rivke's company.

It was insisted that Avrom take the room's only chair. He
protested valiantly, but lost the battle. And so there he sat, while
Blume began telling the assembled company of her two failed
visits in Zavlivoya. Extraordinarily, she began with the mission
to Doctor Artiukhov's, whose reported absence occasioned
great sorrow. Koppel's beardless face was still red and raw, and
the ointment, nearly gone. Quite understandably, however, every thought of the doctor was forgotten when Blume told them
of her abandonment by Dovid, which was taken as a true calam-
ity, and produced a chorus of cries variously expressing disbe-
lief, the demand that the abandoned bride go straight back and
find out just what was going through her bridegroom's head, the
distraught certainty that none of the six girls would ever marry,
the defiant certainty that all six would, a reevaluation of the

merits of Berl Melamed, and the ardent desire that Dovid's bones should be broken as often as the ten commandments, that he should be blessed with ten houses, each house with ten rooms, each room with ten beds, and that he should roll from one bed to the other, night after night, afire with the cholera, that leeches should drink him dry, and that he should become like a chandelier, hanging by day, and burning by night.

Along with these imprecations, protestations, and lamentations came numerous appeals from various members of the family, and from Rivke, for the tsimbalist to weigh in on the matter. This, however, Avrom steadfastly refused to do, having learned his lesson earlier on the walk home.

Amidst all the hubbub, Koppel alone was notably quiet. Indeed, since last night, he had barely uttered a word in Avrom's presence. Always awkward, the head of the family seemed now to have retreated completely into himself. Avrom noticed, however, that Rivke's presence, her tender attentions, seemed to put the patient at greater ease. How much of Koppel's everyday awkwardness — the tsimbalist wondered — arose from simply not knowing how to take care of his girls, and terror arising from that fact? Perhaps all Koppel really needed was to be taken care of himself.

It was not Koppel, though, whom Avrom was most interested in. The moment had come to approach little Yoysif — who, the whole time the rest of the family held their conference, had been lying on the floor by his father's cot.

The boy seemed not to understand at first, when Avrom began to question him as to where he'd found the wheel-spoke. A moment later, Blume most conveniently joined them.

"You remember," she encouraged her brother. "The big metal rod you were doing such a wonderful job of playing with yesterday. Wherever did you find it?"

Yoysif looked around the room, then pointed, toward the front window.

"Out there?" asked Avrom. "Can you show us?"

"Yes, show us, Yoysif," said Blume. "It must have been in a good hiding place."

The boy sprang up, and tore out the door, with Blume and Avrom in hot pursuit. Up to the road he went, and then a short way down it, to the left, in the direction of Zavlivoya. He stopped when he arrived at a clump of bushes, and pointed.

"There in the bushes?" asked his sister.

The boy nodded, and she bent to inspect the place he was pointing to. Avrom, however, remained a little apart, at the very edge of the road. There had been many horses and carriages here last night. It was difficult to see anything very clearly. But Avrom did spot what was, unmistakably, the rut of a wheel, a short distance from all the other wheel marks.

The rut, which might have been made by any common carriage, ran perpendicular to the road, in a line that, had it continued, would have led down to the water, exactly between the clump of bushes where Yoysif had found the spoke and the thicket of birch next to Koppel's house. The ground at roadside had been heavily trampled — some of the steps may have been Avrom's own. Thus, it was impossible to tell for certain what had caused the flattening of the grass and weeds on the way down to the water. But it appeared very much like it had been Arkady Olegovich's dead body, as it was dragged this way, sometime late on the night, or early in the morning, of the Bride of Days, the Sabbath.

Chapter 9

≈

Sparrows and Hawks

I t was simple, thought Blume — but at the same time, com-plicated. There was the spoke, Yoysif's spoke. And there was the wheel to which someone had tied poor Arkady Olegovich Efimovski. Without a doubt, one of them belonged to the other — the spoke belonged to the wheel. And that meant that who-ever had murdered the poor, good man, and tied him to the wheel, had also left the spoke in the bush, for Yoysif to come find. Simple.

The girl shuddered. *Murdered.* How easy it already was to bring that terrible word to mind. And at the same time, how impossible to escape the memory of yesterday's gruesome sight. Last night, it had kept her up for hours, and now it was doing its part again to keep sleep away: Arkady Olegovich Efimovski, so recently so full of life, so handsome on his rides through Ba-lativke, but last night, so stiff and so blue, a cold, drenched, life-less corpse ... and the cold, heartless wheel ...

She wanted to shake herself, to expel the horrible image from her mind. But she couldn't. A movement like that would disturb her sisters, sleeping all around her.

And how could anyone sleep so soundly, with so many disasters whirling around them?

However, Blume was glad to gather all the family's wakefulness for herself. She recalled a Sabbath walk, a few months earlier, with Dovid and her sisters. They had been near Deacon Achilles' house, when an unusual visitor appeared over the lake. It was a bird, enormous and grey, soaring and swooping over the water: a pelican. And without any pause at all, Dovid had produced a few, apt lines of psalm. Like everything else he'd ever said, she remembered it perfectly, even though as soon as he'd said it he added, "You can try to remember that, but I wouldn't bother unless you like that sort of thing." The line was: "I resemble a pelican of the wilderness, I am like an owl of the waste places. I lie awake, I have become like a sparrow alone on the housetop."

Well, there was no sense in having a whole flock of lonely sparrows, was there? Better only herself, lying awake.

Let her sisters enjoy their gentle dreams. But for herself, she couldn't stop thinking about the spoke and the wheel. This wasn't all bad, however: trying to work out the problem of the wheel and the spoke, the complicated part of it, was still better than letting herself be tortured, pricked in her memory by all of Dovid's wonderful sayings and observations and quotations, which were no more or less present in her mind than they had been for a while now, but which in the course of a few hours had become sharp as needles. At least working out the problem of the wheel and the spoke might allow sleep to come take her. Like counting goats.

And so, the wheel. To begin again: the wheel had certainly been brought down from the road, straight past the bush. But beyond that, what did anyone know? This afternoon, the idea that Arkady Olegovich Efimovski had been brought by boat seemed like such a perfect solution. But that wasn't it, after all. He really must have been brought by wagon.

Or, then again, perhaps not. For example, couldn't Arkady Olegovich still have come by himself, and met his murderer at the lakeside? Perhaps on horseback? Still, though, the murderer had surely come by wagon. Because there was no doubt it was the murderer who brought the wheel. No one would carry a thing like that down the road by foot unless it was from very close by. And none of the neighbors was missing a wheel. She would have heard of it.

Then why, why hadn't the noise of a wagon woken them all up?

Unless wheel and dead man both had been carried by boat ... and then the spoke had come loose while the murderer was tying Arkady Olegovich up, and the murderer had thrown it, and it had landed in the bushes?

That was possible, wasn't it? Or — Blume's heart began beating violently at this thought — what if the murderer had pulled the spoke off of the wheel, hit Arkady Olegovich over the head with it, and then thrown it into the bushes?

But then the problem remained, why did he have the cursed wheel with him in the first place?

No, it was all too confusing. The only one who could possibly get to the bottom of it was Reb Avrom. If only he was still awake too.

It was a shame there hadn't been a chance to go over it with him again earlier, after Yoysif had shown them where he'd found the spoke. Well, that wasn't quite true — there'd been a chance. It was just that Reb Avrom had seemed so strange at that moment — preoccupied, even unhappy. She'd never in her life seen him looking like that. When Yoysif pointed out the exact bush, she'd turned around, thinking the tsimbalist would be right behind her. But he wasn't, he was a few steps away. Near enough — only, she'd had the impression, somehow, that he wasn't near at all. Those grey eyes of his, which always looked "a bit here and a bit there," were entirely "there" just then, not at all "here." He didn't even seem to have any idea that she had turned around and was looking at him. Then, his eyes had clouded over, he'd suddenly looked very tired, and, when she asked him what he thought about it all, about what Yoysif had shown them, he only sighed, and said, "I don't know, my dear." And nothing more could be got out of him.

It was all very strange, very puzzling. Very un-Reb-Avrom-like.

And yet — Blume sighed loudly, then clapped her hand over her mouth, hoping she hadn't woken her sisters — should it have really been a surprise? Why should Reb Avrom be different from anyone else? The last two days, the whole world been turned upside-down, and if the whole world was upside-down, then Reb Avrom might as well be too.

~

The moon was nearly full tonight, the lake calm, soundless but for the slow lapping of water against the shore. A breeze had blown up, the birches were rustling, while a goat, one of his neighbor Hezkel's, let out a quiet, quavering groan, about once every minute. All else was silent.

It was this peace, this quiet here by the lakeside, that had first drawn Avrom to settle in little Balativke. And it had acted as a great inducement to his remaining here, despite the village's obvious drawbacks. Avrom had long ago learned the value of quiet surroundings.

In his youth — during one of his "former lives," as he thought of it — Avrom had spent a few months at the feet of the famed rabbi, Yisroel Salanter (the same one who was said to have exerted such a great influence on the Kelmer Maggid.) Although these days the tsimbalist could hardly be called a faithful follower of the great rabbi, he still remembered and held onto certain lessons he'd learned during his brief discipleship. Not least among these was the necessity of calm and reflection for the living of a satisfactory and moral life.

According to Avrom's memory (which he refreshed on occasion with the aid of the written word), Rabbi Salanter believed that one of the chief enemies to living properly was busyness. "The busy man does evil wherever he turns," the rabbi had pronounced, going on to say that, too often, our hurry and worry lead us to become unaware of our own thoughts and feelings, let alone our behavior. Because of this, we must make special efforts, especially on the Sabbath, to set aside time for quiet contemplation and self-examination. It was Rabbi Salanter's advice that this time be devoted particularly to the reading of ethical treatises, and above all to the repetition of key passages from them, till their lessons have been fully inculcated, learned so fully that they will remain in force even during moments of emotional distress.

In this regard, Avrom could not honestly say that he very often followed Rabbi Salanter's teaching — though he didn't entirely ignore it either. But when it came to the general principle of the thing, the tsimbalist was scrupulous indeed. Spending time quietly and alone, making a true effort at self-examination, undistracted and unhurried, was for Avrom a regular practice. He would sit, most often just outside of his dwelling, facing the lake, and he would sift through life's events, his actions and those of others, attempting to let whatever was inessential slip through his fingers and away, so that he could carefully weigh what remained. The quiet of those lakeside moments even seemed — as would perhaps not have surprised the sage of Salant — to have seeped inside of Avrom, so that he carried it with him into the noisy world.

And this was why today had been so particularly distressing. The whole day — and beginning last night — had been strange and unpleasant. The accumulation of one trouble upon another had, little by little and without his noticing, begun to becloud his mind and leech away his tranquility. There had been the horror of the murder. The distressing news of the robberies. Styopa's wickedness. The ugliness of the peasants. Dovid's very disappointing behavior (about which he himself even felt a little bit angry, as though it were he who had been rejected.) And there had been the dreadful conversation with Deacon Achilles, which was, in its way, even worse than the rest — and was perhaps responsible for what happened later in the day.

All day long, he'd tried to do good, for Shimmel Shenkman, for Yudel Beck, for Mirele, for Blume. And he'd accomplished nothing, for anyone. Instead, he'd been overcome by a kind of hopelessness, broader in its scope than the urgent concerns of this one, terrible day, reaching back in time, and forward, to make him feel the impossibility of the world for all of these poor souls, the orphan, the *aguneh*, the unmarried.

It was against this background that he'd gone to look and see where little Yoysif had found his spoke. Up to the road he'd followed the boy, desperate for a thread that might lead him a little closer to the answers he was seeking — he and everyone else. He'd spied the wheel-rut, the flattened grass. And suddenly, with that discovery, his thoughts, like little birds that have been cooped up and then released, shot into the air, and begun to flutter in every direction.

At full velocity they whizzed about, darting from wheel-ruts and flattened grass, to shifty card-sharps and bureaucrats with too many rubles in their pockets; from rashly bestowed inheritances and farmsteads with missing wagon wheels, to snuffed-out candles, half-bare corpses, the coincidental timing — or not — of itinerant preachers' arrivals. His fluttering thoughts set a-sway branch after branch of possibility, while in his head, he heard a kind of chirping, from which he tried to discern what was worth paying attention to, and what was only noise.

But then, before he could discern anything, or fasten on to

the right branch, a second flock of thoughts flew into view, resembling not in the least those who had come before them. For if the first flock resembled so many curious little sparrows, these second behaved more like a lot of hawks, diving down into the midst of their more peaceable brethren, sending them scattering, and dispatching them with savage blows from their sharp claws.

One of this second group had — if a thought can be said to have eyes and feathers — Tatar eyes, and delicate, mustache-like feathers resembling dragonfly's wings. Naturally, it spoke in the ice-cold tones of Nikifor Kharitonovich: *A rut? And some flattened grass? But, my dear Avrom Moisevich, weren't there a hundred ruts? And wasn't the whole place flattened, with half the village milling about by the lakeside, and stamping up and down the bank? Of course a few blades of grass, which you happened to notice out of all the others, were flattened too.*

In fact, there was no doubt in Avrom's mind that this was exactly what the police chief would say, if Avrom attempted to bring the rut, and the flattening of the grass and weeds, to his attention.

And how was Avrom to respond? To say that the rest of the bank had not been flattened so much as it had been trampled — whereas this spot had not been trampled so much as it had been flattened? Not a chance. Even if Nikifor Kharitonovich didn't burst out in anger over the tsimbalist's interference in matters that didn't concern him, the very best that could be expected was that he would laugh and send him on his way.

And while this gloomy certainty was troubling the tsimbalist, a second broad-winged thought descended upon him, having already driven away or cut down its share of the other excited little thoughts. This one did not speak in Nikifor Kharitonovich's voice, but in Avrom's own, which, however, also had in it something of the whining, nasal twang of the fiddler Moishe

Shakhes. It said: *Reb Avrom, my friend, even if, by some miracle, you manage to discover exactly who it was that killed Arkady Olegovich, and how, and when, who do you think is going to listen to you? It's true that Nikifor Kharitonovich is not a bad lot as Russians go, and as fair-minded as you could expect, from one of them. But do you think even* he *will listen to* you — *a Jew?*

﹋

It was no good. She had to get up. Sleep had refused to come.

As silently as she could manage, she rose and pulled the blanket over her shoulders. Then, one slow step at a time, she stole out of the room, and, careful not to wake her father as she crept through the front room, out of the house.

How bright it was out here! Almost a full moon. But cool — there was a breeze blowing. A good thing she had her blanket.

The birches looked even slenderer under the moonlight than during the day. Or was it only that she could see each one more distinctly, separate in their sinuous, silvery contours? She'd spent so little time outdoors at this time of night.

Perhaps that was something that would now change. Perhaps from now on she would be awake at night, while everyone else was asleep.

For an instant, she felt weak, and nearly doubled over, putting out a hand against one of the birch trunks to support herself. It really was true — the world had turned upside down, in only two days. It really was only two days ago that she had been so deliriously happy — happier, really, than she had ever remembered feeling.

What would it be like now, never talking to Dovid? It had already been so difficult, even before she went to his house today, having had to go so long without talking to him. Everything had been too busy, when they were pulling Masha out of the lake, and then afterward, when they were pulling out

Arkady Olegovich Efimovski. And everything had been too busy the night before, at the *shul* in Zavlivoya.

Dovid had been called to the Torah. And how her heart had filled with pride! As she sat there, surrounded by all the Jews of her little town and the larger one, a whole vista had opened before her ... her life together with her handsome bridegroom ... their children ... walks through the town, with friendly, respectful greetings, and admiring glances at her beautiful offspring ... She'd been so deep in her daydreams, she barely noticed when he finished his portion. The only touch of sorrow came from the thought of her mother, who wouldn't be there to share in her happiness.

And then before you knew it, the Kelmer Maggid was up there speaking. And that was a treat in its own way! The great preacher's voice rising and falling, there in the big *shul* ... in that town where, as many times as Blume had been there, she'd always felt like a visitor, a poor country cousin ... At that moment, she suddenly felt that not a thing stood between her and anyone else.

She'd already felt differently, of course, when Dovid had been called up — everyone around her knew, or soon would, that she was his betrothed. The attention paid him redounded on her too. But none of that even seemed to matter once the Maggid began to speak. What need was there for her to be singled out, to be distinguished? Weren't they all, all of them, distinguished in equal measure by the visit, the attention, of so eminent a personage? Weren't they all moved in the same way by his wisdom, by the inspiring images he painted with his eloquent words, and no less by those shining verities of which he firmly reminded them? Didn't they all gasp and sigh in perfect unison when he worked himself up to his greatest fervor, and nod their heads, all together, each time yet one more inescapable truth passed his lips? What a joyous coming together, what a dissolution of all barriers separating one Jew from another!

Well. She ought to have known a joy like that couldn't last. The world is full of hardships and tragedies, which may strike at any time. And all we can do is carry on bravely, and do good for those around us, trying to live out our lives in between the moments of sadness, instead of remaining stuck in them.

In short — Blume stood up straight, and turned her back to the birch, so that she was gazing at the house where her family slept — in short, the money that was stolen wasn't coming back, any more than was Tatte's beard. There was no sense in blaming Dovid for anything. It wasn't his fault if he didn't love her the same way she loved him. In fact, it was lucky, in a way, that he had changed his mind when he had. Just when her family needed her more than ever, here she was, free to give them all of herself. And if she wasn't happy now, she would be later. For now, she could pretend.

Pretending was better than burdening anyone else with her difficulties — they were her difficulties alone. And maybe, if she acted as if everything were all right, eventually, it would become all right. After all, hadn't that been the case when Mama died?

⁓

Sometimes, when he walked to the very edge of the water at night, he could see a light twinkling at Deacon Achilles' house. The deacon was not much of a reader, but some nights, Avrom knew, he practiced his prayers by candlelight. And if Avrom happened to want to get his feet wet that night, and saw the light, he would say a silent hello to the deacon.

He had walked out to the water's edge now, without quite realizing it, even taken off his shoes from force of habit, to avoid getting them wet and muddy. He had been wondering, he now realized, whether Achilles too was brooding over their conversation this afternoon. And that wondering had made him come out here. But when he looked, there was no light from the window down the lake. Achilles slept.

It hadn't taken Avrom long, sifting through everything in the quiet of night, to become aware that he had been unfair, earlier, to Nikifor Kharitonovich. *Nikifor Kharitonovich is not a bad lot as Russians go,* he had thought. *But do you think even he will listen to you — a Jew?*

The idea had rung round and round his head this afternoon, and he'd been unable to do anything better than offer his excuses to Blume, and beat a retreat for home. He'd been taken aback, too. He'd always gotten along with Nikifor Kharitonovich, more or less. But — it made perfect sense when it occurred to him — it wasn't really Nikifor Kharitonovich who was the problem, was it?

Avrom had never been an innocent — at least, he'd never thought he was. He'd never believed, like Dovid and poor Arkady Olegovich, that peasant, Jew, and landowner might all come together, cooperating to usher in a new era of peace and harmony in Russia. That was self-evidently foolish, the product of young, naive minds. He, Avrom, had always believed something quite different — even if he'd never formulated it in words until now. He'd believed that one Jew and one Russian, even one Russian priest, might be friends, even good friends, might get along, even work together toward their own common interests, and the interests of those around them. But tonight he wondered, was that just another species of folly, different from Dovid's, but equally naive?

The difference, of course, was that his point of view was rooted in experience, not in a dream of the future. He thought a Jew and a Russian priest could be friends because Achilles had seemed to be his friend.

And can someone who killed your god be your friend?

This was the obvious rebuttal, and it had an obvious answer: Of course not.

Achilles had a good heart, it wasn't hard to see that. He performed good acts. Of course he did. But Achilles couldn't be expected to overcome a belief he'd taken in with his mother's milk, could he? No. There was an unbridgeable gulf between them. They couldn't be friends, not really. An Achilles might do all sorts of wonderful things for his Jewish neighbors. But what did those wonderful things really amount to? By allowing Father Innokenty's voice to be heard unchallenged by a countervailing voice — which in Achilles' case would have been a loud voice indeed — the deacon withdrew all the good he might have done with his actions. His voice — his booming, loud, peasant voice — could have influenced the folk around him, could have changed the way they looked at things, and thus, the way they acted. It could have, but it never would.

Avrom sighed, as he tiptoed back across the muck. It was a disappointment.

At least he wasn't likely to be disappointed in that way — he thought as he sat back down in his chair — by Nikifor Kharitonovich. The police chief had never seemed quite so much like a friend as Achilles had.

But, to his credit, the chief had never given Avrom any reason to believe that this had anything to do with Avrom's being a Jew. It was just that the chief was a difficult and particular man, and abnormally touchy about anything he saw as interference in his business. As long as Avrom stuck to his duties as barber and confidante, they got along well enough. But Avrom did not presently wish to stick to those duties, he wished to point out to the chief certain facts that might be germane to the investigation of various crimes currently unsolved in Balativke and Zavlivoya.

To be fair, Nikifor Kharitonovich *had* listened when it came to news of the robbery at Koppel's house, and of the menace of the peasants in the woods. But these things were more in the way of providing general information, rather than really interfering. Not like the things he wanted to tell him now. And when he reported to the chief what Foka had told him, about Marfa's nighttime visitor, Nikifor Kharitonovich's impassivity made Avrom wonder whether the chief wasn't narrowing his ears, the same way he always narrowed his eyes.

Undoubtedly, the chief was ignoring others at the moment, too. It was a certainty that he was already under great pressure from the petty-governor. He'd probably heard more than once from Madame Efimovskaya, too, and might be feeling pressure of a different sort from the peasants. Each of these parties, even if they didn't express themselves in precisely the way the miscreant Styopa had, likely shared his desired outcome — the arrest of Koppel. But so far, there was no sign that such an arrest was imminent. Avrom had even heard Nikifor Kharitonovich brush aside Madame Efimovskaya's request for it.

The question was how long he could continue to do so. The chief didn't want Avrom interfering in his business because he didn't want *anyone* interfering in his business. But he couldn't ignore the petty-governor and the Efimovski family forever.

The only person he could afford to ignore forever was Avrom. And *that* was because Avrom was a Jew.

So maybe, in that respect, his unfair thought earlier regarding Nikifor Kharitonovich hadn't been one hundred percent unfair.

It wasn't the chief's fault. Achilles' beliefs, perhaps, weren't even Achilles' fault. It was — Avrom had never thought of things this way before, but tonight it seemed an inescapable fact — it was the land they lived in.

Last night, Nikifor Kharitonovich had arrested Dovid, simply to keep the peace. Sooner or later, he might feel compelled to arrest Koppel for the same reason. He couldn't quite be relied on. The only ones who could really be relied on, to help

Koppel, and Dovid, and Shimmel Shenkman, and any of the other Jews who were currently in jeopardy, one way or the other — were the Jews themselves.

Avrom hated to believe it. But hadn't recent events shown it to be true?

And yet, *if by some miracle* — just as he had put it to himself earlier — if by some miracle a Jew learned the identity of the murderer, and if the murderer was a Russian, how was a Jew supposed to apprehend such a person? That was the biggest riddle of all.

He stood. It was getting late. "The quiet around here is so lonely," his neighbor Rivke had said to him more than once. "All alone, these long nights by the lake ..." He had not often agreed with her. But he felt it now.

A noise, up by the road, suddenly made him turn. Was that a flash of white through the birches? Who was there?

He thought he knew the answer.

But then he felt less sure. No other noise made itself heard, nor did Avrom see any further movement. Everything was still, at his house, and at Koppel's.

A thought came to him, from who knows where: *Koppel's house is so nearby. Then why, the other night, did the thief rob only Koppel, and not me, too?*

Then another movement through the trees caught his eye, this time much closer at hand. Under the moonlight, he saw Blume. She saw him at the same moment and hurried through the thicket till only a bush, thorny and impenetrable, stood between them.

"Reb Avrom," she cried, pushing herself closer. Avrom winced, knowing how sharp were the thorns of that bush. "Reb Avrom!" The moon lit her distressed eyes. "Oh Reb Avrom, whatever will become of us?"

Chapter 10

❧

Under Cover

Most conveniently for him, Nikifor Kharitonovich lived just around the corner from Zavlivoya's courthouse, in an old mansion of which his apartments occupied half the upper floor. The police chief's rooms, which duty forced him to neglect during most of the daylight hours, were dark and drab, decorated in aging, cinnamon-colored wallpaper with gold flowers on it, and filled with heavy furniture of mahogany and redwood. The exception was the room where the chief enjoyed one of his principal pleasures — trimming and shaving — four days a week, including Mondays. This spacious chamber was noteworthy for two features: a tall, curtainless window on one wall, which looked out on the onion dome of St. Vladimir's, and through which morning sunshine streamed on sunny days; and at the room's center, a Voltairean chair, which by the time the chief's barber — that is, Avrom Moisevich — made his appearance, was always covered in a soft, light-colored sheet. House was kept by the elderly Espérance who, most mornings, let the barber in for his appointments. This morning was no different.

When Espérance opened the door, Avrom looked down to greet her, before walking in. The old lady was tiny, barely taller than little Yoysif, and lived in a tiny apartment elsewhere in the mansion. No one knew why she was called as she was, by her French name, rather than by her given name of Nadezhda. In any case, it was never difficult for Avrom to discern, from the manner of her greeting, what sort of a mood the chief was in that day. This morning, she was friendly as she ushered him in.

As soon as the tsimbalist entered the shaving room proper, he heard Nikifor Kharitonovich's voice from the next room: "Just a moment, Avrom Moisevich. Espérance, offer him a glass of tea, won't you? And then fill the bowls for the shave."

A by-now time-honored ritual ensued between barber and maid: Espérance offered tea. But before Avrom had bothered to refuse, she was already turning to fill two copper bowls — they were of Turkish origin — with boiling water from the samovar. Over the many years that Avrom had been shaving her master, Espérance had offered him tea countless times. And countless times, he had declined, explaining that his first cup taken at home always sufficed, and any more, "would make my hand shake" — a condition from which, as it happened, Espérance herself suffered.

As the old woman held one of the bowls beneath the samovar, the narrow table upon which both samovar and bowl rested quivered. A little plate that was sitting there chattered against the bowl, a spoon atop the plate added its ringing voice, while the scattered shell of a boiled egg trembled alongside the more stable morsel of yolk and bread that Nikifor Kharitonovich seemed to have left uneaten.

Meanwhile, a scratching sound came from below. The chief wasn't the only occupant of the apartment who hadn't finished his breakfast: beneath the tall, sunny window, Sumrak the cat was playing with something white, which proved, when the tsimbalist bent to look, to be the skeleton of a carp. Sumrak shared a number of his owner's mannerisms — or vice-versa. When Avrom bent to inspect the skeleton, the cat looked up and squinted at him. He had the same shade of dark green eyes as Nikifor Kharitonovich, bewitching and mysterious against his silvery blue fur. Sumrak belonged to the breed of cats known as "Arkhangelsk blue," which accounted for his name — it meant "Twilight." It was a logical enough choice for a name, but Avrom had also always thought that it had a whiff of gloom about it (even if it was a pleasant sort of gloom) which suggested the possibility of a hidden romantic streak on the part of the cat's owner — who now entered the room.

"A gift of our friend the deacon," Nikifor Kharitonovich remarked in a jolly tone, finding Avrom still doubled over; then laughed, "The whole carp I mean — not just the skeleton. I don't suppose he managed to get you to go fishing with him yesterday?"

"No," Avrom straightened.

"He invited me, but," the chief paused to puff on a half-smoked cigar, "well — you can imagine. Not a moment to breathe just now, let alone fish! A trim today, I think, don't you?" He turned his head so that Avrom could see its rear side.

"As you like."

"Well, what is this?" Nikifor Kharitonovich drew back. "Avrom Moisevich, taciturn?"

Avrom pressed his lips together, displeased with himself. He'd intended not to allow last night's ruminations to show in his demeanor today — and was even resolved to let Nikifor Kharitonovich surprise him, if he would.

"Not at all," he shook his head. "I was just about to thank you for letting Dovid go free."

"Ah, that," the chief chuckled as he lowered himself into the Voltairean chair. "I don't imagine you'll be surprised to learn, you take quite a different view of the matter from our petty-governor. That will do, Espérance, you can go."

With practiced hands, Avrom draped a second sheet over Nikifor Kharitonovich and snapped it flat with a flick of the wrists. "Skorokhodov-Druganin was unhappy, then, that you released Dovid?"

"He is unhappy about several things," replied the chief, and then raised his voice in a fair approximation of the petty-governor's pompous baritone: "I simply can't comprehend, my dear Nikifor Kharitonovich, what would make you set the one Yid free, and not even bring in the other to fill his cell."

Avrom paused in the midst of sharpening his razor. "He's so convinced it was Koppel who murdered Arkady Olegovich?"

"Our excellent Anton Antonovich has, among his many virtues, that of dependability. He always believes whatever is most convenient for him to believe." Nikifor Kharitonovich took another puff on his cigar, then handed it to Avrom. "Would you mind? And Madame Efimovskaya — thanks — believes it too. I heard from the pair of them five times together yesterday. Of course, the lady is to be excused, under the circumstances, but Anton Antonovich? Well, he ought to know what goes into an investigation. In any case, there's no point in holding your young friend for the moment. And certainly not before we discover where that other fine fellow is hiding this time — "

"Ah, so then you've had run-ins with Styopa before," Avrom hazarded.

"Have we! Only little things, mind, but still — a slippery devil. We've tried everywhere, all his usual haunts — his home and elsewhere in the estate village, amongst his cronies here in Zav, both brothels — "

Avrom wondered, but didn't dare ask, whether "everywhere" also included the so-called "Hermit's Cave," a dug out, rocky little hill in the middle of the woods on General Kondratin's estate, which bandits had formerly used as a storehouse for stolen goods, before its existence became too widely known to serve their purpose.

" — and even Hermit's Cave."

"Ah, so you did look there."

Nikifor Kharitonovich gave him a sardonic look. "I see that even when your tongue keeps it hands in its pockets, your brain is still nosing around. Yes, Avrom Moisevich, we 'did look' there. And we found horse-shit."

"You mean, you found nothing?" asked Avrom, taken aback.

"I mean precisely what I say. Some of our famous horse thieves must be using it again — which is all to the good, because now we'll know where to catch them out. Though yesterday, I'm sorry to say, we only found ... what we found. But that's of no relevance right now. Styopa has never counted horse-theft among his accomplishments — even so simple an art as that is too fine for the likes of him."

Avrom, who had been whisking up a bowl of shaving foam, yellow-white and perfumed, paused, and began to say, "Perhaps. But I wonder whether — "

"Avrom Moisevich, I take it back."

"Take what back?"

"You are not taciturn in the least this morning. As usual, you ask for every detail."

"Ah ... I — "

Nikifor Kharitonovich laughed. "What a rare pleasure to see: Avrom Moisevich at a loss. But lucky for you, I am in very good humor this morning. And do you know, it's actually a great boon to me to say everything out loud. For that reason, I will now tell you everything I've learned. Only don't make me angry with more questions, or I'll change my mind."

"I promise I won't ask a thing."

"Excellent. And I even have a question or two for you — put the shoe on the other foot, for a change."

"All right. But please, first, hold still for just a moment."

‿

"Do you remember that little thing you told me?" asked Nikifor Kharitonovich a minute later, after Avrom had finished brushing one side of his face with shaving foam and, with a few light and precise strokes, shaved it. "The little matter of the housekeeper's nighttime visitor — what old Foka told you. Well, judging that it might indeed be worth asking about, I returned yesterday afternoon to the Efimovski mansion to ask whether they'd heard anything in the night."

"Ah?"

"All of them claimed not to have, except for poor Foka, who confirmed what you said, though he didn't like to. Marfa, too, confirmed it — "

Avrom pulled up short, the brush in his hand hovering just by the chief's neck.

" — but only with her eyes. However, something else of mild interest came out of the interviews. The servant, Eremei — "

"Oh, is Eremei back?" (Eremei, along with his wife Pronya, were, next to Foka and Marfa, the longest-serving and sole present members of the Efimovski household staff; but unlike the other two, always traveled with the family.) "I was wondering whether he and Pronya had returned, but didn't — "

"Avrom Moisevich, I warn you!"

"Forgive me."

"As I was saying, the servant Eremei, having arrived with Madame Efimovskaya on Friday night — he and Pronya were with the ladies in Biarritz — told me something which you may agree is of interest. Don't ask me why — he said it was on account of the heat — but he's been sleeping in the stable since they returned. Or at least did on Friday and Saturday nights. And on neither of those nights did he hear a visitor, or anything else. That is" — here, Nikifor Kharitonovich dropped his voice almost to a whisper — "Eremei and the horses were left undisturbed ... if you see what I mean."

Avrom, who was about to shave the chief's neck, paused

with razor aloft, and answered in an equally quiet tone, "You mean that — "

"I mean," said the chief, nearly inaudible now, "that no one from the Efimovski estate made use of any conveyances on either of those nights. Just in case anyone had thought to wonder." Nikifor Kharitonovich's green eyes were quite expressionless as he said this.

A heavy silence ensued, broken only when Sumrak let out an uncomfortable mew.

"Ah," Nikifor Kharitonovich turned in his chair, "are they out again, Susha? Now don't be stupid, my little panther, you know quite well they can't leap all the way to your window." He sat back. "Sumrak becomes frightened when he sees the neighbor's mastiffs in the street. They'd eat him if they could."

Avrom, who was less interested in the cat's concerns than in hearing what the chief would say next, nonetheless found himself looking out the window. To his surprise, the street was entirely bereft of any canine presence.

"Now then, Avrom Moisevich," Nikifor Kharitonovich went on, "I trust you won't be so foolish as to repeat anything of what I say here. You know what an intelligent man I consider you. I should be sorry to be proved wrong."

To this, Avrom made no reply.

"Yes ... well. I said a moment ago that no one from the Efimovski estate took out any conveyance, on either of those nights. Mind you, there's no reason to imagine anyone would have. Nevertheless I ... might have taken a different view, had Arkady Olegovich been killed a week or so ago, instead of this past Saturday morning."

"Wait," said Avrom, and carefully applied his razor to the chief's neck, making sure to concentrate on the work in front of him, rather than on Nikifor Kharitonovich's most intriguing words. The chief himself fidgeted beneath his cover. "There," said Avrom, when he was done.

"I suppose you haven't heard," the chief continued at once, "that Arkady Olegovich gave away his fortune to the peasants."

Avrom said nothing.

"His mother, it seems, has been in serious debt for some time. Well, that's nothing new — which of our august nobles isn't these days? And it's the same story every time. Some Baroness Natalia Petrovna has a dwindling family fortune, but can't bear to give up her yearly trips to Nice, her dresses and jewels in the latest fashion. Or let's say it's a Count Nikolai Nikolayich, whose passionate love for the gaming dice goes sadly unrequited. Expenditure exceeds income, necessity forces a loan from this person, then that person, and that person ... from a merchant, a servant — for example, Madame Efimovskaya has even borrowed by now from her Pronya — or even from a peasant. And do the creditors ever see their money again? Perhaps, if they're lucky enough to have written proof, or witnesses to the transaction, and a little ready cash, they can hire one of these debt collectors who are sprouting up everywhere, and after some months, or some years — or if they're especially fortunate, they might even win a settlement in — however, that's not the point. The point is that while Madame Efimovskaya was in France (I have this on the best authority) she learned from some shyster she met there (but a Russian, still) that she could avoid all her debts simply by devolving her estate onto her sons."

"Ah."

"And she promptly went through with it, with this lawyer's help, right there in Biarritz — without even consulting the sons!"

"Wait," said Avrom again. This time, he applied foam, and then razor, to Nikifor Kharitonovich's other cheek. When he was finished, he fetched a small white towel, which had been steeping in water from the samovar, and with it, concealed the chief's high Tatar cheeks, and his green cat's eyes.

~

"And so," the tsimbalist asked of the little white towel. "Her sons learned of it while she was away?"

The little towel nodded up and down.

"And did Arkady Olegovich give his half away at once?"

Another nod.

"Then I wonder how long it was before Madame Efimovskaya found out what he'd done."

Nikifor Kharitonovich pulled the towel away from his now-rosy face. "She found out yesterday afternoon — from *me*."

"Ah ..."

"Well, really, how was I to know they were keeping it from her?"

"She was displeased then."

The chief sighed. "It was lucky for Arkady Olegovich he was already dead. His mother had obviously expected her two sons to support her — and their sister — in the same style they've enjoyed up until now. Henceforth, the privilege falls solely to Oleg Olegovich — who, at least, is not the sort to give away *his* fortune."

"And her creditors?"

Nikifor Kharitonovich shook his head. "The courts, perhaps ..."

In the silence that followed, Sumrak mewed once more. This time, Nikifor Kharitonovich appeared not to notice. It seemed to Avrom that he was struggling to get something out.

"The end of the subject," the chief finally said, "is that I was curious ... whether Arkady Olegovich's bequest to the villagers was quite final ... or whether it could still have been stopped, if anyone had wished to stop it. However ... it was, in fact, final."

~

"But I see you have your scissors ready," Nikifor Kharitonovich went on in a breezier tone, a second later. "Therefore, I, too, shall move along, and tell you that yesterday afternoon, I sent Ukhovyortov to Chernigov." (Ukhovyortov, Avrom recalled, was the name of the constable who had taken Dovid to jail Saturday night.) "You see, Arkady Olegovich traveled to Chernigov on Wednesday afternoon, and sent a telegram from there on Thursday."

Avrom interrupted by leaning forward, and making two quick snips beneath the chief's chin.

"Naturally, they remembered him well enough at the telegraph office. A handsome young gentleman dressed as a peasant ... it makes an impression. However, after that ... well, let me ask you a question, Avrom Moisevich. If you were told that Arkady Olegovich traveled to Chernigov to find a wedding gift for his brother — some sort of ivory chess set — would you believe it to be true?"

Avrom thought for a moment. "You don't believe it?"

Nikifor Kharitonovich sniffed, and said in a tone betraying some conceit: "I would pose the question a bit differently." (This struck Avrom as rather unfair, since it was Nikifor Kharitonovich who had posed the question in the first place.) "I would say that Arkady Olegovich *may* have traveled to Chernigov with the intent to buy his brother a gift — but that he had another aim, too, which was either an additional reason for going or ... his real one."

As he said this, Nikifor Kharitonovich freed one hand from the sheet covering him, and held up one finger significantly.

"Now let me ask you something else: What do we really know about the murdered boy's activities all winter? We know that he visited peasants, played dress-up, learned how to dance like them. But who else did he see? He was away from home all day, most days. Good. Where was he? Did he really spend every moment with peasants? Or did he see other young people in

Zavlivoya? Was he idling by himself in his orchards? Or did he venture outside the area — for example, to Chernigov?"

Nikifor Kharitonovich paused to let the idea sink in. Avrom, who was now standing behind him, took the opportunity to make several quick snips with his scissors. At the same time, he wondered what exactly was making Nikifor Kharitonovich so uncharacteristically voluble today.

"Marfa the housekeeper can't tell us," the chief presently continued. "She's in the house all day. Foka is practically senile. The Efimovskis' bailiff, Platon Makarovich — do you know him? — spends all his time drunk in the estate village. One thing we do know is that Arkady Olegovich paid no attention whatever to the upkeep of the estate, and didn't keep enough servants, considering that he was actually on the premises. I was treated to quite a generous earful about it from Madame Efimovskaya," the chief laughed. "You should feel sorry for me."

"I feel sorry for you," said Avrom, snipping next to the chief's ear.

"And believe me, even that wasn't the worst of my visit. That shrew Marfa gave me another earful about the other brother, Oleg Olegovich" — Nikifor Kharitonovich's voice rose half an octave — "he didn't hire any help to prepare for his *ball*, he expected two old servants to do *everything*, it wasn't till Saturday when his *mother* came that some servants were fetched from General *Kondratin's* to help get things in shape. Naturally, Marfa only said all of it to distract me from asking about her miserable whelp — though I don't doubt it was all true. The noble Efimovskis appear to have a distinctly impractical — however, our concern at the moment is solely with Arkady Olegovich."

"Yes." Snip.

"Do you know, Avrom Moisevich, what they mean by the word *narodnik*?"

"Those young people who believe that the empire's future lies with the peasants, if only they can be woken up?"

"Well, that's the idea, but it's not only the peasants they'd like to wake up, but also the workers — or at least, as I learned yesterday, the *narodniks* are *allied* with what seems to be a whole rash of 'workers' circles.' Very dangerous business — they could cause real unrest. Of course we've all heard of Berezowski and Karakozov — imagine, wanting to murder our Tsar! — and then Nechayev, who seems to be the worst of all, even if he hasn't tried to assassinate anyone yet. On the other hand, there's something called the Circle of Tchaikovsky, who merely want to circulate forbidden books — though even that — however, in short, all of these little groups are quite mixed up together."

"Ah."

"I myself didn't know everything about it all until yesterday, when I interrogated your young friend Dovid."

"What?"

"Yes, indeed. Oh, he tried not to tell me anything of what he knew — perhaps even believed he succeeded. But as you will have noticed, he suffers from rather an advanced case of enthusiasm. So that in the end quite a bit did slip out."

"Enthusiasm?"

"The symptoms are quite unmistakable, Avrom Moisevich. Glittering eyes, pride, defiance ... He's one of them, you know, though I wouldn't regard him as dangerous in any way. Still, I'd keep an eye on him, if I were you. Keep him out of mischief, if you can. You knew he was a friend of Arkady Olegovich?"

"I — "

"Who, of course, is the reason I mention all of this. Arkady Olegovich was involved in it, and if I'm right, involved up to his shining white teeth."

"Hmm."

"I already knew something about it yesterday morning. But *then*, I was still fixed on his inheritance. Now, instead, I wonder just how far his involvement with these *narodniks* and schemers went. Think — he had great freedom of movement. And by now,

these groups have sprung up in every city of any size, and especially in the biggest cities. For example, Kiev isn't so very far
away. Who's to say Arkady Olegovich didn't go to Kiev last week,
and then to Chernigov Wednesday, for the purpose of passing
messages from one group to another? Everyone knows the mail
isn't safe for secrets — any group that wished to stay under cover would have to make use of messengers, unless they had some
sort of secret code — which, I suppose, is a distinct possibility.
Or — forgetting messages for the moment — there may have
been some other scheme that required him going there."

Avrom, who was still wondering about Dovid, remained
quiet.

"But the most important question, whatever his reason for
going, is *who did he talk to while he was there?* What if, for example, he went to a meeting of a workers' circle in Chernigov, and
in the course of their conversation, he happened to mention
that this 'Kelmer Maggid' of yours was coming to Zavlivoya?
According to your young friend — he was quite proud of the
fact — these workers' circles count among their membership
a number of your co-religionists. And so my first question for
you, Avrom Moisevich, is, how famous is this 'Kelmer Maggid'
of yours?"

Avrom didn't reply right away, but took care to draw a very
slow and deep breath. So here, at last, was the reason Nikifor
Kharitonovich had chosen to be so voluble, and so forthcoming, this morning.

"He is quite famous."

"So that, for example, a Jew in Chernigov, knowing he was
sermonizing in Zavlivoya on Friday night, could have predicted
that every Jew in town would be there?"

"Are you as determined as our petty-governor to find a Jew
behind Arkady Olegovich's murder?" asked Avrom, before he
could stop himself.

"Avrom Moisevich!" exclaimed the police chief, sounding

deeply injured. "How could you believe such a thing? Did I say it was a Jew who killed him?"

Avrom hesitated. "No."

"On the contrary, it is my belief that your neighbor *couldn't have had anything to do with Arkady Olegovich's death* that impels me to look elsewhere for the culprit. How you've wounded me, Avrom Moisevich — you might as well have jabbed your scissors straight into my neck!"

"I ... apologize. I apologize, Nikifor Kharitonovich. Forgive me."

"All right, all right, it's nothing. But now just imagine: Arkady Olegovich goes to Chernigov. He mentions that this preacher is visiting — he would have known about it from your young friend, wouldn't he? — though that's something to check on. All right, someone in the circle there — yes, a Jew — has the bright idea to take advantage of the circumstance to raise money for their cause — certainly by now they have some sort of war chest. And that's something else I must find out, whether Arkady Olegovich set aside any of his money to give to these groups ... In any case, some one of the Jews in the circle has the bright idea of robbing his wealthy co-religionists here in Zavlivoya. Arkady Olegovich is naturally drafted to participate — it's his home territory. He returns with some of them — Jews or not, I make no distinction, Avrom Moisevich. In fact, I'm just as inclined to think they didn't belong to your persuasion — would not a Jew have still felt a little squeamish about the idea? You know better than I do. Though I don't doubt there are some cold-blooded characters in these circles, real reptiles. In any case, the plan is carried out, but in the course of events, something goes wrong. They quarrel, who knows why? — criminal activity, take it from me, always brings out the worst in everyone. Perhaps someone wants to keep the money for himself, that's always the likeliest scenario. And Arkady Olegovich is killed."

Avrom made no reply.

"Tell me it isn't possible."

"I suppose ... it's possible."

"In fact, when you consider it a bit more, you'll find it's the only solution which ties together Arkady Olegovich's death, his involvement with the *narodniks*, his trip to Chernigov, and the robberies."

"... True."

"The only difficulty is ... you've heard of the Third Section, Avrom Moisevich?"

Avrom answered quietly. "I have."

"The difficulty before me," said Nikifor Kharitonovich, "is that I must learn more, much more, about these various groups. And the Third Section certainly knows everything there is to know about them. But if the Third Section were to become involved, there's no telling what might happen, who might get swept up in it. The medicine could turn out to be worse than the disease. Given the excuse of an incident, a murder no less, who knows what they might not ... for example, your young friend Dovid ..."

"Yes," said Avrom. "I see."

"Of course, the main thing is to find out more in Chernigov itself. As I can't go myself — I must remain here to maintain order — I've already sent Ukhovyortov back again. But Avrom Moisevich — I'll need you to do something for me, too."

Avrom's heart sank. "What is that?"

"In our conversation, your young friend would only speak in generalities. But he couldn't be persuaded to name any names. I need you to talk to him, Avrom Moisevich, and find out for me. I need names."

Avrom's heart sank. "I — "

"I should hate to be forced to turn elsewhere for the information." Nikifor Kharitonovich turned his eyes upward, toward the ceiling.

"Then ... I will do what I can," said the tsimbalist.

"Excellent," said Nikifor Kharitonovich — while at the same time, Sumrak let out a loud, satisfied mew. "Now, if you'll just tell me how my health is today — and then of course, wax my mustache for me ..."

Chapter *11*

Travels and Wanderings

T he rest of the morning was a parade of bushy beards and straggling bangs, muttonchops and mustache-wax. Prosaic, by appearances — except that while Avrom's hands were occupied with snipping and shaving and trimming, inside, he was rehearsing the same dispiriting argument over and over again, which went something like this:

To return to the first point — an altogether sickening idea. Sidling up to Dovid under the cover of friendship, and milking him like Masha the cow? Sickening — no other word for it. But — I have to ask once again — is that, alone, reason not to do it? If getting Dovid to reveal names could really keep him out of trouble ...

On the other hand ... My good friend the police chief wishes to keep the Third Section out of his fiefdom. And no matter what his reasons are — the pure and the impure! — everyone in Balativke and Zav will be better off if he does. But — to reiterate — is there really such a good chance of that happening? Even if I accede to his request (or threat!) they'll still become involved — if not here, then in someone else's fiefdom.

To be more specific, let's say Nikifor Kharitonich is right, and Arkady Olegovich was killed by fellow narodniks. And let's say I get him the names, he picks the right one out of the hat, and, voilà, *the case is solved. Is it reasonable to think the Third Section, which has ears everywhere, will fail to get wind of it? Oh, they'll hear all right.*

All right, then what happens? Dovid, who thanks to me has unwittingly betrayed his friends, including not only the murderer but many others — Dovid might still (or might not!) slip free of the Third Section's nets. But his friends, who, in fact, aren't just names to be milked like milk, but real people, and real people who are well-meaning, even if they're foolish — or at least, they're well-meaning when compared with the tsar's spies ... They'll all be netted like a school of minnows, and ground up like pike.

And what, exactly, will that make me?

This was the question he kept coming back to, after circling through the rest of the argument. Once, he even yanked a lock of the health commissioner's thinning hair asking it.

Thank goodness the morning's last client was the pensioner Parfyon Panteleyevich Shchegolev. Unlike the others, whose dull monologues necessitated only a few understanding grunts and agreeable chuckles — making it all too easy to remain lost in ugly thought — the old pensioner was impossible to ignore. A lucky thing, on a day like today.

The happy truth was that Parfyon Panteleyevich, who lived alone on the eastern edge of town, was nothing less than a fountain of stories, which would come shooting out of his mouth in a never-ending stream, to fall lightly and musically upon Avrom's ears, and wash away any troubles that may have clung to him when he stepped through the door. The work was easy, too: rarely did Parfyon Panteleyevich require any trimming or snipping (though he did like to be shaved.) Instead, on most visits, he requested only that Avrom apply a fresh dose of indigo to darken up his naturally white hair and beard.

While Avrom worked, Parfyon Panteleyevich would regale him with one tale after another, specializing in anecdotes from his own youth, which were mostly of a distinctly amorous nature.

The tales' elements were by now familiar: a much younger Parfyon Panteleyevich, some "indescribable" beauty (whom the pensioner nonetheless described at great length and in vivid detail), an angry father or fiancée, and a narrow getaway. The stories always amused, in their general outlines. But there was also about them a certain touching quality, a sense of deep nostalgia and longing. Anyone listening to him could tell that Parfyon Panteleyevich wished those days had never passed — a desire almost anyone might fall prey to now and then, especially those who have not exchanged the pleasures of youth for other, more domestic felicities — but Parfyon Panteleyevich wished it more than other people did, wished it with nothing less than a burning fervor which shone brightly through its light comic clothing.

This, clearly, was why he insisted on the indigo treatment: to restore some small degree of his lost dash and charm. Alas, it was a misplaced effort. The dye did darken his hair and beard. But the effect, set against the his wrinkled skin, was more ridiculous than rejuvenating. Avrom might even have felt he was cheating him — dye didn't come cheap — if not for the fact that their weekly mains-à têtes unquestionably ameliorated the loneliness and relative poverty of the pensioner's current state.

Today, though, it was Avrom who got the best end of the bargain. Parfyon Panteleyevich's latest anecdote, a particularly risqué one involving an entire Georgian dance troupe and a false beard, completely succeeded in putting Dovid, Nikifor Kharitonovich, the *narodniks*, and the Third Section out of his mind. By the end of the story, his spirits had halfway recovered, and the last line — "And for all I know, the beard is still there!" — drew a full laugh from his belly. If only the next words out of the old man's mouth hadn't given him something new to worry about!

"And now, Avrom Moisevich, I have a little question for you," the pensioner smiled with his remaining teeth. "I've been invited down to Zavlivoya Inn this afternoon for a round or two of *préférence*. What I wonder is ... do you suppose the dye will have set by then? That is ... will I look fit, d'you think, for the delightful young ladies they have down there?"

This "little question" instantly brought an unwelcome image to Avrom's brain: Parfyon Panteleyevich in some dingy little room at the inn, with Mirele, the orphan girl. Was that the sort of "delightful young lady" he meant? Parfyon Panteleyevich was an amusing old soul, certainly. But that image ... Well. If everything that had happened since yesterday's visit to the inn had made Avrom forget the extent of his dereliction toward the orphan girl and her deceased parents, this brought it back in full force. No matter that he'd forgotten her for a long, a shamefully long time. Her fate was not, for that reason, any less important than Blume's or Dovid's. To the contrary! Add in the fact that he had a chance to materially improve her lot (something less clear in the case of the other two young unfortunates) and, despite everything else swirling around him (or perhaps because of it?), a visit to Yudel Beck's inn suddenly seemed a rather urgent necessity.

And, as soon as he'd finished rinsing the excess indigo from Parfyon Panteleyevich's fan-shaped beard, that was exactly where he hurried.

~

But man proposes, and God laughs. Once Avrom arrived at the inn, his plan to rescue the orphan girl was foiled by the simple fact that she was nowhere to be seen — he walked all around the haze-filled room to make sure. Worse, no one could tell him a thing about her, not the girls she'd been sitting with yesterday (who when asked where he might find her, met his question with dumb stares) nor the tuneful Ukrainian and mournful gypsy (who didn't recognize Mirele's name or description, or pretended not to.)

Two coins, for a glass of schnapps each, produced better results from another pair, a lanky blonde and a freckled redhead, dressed as Mirele had been yesterday. But only a little better. They agreed the orphan girl existed, and recalled speaking with her once, or maybe even twice. But more than that they seemed reticent to say. Any speculation as to her present whereabouts or place of residence was out of the question.

Well, what now? Of course! Yudel Beck would know.

On his way to the back of the room, he saw that yesterday's gamblers were at it again. And surprise, surprise — the ill-favored Pugovitsin once again had a healthy pile of cash and coins in front of him. But hadn't he been cleaned out yesterday?

Curiosity getting the better of him, Avrom paused to congratulate the bureaucrat on his restored fortune.

"Thanks," Pugovitsin looked up, shaking his head and waving his hand nervously. "But if you don't mind, save your congratulations till I've managed to hang on to it." And he scattered a few small coins on the floor.

Avrom had a feeling this superstitious behavior wouldn't bring Pugovitsin any luck. It was obvious the three merchants were cheating again: as soon as Avrom arrived, they'd sat up very straight, and now they were fidgeting like a trio of squirrels. As Avrom looked around the table, however, he saw that this afternoon, they themselves were being out-gambled. A fifth player sat at the table: not the Pole, who must have been put to work today by Nikifor Kharitonovich, but an altogether more sympathetic character, if one still less fortunate in appearance than Pugovitsin. The plump, clean-shaven face beneath the man's ginger curls was rashy and red, and his spectacles were so thick, the eyes behind them could scarcely be made out.

"Anshel Pempik," the newcomer introduced himself, smiling engagingly as soon as Avrom turned his way. A Jew then, despite his clean-shaven face. And another merchant, as he went on to explain. From as far away as Lemberg (he said it in some sort of exotic accent, Polish or perhaps Austrian), only passing through, and unlikely to spend the night — "though your town *aynd* the waters of its *like* are *livly* indeed."

Well, it seemed they knew how to gamble in Lemberg, no matter how they spoke. The newcomer had an impressive stack of bills in front of him, while the three cheats had few. Perhaps, thought Avrom, with a lighter heart than he had felt most of the day, there was justice in the world after all.

~

Yudel Beck was as rude as ever.

He giggled unpleasantly upon hearing Avrom's inquiry: "Well, well. So even the famous Reb Do-Gooder has his weaknesses. Let it be a lesson to us all! On the other hand, why not? Any traveler in the wilderness will get hungry sooner or later, tee-hee. So the tsimbalist's taste runs to young Mireles, hmm ..."

"No, it's — " Avrom was about to correct Yudel Beck's misapprehensions. But then he thought better of it. "It's ... only the one Mirele. Mirele herself. I dearly desire to see her."

"Dearly desire?" the innkeeper guffawed. "I see you've really got it bad. But why so picky? There are a number of beauties here, and of the same type — that one there, for example, another Queen Esther. I'm sure she'd be *honored* to do business with such an *eminent* barber as yourself."

"It's Mirele I'd like to see."

"Well, in that case, bad luck for you."

"Bad luck? Why so?"

"Because you won't find her."

"You don't mean I have to go look for her at one of those places at the end of Post Office Street, where — "

"You can look wherever you like, but you won't find her in all of Zav. She's left town. Or so at least I've heard."

"Left town?" Avrom protested. "But I saw her just yesterday."

"And been thinking about her ever since — I can see how it is," Yudel Beck's whiskers shook with glee. "It just goes to show — if you didn't hold your nose so high in the air, and came around more often, you'd have gotten a chance by now to wet your whistle."

"Reb Yudel, you ... you're ... you're right, of course. But ... can you tell me where she went?"

"I couldn't say for sure."

"No idea?"

"I'm afraid I can't help you."

~

Like a treacherous chasm, or the mouth of a hungry lion, the rest of the day now yawned. And with what was he to fill it? Nothing could be done about Mircle if he couldn't find her. That would require some thought. There was, of course, Nikifor Kharitonovich's "request" concerning Dovid. Nothing stood in the way of Avrom's going to talk with that young man this very moment. True, he didn't know where Dovid was, but that was not so mysterious a matter as Mircle's whereabouts. Chances were good that Dovid was a mere fifteen minute walk away, at the *besmedresh*, the study house next to Zavlivoya's *shul*.

It was therefore time to come to some sort of decision on the subject. Would he ruin Dovid's life, or would he ruin the lives of many people, possibly including Dovid? Avrom walked in the direction of the *besmedresh*, going once more over the same old argument. And at last, he came to a decision — though a decision that was really no decision at all. He'd find Dovid, because he'd been wanting to talk to him anyway. Then, when they were talking ... he'd see what would happen.

And this way, he might also finally get a chance to meet the Kelmer Maggid. The Maggid — if he was still in Zavlivoya at this late date — would probably also be at the *besmedresh*.

However ... the visit to the study-house was no more suc-
cessful than the trip to the inn had been. In the first place, the
Kelmer Maggid wasn't there. As an admiring Berl Melamed
reported: "You know, Reb Avrom, he's a very quiet sort, and likes
to listen to what we have to say more than to hear himself speak
— as it is said, a wise man hears one word and understands two.
But, as he said, sometimes if he's with people too much, his
mind becomes beclouded, and he needs to go off by himself
somewhere, for silent contemplation and self-examination. It's
his habit at such times to go out walking alone in the woods. So
that's where he went."

And Dovid?

"Oh — *him*." The Hebrew school teacher's tone took on a
dark hue as the subject turned to his erstwhile rival. "As I've noticed more than once, and even pointed out to those who would
listen, that fellow likes to steal other people's glory, make himself
look good in order to trick the people around him and get what
he wants, if you know what I mean. And here's a good example,
if you don't believe me. As soon as the Maggid left today, that
Dovid said *he* needed solitude too, and that a walk was just what
he needed — like he's another Kelmer Maggid! So he left, to who
knows where. But Reb Avrom, why do you look so happy all of
a sudden? And where are you going? You've only just arrived!"

⁓

Avrom was happy, of course, because being unable to find Dov-
id, he wouldn't be able to ask him any compromising questions.
But as to Berl Melamed's other question: where *was* he going?
He simply didn't know.

In fact, however, for the moment the question turned out
to be immaterial. As soon as Avrom exited the *besmedresh*, he
found his bass player, Kuz'ma, waiting for him.

"Well. *Sholem aleikhem*, Kuz'ma. What are you doing here?"

"I followed you from the tavern, Avrom Moisevich."

"Did you? The whole way? Then why didn't you call out?"

"Well ... I'd been in my drink, and ... somehow I was feeling too sleepy to shout."

"Ah ... well, and did you have a reason for following me?"

"I did. I wanted to ask ... when do you suppose we might get our pay?"

"Ah, that. Perhaps soon, I suppose. It's a delicate matter."

"It's just, I could do with the money."

"Are you in need of a loan?"

"Oh no, Avrom Moisevich, not that."

"Are you sure?"

"I couldn't ... Avrom Moisevich, I heard what you were asking about in the tavern. When you were talking to Beck."

"I don't know how I didn't notice you there. But do you know something about it?"

"The girl you were looking for — "

"Yes?"

"Well, you see, there was a foreigner hanging about the tavern lately. A Prussian, or some. I didn't catch his name, but they called him, what was it they said, a *khaper*."

"A recruiter? From the army? But why wou-"

"Not from the army, Avrom Moisevich. He was recruiting girls. That is, Beck was selling the girls to him. And no one was to know anything about it. But I heard."

"It wasn't the man at the tavern just now?"

Kuz'ma shook his head. "No. They went on their way this morning."

"To where? In which direction?"

"I'm sorry, Avrom Moisevich. I didn't go outside to see."

⁓

Kuz'ma's information was disheartening. But, if it were possible to enlist Nikifor Kharitonovich's aid in the matter, then it might also prove useful.

But where was the chief to be found? Avrom didn't have the heart to go looking for yet another difficult-to-find person, not on this day. And so instead, he directed his steps homeward.

And this proved a wise choice indeed. For who did he see when he had nearly arrived? None other than Nikifor Kharitonovich, crouched at the side of the road a few steps from Koppel's place.

The chief was bent over, studying the ground. But at the sound of the tsimbalist's steps, he raised his head.

"Well, Avrom Moisevich. Any luck yet?"

"Luck?"

"With our young friend," the chief stood, rubbing dirt from his hands.

"You mean Dovid?"

"Yes, Avrom Moisevich, that is who I mean."

"Ah ... No, I haven't been able to find him yet. But what brings you here?"

"What brings me to the scene of Arkady Olegovich's death? A strange question."

"Of course ... It's just that it's been two days now since--"

"Yes, two entire days. Or at least a day and a half. I've been quite derelict, haven't I?"

Avrom realized, too late, that the chief was in a foul humor.

"If only I hadn't wasted my time looking for Styopa," Nikifor Kharitonovich went on, "or answering the door when our petty-governor and Madame Efimovskaya came calling. I even had a visit from General Kondratin this morning, who is most anxious for me to arrest a Jew or two--or at least a peasant, since it may just as well have been one of them. No doubt, I should have left my door closed to the general as well. But at least I'm here now."

"I didn't--"

"Never mind. Since you haven't done what I asked, perhaps instead you can answer a question for me."

"Of course, what is it?"

"This: when you see fishing boats on this part of the lake, how close in do they come?"

"Fishing boats?" Avrom considered. "I suppose not so very close. Sometimes, the fishermen tell me they can hear conversations right here on shore, from their boats. And it always strikes me that our words have traveled quite a long way to be heard. But of course, that's how it is on this lake. Still, it's always a surprise. So, not very close. I suppose they *could* come closer, though, if they wanted. It gets deep quickly from the shore."

"In other words, you have nothing useful to tell me, on any subject." The chief scanned the ground. "A pity there were so many wagons, and so many pairs of feet, up here."

"I could show you where little Yoysif found his wheel-spoke ... that bush over there."

"Oh yes?" Nikifor Kharitonovich took a step in the direction Avrom was pointing.

"And then, I also--" Avrom went on.

But: "That will do," Nikifor Kharitonovich interrupted. "My day is vanishing far too quickly. Can't you all leave me in peace for one uninterrupted minute?"

～

... And once again, the day yawned.

But this time, the tsimbalist had something with which to placate the lion and bridge the chasm. No Dovid, no Mirele, no Kelmer Maggid, no "recruiter"? What else should a tsimbalist do, but play on his tsimbl?

And what better way to forget about Mirele, when the thought of her occasioned such guilty feelings?

Not that he needed any such excuses. An hour or two with his tsimbl was even better, in Avrom's judgment, and in the judgment of his heart, than a solitary walk in the woods, or, let's say, a quiet evening staring at the lake. Though in fact, the three things were not unrelated--at least not in Avrom's mind.

Avrom had been struck, and forcibly, by Berl Melamed's words: "If he's with people too much his mind becomes be-clouded, and he needs to go off by himself somewhere, for si-lent contemplation and self-examination." Where had he heard that before? The Maggid must indeed be a disciple of the great Rabbi Salanter.

Although ... not a *strict* disciple. More one after his own heart. Had the Maggid's experience with Salanter, he won-dered, been similar to his own?

Avrom had learned from the great rabbi the importance of contemplation, and that it was something best done away from the hurly-burly of the everyday world. Salanter, though, had never specified that it should be a *solitary* practice — not in Av-rom's hearing at least. Avrom preferred solitary contemplation, and it seemed the Maggid did too. But Salanter had advocated something else: the construction of special buildings, "ethics houses," which were to be built next to the usual study houses, in order to provide a sort of communal privacy.

Why communal privacy? Because that style of repetitive reading that the great rabbi recommended, the repeated utter-ance of key passages from his chosen ethical treatises, had a very peculiar, a truly eccentric feature. Salanter's idea — de-signed to most effectively inculcate the moral lessons of his chosen treatises — was that the first time a given passage was read, it should be read very quietly, very neutrally, but that each subsequent iteration was to be progressively less quiet, less neu-tral. The second or third utterance was to be mildly emotional, the fourth or fifth downright passionate, and the last, urgent and vivid, so that the words being spoken took on real life

— even a kind of physical form, like a silhouette hovering in front of the utterer, who could then, as it were, step into it, and be joined to it. That, at least, the idea of a physical form, was Avrom's way of imagining the process, though the rabbi had never described anything of the kind.

Salanter recognized that shouting out passages in an ecstatic manner was not something everyone would feel comfortable doing. Hence, the "ethics house," where, because everyone was behaving in an equally eccentric manner, the eccentric would seem more or less normal.

During his few months with the rabbi, Avrom had spent a great deal of time in the "ethics house." He threw himself into his readings, hoping to make the words appear before him in the vivid way he imagined. Only, he couldn't do it. What would happen was that, after the first several utterances, as the young Avrom attempted to inflect his words with more emotion, he encountered a barrier between himself and the words, a form of shyness perhaps, though it wasn't exactly a fear of other people as much as — well, he didn't know at the time what it was, only that he was unable to overcome it. He *wanted* to fill the words with passion, as he saw and heard others do. But he couldn't forget himself to a sufficient degree, couldn't allow the words to find their own life, to blossom.

And it was this that eventually led him to wander on from the rabbi's tutelage.

It couldn't be, could it, that the Maggid had encountered the same difficulty?

No. It seemed doubtful. The Maggid had no trouble allowing himself to be ecstatic in front of whole crowds of people, had no trouble embracing the meanings of the words he said, no matter how flowery and high-flown. But perhaps there was another side of him, a much more private one? Perhaps he was comfortable *before* people, but reticent *with* them? Why not? People came in all shapes and sizes, and for everyone, there was a different way of doing things — as Avrom had found out about himself, not so long after he left Rabbi Salanter.

This was when he was almost seventeen. Despite his advanced years, he had apprenticed himself to an old barber who was also a tsimbl player. Artchik had his own shop, which Avrom was charged with sweeping and keeping clean — the old man was quite meticulous. In addition to cleaning, Avrom's duties included sharpening the scissors, grinding the powder for shaving foam, and so on, and carrying Artchik's tsimbl to weddings for him. In return, he received meals and lodging, but so far as the tsimbl went, little in the way of useful instruction. At least he was free at night to stay in the empty shop as long as he liked, and practice. He was even allowed two candles a week, so that when he practiced, it was not *always* dark.

One night he was in the empty shop, playing. It was almost dawn. He had no candle. Despite the darkness, it had been more than an hour since he'd played a note amiss — so far had his mastery progressed. Yet he was overcome, at that in-between hour, by an unmistakable feeling of dissatisfaction, which began as a nagging whisper, and then began to fill his ears.

There was nothing glaringly out of place to occasion this feeling. In the two years he'd been with Artchik, on two occasions when the old man was laid up with a stomach ailment, Avrom had filled in for his master, and encountered no difficulty fitting right in with the band. The technique of the instrument had come quite naturally to him. (He attributed this, in part, to the years' worth of piano lessons he'd taken while still a child in his father's house.) The sticks felt perfectly balanced in his hands, the entirety of the motion, the forth and back of the arms, and in counterpoint with it, the gentle down and up of the wrists, gave him immense physical pleasure. The sound with which the instrument filled the room also filled him, made his whole body vibrate.

But that night, he became aware that the music he was playing was lacking in life. Not in *liveliness*. But in a true, animating spirit. The way he played might be nice to listen to. But what it ought to do, what he wanted it to do, was to take anyone who might be listening, and transport them, somewhere else, somewhere far away, the way that ... the way that the firebird, in that famous legend the Russians told, carried away the tsar's apples. (That was the image that came to him, there and then, even if it didn't make any sense.)

Whether it was that night, or the night after, he didn't know anymore. But on of those nights, he found himself applying to his own practice on the tsimbl Rabbi Salanter's eccentric technique for contemplation. He played a certain passage in a neutral, exact manner; then repeated it, with more emotion — or character, or spirit, whatever you wanted to call it. And so on till ... the music did have life. That barrier that had existed between himself and the words of those passages? It was not there, when it came to the notes emerging from the tsimbl. (Not even later, when there were people there to listen.)

He practiced like that until morning arrived, and the barber opened the door of his shop. That same day, he left his apprenticeship with Artchik. But all these years later, he still practiced his tsimbl the very same way.

~

And that was how he played today, filling the yawning afternoon with song. He played every piece of music he knew, barely stopping to rest. His arms, far from tiring, seemed to heal from the wear and tear of barbering. He forgot all his troubles, forgot for a little while the existence of other people, as the sound of his tsimbl floated, away over the lake.

He only came to himself when, stopping to take a breath, he happened to glance up toward the road, and caught sight of the very young man he'd been looking for earlier.

Chapter 12

Relations Between the Faiths

He saw Dovid before Dovid saw him.

The elusive young man was standing practically in Avrom's yard, close enough for the tsimbalist to see every detail of his familiar appearance: the handsome profile with its high forehead, the chocolate-brown beard, silky and elegant, the black coat short as Avrom's own. But as close as he stood, it was obvious Dovid was looking elsewhere. He was staring at Koppel's house — or rather, Blume's.

For a split second, Avrom observed him, himself unobserved. Then, several things happened, very quickly. First, Dovid must have noticed the tsimbl go silent, because he spun to face the lake, and Avrom. Their eyes met; and Avrom couldn't help but think Dovid looked like a thief, caught in the act. His face, which usually wore a confident, relaxed expression, had on a guilty and uncertain one, which was also not without a hint of helplessness.

Determined to put him at ease, Avrom raised his arm in welcome. But even as he did so, a noise, the creaking of a hinge next door (it sounded like Masha's little barn), made Dovid's eyes widen. For an instant, he turned to look back, then whirled the other way and took off at nothing less than a full run, in the direction of Hezkel the Woodcutter's place.

Avrom hesitated a second, then, without bothering to ask himself why, bounded toward the road in pursuit. But he was intercepted almost at once.

How beguiling it was, listening to Reb Avrom play on his tsimbl. And painful, at the same time. Just little fragments of music, over and over again: the first like a caress, the next like a hand on the shoulder, gentle but firm, so you couldn't help but pay attention — even if you were busy with something altogether less exalted, like trying to squeeze four rounds of cheese out of three buckets of milk, with something left over for butter too. And then the last time, the music would push against your chest and make your heart cry out. Yet afterward, for some reason — who could understand these things? — you felt consoled.

They said Reb Avrom could have been another Gusikov, the most famous tsimbl player of them all, who toured all of Europe and became a real millionaire. How lucky — what a source of pride! — that they had Reb Avrom here in little Bala-tivke. It would have made her wedding so perfect if —

No. She mustn't think about that. If she wasn't careful, she'd get her tears in the milk. *That's it, Blume. Just listen to the music, and churn.* It was even possible to do it in time to the music.

Except that the music stopped. That was all right, though. That meant she could go ask him.

"Reb Avrom, how nice to listen to you play your music — and all afternoon, no less! What good it does a heart."

Avrom answered in a rush: "I'm-happy-you-enjoyed-it-my-dear-but-tell-me-what-brings-you-here?"

Well, thought Blume, how unlike Reb Avrom to be in such a hurry. "Only a little question, but I can come back later if — "

"Yes, that would — "

And why was he turning his head and looking the other way? "I only wanted to ask the way to the Tatar's who lives in the forest. Tatte didn't want me to go alone, and won't tell me the way. But with Rivke watching him I thought I could slip away now."

"The Tatar healer? Well — all right, that's told quickly enough."

Yes, he really was in a hurry — he didn't even ask why she wanted to go see the Tatar!

"Do you know the little path that runs near Itzik Leyba's house?"

Well all right, the path by Itzik Leyba's, that was easy enough. The old man lived one house before Rivke, though his family was so large — twelve children and who knows how many grandchildren and great-grandchildren, and half of them still living together — that they also occupied the house next to Hezkel's, that is, one house closer still. And Itzik Leyba himself, poor man, still went to work at the pitch-works in the middle of the forest, though he was past sixty. Imagine, feeding forty people. Or was it fifty? It was so difficult to remember.

But what was Reb Avrom saying now? The first fork left, the next fork right, the last fork left? Or was it the other way around? She should have been paying better attention, instead of thinking about the size of Itzik Leyba's clan!

"... And then go along for another few minutes till you see a little hut with a mud roof, it isn't more than three *versts* — but I fear it's too late to go now and get back before dark, if you like, I'll go with you after market tomorrow, how does that sound?"

"Oh, that would be — "

"Excellent. And now I must — but my dear, you *are* all right today, aren't you?"

"Yes, Reb Avrom, but — "

"You only just came outside, didn't you? You weren't in the yard for a bit?"

"No, but — "

"Ah, I'm glad to see you laughing, but — why are you laughing?"

"Because Reb Avrom, you still have your tsimbl sticks in your hands. You're not going to walk down the road like that, are you?"

~

At first, he didn't see Dovid. The young man must have run a good distance. Avrom shook his head. How could anyone be so afraid of a sweet girl like Blume? He was the one who had made *her* cry.

Ah, there he was — no longer running, thank goodness, in fact, walking as slow and aimless as could be, but nonetheless, a good four houses ahead. Here was Hezkel's place, and Dovid looked to be roughly even with Rivke's house. Yes, he was stopping to look at the flowers. And that was the little spaniel, barking.

"Dovid," he called out. But Dovid didn't hear — the little dog was barking too loud.

By the time Avrom reached Itzik Leyba's house, Dovid was nearing the village oven. And when he came to Rivke's, Dovid was by the bathhouse. Why didn't he stop already, and turn around? If anything, his pace had quickened again. It was as if Blume exerted some gravity-like power upon him: the further he was from her house, the lighter his step.

Avrom was about to call his name again when he saw Rivke, standing by her door with a half-smile on her full lips.

She looked in the direction Dovid had just gone. "What's *he* doing here?"

"I don't know myself," Avrom spoke quickly, "but — "

"Poor Blume," Rivke interrupted. "Abandoned, and just a few days before the wedding."

"Yes, and now — "

"Unless someone else decided to marry her." The smile left Rivke's lips. "Do you know of anyone else who might wish to marry her, Reb Avrom?" She stared intently at the tsimbalist.

"I? Who knows? It's much too soon for such talk. And I have no time for it."

He hurried off, and saw up ahead a half-minyan of Jews, laughing loudly as they departed the bathhouse. Beyond them, Dovid was now almost too far away to see.

Balativke was a tiny town, but long. To walk from one end of its lone, muddy street to the other took a good half hour or more. But Dovid — to Avrom's increasing mystification — went the whole length: past the dilapidated bathhouse, the sickly yard full of half-chewed cabbages and wilting carrot and parsnip tops euphemistically known as the communal garden, the dark wooden *shul* and its accompanying *besmedresh* that looked more like an outhouse than a study house ... and on, past Mendel the butcher's and Motl the tinsmith's and all of the hovels occupying the village's especially dismal north end, up to and including the smallest (where Bentze the bathhouse attendant and bookbinder lived with his wife Dinka, who kneaded matzohs before Passover and knitted socks and gloves the year round) and the largest (occupied by Issachar Ber the tanner) till at last, he reached the village swimming hole (where even out in the water you could smell the lye, dung, and urine Isachar Ber used for tanning hides.)

Just what was Dovid doing, walking so far? It couldn't be, not any longer, that he was trying to avoid being seen by Blume. What, then?

Another interesting question: What was he himself doing, following Dovid so far? This was a different kind of question, but strange to say, Avrom found it nearly as difficult to answer as the first. Several possibilities kept tugging him in different directions, even as he walked straight ahead. Did he wish to help Dovid out of whatever difficulty he'd found himself in, or was it really that he wanted to call him a nitwit for abandoning Blume, and a scoundrel for making her cry? Was he finally going to ask about the famous friends in Chernigov — or was it none of these things, but instead, raw and unadulterated curiosity leading him on? Dovid certainly had *some* secret, that was clear enough. Maybe it was about to be revealed.

Before long, Avrom made one interesting discovery: he became aware that, somewhere along the way, he had become worried Dovid might suddenly turn around and spot him. For example, at this time of day, shadows extended over the left side of the road. Which side of the road did Avrom start sneaking along? The left — all the way at the edge.

When Dovid reached the *besmedresh*, Avrom was not far behind, just coming to the *shul* (which cast what looked to be a particularly helpful shadow — the *shul* was tall enough to have attracted a stork to settle atop its roof.) Borekh Mordkhel the beadle was outside sweeping, and greeted Avrom loudly and enthusiastically as he approached. At once, Avrom leaped to his left, to hide around the corner of the building — from where he peeked out, down the street. A good thing he'd leapt, even if Borekh Mordkhel was giving him a very funny look. Dovid had paused, and was looking back over his shoulder. But he didn't see the tsimbalist.

～

North of the swimming hole a small road branched off to the left, which several *versts* distant, led to the manor of Count

Bestuzhev, owner of all the land hereabouts. Not long after, the main road itself swung inland, away from the water.

It would have been an excellent place to erect a village, much better than the swampland to the south — if only Count Bestuzhev had thought so too. But this region, as everyone knew, was the count's favorite hunting ground. Forest grew up on both sides of the road, wild and luxuriant, tall oak, expansive alder, slender birch, short, squat hornbeam. Branches hung out from left and right to get tangled overhead. Roots and mushrooms poked out from the road, the ground smelled pleasantly of mold, while the temperature was distinctly cooler than in the village.

From time to time, a warden could be seen riding in these parts, looking for trespassers — mushroom pickers and picnickers, but especially poachers, such as the ones who according to popular suspicion supplied Issachar Ber his hides. Otherwise, apart from occasional traffic between Zav and towns to the north, this piece of road was generally quiet, and at the moment, perfectly so.

It was so quiet that Avrom noticed his own footsteps. And when he paused in his stride, he could hear Dovid's, too, up ahead, even though at the moment Dovid was out of sight, somewhere around the next bend in the road (which had gotten hillier and curvier since leaving the lake.)

He started forward again, then stopped. Hmm ... If he could hear Dovid's steps, then Dovid might hear *his*, too. Therefore, wouldn't it be better to fall back? Yes, wait for any sound of steps to disappear; then wait a while more.

Good. Now he couldn't hear a thing, not even a snapping twig or a rustling branch. It seemed even the animals of the forest were asleep, or absent.

Up ahead, the road was lit by a gentle green glow: sunlight streaming through the leaves overhead. The trees were thinner here, mostly birch and beech. The far limit of Count Bestuzhev's lands wasn't far off. Soon would come the old wooden bridge over the stream, really more of a trickle, that marked the end of the property. Though Avrom rarely came here anymore, he still knew the route well. At one time, he had traveled this way as often as once a week. Nonetheless, the bridge appeared before he expected it. A good thing he was taking care to be quiet. Dovid was standing on the bridge.

He was entirely motionless in the sunlight, his peaked cap in his hand. His hair must have been damp — it lay flat against his head. His face shone with perspiration, too, and though he was looking down at the water, his eyes were almost closed. His eyelids looked enormous and smooth, his posture limp, even defeated. What thoughts, Avrom wondered as he hid behind a thick, furrowed hornbeam, could be passing through his mind?

Suddenly, Dovid's head shot upward. Without warning, the air was filled with a racket. Avrom too was startled, his foot slipped, and he scraped his hand on the bark of the tree. A great wood grouse had flown up, violently flapping its clumsy wings. It must have been concealed in the brush near the bridge. The bird's path took it within an *arshin* of Dovid's head ... but Dovid watched calmly. Apparently, a bird flapping next to your head was less frightening than a girl.

The grouse flew in spurts: flapping wildly, then gliding. In this jagged way — preposterously, it made Avrom think of a knight, in chess — it disappeared in the direction of the lake. When it was gone, Dovid did nothing but wrinkle his nose, and then continue on his inexplicable way north.

Count Bestuzhev's neighbor across the stream was the merchant, Saveli Savelyevich Baryshevsky. Though of humble origins, Saveli Savelyevich had acquired, ten or fifteen years ago, a vast fortune, and six or eight years ago, a slightly less vast estate. Tatiana, the merchant's daughter, used to take music lessons from the tsimbalist. And that was why Avrom used to come this way so often.

Saveli Savelyevich's mansion, which he had christened Bol'shaya Sosna, or "Big Pine," lay at the end of a winding and climbing drive, the entrance to which was a mere ten minutes' walk past the old wood bridge. Bol'shaya Sosna was surrounded, as was to be expected, by pine trees, and already here at the estate's edge, that majestic race had begun to supplant the more deciduous species amongst which Count Bestuzhev preferred to hunt. On this higher ground, the weather was still cooler, and the light coming through the trees less green and gold, more silvery. The sun was barely visible any longer.

From somewhere off to the left, a rustle through the trees: a reminder of something Avrom had forgotten. Late afternoon had not been his favorite time to teach young Tatiana. Once the sun began its descent, the road home through the forest grew dark quickly. And the woodland beasts that might appear scarce in the daytime proved, by night, to be anything but.

Dusk was already threatening now. And was that another beast stirring from its sleep, this time to the right?

It's one thing to indulge your curiosity — thought Avrom to himself — *and another to indulge it when there might be wolves and bears about.*

And then an extraordinary thing happened: under the influence of the rustling and stirring coming from both sides, Avrom's attitude toward Dovid's long walk underwent a complete transformation. Suddenly it seemed obvious: there was no good reason to think Dovid was doing anything but walking aimlessly. And it was actually tedious, pointless to follow him.

Yes. If you looked at it logically, without letting false hopes and sentiments interfere, everything was very simple — even if for the last hour Avrom had been entertaining other ideas: Koppel's house had a window at the front, and a window at the back, and no window at the side. Dovid had been standing where he was, close to Avrom's but with a view of Koppel's — or rather, Blume's — because he was screwing up his courage to do something, say something, and didn't want to announce his presence before he was ready. He'd probably sprinted past Blume's to get to Avrom's in the first place. Then, Blume had come out, he'd gotten scared away ... and the rest had been one long, pointless walk.

There was no telling how long Dovid would keep walking. But it was time for him, Avrom, to give up.

A moment later, he did just that. In the event, however, it had nothing to do with either the threatening dusk, nor the pointlessness of following Dovid. On the contrary: turning back toward Balativke, he had the feeling he understood everything much better than before, quite clearly indeed. He'd just seen young Dovid disappear, up the drive to Bol'shaya Sosna.

~

Dark had come by the time Avrom passed the *shul* again. He'd been walking slowly, not wanting to arrive too quickly back at his house — not for any lack of desire to be at home. It was because he didn't wish to see Blume.

The thing that wasn't yet clear to him was whether he would do better to tell her, or if he ought to wait for Dovid to do *that*, at least. It was something he should have done long ago, before things reached this point. But obviously, Dovid hadn't had the courage for that. Sooner or later, though, at some precise point when his secret became public, he wouldn't have any choice, would he?

Avrom shook his head, not for the first time on the long walk home. The simplicity of the riddle's solution was exceeded only by its strangeness. Who ever could have guessed it? Although he *had* suspected Tatiana was in love with a Jewish boy — hadn't he said as much to Pasternak? And it seemed to him

— he couldn't be sure, everything had happened so quickly and it had been so dark, but he was almost convinced it was true — that at the lakeside the other night, when Tatiana had screamed, it had come immediately after Dovid was felled by the Pole.

Still, it wasn't reasonable to think he could have imagined the truth on such a flimsy basis as that. No one else could have guessed it either.

For that matter, how had such an unlikely thing begun? How had Dovid and Tatiana met? And what would happen to them now? Both were sure to be disowned by their families — no, by everyone they knew.

That didn't have to include him, though. He didn't have to be among those who ostracized Dovid. He would lay into him for the way he'd treated poor Blume — that was another thing entirely. And he'd never defend him in her presence. But he would not, he resolved, add his voice to all the others which were sure to rise up in condemnation. And if there were anything he could do to help him through the coming difficulty, he would do it. This village of Balativke, though, it surely would be no happy place for Dovid to visit, ever again.

Avrom looked around. The complexion of the village seemed to have changed in just the last hour or so — almost as if, during his absence, everyone else had discovered the same secret he had. His sensitive nerves detected something tense, closed, in the air around — surely only the product of his imagination, though, no?

Going by Rivke's house, he saw her sitting at her window, staring out. And when he passed Itzik Leyba's house, there were *three* faces in the window. What were they all staring at?

Down the road he glimpsed lights in the darkness. But they looked just like the torches from the other night! Hurrying past Hezkel's, he heard the first loud voices, many of them, all talking at once. Among them, a booming bass stood out. If he didn't know better, he'd have said it belonged to Deacon Achilles.

No — that really was Achilles' voice. "Go away!" it was shouting. "Go back to your village!" And the others were saying, "Come out!" "Make him come out!"

They weren't saying it in Yiddish.

Avrom ran forward, suspecting the terrifying truth, then skidded to a halt near Koppel's, where he could see it for himself. They were peasants. They were armed, with torches, knives, clubs. And they were gathered in front of Koppel's door.

Was everyone there, inside?

The whole mob must have been inflamed by drink. Avrom could smell it, the distinctive and revolting odor of yesterday's liquor, coming out of their sweat glands and mingling with the scent of today's fresh dose. They were the same ones who'd been there yesterday morning in the woods — they must have been drinking without pause since he'd last seen them. And at their head once again was that diminutive cousin of Styopa's who so resembled him, the one who had laid hands on Pasternak's muzzle. He was standing — no, crouching — in front of Koppel's door, a torch in his hand, and he was braying in a taunting tenor:

"Come *ou — out*. Please, little Yids, come out. We want to repay you for what you did to our darling benefactor!" With each of the last syllables, he shook his torch at the house. It looked as though, if they didn't come out, he planned to burn them out — and might burn the whole place anyway. But blocking his way to the door, and towering over him, was Deacon Achilles, who for his own part, was brandishing not a torch but a horse whip. "Stay inside," Achilles warned those behind the door, while he shook his whip at the crowd. "Go home!"

"Come now, deacon," said Styopa's nasty lookalike. "Surely you wouldn't use your lash on a good Orthodox believer?"

Achilles shook the whip again, suggesting he would, and swore, "As the Lord is my Light and my ..." As often happened with the deacon he was unable to get the whole sentence out.

The other finished for him: "As the Lord is my Light and my *Salvation*, deacon. And by the way, is it true you got lost during the service yesterday?" He grinned at his companions, inviting their approbation, which a few granted it with nervous laughter. The others glanced at their feet. Such brazenness toward a priest was too much for them.

"Hey Andryushechka," called out a woman Avrom couldn't see. "Why not just go right under him?"

"A fine idea!" Andryushechka replied, and, wasting no time, darted forward, the flame of his torch licking close to the house's rough wood wall.

Achilles' wrist was quicker than his tongue. Before Andryushechka had taken two steps, his torch dropped suddenly to the ground — the deacon stepped on it with a crunch — and his fingers flew to his mouth. Glaring fearfully up at Achilles, he cried, "It hurts!"

Seeing such gutlessness from their leader, others in the crowd exchanged disheartened looks. But not all were of the same mind. One young buck at the back shouted: "Let us through, deacon. They killed our darling benefactor!"

Achilles shook his head. "That's ... something for the judges to ..."

"And shed the blood of our Blessed Savior!" put in a woman of Amazonian proportions standing just behind Andryushechka, who carried a torch in one hand and a sickle in the other.

"That's ... for God to ..."

Meanwhile, a crafty character in a straw hat, standing quite close to Avrom, had a new idea, and whispered it to his neighbor: "Let's sneak around to the side and start a fire there — smoke them out!"

"Right!" the neighbor replied. "The deacon can't stand in two places at once."

The pair took a few steps, when they saw Avrom right in front of them. At first, they goggled in surprise, then the one in the straw hat joyfully trilled, from beneath his yellow mustache, "Look here! Look everyone!"

The same disembodied female voice that had been giving Andryushechka advice screamed a reply: "Get him!" And the mob surged sideward.

Twice in the last three days, Avrom had escaped harm — when Styopa attacked Koppel instead of him, and when the Pole rode up yesterday morning. This time, it didn't look as if he would be so lucky: nothing stood between him and the mob, he had no weapon — the tsimbl sticks that were still in his pocket hardly counted — and he'd never been in any kind of fight in his life. Not to mention that a Jew wasn't supposed to fight back if attacked by an Orthodox.

He fumbled for the sticks, cleared his throat, though he had no idea what he could say to turn them away, opened his mouth —

"Hold!" shouted Achilles — with such authority that it stopped them all short. Then, with an uncharacteristic flash of inspiration, he added, "He's Nikifor ... Kharitonich's barber."

This important piece of information gave the mob further pause. And when someone muttered, "It's true," and someone else added, "I've seen them together," the will to fight seemed to seep out of them.

But not for nothing was Andryushechka his cousin's cousin. Seizing the amazon's torch, he made another attempt to dart past the deacon. This time, Achilles eschewed the whip: he stopped him with a mighty clout from his fist, which sent the cretin to the ground howling in pain.

"Anyone else?" Achilles glared all about. He found no takers. Someone mumbled, "Father Innokenty will hear about this." A few edged backwards, not wanting to show their backs to the deacon. The crafty character in the straw hat, on the other hand, feinted forward, making Avrom leap back, then laughed and walked away with a springier step than most, toward the wagons in which they had all arrived. Meanwhile, the amazon crouched down to tend to their fallen leader.

"Come, Andreichik," she said, running a gentle hand, which was missing its pinky, through his hair. "Time to get us home." But he shrugged her off as she pulled him up, and hurried limping toward the first of the wagons. Gathering her extinguished torch up off the ground, the amazon went trotting meekly after him. The wagon was already moving when she hopped heavily in.

As for Avrom, he watched the last of them go. When they had, he, with one or two new thoughts in his head, made his way to the door of Koppel's house, and followed Deacon Achilles inside.

Chapter 13

Wheels

O n Tuesday morning, Zavlivoya's Jewish quarter was awake even before the sun. First came light: one candle and then another flickering to life in the dark. Then sound: whispers, coughs, someone spitting, the swooping diphthong of a morning prayer. Buckets bounced up and down wells, samovars hissed, doors creaked open. Before long, dark-clad figures slipped out into the street, more shadow than substance in the dawning light. Their steps nocturnal and cautious, their voices low, they passed by square grey windows behind which their neighbors still slept — till brightening light and swelling numbers emboldened them, and converging into one, northward flowing current, they banished the last of the morning silence with their greetings and conversations.

"Good morning," called out half of them at full voice.

And "Good morning and good year," returned the other half.

"Fine weather for market," pronounced one matron in pelerine and bonnet, with a brood of children in tow. "Not a cloud in sight, the Almighty be praised."

"The Almighty be praised indeed," agreed a forty-year old

man looking up at the lightening sky, the sawdust specking his long cotton *khlat* just visible in the early light.

"You could do your praising at *shul* for once, Reb Shabshel," said a long-bearded *alter* walking close by, clad in cheery white tunic, blue breeches, and yellow stockings and *yarmulke*. "Why not join us, instead of going straight to market?"

"I would if I could, Reb Nokhum Grinshpan," sighed the younger man, and then let out a deep, hacking cough. "But time is money."

"If time is money, then *I* don't have any time either," replied the *alter* to general laughter. "But I'm still going to the service."

"If only market started later I'd come with you to *shul*," parried Shabshel. "But by the time you're getting to the *aleinu*, the peasants I sell to will be getting back in their wagons to go home."

"Now, now, Reb Shabshel," laughed Nokhum Grinshpan, "you know very well services start an hour early on Market Day, just to accommodate a devout Jew such as yourself. Let the ladies go off to set up shop, and you come pray with us men." He paused where the street went right, in the direction of the synagogue.

"It's true services start early today," Shabshel started to cough again. "But they'd have to start in the middle of the night for me to be ready when market opens up. Besides, you know what they say — the further from *shul*, the closer to God." With which, he spun on his heel, directing his steps toward the market square.

Just behind him, two women were walking.

"Did you see the way Grunya is gussied up today?" said one of them. As soon as she spoke, Shabshel saw a third woman, walking just in front of him, flinch. "A *shterntikhl*, just to go to market."

"Just to go to market," repeated the second woman, and added, far louder than necessary if she only wanted to be heard by her friend, "She must have forty pearls on her head."

Shabshel confirmed that the headband of the woman in front of him did have, if not forty, then at least thirty pearls on it.

"That's Grunya for you," the first woman went on. "Always showing off. Why, just look at her bonnet. It's sewn with *shpanyer arbet.*"

The second woman whistled. "Your eyes are as sharp as ever, Feyga. That *is shpanyer arbet* — and with silver thread running right through the cord. No wonder she thinks so well of herself."

The two women paused expectantly. But the subject of their gossip stubbornly refused to turn around or even show any sign she was listening, instead walking on with her hands stuck haughtily inside the *bristekh* that hung down her front. At length, Feyga went on.

"Of course she thinks well of herself. She has a shop, while we only have stalls. All of those shop ladies think they're better than everybody else."

"Yes, and why? Just because they had mothers or grandmothers who lucked into the leases in the first place."

"And husbands on the *kahal,* who won't hear of changing anything from the way it was a hundred ago, even when the old ways are so obviously unfair."

"What *kahal?*" butted in Reb Shabshel. "Everyone knows the *kahal* was abolished a long time ago, that we Jews don't have any say over anything anymore, even when it comes to our own private matters."

"Listen to him," said the first woman. "If he were twice as smart, he'd be an idiot. What everyone knows is that the *kahal* still has a spoon in every pot — which must be why they won't change a thing. They'd have to admit they're still alive and kicking. And so the rich get richer, and the same few families keep the leases to the shops. I wonder what the Kelmer Maggid would have to say about *that.*"

This last remark appeared to have the effect that none of

the women's other remarks had: the woman named Grunya turned around, pulled her hands from her *bristekh*, and opened her mouth, which sat directly beneath a healthy mustache.

"The Kelmer Maggid? What does he have to do with anything? I keep an honest shop, I work my fingers to the bone — and if I charge more than the two of you, it's because that precious lease you want so much costs an arm and a leg, just like my merchandise, which is of the first quality, not like the *dreck* you two pass off on the yokels. The sole and solitary pleasure I get all Market Day is watching the likes of you wrestle your stalls into place sweating like pigs before the first customers have even arrived. Ha, what a sight! Oh, it's a real treat, listening to the two of you talk badly about other people just because you're jealous of them. But if you really want to complain about somebody, why not this one?"

She pointed at Reb Shabshel, who was trying to pass her on the narrow street as she stood venting her spleen and blocking the way.

"*He* has a lease, and doesn't even use it! The lease that was entrusted to him, that his father and grandfather held before him — he takes it and turns his place into a barber shop — all for a bit of profit. So tell me, why don't you Kelmer Maggid *him*?"

~

Reb Shabshel Urvand did indeed hold a lease to a shop, on the north side of the enormous market square, in the shadow of St. Vladimir's. (Shops lined the square's north, south, and east sides, while the fourth side was open.) He held the lease, and five days a week, labored in his shop, making chairs, toys, and utensils: he was a woodworker. But he preferred, when Tuesdays rolled around, to sell out of doors, getting a lungful of fresh air, and at the same time, displaying his wares to greater advantage in the light of the sun.

Near to his shop was a little area where a few barbers always set up, spending the morning placing bowls upside-down on peasants' heads and snipping all the hair that spilled over the sides. In former times, it had been a wide space, but a few years back, Shabshel had managed to lease half of it, to the chagrin of the barbers, but to the relief of his sawdust-addled lungs.

There was only one little problem with this arrangement: namely, that a prime piece of real estate was left completely unused on what was by far the most lucrative day of the week. With luck, however, everything is possible. A perfect solution soon presented itself. One of the barbers, Reb Avrom, the one who also played the tsimbl so magnificently at weddings from time to time, was unhappy cutting hair out of doors with the other barbers. His usual clients — he said he made house calls four days a week — were accustomed to a modicum of privacy, which allowed them to speak freely, a pleasure at least equal to that of being shaved. And they expected a comfortable chair, such as they might find in their own homes. Meanwhile — as the barber put it — the woodworker had his little patch of square, and his shop, but as everyone knew, you couldn't dance at two weddings with one *tukhes*. Well, suggested Reb Avrom: Why didn't Shabshel Urvand rent him his shop for the day, at a nice price, and just do him the favor of leaving a nice chair for his own clients' *tukheses*?

"Why not?" Shabshel Urvand had replied. And ever since, the two men had met at the shop door every Tuesday, shortly after dawn. The woodworker would begin carrying out his stock, while Avrom — who had to wake up very early indeed to get to Zavlivoya in time — proceeded to attack the Augean mess the woodworker had somehow managed to create in the same number of days it took God to create the world. By the time the first customers arrived, the place was always spotless.

~

Avrom had just finished cleaning up this morning, and was standing outside by the shop door, when the first of the wagons rolled into the square. The sun was up and visible over the hill where Grinberg's fine house stood. In front of the shop, Urvand had his wares artfully arranged. To the right, one of the other barbers had arrived — he and Avrom exchanged friendly nods. To the left, in the spot reserved for visiting merchants, were the three northerners whom Avrom had twice seen cheating at cards, with a variety of expensive-looking items spread out in front of them.

At the square's open west end, the wagon pulled to a stop. Two peasants hopped out, man and wife. Unhitching and tying up their horse, they raised from the wagon's rear two crates, from one of which a chicken was attempting to escape. And without further ado, husband and wife plunged into the thick of stalls.

A minute later a second wagon pulled up behind the first, then a third, both of them depositing peasants who had brought what looked like bags of vegetables. Before long, a whole row of wagons was parked at the square's end, with more arriving, from north and south, from down the west side of the lake and the east, from villages attached to the estates of Count Bestuzhev and General Kondratin and the Efimovskis and the area's other luminaries, and from every other village for twenty *versts* around.

The wagons didn't only carry peasants. Here came Balativke's own Malke Rukhe, wife of Issachar Ber the tanner, who on Market Days took charge of selling the hides her husband tanned. (Like most Jewish men, Issachar Ber himself understood neither Russian nor credit.) And who was that, crammed into the space not taken up by hides, and holding tight to their packages of butter and cheese? Koppel's three oldest daughters, Blume, Zlata, and Tzippe, hitching a ride with the tanner's wife.

Avrom saw the girls hop down and enter the labyrinth of stalls, where the wheels of commerce had by now begun spinning at a dizzying pace. Everywhere you looked, peasant and Jew were driving razor-sharp bargains, exchanging goods and money of every kind with lightning speed — calico and kopeks, bread and bagels, parsley and parsnips, rubles and ribbons, buttons and thread, flour, iron pots, roast pig and rosaries, eggs, kerchiefs, onions and potatoes, horse collars and horses and turpentine — what was there that wasn't for sale at the Zavlivoya market? At the same time a hum rose up as if from a colony of mosquitoes: the buzz of ubiquitous bargaining and dickering, mingled with the pleading of beggars and squeaks of urchins, a tribe of whom had sprouted up like mushrooms after the rain as soon as the wagons arrived and were already running wild through the stalls. Punctuating all these noises was a regular slapping of hands, each time a deal was made.

"*Sholem aleikhem*, Reb Avrom."

The tsimbalist's survey of the scene was interrupted by a familiar and welcome face looming up in front of him: Hertzik Katznelson, a kind and cheery locksmith who often showed up Tuesdays for a quick snip. Barely had Katznelson come and gone when Zalman Nisnevich, Count Bestuzhev's estate manager, arrived for a trim, followed by Egorsha Kolbov, a plump and wealthy peasant who had a large farm on the east side of the lake, north of General Kondratin's estate, and a little east of where that old rascal Parfyon Panteleyevich lived.

When Avrom opened the door to Kolbov, a tantalizing smell of baked goods and — in truth — roast pig wafted in with the farmer. Throughout Kolbov's haircut, Avrom could think of nothing but eating a bagel, and no sooner had he finished with the farmer than he ran to get one, which he ate standing by his rented door, watching still more Market Day faces, familiar and unfamiliar, pass by.

There, just approaching: Sofroniya Amvrosievna, Father Innokenty's pink-skinned and white-lipped wife, before whom the market's urchins scurried away in terror. And there, someone you didn't see on just any Tuesday: Savely Savelievich

Baryshevsky, Tatiana's merchant father. Too wealthy to bother with buying and selling at such a local level, Savely Savelievich seemed today to have some personal business to conduct. He was walking with Oleg Olegovich Efimovski, with whom he appeared to be engaged in grave discussion. The young noble's demeanor was as mournful as his dress. When the merchant addressed him, all apology, Oleg Olegovich smiled sadly, and shook his head. When Savely Savelievich turned to him pleadingly, Oleg Olegovich nodded and took the merchant's hand in a frank grasp. What might the two of them be talking about? Of course — the interrupted engagement. Unless Avrom was wrong, they were renewing their intentions, here and now. Poor Oleg Olegovich, Avrom thought. He had just lost his brother. Soon, he'd learn that his promised bride loved someone else.

Oleg Olegovich's sister, Aglaya Olegovna, was here too, looking in on the shops not far away. She was dressed in elegant black, and accompanied by a hobbling Foka. Avrom saw the young woman pick up a piece of black cloth, study it, sadly shake her head, and then put it back down again. Brother and sister both were putting a brave face on.

Quite a contrast was the next face Avrom saw, someone altogether less sympathetic, idling but two or three *arshins* away: last night's delightful fellow who had made Avrom's life flash before his eyes, the one with the straw hat and yellow mustache. Would the man turn? And if he did, what then?

Perhaps that dubious protector of Jews, the Pole, would come to Avrom's rescue once again. The constable was here patrolling the market, to ensure that peace reigned amidst the commerce. Avrom saw him take notice of the three northern merchants, stop, bend to inspect the fancy goods they were selling ...

Hmm, Avrom wondered. And meanwhile, how was that poor gambler, Pugovitsin, whiling away the time, without his three friends around to cheat him at cards?

Ah! And there, halfway across the square, the most interesting face of all, though still in the distance (and in fact, Avrom had yet to get a close-up look at it): the Kelmer Maggid's. The Maggid was strolling about, looking this way and that ... no doubt putting the fear of God into every merchant there.

Avrom wondered: How many kopeks fewer would all the merchants be charging today? And how long would their discounts last, once the Maggid left town? Still, in bad times, as the saying went, even a penny is money. Now ... if the preacher would only come a little bit closer, it might finally be possible to draw him into conversation.

"Avrom the barber?"

Alas — here was more business to attend to. But if it was only a trim or a shave, there might still be a chance to catch up with the Maggid.

~

The man standing in front of him was vaguely familiar: tall and vigorous-looking, with a long, rectangular face, and his arm in a sling.

"A cut or a trim?" Avrom asked, looking up to survey the man's shaggy head of grey hair.

But the man surprised him. "Neither. I'm here on General Kondratin's behalf. I'm his valet."

"Ah, are you the one who does such a magnificent job shaping his beard?" Avrom asked, thinking of the general's impressive appearance at the Efimovski ball the other night. "It's as neat as a spade."

"Ah, well ... thanks." The man looked embarrassed. "It is me that does that, usually. Only, as you can see ... the other day I had a little accident."

Avrom looked at the sling, than again at the man's long, rectangular face. "Yes, now I remember. It was you fighting at the inn on Sunday."

The valet drew back, a worried expression taking hold of his features. "Were you there? That *was* me — but ... you won't tell His Excellency, will you? He was angry enough when I told him it was an accident. Back when we were serfs, he would have whipped me for it."

"You have nothing to fear from me," Avrom shook his head and smiled. "And I don't know when I might have a chance to tell him, unless you've come to ask me to play music at his — "

"No, it's not that. Since my arm is hurt, he sent me to ask if you'll come to his estate tomorrow to — "

"To try to duplicate your excellent work?"

"Ah, you flatter m — "

The valet's reply was drowned out by a sudden wail. A few steps away, at the stall where the northern visitors had set up, Avrom saw Aglaya Olegovna standing — or no, now she was half-collapsing, gripping the table in front of her. As best Avrom could tell, she was wailing about a chess set: "A Kholm ... chess se — ... but if you had only ... a week earlier ... where did ..."

The poor young woman couldn't quite seem to speak. Her words were broken up by heaving sobs, increasingly loud and hysterical — which in one, dangerous moment, as she stood up again taut as a fishing line, were replaced by loud inhalations, jagged and spastic.

"In here," said Avrom, grasping her arm and pulling her toward his door.

~

A moment later, Aglaya Olegovna was inside Avrom's shop, seated on the comfortable chair left by Shabshel Urvand. Old Foka stood against the wall, speechless and terrified, while Avrom handed the young noblewoman a glass of the rum he used as an aftershave, and then gently patted her arm as she drank it down.

"There," he said, as she sputtered and coughed.

And then again, "There," as her breathing grew quieter.

"There. That's better now, isn't it?"

Aglaya Olegovna nodded, taking in a deep, slow breath of air, and then blowing her nose. Without warning, she laughed.

"*Cher maître,*" she said — it was what she had playfully called him when she was his music student. "You must think me terribly silly, getting so upset over something so stupid ..."

"I don't," Avrom gravely replied. "Your brother — "

He broke off as she sat up and looked around the room. "Is this your shop?"

"It's my shop on Market Days, yes."

"It's very clean. And quiet ... I don't suppose you've got a mirror. You do? *Merci.*"

The young noblewoman tidied her hair, dried her eyes with a black kerchief, and then spent a minute studying her delicate, vulpine face.

"Hmm ... I don't *look* old, do I? *Do* I, *cher maître?* You're used to looking at faces."

Avrom remained silent.

"They say I'm beautiful ... But I feel so old ... so many memories behind me already ... I even remember when we nobles weren't such a useless, dying breed." She laughed again, sounding very sad as she did so, and slumped into the chair.

"*Mademoiselle* ... Forgive me, but ... may I ask ... the Kholmogory chess set your brother went looking for ..."

"Oh, do you know about that?" The young woman blinked several times quickly, and pressed her lips together.

"Forgive me, I heard the details of the — "

"Never mind that," she said, her demeanor changing quick as quicksilver. "What is it you wish to ask?"

"I wished to ask whether you believe your brother would have traveled to Chernigov solely to hunt for a chess set."

Aglaya Olegovna let out a sound that could have been either

a laugh or a whimper, then picked up a pair of scissors lying close at hand.

"What an awful noise they make," she remarked, opening and closing the scissors. "How do you stand it all day, with your musician's ears?"

"Oh ... I never considered — "

"You mean to ask, I suppose, would he have gone still, if he'd known these merchants would turn up here with the very thing. Is that it? But *cher maître*, how could he have known? Those Kholmogories don't just fall out of the sky." She opened and closed the scissors again, and made a face. "And at our stupid little Zavlivoya market? No, Arkasha never would have dreamed he might find one here."

Avrom nodded slowly. "I'm sure that — "

"If he'd thought he could find one here, it wouldn't have been worth the trouble. Do you see what I mean? Our old set was like something out of a fairy tale. Our father was journeying up north when he found it — you see, that's exactly what I mean by feeling old."

"You mean — "

"All of those wonders from our childhood. They're untouchable. Impossibly far away."

"Ah."

"And now it's even worse. Arkasha is gone ... and Olezhka and I are completely useless."

"Hardly so, you — "

"You're very kind. But — oh!"

~

Someone was knocking at the door. Avrom went to send the customer away — it was Nikifor Kharitonovich, who didn't look pleased to be told to return later, or to have his view into the room blocked. As soon as the door was shut, Avrom ventured: "It seems the chess set would have had a special importance to you and your brothers."

"Well ..." Aglaya Olegovna continued to worry the scissors. "... a special importance ... oh, I don't know. What you must understand is that our childhood was really perfect — idyllic. And we did all *sorts* of things together. The three of us were inseparable. That was before the serfs were freed of course. After that," she sighed, "we all seemed to go our separate ways. As if we knew, there and then, that we had been, *trakh tibidokh*," she wiggled her fingers as if casting a magic spell, "turned into dinosaurs. But I suppose you need me to leave so you can go back to work."

"Not at all," replied Avrom, taken aback. "Please rest."

"Oh, well then ... *merci*. Foka, old dear, one of my *pakhitoskas*."

The ancient servant, who had been utterly silent till then, apart from a disapproving cluck at the mention of the liberation of the serfs, handed her a slender cigarette, and lit it for her. Aglaya Olegovna sat straight again, propping herself up on one hand, and faced Avrom as she smoked, with her head tilted downward and her eyes raised.

"Have you ever wanted to go back in time, tsimbalist?" she asked. "Tsimbalist — is that a word?"

"I—"

"That's all I've wanted the last few days — to go back in time." Avrom gave up trying to reply.

"Arkashenka was so adorable, he used to follow us everywhere. The three of us would get into all kinds of mischief together — it was always Olezhka leading the way, right into the teeth of trouble. Arkashenka would be so afraid our father was going to beat us, but when we were called to account Olezhka would make up the most fantastic stories on the spot to get us out of it — talk about fairy tales! ... In a way, it's Olezhka's fault that Arkasha's dead ... if he'd set a better example ... He was so full of clever ideas as a child, he could really have done the world some good if he'd put his mind to it, and instead he's spent the entire last decade drinking and gambling. And so ... without anyone to look up to, Arkasha remained a child, do you see? ... Oh! But don't imagine that I'm any better. I'm quite awful, much worse than you can imagine. All I know how to do is spend money, and break hearts. Do you know I've turned down five proposals?"

Aglaya Olegovna looked around for a place to put her spent cigarette, till Foka came to her rescue.

"It's not my fault, though," she talked on. "It's my fate always to be alone. The only man I was ever in love with never even noticed me. Men find me interesting because I'm tragically unhappy, but in a few years, I'll be too old even for that. Then it'll really be a hopeless case!" At this, she burst into another disconsolate laugh.

"I'm sure that — "

"No, it's true. And so as I said, Arkasha was just as incapable as Olezhka or I of acting even slightly responsibly. If only he'd grown up, if he'd fallen in love, really in love, with a woman — they all adored him — or acted in his own interests in any way! But instead, the past year, he was obsessed with these peasants, by all accounts, gave away all his money to them — as if they know how to spend it any more wisely than we do. And he was living like a peasant, too. He really let the house go — *Maman* is very angry about it, says it was really unfair to the servants for him to keep such a small staff if he was going to live there. Foka had to take care of the horses *and* the garden — now don't get upset, Foka, it's *Maman* saying it and not you — and Marfa only had help in from the village one day a week to keep up the house."

The old servant made a noise of protest.

"What is it, *dyadka*?"

"He ... was kind to us."

To Avrom's great surprise, this fine sentiment seemed to make Aglaya Olegovna grow very angry.

"Our Foka is like an old dog, tsimbalist," she said in a clipped tone. "He's overwhelmed whenever anyone shows him any hint of kindness."

"Ah."

"I assure you, it's true. Just listen to this: Last week, Olezhka announced his engagement party *one day* after the market here in Zavlivoya had already gone by — exactly the sort of thing we dinosaurs would do — and so our poor doddering servant, besides having to do extra gardening and cleaning, was forced to spend all Thursday going with Marfa to the market in Sosnitsa — all that way away! How many *versts'* ride? Just to get what could have been gotten here in Zavlivoya, if Olezhka had been slightly thoughtful. But instead of complaining, Foka won't stop going on about how *kind* Olezhka was, to *let* him and Marfa go cherry picking Friday, while Olezhka took some of the other work on himself. Well, do you think my brother got his hands dirty with the gardening? Of course not, he only went to Yudel Beck's for the champagne, which he would have quite enjoyed anyway, and then fetched *Maman* and me from the train. What do you think, tsimbalist, was it *kind* of him, to *let* them go cherry-picking? ... Mind you, I'm not blaming Olezhka for a thing. The point is, it was only Arkasha who was stupid enough not to look after himself before others. Imagine, riding all the way to Chernigov on someone else's behalf! Everybody loved Arkasha for being kind, but if he'd ever grown up, acted for himself for once, not been so blessedly kind, then this morning, we wouldn't have been burying — "

Aglaya Olegovna didn't finish her final sentence. All through this last speech, she had been working herself into a higher and

higher pitch. Now, she burst out once again into the same hysterical tears and jagged, violent intakes of breath that had first
drawn Avrom to her side.

   It took another glass of rum, and several more pats on the
arm, before she was calm enough to leave.

⁓

Nikifor Kharitonovich's return visit was brief. He required only
a shave today, along with Avrom's daily pronouncement upon
the state of his health — and he was in a hurry besides. He exclaimed when Avrom told him about the incident at Koppel's
house last night. "They're conspiring to never let me proceed
with my investigation! As if I had a single deputy to send down
to the Efimovski village today. No one harmed though? What's
that? Yes, I suppose some of them *are* here at the market. Well,
all right ... you can point them out to me when we've finished."
He narrowed his eyes when told that Avrom had not yet had an
opportunity to ask Dovid about his friends in Chernigov. "I
thought I made it very clear what is at stake, Avrom Moisevich
— and what could happen if you are unsuccessful."
However, the police chief was all smiles when it came to report-
ing a discovery of his own. "You know the farmer Kolbov, who
lives near General Kondratin? You say he was just in here an
hour ago? Well, while he was in here, I was looking about the
market, and what do you think I noticed? Kolbov's wagon has
one brand-new wheel on it. I asked him about it a few minutes
ago — it was just after you so considerately refused me entry.
He told me the *old* wheel was stolen from his yard — he'd been
about to repair it — last week. He didn't see who took it. But ...
if anyone had been coming from Chernigov, and decided to
travel down the east side of the lake, to come into Zavlivoya
without being noticed, for example ... Kolbov's farm would
have been right on the way."

Chapter 14

Found Objects

I t was apparent the moment Avrom opened the door that another disturbance was underway in the marketplace.

"Then whoever you bought them from stole them from *us*," a young woman's voice was shouting in Yiddish, from the area where the three Lithuanians had set up.

"Go bend *their* ears, then," a man's voice shouted back in the same tongue, "and leave *us* alone."

"What's going on here?" Nikifor Kharitonovich rushed outside. "Speak Russian."

The young woman whirled around. It was Zlata, Blume's younger sister. "These *ganovim* have our things, everything that was taken from the house — Mama's jewels, the candlesticks, everything. You'll make them give it all back, won't you?"

"Show me," said the police chief, and Zlata pointed to a pearl necklace, an assortment of other jewelry — a ring of silver and amber, a gold wedding ring, and a few bracelets — and a *kiddush* cup, menorah, and candlesticks.

"You," Nikifor Kharitonovich addressed the tallest and thinnest of the Lithuanian merchants. "Where did you come by these things?"

"These?" replied the merchant. (His name was Zusman, Avrom recalled.) "Why, we bought them."

"And for good money," added one of his fat, fair-skinned, green-eyed partners. (Lemel, wasn't it?)

"Your Nobleness, I assure you," the third of the northerners (Selig?) leaned forward. "We got them from an unimpeachable source."

"Oh yes?" Nikifor Kharitonovich said in his iciest tone. "And what unimpeachable source was that?"

The three merchants exchanged glances.

"Well? If you don't tell me, I'll have to assume it was the three of you who stole them."

"Stole?" Lemel exclaimed. "Now listen — "

"Oh no, you can't pin it on us," protested Zusman, "it's an — "

Selig jumped in. "Your Nobleness, it was your own constable who sold them to us — Faddei Kazimirovich."

"The Pole?" cried everyone in the sizable crowd that had already gathered round.

"Faddei Kazimirovich?" repeated Nikifor Kharitonovich. "Why, I'll ..." He cast his eyes furiously about, and after a few seconds, spotted what he was looking for. "Try to slink away, will he?" he growled, and shot away into the crowd. A minute later he returned, pulling the Pole roughly by the arm.

The constable's dull, open face was arranged into an expression of innocent puzzlement as they came. But the moment they arrived at the stall, he gave himself away. He looked straight at the pearl necklace, and then, as if it had burned his eyes, moved his gaze in quick succession from Zlata, to Nikifor Kharitonovich, and finally, to the ground.

"Faddei Kazimirovich," Nikifor Kharitonovich curved his mouth into a dangerous smile — and it goes without saying, narrowed his eyes. "These merchants claim to have bought a few items, these here ... yes, look, that's right ... from you. Is that the truth?"

It took the Pole only an instant to scan the items in question, but longer to decide whether to tell the truth. A guilty glance at the merchants decided him: "Y-yes. It's true ... So what?"

The police chief's smile widened, while his eyes narrowed to the point of invisibility—a perilous sign. "He asks me *so what*," Nikifor Kharitonovich said to Zlata. "So what," he twisted the Pole's arm, making him wince, "is that these items may have been stolen. So please tell me, my dear constable, where did you get them?"

The Pole seemed to have taken full cognizance of the narrowness of Nikifor Kharitonovich's eyes. At least, his voice trembled as he replied: "Oh, th-they're just ... heirloom-ms. Th-they were my m-mother's."

"Is that so?" Nikifor Kharitonovich laughed silkily. "Do you know, this case is positively teeming with mothers? Zlata —that's your name, isn't it?"

"Yes," replied the girl.

"Do you know where *your* mother got these things?"

"Yes ... she told us ... this, and this ... and this ... they were all heirlooms. I don't know where *these* came from. But the necklace— Mama bought that at Feldshteyn's shop, just over there."

Nikifor Kharitonovich looked around the square again, suddenly pulled a little whistle from his pocket, and blew on it, producing an earsplitting shrill. A moment later, a square-faced man with bright eyes and a small, dark mustache beneath his peaked official's cap came running up.

"Ukhovyortov, fetch the jeweler Feldshteyn."

The newly-arrived constable, surveying the situation, pointed at the Pole and protested, "Why not send *him*?" But when his circling gaze arrived back at Nikifor Kharitonovich's face, he rushed off without any further questions. No more than three minutes later, he returned alongside a tall Jew with a long, distinguished nose and large, intelligent eyes.

"Izrael Samoilovich," Nikifor Kharitonovich addressed the new arrival. "Would you do us the kindness of inspecting that pearl necklace? See if you happen to recognize it."

Feldshteyn raised his hand to his face — Avrom now saw he was carrying a jeweler's eye loupe — took one look and announced: "I do recognize it."

"Well?"

"An inexpensive piece — the pearls are not of the first quality, but they do match well. I remember clearly, I sold it ten years ago or so — to Sora Hinde the dairywoman."

"Mama!" Zlata cried out.

"Thank you," Nikifor Kharitonovich graciously replied. At the same moment the Pole's face contorted in pain, as his arm was twisted once again. "And so ..." The chief's voice was so cold that Avrom actually shivered. "Let me ask again, my excellent constable. Where did you get these things? Did you take them from this girl's house?"

"I'm no thief!" shouted the Pole. "I — ouch — I found them."

"Oh, you *found* them. And where was that?"

The Pole didn't answer at once.

"I see," said Nikifor Kharitonovich. "It *was* you who stole them. In that case — "

"No — ouch — let go, will you? I'll tell you. I found them when I was searching Styopa's place, in the village."

"What? And you say you're no thief?"

"He's fled! His place is abandoned. They were up for grabs."

"And you grabbed them." Without thinking about it, Nikifor Kharitonovich addressed Avrom. "We can assume, then, that it was Styopa who stole them."

"Indeed," replied the tsimbalist.

Immediately, the chief seemed to realize he ought not to be discussing the case with the tsimbalist in public, and turned quickly away, taking his discomfort out on the Pole: "And what about the money, you miserable crook?"

Faddei Kazimirovich cowered before this new accusation. "M-money? I don't — "

"The money Styopa stole along with these things. Come now, I may soon lose patience."

"I don't know anything about that, Nikifor Kharitonovich, I swear on all that's holy!"

"Oh yes? Well, we'll see when we search your place. Meanwhile — Ukhovyortov? Take this scum, and put him in the jail."

"What?" protested the Pole. "You can't put me in there."

"Must I, chief?" asked Ukhovyortov. "He's always been a good sort — "

"No, wait," said Nikifor Kharitonovich.

This time it was Avrom who cried, "What?"

"Izrael Samoilovich," the police chief turned again to the jeweler Feldshteyn, who was still standing there. "Your house was robbed the other night, too. I can't help but notice that a number of these trinkets," the chief drummed his fingers lightly on a silver wine cup, a fancy spice box, and a diamond-and-pearl *shterntikhl* headband, "resemble the things on the list you made me. Could you have a look, and see if you recognize them?"

Feldshteyn took a careful look at the northerners' array of merchandise. But to Nikifor Kharitonovich's obvious disappointment, the jeweler's reply this time was "I do not."

"We're no thieves," said the merchant Zusman angrily.

"We'll see about that," said Nikifor Kharitonovich. "Ukhovyortov, take Faddei Kazimirovich — "

"You can't put me in there — "

"And when he's safely locked up, bring Grinberg and Rosengauz here."

~

The two constables had barely left when a little urchin ran up.

"Come quick," he tugged Nikifor Kharitonovich on the

sleeve. "Deacon Achilles says Verusha's Ivan is selling stolen horses."

The police chief looked down at him in surprise, then directed a stern look at the three northern merchants. "I won't be far away," he warned, then hurried off.

Most Market Days, Avrom did his best to give a wide berth to the horse market: even days later, the grounds there gave off a revolting odor. Now, though, he couldn't contain his curiosity. A few seconds after Nikifor Kharitonovich followed the little urchin, the tsimbalist followed. Cutting a path straight for Deacon Achilles' highly visible head, he even arrived at the corral belonging to Verusha's Ivan at almost the same moment as the police chief.

Verusha's Ivan (so called to distinguish him from another horse-trader named Ivan) was standing squeezed up against the railing of his corral, interposed between Deacon Achilles and one of the horses, a white stallion who made all the other horses in the market look dingy and drab. The trader was tall and rangy, with a long blonde beard, but he looked small next to Achilles.

It looked as if the deacon, for some reason, was trying to reach out and touch the horse, but Verusha's Ivan kept moving to get in his way. When he noticed the arrival of the police chief, however, the horse trader stopped moving, and Achilles, seeing where his eyes were looking, turned around at once.

"Your Nobleness," the horse trader opened his mouth. "I'm glad you're here. Deacon Achilles is pestering me, and keeping me from doing business."

"Nikifor Khari ..." said Achilles. "This is Star ... Arkady ... 's horse."

"The good deacon is confused," Verusha's Ivan was quick to contradict. "That poor young man's steed had a little brown mark on his neck in the shape of a star. Everybody knows it. But look here. This beauty is of the purest white."

Nikifor Kharitonovich looked inquiringly at Achilles, who uttered one clear word: "Paint."

"Nonsense!" exclaimed the horse trader. "Deacon, you ought to be ashamed of yourself, such a horse lover as you are. You're insulting this beautiful animal — you can see for yourself there's no hint of variation in the color. ."

"Nikif— " began Achilles, but the police chief said, "Enough!"

The little urchin was next to Nikifor Kharitonovich, hopping back and forth in anticipation of what might happen. Now, the chief bent down toward him, and asked, "What name do you go by, my young friend?"

"Senka." He had a voice like a flute.

"Very good, Senka," said Nikifor Kharitonovich. "Now, I need you to do an important service for me. Take these three *kopeks*, go to Brukha the oil seller, and tell her I need two *kopeks'* worth of turpentine. You can keep the other one for yourself."

The boy ran off without a word, and everyone fell silent, waiting.

As had happened at the stall of the visiting northerners, a crowd had by now gathered round, this one comprised of the horse market's other buyers and sellers. Avrom thought he could read in the faces of the other traders pleasure over the predicament Verusha's Ivan found himself in, tempered by a mingled solidarity and concern — there wasn't one among them who hadn't pulled similar tricks in his time.

The tsimbalist hadn't noticed anyone standing next to him, but he suddenly heard a whisper in his ear: "What an idiot that Verusha's Ivan is. A real *shabbes mikra koydesh* and *leymener goylem* rolled into one. A piece of meat with eyes, if you know what I mean. If it'd been me, I would have taken the horse to the market at Konatop. Who would ever recognize it there?" It was Yasha, one of the Jewish traders.

The next moment, Senka returned with the turpentine.

~

The horse was Star, of course. One good rub of turpentine, and his well-known brown patch appeared in all its glory.

At once, Verusha's Ivan tried to laugh off what he had done. "I just thought the horse would look better if he was all white, Nikifor Kharitonovich. Don't you agree that he — "

"Why did you kill Arkady Olegovich Efimovski?" asked the police chief.

"Kill Ark — you don't think I — Nikifor Kharitonovich, I only took the horse from where — it wasn't me, I had nothing to do with it, I swear on all that's holy!"

"You too, hmm?"

"What? I — "

"Explain, then, how you came into possession of the horse. And why did you paint it?"

"I painted him because the Efimovski boy was, pardon me, dead. It seemed — "

"When?"

"On Saturday last."

"And where did you find him?"

"At the Hermit's Cave. He was there, tied up inside."

Nikifor Kharitonovich glanced at Avrom meaningfully, then asked, "That was also on Saturday?"

"Yes."

"And how did you happen to find the horse there?"

"I didn't happen to find him at all, Your Nobleness," replied Verusha's Ivan. "Saturday morning, I was minding my own business, when that Styopa came along."

"Styopa?"

"That's right. He asked me if I'd like to know where to find a horse, and I said — "

"Wait a moment — do you know where Styopa is now?"

"No idea, Your Nobleness."

"All right, go on."

"I said I wouldn't mind knowing, and he said if I gave him fifteen roubles he'd tell me where to find a fine stallion. He said I could take it, he didn't know how to sell a horse, as long as I didn't touch the wheel and anything else he might have left behind — "

"The wheel?"

"There was an old wheel in the cave — but I didn't take it, I don't just take what doesn't belong to me, Your Nobleness."

"Tell me more about the wheel."

"It was just an old, rusty wheel. Styopa said he was going to sell it himself ... So, as you can see, I didn't do anything wrong at all."

"No, of course you didn't, my friend," purred Nikifor Kharitonovich. "Tell me — did you recognize the horse?"

"Of course I recognized him — everybody knows Star. Right away I thought, well, Ivan, are you the sort who'd just sell a horse that belongs to someone else? No, you're not. You'll just have to take him straight to the Efimovski estate and return him. Only I was in a real anger at the same time, and wanted to find that Styopa first, to get back my fifteen roubles. So I tied Star up at my place, and went looking for him. It was just a few hours later that I heard about poor Arkady Olegovich."

"And the first thing you did when you heard was paint the horse." Nikifor Kharitonovich pulled out his whistle. "I'm putting you in jail, Ivan."

"What for?"

"Because if you're telling the truth, you took a horse that wasn't yours and disguised it to sell. And if you're lying ..." The chief blew on his whistle.

Everyone expected a constable to run up. But Ukhovyortov must have still been busy with Grinberg and Rosengauz. He didn't immediately appear, and then continued not to appear.

Avrom was unsure of how much time went by waiting. He was rather distracted, thinking that Nikifor Kharitonovich's theory of the crime had changed awfully quickly. The chief seemed to have decided, first of all, that the thefts of the three wealthy Jews' houses, and of Koppel's, were unrelated. Apparently, Styopa had robbed Koppel, and the three merchants had robbed the three Jews. Well, that was possible — and if it *was* the merchants, it should be proved as soon as Rosengauz and Grinberg came. Although, if they had Rosengauz's things and Grinberg's, what had they done with Feldshteyn's? Nikifor Kharitonovich could be in for a good deal of embarrassment.

At any rate, there was another question: Did the chief think the merchants were connected in some way with the *narodniks*? Or had he thrown the idea of *narodniks* unceremoniously aside? It would be nice if he had — no more asking Dovid for the names of his friends.

A second blast of Nikifor Kharitonovich's whistle interrupted these speculations. This time, Ukhovyortov came running.

"Chief," said the breathless constable, "the two Jews are waiting for you at the stall."

"Fine, Ukhovyortov. And now I have another task for you. Take this wretch to the jail — I'll explain later. Then come right back. I expect I'll have need of you again, quite soon."

⁓

By the time Nikifor Kharitonovich returned, accompanied by Avrom and an increasingly large crowd of gawkers, Grinberg and Rosengauz had already had a chance to inspect the northerners' merchandise. Grinberg, who had a long white beard and a bald pate beneath his felt hat, gave the police chief a curt shake of the head, his lower lip thrust forward. Rosengauz, who had a short grey beard and a bald pate beneath *his* felt hat, was more expansive.

"They're *like* the things that were stolen from me. But they're *not* the things that were stolen from me."

"You see?" the merchant Zusman thrust his pink face forward, and his green eyes glittered. "Now will you let us do our business? You've already lost us a fortune." Then he addressed the crowd that had gathered: "Come closer, all of you, don't be afraid of the chief of police — now he's going to leave us in peace. Items of the finest quality, at prices to keep 'em movin' — one hundred percent legitimate — as your chief has just proven."

Laughter erupted from the crowd, as customers pressed in close. Nikifor Kharitonovich flushed a very dark color, and took Zusman by the collar.

"You're staying at Yudel Beck's inn, yes? Well then, I want one of you to come with me, while I search your rooms — I think I'll choose *you*. Avrom Moisevich," he said more quietly, "I need you to do a favor for me. When Ukhovyortov returns, tell him to join me at the inn."

⁓

A few minutes later, when the constable returned, Avrom did exactly that, and then hurried into his shop. Two customers were waiting: the health commissioner, and Doctor Artiukhov, with whom Avrom discussed Koppel's outlook, and the fact that the doctor had decided to write a little work of fiction based on the events at the market this morning — he had already published two or three other little pieces in a literary magazine. Avrom finished trimming the doctor's hair and made it outside just as a triumphant Zusman was strutting back to his stall.

"A clean bill of health, boys," the northerner winked at his two partners.

"Where's our friend the police chief?" called out Lemel, who was daringly slipping a bracelet onto a young Russian lady's delicate wrist.

"Oh, he won't be back here any time soon," Zusman laughed.

"Went off with his constable, saying something about a cave. Probably wants to hide in it, tee-hee ... But say, who's hungry? My mouth is all a-water from the smell of that roast pig."

~

Two hours later, the market was winding down. Half the wagons were gone, with more being hitched back up. Most of the stalls were empty or on their way to being so: as peasants departed town, lady merchants were decamping in order to catch them on the way out and pick up unsold produce on the cheap. Other peasants, meanwhile, were heading for the public bath or the tavern, while at the market, a few late-arriving customers were hurrying about trying to find what they needed before everything closed down entirely.

The woodworker Shabshel Urvand had already begun carrying a number of his smaller toys and utensils back indoors, while Avrom stood outside his rented shop, with the expectation that he'd finished work for the day. On his mind were two questions, neither of which had anything to do with the momentous events of the morning: was he more likely to find the Kelmer Maggid right now at Grinberg's house or at the *besmedresh*? And would he have time to go for a quick visit to the holy man before accompanying Blume to see the Tatar healer?

It was the second of these questions which promised to be answered first. Blume appeared in front of him.

"Good day, my dear," he greeted her. "And *Mazel Tov.*"

"Thank you Reb Avrom! What a wonderful morning!"

"Yes, indeed. You got your things back — all of your mother's jewelry."

Tears sprang to Blume's eyes. "Yes ... yes ... It's true what they say. With luck, everything is possible."

"And how did you sell?"

"Oh, even there we were lucky. We sold everything, and

found a few bargains, too. Do you know, I was able to get a hand-ful of poppy seeds, a handful of caraway, and a handful of *cher-nushkas*, all for only three kopeks! But that's not the important thing! The Tatar healer was here today, so I was already able to get Tatte's ointment from him."

"Ointment? But didn't you get that from Doctor Artiukhov?"

"No — why did you think I wanted to go to the Tatar?"

"I didn't th— but why not from Doctor Artiukhov?"

"I kept trying to go to the doctor's and he was always away. Yesterday I went again, and this time he was in, but what do you think? The ointment was out! He'd just sold the last of it."

"I see."

"Imagine, if I'd only arrived ten minutes earlier, I'd have gotten it, instead of that awful man." She gestured with her thumb at the stall where the three Lithuanians were packing up their wares. "But instead — "

"Who got it?" asked Avrom.

"One of those two brothers there, the ones who had our things — I knew exactly who Zlata was talking about the min-ute she described them. He I think it was *that* one — was just coming out of the doctor's when I was going in, and he had the ointment bottle in his hand, I saw it. I didn't know it was the *last* bottle till I went inside. But Doctor Artiukhov told me he gets the ointment from the Tatar, so now I finally have it!"

Avrom thought for a moment, and then said, "That's won-derful, my dear. And I'm very happy you got your mother's things back. Now, will you forgive if I say goodbye for the moment?"

"Where are you going?"

"I want to visit my friend Hertzik Katznelson — the lock-smith."

Chapter 15

Keeping Secrets

A ray of sunlight crept in through the high-up window, brightening the airy room, and the Kelmer Maggid ran a light hand through his voluminous brown beard and nodded sagely.

"Yes," he pronounced his considered opinion. "Yes. What you say is true."

The holy man was seated in a place of honor, in a Voltaire-an chair at the center of Reb Lev Grinberg's salon. Surrounding him were two *minyans'* worth of Jews, perched on Grinberg's elegant furniture, and talking amongst themselves. In a humbler chair, directly in front of the great man, sat Avrom.

"To go off in solitary meditation," the Maggid elaborated, "is as you say, not exactly what Salanter taught us. Between the two of us only, however," he lowered his voice, "I always found it trying, hearing other people shouting like that around me in the Ethics House."

"Perhaps," said Avrom with a rueful smile, "that was my problem too, and it was just that I never realized it. In any case," he looked into the Maggid's brown eyes, "it's a true honor to meet you and have the opportunity to discuss these matters. A rare and sweet chance, indeed."

"A pleasure to speak with you, too, Reb Avrom. If it were not that I am leaving Zavlivoya so soon, I'd urge you back for another discussion."

"You say the train leaves from Bakhmatch at two o'clock?" asked Avrom.

"Yes — which means I ought to depart from here, God willing, within the half hour."

"It's good of Reb Lev to send you to the train in his carriage."

"He can spare it, I think."

"I think so," Avrom laughed, "since he has two of them." He looked around the room. "Quite a house, isn't it?"

The preacher glanced around too, and shrugged. "I suppose so. It makes no difference to me what sort of a house I stay in. It was good of Reb Lev to put me up, of course."

"They say you had the misfortune of losing a prayer shawl when this house was robbed the other night," Avrom ventured.

"Indeed," the Maggid sighed. "But no matter. We mustn't let ourselves be overly concerned with the things of this world, lest they distract us from thoughts of the world to come. If I care how many prayer shawls I own, then I may care how much money I have with which to buy more prayer shawls. Then I might try to cheat my neighbor — God forbid — in order to have more money. You see how it is? However, I'm sorry that Reb Lev lost so many things."

"Yes," agreed Avrom, "it's difficult to detach ourselves entirely from the things we own. I'm sure that's the case for Reb Grinberg, too, even though he owns so many things — or because of it." Avrom dropped his voice even lower. "I have to admit, though, as much as it shames me — I'm curious to see how the man lives. I've never been in his house before. Would you excuse me while I take a little look around the rooms?"

Avrom was not surprised when the Maggid replied with a disapproving nod.

"And thank *you* for honoring my house with your presence," said Reb Lev Grinberg half an hour later, as he embraced the Maggid. "The Jews of Zavlivoya will remember your visit always, and cherish the memory ... And so, I'll just send the servants up for your books and things ..."

"Fine," said the Maggid.

"Wait," said Avrom, standing with all the others in a ring around the two men. "I had an idea ... a silly idea perhaps, but ... the Kelmer Maggid has done us an extraordinary favor by visiting Zavlivoya. Would it not be seemly for us to return that favor, by doing a special service for him?"

"Hmm," said Grinberg, looking dubious — no doubt, he thought he'd done enough favors for the preacher already. "What sort of service would that be?"

"I thought," said Avrom, "that instead of sending your servants, a few of us — eight of us, I suppose — how many trunks are there?"

"Two," replied the Maggid.

"Good. And are they large?"

"They're quite heavy — I have many books."

"Then, I propose that eight of us go up, and carry the Maggid's trunks out to the carriage ... as a sort of honor guard."

"I don't — " began Grinberg, but he was drowned out by Berl Melamed, who exclaimed, "What a fine idea! Who wants to volunteer?"

"I will!" Avrom boldly cried.

"Well then," said Berl Melamed, "I will, too!"

"And I will! I will," shouted twenty other voices.

"Now, now," said Berl Melamed, "first come, first served. That will be me, and Reb Avrom, and ... all right, you, and you, and you ..."

The trunks, each of which had a padlock on it, were heavy indeed, and large — it was a good thing there were eight men to share the burden. Grinberg and the Maggid supervised the operation: one, two, three, hup — now through the doorway — don't scratch the paint — you two first — ready? — down the stairs — just three more steps — not too fast now! — through the door — now five steps more, down to the drive, and — watch it — careful — careful! — no!

The accident began on Avrom's end. Somehow, even though the chest was quite heavy, he raised his arms up quite suddenly, tipping the trunk downward toward Berl Melamed. Berl's knees buckled, but then he managed to steady himself, and for a moment, it seemed as if everything would be all right. But the Hebrew school teacher must have jumped back up with too much force — down went Avrom's end. For some reason, Avrom now moved around to the front of the chest. But that made the corner he had been carrying tip down even further. Next thing you knew, the front of the chest was facing the ground, Avrom was underneath it on his knees, the chest shook up and down a little, and then — who knows how — the lid came open.

A few books fell out first — and then a few other items which were most definitely not books. Most of the chest's contents were tightly wrapped in cloth, but as its bearers lost their grip and it tumbled down the bottom stairs (Avrom just managed to scramble out of the way) more and more little things came loose: a silver spice box, a string of pearls, a diamond ring, an emerald-and-pearl *shterntikhl* headband.

For a few seconds, everyone stood with mouths agape, including — or especially — the Kelmer Maggid. Then he said, in a weak and baffled voice, "The lock ..."

This was followed by Grinberg saying, in an awestruck and baffled tone, "My ring."

And Berl Melamed, heartbroken and baffled, whimpering, "the Maggid?"

And then all hell broke loose. Hands started to pull all the items free from their cloth wrapping. Avrom, unseen by anyone else, produced a skeleton key — now why did he have that with him? — and opened the other chest, which was similarly stuffed with precious items. The Maggid edged toward the horse hitched in front of the carriage, Grinberg pointed at him, hands reached out to take hold of the criminal, and then Avrom whispered something to Berl Melamed, who shook his head, until Avrom whispered again, more insistently. Then Berl went up to the Maggid, grabbed his long brown beard, and pulled. It came right off.

The skin underneath was significantly less red and rashy than it had been the day before — the Tatar's ointment was obviously most effective. The thick glasses had been a surprisingly good disguise. Even with the beard torn off, Avrom would still not have recognized Anshel Pempik, the traveling merchant with whom the three Lithuanians had been playing cards yesterday, had he not been expecting to see him. The only remaining question was how long it would take for the false preacher to finger his three partners.

"Just do me a favor," Avrom whispered to Berl Melamed as someone went running to look for Nikifor Kharitonovich. "If anyone asks what made you pull his beard off? Don't tell him it was my idea."

⁓

In fact, it didn't take long at all, even before Nikifor Kharitonovich arrived, for the Maggid (or whatever he was) to tell all. Pleading his case to Grinberg and all the others gathered round, he claimed to be "only a poor actor from Odessa," by the name of Jakob Pinsky. The masterminds behind the robberies were the three Lithuanians — the Epshteyn brothers and their accomplice, Zusman Goldfarb. They had forced him, more or less, to impersonate the Kelmer Maggid — a very holy man for whom, by the way, he had the utmost reverence. It had actually sickened him, taking advantage of the great preacher's good reputation, in order to enable his partners to rob houses — which he himself, of course, had never personally participated in. Why, just look at his face. That was the body crying out, because the soul was unhappy. And by the way, might it be possible for him to just get into his luggage, where he had a bottle of the most miraculous ointment? What was that? Had they ever run their scam anywhere else? Why, Reb Lev — heaven forbid! Of course not!

Within a few minutes, Nikifor Kharitonovich arrived, accompanied by his constable Svistunov, and was told the same tale. The chief proceeded to have a private chat with Reb Grinberg, a short distance away from the house — during which, several times, he glared at Avrom. He then strode purposefully to his horse, calling out, "Svistunov — take the actor, if that's what he really is, to the jail, and then meet me at the inn to help round up the other three. And make it quick."

He jumped up onto his horse.

"And Avrom Moisevich — I want you at the jailhouse, too."

~

Avrom wasted little time obeying the chief's request, which had been delivered in a notably chilly tone. He only stopped off at Hertzik Katznelson's on the way, to return the little skeleton key.

Upon walking in, he announced to Ukhovyortov, who was on guard duty, "I'm to meet the chief."

"Fine," said the constable. "Take a seat."

"Ah, he's not here yet?"

"Take a seat."

A few minutes passed.

"Quite a busy day, here at the jail," Avrom remarked.

Ukhovyortov made no reply.

"I expect they're going to be bringing in another three prisoners any moment."

This time, the constable rustled his newspaper, but otherwise remained silent.

It really had been a busy day, though, thought Avrom, with so many new prisoners. First, there had been the Pole. Then, Verusha's Ivan. The Maggid, or, that is, the actor Jakob Pinsky. That made three. And Lemel, Zusman, and Selig would soon make six. With any luck, Styopa wouldn't be far behind. How many could Zavlivoya's little jail hold? Certainly not an unlimited number. No one had better commit any other crimes in the next few days! Avrom smiled to himself, then noticed Ukhovyortov giving him a sour look, and stopped.

Of course, there was still the murderer to think about — easy to forget in the midst of all these other revelations. Unless the murderer and Styopa were one and the same — which seemed even likelier now than it had before, what with that repulsive character knowing just where the wheel was to be found. It was still hard to understand, though, how everything might have happened, and why Styopa might have done it.

⟨~⟩

It had been about one o'clock when Avrom got to the jailhouse. From then on, time had been moving extraordinarily slowly. And yet the clock had somehow arrived at one-thirty, and then at two. Next, two-thirty came and went. And now, it was even past three. Yet for some reason, Nikifor Kharitonovich had still not gotten back.

It was hot in the jailhouse.

⟨~⟩

At three-thirty, the chief finally walked in. He looked road-weary, and purple in the face. He was accompanied by Svistunov, and precisely no one else.

"Avrom Moisevich," he said, his voice as frosty as the room was warm. "Come." And he turned around and walked back out the door.

What could Avrom do but follow?

They walked down the street, then around the corner; straight for two blocks, and around another corner; and finally, three more blocks down, around to the left, and a block more, till they arrived by the lake. All the time they walked, Nikifor Kharitonovich looked straight ahead, his face impassive. He said not a word.

At the lake's edge, there was a seawall, with an expanse of grass running right up to it. Standing in the middle of the lawn, in the shade of a slender young linden, the chief finally spoke, his words seeming to come out of a very small, narrow, constricted hole: "Well, Avrom Moisevich ... Grinberg tells me it was you who dropped the chest that came open."

"I don't know how it happened," Avrom hastily replied. "Clumsy — though I suppose it was lucky, too."

"Quite."

The chief extracted a cigar from a pocket, savagely bit off its end, and lit up. There was a breeze by the lake — it took two matches.

Nikifor Kharitonovich watched the smoke of his cigar rise up among the leaves overhead, and then remarked: "It's extraordinary. How do you imagine the Hebrew school teacher thought of pulling the man's beard away?"

"Oh." Avrom didn't know what to say. "Perhaps ... one of those ... mysterious inspirations."

"Oh," Nikifor Kharitonovich put his hand on his chin and nodded his head in an exaggerated motion. "Yes, of course, one of those mysterious inspirations." He stretched the words out mockingly, then added, "I'll be sure to ask him exactly what inspiration that was."

For a moment, neither of them said anything.

Avrom spoke first. "I suppose that you have a clear picture of everything that happened now with the robberies? The part I don't understand is how Styopa managed to get Koppel's goods from the three Lithuanians, after they had stolen them from Koppel."

"Ah, there you're mistaken," Nikifor Kharitonovich condescendingly replied. "The Lithuanians never stole Koppel's things. You've confused everything."

In fact, Avrom hadn't confused anything—he didn't believe the Lithuanians had stolen Koppel's things any more than Nikifor Kharitonovich did. The chief was in a dangerous mood, however, and Avrom felt it might help smooth things over, if he pretended to be mistaken. "They never stole—"

"No. The thefts here in Zavlivoya and the theft at your neighbor's house were entirely unrelated. That is, they were connected only by the false preacher's sermon."

"Ah ..."

"Yes, it's quite simple, and even obvious, if I may say so. The sermon, you see, assured that all the Jewish houses for *versts* around would be empty. And two separate thieves, or sets of thieves, took advantage of that fact."

"So ..."

"All right, Avrom Moisevich, what I assume happened here in Zavlivoya was something like this. The preacher—we'll call him that for the sake of convenience—arrived with two trunks, which would have been full of, oh, let's say junk—but something sufficiently heavy to pass for books. Did you notice that there were a few actual books in among the stolen merchandise? But there were none on the lists Grinberg and the others provided. They would have been in there, and right on top, for appearances. So that the preacher could pull out a book from the trunk, and thus make it seem as though the trunk were full of books."

"Of course ..."

"Now, the preacher secured an invitation to stay at Grinberg's, which was risky for him, but at the same highly convenient, for reasons which you shall hear in a moment. Meanwhile, the other three also arrived. They spent their time learning the lay of the land, finding out who was most worth robbing, and so on. Good, now it's Friday night. All of your people flock to your synagogue to hear the preacher — how was he, by the way?"

"Convincing. I think he must have memorized some of the real Maggid's sermons — a few of them have been published. And even in private, he seemed to know what he was talking about. He's either very sharp-witted or well-informed — or perhaps both. But he also did keep his mouth shut much of the time he was here, by all accounts. Perhaps he couldn't keep going without giving himself away — "

"All right, that will do. Now, the three thieves: I would guess they went to Feldshteyn's first, and then to Rosengauz's. Rosengauz lives quite near Grinberg. They certainly ended at Grinberg's, where they robbed the house, took whatever trash they'd stuffed into the chests *out*, and stashed everything they'd just taken *in* — except for the cash."

"So the things they stole on Friday — they weren't selling any of that today?"

"Not at all. With the exception of the things they bought from — " The chief's face flushed an unhealthy violet, and he took a long and greedy puff on his cigar. "With the exception of the things they bought from Faddei Kazimirovich, the items they were selling today will have been the fruits of a similar charade they pulled somewhere else. That is my assumption, at least — and it's something I'll be able to confirm soon enough."

"Aha ... and so what about the robbery at Koppel's?"

"Yes ... It is understandable, perhaps, to fall into the error of thinking that because the Lithuanians had your neighbor's things for sale, they had something to do with that robbery, too. But as I said, I don't believe that to be the case. In the first place, the chests were full. Why steal more than they could stash? And in the second place, if they'd had any idea the items were stolen, they'd never have sold them here in Zav ... And in the third place, if they were going to rob a fourth house, why not another in Zav, rather than out in the middle of nowhere ... that is ... I mean to say ... In any case, it's clear enough it was Styopa who robbed your neighbor's house."

"I agree," declared Avrom.

It was the wrong thing to say, or the wrong way to say it — as if he'd thought it all along (which was, in fact, the case.) Nikifor Kharitonovich flared up at once: "I don't recall asking for your opinion, Avrom Moisevich — or for your help."

"My help?"

"Yes, indeed. Those locks. I'd dearly love to know how they came open. Among other things."

"What I wonder," said Avrom, in a humble tone he hoped would mollify the chief, whose face was turning purple again, "is why Styopa had the wheel at the cave, but Koppel's things at his house. And how he got a hold of Arkady Olegovich's horse. And of course, where he's hiding."

"He's *not* hiding."

"What? What do you mean, did you find him?"

"In a manner of speaking."

"Then, where is he?"

"He is nowhere, Avrom Moisevich. He is dead."

"What?"

"Indeed."

"But how — why do you only now — "

"Well, well. Would you look at this? Now we *see*, when *he's* the one left in the dark, Avrom Moisevich doesn't find it quite so enjoyable, having people keep secrets."

"I don't — "

"Would you like to know, my friend, where I've been for the last several hours? Did it not seem strange to you that I was so slow in returning, did it not make you want to ask me, the way you always do, what in the world could be the meaning of it, why I arrived with not even a single Lithuanian in sight, let alone three?"

"It ... did."

"And yet, I flew like the wind from Grinberg's house to Yudel Beck's inn. How could I have missed them? But they were already gone — and in an obvious hurry. They threw a little money Beck's way as they ran out, and by the time he followed them outside they had vanished. Yudel Beck was of no help whatsoever in locating them. All right, I thought, the preacher was supposed to take a carriage to Bakhmatch to catch the train. They must have planned to meet him there. But instead, we'll meet *them*. And that's what we did, Svistunov and I, or tried to do. But the train came and went, with no sign of our trio. Perhaps, I thought, they saw us, and hid out. Let's search the inn, and the town. I was forced to enlist the aid of Kornilii Filimonovich, the police chief there. He had a very nice laugh at my expense. Unable to apprehend a few Jewish merchants? Nikifor Kharitonovich can't be very much of a policeman, old Kornyukha must have thought. But even with his help, we couldn't find a trace of them. Back we came to Zav, and canvassed for information. It took some time to find anyone who'd seen them go, but we finally turned up one witness who saw them ride south, in the direction of Pryluky. Irakli Tengizovich is lucky. He'll get a nice laugh, too."

"The — "

"Yes, Avrom Moisevich, Irakli Tengizovich is the police chief in Pryluky. I've had to wire there, and to a few other towns, too: Please, will you catch my petty criminals for me? I didn't put it that way, of course, but I may as well have. And yet, had anyone who might have known anything about the matter thought to tell me earlier, I could have caught the thieves before they ever left."

"Nikifor Kharitonovich ... I apologize."

The chief stared at Avrom for a few seconds, then walked away along the seawall. When he came back, he only said, "I'd like to know how you discovered it."

"Oh ... Really, it was luck. It seemed, after you searched the inn, that if those three merchants were the thieves, which seemed likely — you were right to notice the similarity of their merchandise to the ... as of course you would be ... *right*, that is ... anyway ... if they were the thieves, and the stolen merchandise wasn't in their rooms, then either they had another hiding place — unlikely, since they're not from here ... or else there was a fourth partner no one knew about. Here's where I was lucky: the other day I was at the inn, and the three of them were gambling with a stranger. He had a clean-shaven face, with very red, rashy skin, and thick glasses that completely concealed his eyes. Today, I learned from Blume — that's Koppel's daughter — "

"Yes, Avrom Moisevich."

"Sorry ... well, I learned from Blume that one of the merchants, Lemel, had bought a skin ointment from Doctor Artiukhov. I didn't know why he would need it. But the Maggid's, I mean Pinsky's face ... it must have been irritated by the adhesive from the beard ... If I hadn't happened to be at the inn that day, and then talked to Blume — it's no virtue of mine, just luck, that allowed me to put it together. Ah, and then the other day, someone also told me a story about a false beard. It must have been on my mind still."

"That's all very well. But when you 'put it together,' as you say, you chose not to tell me."

"It was impossible to be certain, and given his stature ... if it had turned out to be the real Kelmer Maggid, it would have been outrageous for you to search his trunks. I went to break into them to make sure, and you know what I found, of course. But by that time, he was on the verge of leaving. And so ..."

"Come," said Nikifor Kharitonovich, in a somewhat less cool tone. "Let us walk back."

"Nikifor Kharitonovich," said Avrom, walking with the chief away from the lake. "I hope you won't refuse to tell me about Styopa now."

Nikifor Kharitonovich did not reply right away.

"No ... I won't refuse. However, there is precious little to tell. You were there to hear what Verusha's Ivan said. After the search at the inn came up empty, Ukhovyortov and I went to the Hermit's Cave. I'm not sure what I hoped to find, but ... it was a surprise, certainly. He was stabbed, several times, and — this is interesting — from the front. He bled to death. And if he had anything with him, any of the money — whoever killed him took it away."

"The knife?"

"Common."

"When did it happen?"

"I sent Ukhovyortov for Doctor Artiukhov. He said it was most likely Sunday — some time after I searched the place, obviously. He was definitely killed there in the cave."

"And so ... what now?"

"Now, I'll go to General Kondratin's. When I sent that idiot Ukhovyortov for the doctor, he didn't come back. I needed a constable, so I returned to Zav to fetch Svistunov. That's when they ran in to tell me to come to Grinberg's. I haven't had a chance to learn a thing ... I have hopes that General Kondratin or someone from his household might have seen something — the cave is on his grounds, after all. It's very difficult. I'm down a constable now."

"Nikifor Kharitonovich, I'd like to apologize once again," said Avrom, who had noticed that the chief, despite his now calm demeanor, did still have an unhealthy purple glow about his skin. "I —"

"Nikifor Kharitonovich!" yelled Svistunov, running towards them a block away. "There you are! There's been a fire!"

"Where now?" The chief ran to meet his constable, with Avrom right behind.

"The Efimovski village," panted Svistunov. "They've heard about Styopa — and they've gone and burned down the Jew's tavern!"

Chapter 16

Visits

Khana Lipkin was in the kitchen, standing on her tiptoes. The wash-basin sat up on the table, high enough that Khana could barely reach over its top edge. Inside the basin was a baking pan, made of copper, with an inner coating of tin.

Though the pan's exterior was tarnished and stained, the coating already shone like a mirror. That, however, made no difference to Khana: without any active guidance from her brain, but with the avid participation of her shoulder, her arm kept going round and round a strenuous, circular track. Her head, with its prematurely white hair, was bent over her work. Her eyes looked elsewhere, or nowhere.

Who knows how long she'd been scrubbing? Inside her kitchen that afternoon, each second lasted an hour, and each hour seemed like a day. Except for the quiet scraping of pan against basin, the house was quiet — until, at a certain moment, she gave the pan an especially vigorous thrust. The pain on its backside made it cry out in its harsh metallic voice. And Khana was brought to herself.

At once, she abandoned the wash-basin, strode out of the kitchen, opened the door of the house, looked out into the street.

She didn't see what she'd hoped for. Still, she hesitated, not wanting to close up again. Perhaps she could go weed the garden ... but no, she'd just done that. One of the cucumbers had been almost ready to pick ... but that had only been an hour ago. It wouldn't be any readier now. Letting out a long, long sigh, she shut the door.

She wasn't tired, or shouldn't have been. She hadn't worked any harder than on any other Market Day. Last night, as always, she'd made the dough, let it rise, punched it down, and gone to sleep at midnight. At three, she'd gotten up, shaped the loaves, stoked the fire, baked all the bread, and finished by making a batch of *pletzlekh*, three raisin cakes, and eight lengths of *kmishbrot*.

With the *kmishbrot* still warm and soft, she'd wheeled everything to market. And there, the morning had proceeded as expected. Every crumb sold. Nearly every one of her usual customers came. Few of them left without saying that her goods were the best at market.

On any other day, it would have been enough to fill her with joy. But not today, when her favorite customer hadn't come. Or better to say, couldn't come.

She'd tried, poor thing, Khana had seen her trying. She'd gotten up, begun to approach, a look of resolve stamped on her pretty face. She'd taken one difficult step, and then another. But then her sister Zlata pulled her back, and from the look of it, scolded her.

Later, Zlata went to look around the market, and Blume got up again, with the same look on her face. She took one difficult step, another, another. But halfway along, her lip started to tremble, she shook her head. It even looked, this time, as she turned her back, as if she let out a sob.

When everyone started exclaiming about how the girls had recovered their stolen possessions, Khana rejoiced inside. But a sense of delicacy prevented her from joining the crowd gathered to congratulate them. None of the three had even managed to look her in the eye, though they were only a few stalls away.

Then later, Zlata left again. When she came back, she had under her arm one of the loaves made by Rivke the *aguneh*. Well ... Rivke made good bread, by the look of it. And after all, that sad woman did have to make ends meet somehow. Nothing wrong with buying bread from Rivke. Why was it, then, that it nearly broke Khana's heart, seeing that fat, round loaf sunning itself atop the girls' rickety little table?

The worst part of all was that she couldn't blame them, not a bit. The fault was entirely her son's.

If she'd been superstitious like the other ladies, she might have thought Dovid had been taken by an evil spirit. "He simply isn't himself. He isn't himself." That's what she kept repeating. When he wasn't closed up in his room — he had the room to himself, now that his brothers were married — he was out wandering, nobody knew where. He was slow to respond when spoken to. And when he was alone in his room, he'd taken to mumbling to himself.

Khana could hear the things that escaped his lips. For example: "Ah, what a terrible thing it is to be in love." And, "I must tell Blume. In fact, it's kinder that way, if I could only bring myself to do it."

The day before yesterday, she'd heard him ask: "Is it a grave mistake, to let ideas take precedence over the natural leanings of the heart?"

But the worst was when he said, "If I could only cut my heart out of my chest ..." And then he'd laughed.

She didn't understand any of it. Dovid had a good and beautiful girl who loved him. Why make trouble? What was clouding his heart so, that he had to run away from Blume? And why didn't he confide in his mother?

On the kitchen floor, a basketful of beautiful mushrooms, bought from one of her faithful peasant customers, sat waiting to be united with the two handfuls of buckwheat groats purchased from another of her usuals, along with an onion, an egg, and a healthy spoonful of *schmaltz*. It should have been the last Market Day supper before Dovid got married. But who knew if Dovid would even be at home? It seemed almost pointless to cook them up.

For the first time she could remember, Khana was tempted to sit down, take a rest, and leave the work for later.

~

The first knocks were peremptory, the next, insistent.

"Just a moment, just a moment," Khana called out, hurrying from kitchen to door. "Why, Reb Avrom!" She looked up at her visitor. "What in the name of the Master of the Universe — "

"Khana, is your son at home?"

Something terrible had happened, she could hear it in his voice. "Oh God, Reb Avrom, what is it?"

"Ah, pardon me, Khana." His voice instantly transformed, gentle and warm now. "I didn't mean to frighten you. It's just that there's something I need to tell Dovid as soon as possible. I don't suppose you have an idea where he might be?"

She wasn't fooled. "Reb Avrom," she demanded, "tell me what's happened."

He stared at her for an instant, then nodded. "All right. There's been a fire at the Efimovski village. They've burned down Shimmel Shenkman's tavern."

"*Oy, Got zol ophitn!* How terrible! Was anyone — Reb Avrom, I'm afraid to ask."

"No one was hurt. They'll only lose everything they own ..."

"Oh, the poor children ... and Khaia Tauba ... first of all we must find them a place to sleep ... of course she has her sister here in Zav, but if there isn't any room there, we'll make them a place here ... provided we can round up the bedding from somewhere. But how will they get here, they mustn't walk in their current — "

"Khana, of course you would think of those things," Reb Avrom interrupted her. "You're far too good. But I just came from the *besmedresh*, and saw Khaia Tauba's uncle Zorakh there. He's on his way to the village now in his wagon, to bring them to Zav."

"Ah, good, then — "

"Listen, Khana, there's something else I must tell you. The tavern was burned down by the peasants in the village ... They've been somewhat ... they've been in a state of disturbance ever since the Efimovski son was found dead, he was a great benefactor to them. But it was something else that pushed them as far as burning down the tavern. The man Dovid fought with — he was named Styopa — he was one of the villagers, more or less. Today, he was found dead, too."

"*Got zol ophitn!*" Khana said again, and then froze. "Reb Avrom ... why are you in such a hurry to find Dovid?"

"I ... Khana, I'm certain nothing will happen to your son — "

At this, her fingers flew straight to her mouth.

" — but after the fight they had, it could be that the villagers might think — "

"No, not that he — "

"It could be that they'll blame Dovid."

"Oh God!"

"And for that reason, it's very important for him to stay out of sight for a few days, do you see? Away from Zavlivoya, certainly, and especially not anywhere to the south. Until the police can discover who — "

"Oh God, what will we do? Where's Shmerl? He's been away all afternoon! Why doesn't he come home at a time like this?"

"Where is he?"

"At the bathhouse, I suppose, or else at the *besmedresh*, I don't know where."

"Not the *besmedresh*, I was just there. I'll go to the bathhouse and tell Shmerl to come to you. With any luck, Dovid will be with him. All right?"

Reluctantly, Khana nodded.

"Now, I'd be happy to have Dovid come stay with me, if you think it would be a good idea ... only ..."

Khana bit her lip and clasped and unclasped her hands, thinking and panicking at the same time. "No," she finally shook her head. "What with you living so close to — but Reb Avrom, you mustn't think less of him, Dovid isn't himself lately, and — "

"That's of no importance right now. However, you're right of course ... All right, Khana, when he returns here, tell him to come to me, and I'll find another place to hide him. But meanwhile, if he's not at the bathhouse — can you think of any other place he might be?"

Tears sprang to Khana's eyes, and she shook her head. "He hasn't been himself, I don't know where he goes. He could be anywhere — but you'll keep him safe, Reb Avrom, won't you?"

"Of course I will."

~

"Well, Mykola," Nison Vainberg asked of the peasant slumped forward on the table, "did you get your fill of blintzes? Gapka tells me there's one more, just waiting to hop out of the pan and onto a plate — and from there, who knows where?"

The peasant raised his head, which was shaved except for a shock of blonde falling across the forehead. "I won't refuse another," he slurred. "But mind, bring me something to wash it down with."

"Naturally!" replied Nison.

He skipped into the kitchen to fix up a glass of the house specialty — cold vodka, with orange peel floating in it, just like they made it in Odessa — and bustled right back out, the vodka in one hand, and in the other, a plate upon which a plump cherry blintz lay sprawled out like an odalisque in a harem.

"Well, Mykola — " Nison began. However, Mykola was asleep again.

"That's all right," said Nison in a quiet voice. "Let him rest. So as not to let this little treasure go to waste, though ..." He picked up the fork that lay side by side with the blintz, smacking his lips in anticipation.

Nison looked the blintz in the eye, suspending his fork in the air, as Abraham must have suspended his knife when preparing to sacrifice his son Isaac. He smiled down — and could have sworn that the blintz smiled back. Then he put down the fork, took a swig of vodka, and let out a long, contented sigh.

Life, it turned out, was — *borukh hashem* — a fine thing indeed: rolling in blessings, the same way the golden, fragrant delight he was shortly to offer in sacrifice was rolling in juicy red cherries. For example: you could spend two hours at *shul* in the morning, praying to your heart's content. And you could still arrive in time to open up your tavern, before anyone had yet finished their business at market. And then, even if Yudel Beck did have the biggest tavern in town, at least one day a week, your place could do the better trade, on account of its being just around the corner from the market square. And after such a day of trade, even subtracting the eleven twelfths of the profit due to Count Bestuzhev, you still had more than enough to welcome the upcoming Sabbath in style. All without getting your hands dirty the way Yudel Beck did, with those various filthy "sidelines" of his that made Nison blush just thinking about them.

Also: if you were lucky enough to strike up an acquaintance with the peasant who sold you your grain, *and* if you invited him for a visit on Monday nights before market, *and* if you let him leave his wagon in your yard during market, instead of in the middle of that dung pile where the other peasants parked ... then he might surprise you now and then with a present: for example, a whole bushel of fresh-picked cherries, which your Gapka could then make into a nice, cold summer soup to attract the hot market-goers.

And there would even be enough left over for blintzes — which, among all the fine things, were the finest of all.

~

The fork was halfway to his lips again when the tavern door flew open. Well, another customer, praise God — but at a most inopportune moment.

The visitor was lit up from behind by the afternoon sun. But his outline was familiar.

"Reb Avrom the barber is it?" Nison came over to greet him. "Yet another blessing. What brings you here? A drink?"

"No, thank you," the barber replied. "I come on business, of a kind. I've just been to Yudel Beck's — I don't suppose he came by the other day to give you a warning?"

"A warning? Why, that *balaveranik*, if he thinks he has the right, just because we're both — " Nison fell silent as the visitor held up a hand.

"All right," said Reb Avrom, "I see he didn't come, even though I asked him to ... but there's no point in troubling you with that. The point is, Reb Nison — I don't suppose you've heard about what Father Innokenty has been saying lately?" There was something ominous in the barber's tone. "The father has been reminding the good folk around here of the hatred they ought to bear for us. And especially, for the tavern-keepers."

"The tavern-keepers?" Nison sputtered. "What's wrong with us? That is — of course, with Yudel Beck it's obvious, with the *mieskait* he gets into. But the rest of us? All we're doing is trying to ..."

The visitor shrugged. "You must have heard, in your line of

work, that there are those who consider drink to be a corrupting influence on the peasants. And therefore, they blame the peasants' plight on those who supply them drink." The barber cast an eye behind Nison into the room, and raised an eyebrow as if to ask, "Who is that?"

"My friend, Mykola," Nison whispered.

"Ah — a dependable type?"

"Certainly."

"Good. Now, Reb Nison, here's the worst part of the news. Today, a certain Styopa, who is more or less one of the villagers, down at the Efimovski village — "

"Ah, I know that *zhulik*, he comes in here from time to time. I wish I could throw his kind out, but of course ... I can't."

"You're in luck then. Styopa won't be coming around anymore."

"Oh? And why not?"

"Because he was found dead today — "

"Ah."

" — and as a result, they've burned down Shimmel Shenkman's tavern."

"*Oy, Got zol ophitn!* Was anyone — "

Reb Avrom held up both hands. "Luckily, no one was hurt."

"And ... are they in need of any aid? A place to sleep?"

The barber smiled sadly, and shook his head. "There are many good Jews in Zavlivoya ... and you are one of them. However," he said more briskly, "I think that the most important thing at the moment is for you to look after yourself and your family. That's the reason I've come — and also, to ask if you wouldn't mind spreading the word to anyone else who keeps a tavern in Zav."

"Of course, right away, God willing. There are four of us, not including Yudel Beck. But Reb Avrom, you've frightened me."

"I'm sorry."

"No, it's not that, I thank you for coming, of course. Only tell me, what can I do, to keep my family safe?"

The barber glanced around the room — it appeared as though he were looking for something in particular, but did not see it. Finally, he whispered, pointing at Mykola, "I'd try to keep him around for a bit, if you can."

"Ah ... keep — yes, a fine idea, that's a ... and, well ... anything else?"

"You are a man who prays, I think?"

"What? Oh ... yes ... well, then ..."

"Well, then ..."

"Thank you, Reb Avrom."

"Of course."

The barber — or should he, Nison wondered at that moment, think of him not as a barber but rather as a tsimbalist? Yes, now he remembered, that was the thing Reb Avrom was best known for in Zav. He was the tsimbalist.

And so ... the tsimbalist exited, closing the door behind him. And Nison returned to the table where his blintz still waited. He sat, lifted his fork, suspended it once again in the air. Now: how could he entice Mykola to stay a little longer?

He looked at his friend the peasant. At that moment, Mykola stirred, and raised his head once again.

Without pause, Nison pushed the plate forward on the table, and thrust the fork, handle first, in Mykola's direction.

"There you are, my friend," he said. "Eat up. Oh, and did I tell you? Gapka is planning to make blintzes again *tomorrow* — God willing."

⁓

The *besmedresh*. Khana Lipkin's house. The bathhouse. The *shul*. A few other houses where Dovid might be expected to

turn up. Yudel Beck's tavern. Nison Fainberg's tavern. And —
why not? — Deacon Achilles' house. It had been a full world tour
of searching and warnings. By the time he reached his own village, Avrom felt the weight of the day each time his feet struck
the ground.

He'd managed — he thought and hoped — to warn all the
tavern-keepers, all but one. And he'd urged Shmerl Lipkin to
join his wife at their home. But he hadn't found Dovid. And
there was still one more tavern-keeper unaccounted for. Therefore, two more places to go. Without stopping for even a moment at his own house, Avrom continued up the lake road.

The first destination was a matter of simple logic. If Dovid
wasn't at any of the places where he wasn't, he must be at the
place where he was. On the other hand, he couldn't actually be
inside, could he? No, out of the question — if for no other reason than the conversation Avrom had witnessed between Savely Savelievich and Oleg Olegovich this morning. It would be a
long while, and maybe an eternity, before Dovid would be welcomed *inside* the house at Bol'shaya Sosna.

Saveli Savelyevich's grounds, however, were extensive. And
heavily wooded. What if Dovid and Tatiana had a regular meeting place, somewhere on the estate? Yes, that seemed likely: a
spot that was easy for Tatiana to steal away to, but not so close
to the house, or so visible, that there was a grave danger of the
lovers being caught.

A memory came to Avrom from his days teaching music to
Tatiana. As you proceeded up the road that led to the house,
there was a sort of turnoff to the left ... more of a grassy path
than anything else, but certainly wide enough, and clear enough
of trees, to walk along. He didn't have any idea how far it went,
or where it led. But perhaps it was worth taking a look.

～

Upon arriving at the road to Bol'shaya Sosna, the tsimbalist began to proceed with greater caution. And when he came to the turnoff to the grass path, he went quiet as a rabbit. If the unlikely couple were indeed where he guessed they were, he didn't wish to announce his presence ahead of time, lest they run away. This time, he really did need to speak with Dovid.

The afternoon was growing long. Sunlight came obliquely through the the trees to Avrom's right. The grass on the path was colored a bright, springtime green.

After no more than twenty paces, the path turned towards the house. Now Avrom understood why he hadn't known before how far it went. Unless you came to this point, it looked as if the path dead-ended in the trees.

And then, after only twenty paces more, the trees parted, holding out their branches to welcome the tsimbalist into a wide clearing. A kind of bristling lawn of green and purple sparkled in the sunlight before him, made of tall grass and wildflowers. Along the clearing's edge, bushes grew, with great clusters of pink and white petals blossoming from their branches. In the midst of the lawn, two enormous flat rocks were lying side by side. They might have been expressly placed there, for the purposes of two lovers.

The entire scene so closely matched the trysting place of Avrom's imagination that, at that moment, it was impossible to imagine Tatiana and Dovid hadn't chosen it for their clandestine encounters.

And then he saw it, caught in the narrow space between the two, complementary rocks: a kerchief, sewn of silk, and dyed in pink and champagne. There were not so many ways a woman's kerchief could end up caught between two rocks. Tatiana and Dovid had certainly been here.

There was one problem, of course. They were not here now.

～

It was another six *versts* to the North Village. Avrom had only been here once, but he had no difficulty recognizing Gitl-Golda's tavern.

Fifteen heads turned as Avrom stepped inside. The place was full of peasants, spending the money they'd earned at the Zavlivoya market that morning, and in a merry mood.

"Reb Avrom," called out the tavern-keeper. It had been more than a year since the tsimbalist had seen her, but the vital and vigorous smile on her seventy-year-old face was exactly as it had been each time they'd met. "Welcome. Have you come to bring us music? No? No tsimbl hiding under your jacket? Well, too bad for us."

"No music this time," Avrom called out. He drew closer. "I hoped to have a private word with you, Gitl-Golda."

"All right, just a moment," the tavern-keeper bowed her head, then wiped her hands on her apron. "Is anyone," she said more loudly, "in need of anything at the moment?"

Five minutes later, Avrom was inside her house behind the inn, and Gitl-Golda was offering him refreshment.

"A little vodka? A glass of tea? What about a bowl of summer borscht? No? Come now, Reb Tsimbalist, you look, though I don't wish to insult you, more than a little bedraggled. How can we undraggle you?"

Avrom looked down at his clothes, which were dusty, as were his hands. "I suppose," he said, "that what I'd really like to do is wash."

"Fine," she said. "The well is just over there. But I'll get you a bowl of the borscht, too. Cold and red — you'll see, it'll clear your head."

She waited till he'd taken a spoonful of the soup before she agreed to talk about anything else.

"And now, what was it you wished to discuss?"

"Well ..." He proceeded to tell her what he'd told everyone else that afternoon: about the murder of Arkady Olegovich, which she'd heard about, of course. About Father Innokenty's words, which she hadn't.

"And today, they burned Shimmel Shenkman's tavern in the Efimovski village."

"*Oy, Got zol ophitn!*" cried the tavern-keeper. "How terrible! Was — "

"No one was hurt."

"Thanks to the Almighty for that, at least ... Well, I thank you for the news, Reb Avrom. But I'm sorry you traveled so far — surely, I would have heard soon enough. Now, eat the rest of your soup."

"Ah, but I haven't finished. You see, the villagers were set off by the murder of one of their own, a certain Styopa. But that was only the match that set fire to the straw, which had already been soaking in oil. The villagers have been in a ferment since Efimovski's body was found. So I thought that you, too, ought to be on the lookout for trouble. Perhaps, when your villagers hear of the fire, that will be their match."

"The villagers here? But why should I fear them? I've helped deliver half of them into life, and there isn't one who hasn't come to me for advice some time or other."

"Ah, is that so? Your tavern certainly does seem ... different from some of the others."

"A tavern is what its keeper makes it."

"I see ... still, though, I thought because Arkady Olegovich was so beloved in this village, came here so often — "

"What are you talking about, Reb Avrom?"

"I'm trying to say that the villagers here must be especially upset by his death, since — "

"I don't think the villagers here care one way or the other ... oh yes, I remember now, the young man did visit here once or twice, a few months ago. But not since. And when he did come, they all thought he was a fool ... he told them not to come to my place so often to drink, wanted to learn their dances, and I don't know what other *mishugas*. Beloved here? No, Reb Avrom, you've been misinformed."

Avrom didn't know what to say.

"Now, finish your — " Gitl-Golda began to say, but he held up a hand to silence her, and sat there, moving his lips, but not uttering a word, for several long minutes.

Finally, he spoke. "I've been misinformed — or else, someone else has been." He looked up. "Answer me a question, Gitl-Golda. You know Yudel Beck, don't you?"

"I do."

"Well ... Do you believe he might be capable of murder?"

Chapter 17

Houses

The tsimbalist was walking by Achilles' house next morning when the deacon hurried outside.

"Good morning, Avrom Moisevich."

"And a good morning to you, Akhilla Gerasimovich." Avrom looked up at the almost perfectly blue sky. Only a very few puffs of white floated here and there, one of them shaped just like a carp. "A fine day," he remarked.

"God be praised," mumbled Achilles, looking at Avrom with a diffident expression which also seemed to indicate some sense of expectation. It was plain that the deacon was unsure, after the events of the last few days, where the two of them stood with one another.

Avrom was not sure that he himself was any less unsure. For a few seconds he didn't say anything, then found himself stupidly replying to a question the deacon hadn't even asked: "Yes, I'm off to my appointments — a full morning ahead, you know."

"Ah." The deacon struggled to get a question out: "And after ... what about ... singing?" He said the last word with a gusto lacking in his usual speech.

However, it was certainly no day for singing, and Avrom said as much.

The way Achilles deflated made him look, despite his immense size, like a sad little boy. But he found the courage to try again. "And what about ... fishing?"

The tsimbalist sighed. "I would absolutely like to fish with you some time. But it's not a very good day for that either. However, I wish you a fine catch."

"Maybe Nikifor ... Kharitonovich then," sighed the deacon to himself.

"I'm afraid he's likely to have a busy day, too," Avrom said as gently as he could. "He has a murderer to catch."

"Ah ... yes."

"I'll say hello again later, Akhilla Gerasimovich. And we'll fish together soon."

—

Avrom was afraid of what Zavlivoya might hold in store this morning: smoke, fire, news about Dovid — and specifically, news that Dovid had been found, not by someone who wished to warn him of possible harm, but instead by those who wished to harm him.

Upon arrival, however, Avrom saw no sign that it was anything but a typical, sleepy Wednesday in the town, as sleepy as always on the day after market. He learned from a quick visit to the Lipkins that Dovid had spent the night away from home, that no one had visited the house for any reason the evening before, and that Dovid's parents were sunk into the deepest depths of worry. He was surprised, but pleased, that no one had visited the house. He was equally surprised, but not at all pleased, by what he found at his next stop.

"He's not at home," said Espérance, when she opened Nikifor Kharitonovich's door. "Didn't sleep a wink last night, he said, and went out immediately after the petty-governor left."

So the chief wasn't home. And Skorokhodov-Druganin had been to see him. Two pieces of bad news.

⁓

He dispensed easily with the usual round of Wednesday customers. Full of impatience, he did his snipping and shaving more quickly than habit decreed, and though he interrupted his route halfway through with a quick trip back to Nikifor Kharitonovich's rooms (the chief was still absent) he nonetheless arrived well ahead of time at Parfyon Panteleyevich's house on the edge of town.

Before the old rascal had time to launch into any of his stories, Avrom brought up the subject foremost on his mind: "Parfyon Panteleyevich ... it's a bit of a delicate question, but ... those places at the end of Post Office street — you visit them from time to time, don't you?"

"Er, that is ..." The old man blushed. (Avrom noticed that it made his skin match his dyed beard a bit better.) "...Yes. Indeed, undoubtedly, from time to time. As it says, 'even when Ivan grew long in the tooth, he kept his liking for the tastes of his youth.'"

"Indeed," said Avrom. "And so, I wonder if you ever happened to see, in your visits there, a girl by the name of Mirele: dark, slender, great big eyes with a good deal of black painted around them?"

"Why, yes ... I ... never met her personally, other than to exchange a word, so to speak, but — "

"Fine. In that case, I wonder also ... among the other gentlemen who you might have run into there — "

"Oh, I'm not one to tell tales, Avrom Moisevich. Come now, what about my shave? Let's get started."

"Yes, of course, Parfyon Panteleyevich ... I didn't mean to pry." Avrom began stropping his razor. "It's only that our police chief—you did know that he's one of my clients as well, didn't you? Of course you did. Well, he's been investigating these murders that are turning Zavlivoya upside-down, and—between you and me—he's entirely stumped."

"Is he?" asked the old pensioner, sitting forward in his chair.

"Alas, yes. Out of ideas, he says ... except that he seems to have had some notion ... yes, and so this very morning he asked me the question I was about to ask you. Of course, I would have liked to have been able to give him an answer—if only to have a story to tell the next time I visit Yudel Beck's tavern. Only, since I've never been to the establishment ..." Avrom let out a deep sigh.

"And what was the question, again?"

"Oh ... well, now that I think of it, it's probably of no importance."

"Oh, one can never be sure. Let's have it."

"You're sure? Well, Nikifor Kharitonovich wanted to know whether I'd ever seen Arkady Olegovich Efimovski visiting one of those establishments."

"Oh," the pensioner sat back in disappointment. "That's ... that's rather a pity."

"Then you never did either?"

"No ... I can't say I did."

"You're ... quite sure?"

"Quite ... however ... that does remind me of a story."

~

During the lull following the excitement at market yesterday morning, General Kondratin's injured valet had stopped by Avrom's rented shop again, to confirm that the tsimbalist would be able to come and trim his master's famous beard. As the general's estate was not far from the eastern edge of town, where Parfyon Panteleyevich's house stood, Avrom decided he might as well get the job out of the way now, before returning to look once more for the chief.

A half hour's walk through the woods brought him to the vicinity of the general's mansion. Its steel-grey dome was already peeking out above the trees like a Mongol warrior's helmet, when a horse came charging down the road, and then reared up. Atop it sat Nikifor Kharitonovich himself, his narrow eyes hot with rage.

"Dear God, Avrom Moisevich! Is there any place on God's green earth you're not ready to poke your nose into?"

Avrom opened his mouth, and then closed it again in genuine confusion.

Meanwhile, the chief laughed bitterly. "I see now it was a mistake to tell you I'd be returning to General Kondratin's. Thanks to that fire I couldn't come till this morning. And who do I see the moment I leave? Just waiting to ask your own questions behind my back, are you?"

Avrom strode straight over to where the chief sat on his horse. "I can imagine that it looks that way to you, Nikifor Kharitonovich, but the only reason I'm here is to trim General Kondratin's beard. His valet broke his arm, and came to ask me to do his duty for him."

"Ah ... well ..."

"The truth is, though, that I've been looking for you all morning. After yesterday, I'm particularly anxious to be entirely forthcoming with you. It so happens that once again, I think I may have been lucky enough to stumble on something of the greatest importance. But Nikifor Kharitonovich, are you feeling all right?"

He'd just noticed that the chief, who'd been looking somewhat purple yesterday, was nearly the shade of an eggplant today.

"It's nothing, I slept poorly and ... well, the truth is, Avrom Moisevich, this case, all these cases, the number of details ..."

"You have many things on your mind, and you can't relax."

"It's a matter of too much blood, that's all. I've always had an excess of blood at times like this. I don't suppose I could persuade you to apply the leeches?"

"I've told you my viewpoint on such things, Nikifor Kharitonovich. If you really insist on having your blood let, you'll have to go to one of the other barbers. But I don't recommend it."

"What about a tonic, then?"

"This isn't the sort of a case for which a tonic — "

"Well then what do you suggest?"

"A distraction of some kind — and as soon as possible. You must put yourself into a position in which the most natural thing is to think of something else. If you push your brain and body too far, it's inevitable they'll rebel."

"But *now*, Avrom Moisevich? I have a murderer to find. And those three merchants are hardly likely to turn up on their own."

"Of course, you have many burdens. But some knots, one does better not to pull — they only get tighter. In other words, if you let your mind do its work behind the scenes while the soul is at rest, it will perhaps come to a solution more quickly than if you had been thinking about the problem the whole time."

Nikifor Kharitonovich considered Avrom's words for a moment. Then he said: "Nonsense. Now ... what was it that you wanted to tell me?"

"Very well, suit yourself. As for my idea, it's a bit ... half-formed. I'm in need of your expertise to fill in a few holes, so to speak. Would you mind if I asked a question or two? Otherwise I fear what I say won't make any sense."

"You may ask a question or two, as long as one doesn't turn to ten, and two to a hundred."

"With a strong hand and an outstretched arm," Avrom laughed to himself.

"What's that?"

"Nothing, nothing."

"Your questions, then?"

"Yes ... first of all ... pardon me: who, Nikifor Kharitonovich, is in charge of the prostitution in Zavlivoya? That is, who owns, or runs, those ... houses."

"You believe this question has something to do with Arkady Olegovich's death? And Styopa's?"

"Yes, I do."

"All right. In that case: there are two whorehouses, rivals of a sort, though they cater to somewhat different clienteles. One is run by Yudel Beck, or by his employees at least — he has a few Ukrainians working for him."

"Exactly as I suspected."

"And the other is run by a lady named Fruma."

"What? Not the Fruma who's married to Khaim Natan who — ?"

"I wouldn't know. The lady lives on the Pryluky Road."

"My God! It just goes to show that you should never be surprised by anything. Her husband is the *parnas* of the *khevra kadisha*!"

"The what?"

"The head of the burial society. A very respectable position."

"I see. That's proof then."

"Of what?"

"We Russians and you Jews are not so different, after all."

"No indeed ... now Nikifor Kharitonovich, tell me: all of these ... young ladies are officially registered, are they not?"

"Yes, indeed."

"And so everything is on the up and up?"

"Oh, Beck and this Fruma pay their bribes, the same as anywhere — to the health commissioner and ... others. But let's get to it now: what was it you wanted to tell me about?"

"Nikifor Kharitonovich, I don't suppose you would consider dismounting. My neck ..."

Slipping from his horse, the chief pointed to a low stone wall separating General Kondratin's grounds from the road. "There. We'll sit."

"I do have one more question," said Avrom when they were seated.

"How fortunate. That is exactly the remaining number I'll agree to answer."

"The question is this: did Styopa, to your knowledge, ever do work for Yudel Beck?"

"Alas, I don't know the answer. It's not unlikely, I suppose. But now, Avrom Moisevich — "

"Yes, all right. Let me begin by telling you that I knew — or, I should say, I *know*, though I have a terrible feeling that *knew* is the more accurate ... no, I *know* a girl named Mirele, who seems to have become one of Yudel Beck's ... employees. I don't know for how long."

"Hmm."

"Do you know of her?"

"I don't keep a close watch on those places."

"I see ... I also, I'm afraid, don't keep a watch on Mirele. But I saw her on Sunday morning. A few minutes later, however, she was gone, and she seems to have entirely disappeared ever since. The workers and regulars at Beck's tavern would barely admit to knowing her, and then Kuz'ma told me that there was a sort of "recruiter" in town, and Beck sold Mirele to him. In other words, it's because of him that she's quite suddenly disappeared! Supposedly, she left town, but now I'm afraid of what may have happened once they left."

"All right," replied Nikifor Kharitonovich. "And what else?"

"Oh ... well, ah ... turning to Arkady Olegovich, then: everyone has been under the impression that he spent all his time riding out to peasant villages, but I've just learned that he almost never visited the North Village. I can't say what the truth is as far as the other villages go. But, speaking of the North Village, where was he all those times when he was supposed to have been going there? And a second question: why would a nobleman like him take such a very friendly attitude toward my people? It is not, as I'm sure you know, quite the usual thing."

"And so you asked yourself these questions, and the answer came to you: a nobleman might naturally take this attitude and tell false tales about where he's spent his time, if he had fallen in love with a Jewess."

"Yes," said Avrom, stunned. "How did you guess?"

"Logic."

"And in fact, such things happen more than you might think, in the most unlikely ways. I could give you other examples, right here in Zavlivoya."

"That won't be necessary. And so then, I suppose, the next step is to assume that a man in Yudel Beck's position has some very nasty secrets, that a girl working for him has a good chance of having stumbled across them, and that, if she had a lover, she'd be likely to tell him about them. It might then happen that the lover, for some reason, threatens to expose Beck. Or maybe Beck just assumes that the girl has told her lover, and that it's better to silence him. Is that the idea?"

"Nikifor Kharitonovich ... that's it exactly. You've read my mind. And I would add that, prior to yesterday, it seemed that Arkady Olegovich's murder was connected to the thefts. Well, why should it not, instead, be connected to another unusual and suspicious occurrence — Mirele's disappearance? As for Styopa, perhaps it was he who murdered Arkady Olegovich, and then, after Mirele was made to disappear, they did away with him, too."

Nikifor Kharitonovich extracted a half-smoked cigar from his pocket, lit it, took a puff, and then said, "Well done, Avrom Moisevich. I congratulate you."

"Thank you."

"But I'm sorry to say, I don't like it."

"You don't?"

"No."

"Oh."

"I apologize."

"And what is it about it that you dislike?"

～

"To begin with," said Nikifor Kharitonovich, "it is entirely possible that Yudel Beck has some nasty secrets. It is also possible that he would kill over them. And it is possible that Arkady Olegovich fell in love with this girl ..."

"Mirele."

"Yes. As I say, it's all possible. But personally, for whatever reason ... none of it feels right to me. Also, I can hear in your voice when you say her name, you are very concerned about this girl — Mirele, is it? That fact alone could be enough to corrupt your logic, and make you see things that aren't there. In fact, what reason is there to believe she isn't simply being transported to Vienna, Prague, or if you like, Constantinople. But more importantly, there are too many things your theory doesn't take account of — beginning with and especially, the fact that the whole course of events commences with Arkady Olegovich's trip to Chernigov."

"Ah."

"And the other fact that, thenceforward, he disappeared from view. In fact, as my trip here this morning has proved useless, I've decided that the next thing I must do is to travel to Chernigov myself."

"Oh?"

"Yes, for several reasons. Arkady Olegovich didn't spend the night at any of the inns there in Chernigov. But there are plenty of inns in the villages nearby. And I'm not convinced that Ukhovyortov was entirely ... zealous, shall we say, in exhausting every investigative possibility when he visited the telegraph office there. Or the shops selling antiques, either."

"So you will go to try again."

"Yes. And while I am away, Avrom Moisevich, I hope you will not pursue this theory of yours."

"There would be little I could do without you here. I am quite a powerless individual: I believe the exact term is 'lowly Jew.' Even if I discovered exactly who the murderer was, and why he did it, I couldn't do a thing."

The chief put out his cigar underfoot.

"You misunderstand. I am quite aware that you cannot arrest anyone. But things have arrived at quite a delicate balance here in Zavlivoya. You could still stir up trouble, muck up the works. What we need now, however, is not chaos but order. No more murders, no more fires. Avrom Moisevich — no, don't protest. What you must get into your head is that society is a kind of machine, made up of many interlocking parts — like a locomotive, for example. And for the whole to work properly, each part must stick to the function it was designed for — otherwise, chaos is introduced, and we might run right off the rails. I am a policeman. It is my function to investigate crimes, and apprehend criminals. You are a fine barber, and they say you play music well — I have no ear for it myself, but it's what everyone says, so it must be true. Bravo — you excel at two functions. Now, when it comes to untangling knots and turning up secrets, I won't deny that you're clever, and have fine instincts. And I let you ask me questions just now, and tell me your theory, because I could see you felt bad about what happened yesterday. But from now on, Avrom Moisevich, I must insist that you limit yourself to your proper function."

"But if — "

"No, no. You are far too convincing a talker for me to let

you get past that first "if." From now on, when you try to bring any of these questions up, I shall simply close my ears, and go *la la la.*"

Avrom stared at the chief, quite shocked. "May I at least, solely out of concern, ask what you found when you went to the Efimovski village last night?"

"Certainly you can, *that* is an entirely reasonable question. I found that the fire had already been put out. But the tavern is hopeless. I arrested the instigator — he's a cousin of Styopa, the one you mentioned, Andryushechka. And I believe I frightened the other villagers enough to keep them from doing any more damage."

"I worry that they might try to harm Dovid, since he just fought with Styopa the other day. They might think that — "

"Speaking of that — this I *will* share with you. Skorokhodov-Druganin came to see me about Dovid this morning." Nikifor Kharitonovich turned a still darker shade of aubergine. "He is another who doesn't understand how the machine ought to work ... He wants me to arrest your young friend."

"For what?"

"The murders of Styopa and Arkady Olegovich, of course."

"I thought he believed it was Koppel who murdered Arkady Olegovich."

"I believe I've mentioned the malleability of our petty-governor's opinions. In any case, I told him that if I saw Dovid anywhere in Zavlivoya, I would do as he asked."

"I see," said Avrom, his mood growing worse and worse.

"Yes. *If* I see him, *anywhere in Zavlivoya,* I will arrest him. However, I'm confident that he has friends who are intelligent enough to advise him to keep *away* from Zav."

"Ah," said Avrom, catching on. "Yes, I imagine that he does. The only problem is that no one seems to be able to find Dovid."

"Is that so? Well, if no one has found him yet, you must hope that things continue that way ... You see, Avrom Moisevich, I'm not so heartless, am I? I simply wish to keep the order, for the sake of everyone."

"I understand," said the tsimbalist, not very expressively.

A noise in the trees nearby made Nikifor Kharitonovich look away for a moment. Then he grinned, baring his teeth.

"You'll see, Avrom Moisevich. When you think it over, you'll see I'm right. Ah, but before I go to Chernigov ... I *will* need a shave and a wax."

"Of course," Avrom inclined his head. "I am always happy to perform my *proper function*. I'll come the moment I've finished at General Kondratin's."

It took Avrom only a few, irritated steps to arrive at the avenue leading to General Kondratin's house. The house was not, in its outlines, unlike the Efimovski mansion a short way down the road. The rotunda's dome was steel-grey instead of sea-green, the façade ochre rather than yellow. The outbuildings were connected to the main house by two long arcades, the avenue paved with gravel, without any trees shading it, and the lawn more verdant, with little yellow flowers popping their heads up here and there. On the whole, however, the house was of similar vintage to the Efimovskis', and promised the same sort of inhabitants.

Avrom was halfway between the road and the house when the general himself appeared, accompanied by his wounded valet, who carried a hunting rifle in his good hand. Avrom saw the valet point, and the general changed course, walking toward him.

"You're the barber," the general barked when they were close enough to speak.

"Yes, your excellency."

"You believe you can replicate the way my idiot valet trims me?"

Avrom glanced at the valet, who flushed a deep red. "I will do my best, your excellency."

"You should have come earlier," the general looked him up and down. It was difficult to tell what he thought of what he saw.

"I apologize, your excellency. Many clients rely on me Wednesday mornings."

"Clients? Are you a lawyer, then? I believe they're allowing you Jews to become lawyers now. Colossal mistake. The result is that you have a barber thinking he has clients."

Avrom did not reply.

The general glared at him, then announced, "I'm going hunting now. You'll wait for me out here."

"Unfortunately, your excellency," said Avrom, "I am not able to wait. The police chief, who I just saw, has ordered me to come and shave him within the hour."

"Did he? Intent on ruining my entire day, is he? And I'm to be at a Jew's beck and call?"

"Perhaps if I came back another time — "

"No, you'll trim me now."

"Very good, your excel — "

"Hup to, then, hup to. No point in wasting any more time gabbing out here. Zhilin, you numbskull, the door! And then run and get me my chamberpot. You know that getting a trim always gives me the waters something fierce. Now, hup to!"

Chapter 18

The Fate of a Bride

The house's interior was surprisingly dingy, despite showing signs that it had once been quite grand. The paper on the walls was stained and peeling, the silks and velvets on the furniture ripped and faded. It was, Avrom realized, a singularly masculine domain. Now that he thought of it, there wasn't any garden outside. In fact, he couldn't remember ever having heard that the general had a wife.

Zhilin led him through the entry-way, down a corridor, and past several rooms, to a porch at the house's rear where, the valet explained, the general preferred to have his beard trimmed. The general himself seemed to have disappeared somewhere along the way. And nearly as soon as they'd reached the porch, Avrom found that, while he had his back turned to gaze out over the woods (in the direction, he thought, of the Hermit's Cave), Zhilin had slipped away, too.

But soon enough, Kondratin reappeared. The reason for his disappearance was explained by the housecoat he now wore in place of his hunting outfit. Depositing himself in a redwood rocking chair, the general began the appointment with an admonition: "Mind you don't get any clippings on the coat."

Avrom looked around for something with which to catch the cut hairs. "Is there a ..."

"Your *hand*, Jew," Kondratin said in an exasperated tone, holding up his own cupped hand by way of illustration.

Once the trimming proper began, however, for several minutes at least, the general remained silent — an ideal condition in Avrom's opinion, not least because it would enable him to finish his work as soon as possible, and leave. Kondratin limited himself to a few exasperated sighs and irritable snorts to express whatever inner torment he was feeling — at first. But Avrom was certain the general's restraint couldn't last indefinitely. And he was quite right. Before long, Kondratin burst out with the first of what Avrom was sure would be many complaints.

"The nerve of that Nikifor Kharitonovich," the general growled. "Nosing all over my property without permission. I'm of half a mind to have that cave sealed up, only he'd just as likely dig his way in, the prying, arrogant ..."

He glared at Avrom, who took a few seconds to understand that this was his cue to say something, which he then did: "Indeed."

Apparently, this was the proper response. At least, the general immediately went on: "And for what? Because somebody rid the world of a ne'er-do-well miscreant, and before that, a noble who would betray his own. When they find the one who did it, instead of putting him in a cell, they ought to give him a medallion."

Here, he glared at Avrom again, who began to understand just what it meant to fill in for the general's valet — and also, why Zhilin had so quickly made himself scarce. More promptly this time, the tsimbalist said: "Indeed."

"The very idea of it!" the general went on at once. "Giving away all that money to his filthy little serfs — pardon me, *villagers*. We had a few soft hearts like that in the regiment, until we whipped it out of them. No clippings on the coat, I said!"

"Pardon me."

"Oh yes, we whipped it out of them. And someone ought to have whipped it out of Arkady Olegovich a bit sooner, before he had time to give all that money away. Now what is his mother to live on?"

"Indeed."

"Though it's entirely her fault the whelp turned out as badly as he did. And it serves her right, too. Agrafena Ivanovna was well aware that I was ready to take the orchards and village off of her hands, for a perfectly reasonable sum, perfectly reasonable. Instead of which, she gave them to her sons. And just look where they all are now!"

"Indeed ... but," Avrom ventured, while making a careful snip on the right side of the general's beard, "what about the other brother?"

Kondratin started, evidently amazed that a barber might say something other than "Indeed."

"You think you know something about anything, do you?" he barked. "The brother's hardly better. Oh, once upon a time it seemed as if he had proper pride, but that was before that filthy merchant's daughter came into the picture. Revolting as her father and *his* airs — and she'll pull Oleg Olegovich down into the gutter with her."

"Indeed ..." Avrom made a careful snip on the left. "But I meant, what about the brother's money? Can't he still support his mother?"

"Why, of all the uppity, presumptuous ... as if you Jews had any right to hold an opinion concerning those who are your betters. Not only that, you're living proof of the old saying: whatever a fool does, he'll do it wrong."

Avrom failed, this time, to say "Indeed," but the general went right on.

"Here's all you know. Oleg Olegovich is up to his eyeballs in gambling debts. *I* play *préférence* with his lawyer every

Thursday, so I know all about it. He may be all right for now,
but once his creditors hear that he's received half his mother's
estate, they'll swarm to him the way you Jews do to a kopek.
Why else would he want to marry that slut of a merchant's
daughter? I have it from his lawyer that Arkady Olegovich demanded a king's ransom for the dowry from Saveli Savelyevich." The general chortled. "I'll bet he'd like to get a hold of his
brother's murderer now, but not out of brotherly love. I'll bet
he'd just like to wring the rascal's neck. About to get his hands
on all that money from the dowry, and now he has to wait till
the period of mourning's over, hee hee."

Kondratin laughed so hard that he had to blow his nose
and wipe his eyes, then said, "Hold on a minute, I have to piss."

"It's all right," said Avrom. "I've already finished."

"Oh you have, have you? Hand me my pince-nez then, and
that mirror. Let's have a look. Well ... I don't suppose you did
any worse than that lunkheaded valet of mine. Go find him,
and he'll give you your kopek."

"Thank you, your excellency," said Avrom, marveling at his
own strength of character. Despite his most fervent urges to do
otherwise, he'd made both sides perfectly even.

～

"Reb Avrom!" He'd barely regained the road when he heard the
whisper.

Turning, he squinted into the trees at the side of the road,
then whispered back: "Who's there?"

In answer, a nose emerged from the leaves. It was soon followed by a pair of coal-black eyes.

"Reb Avrom," came the whisper again, "is it safe to come
out?"

The tsimbalist stared. "Dovid? Dovid! But what are you
doing here, of all places?"

"Is Nikifor Kharitonovich still there? I saw you with him before. What were you talking about? Was he looking for me?"

"He's gone, Dovid, there's no one around. But why are you here?"

"I was hiding in Hermit's Cave," the young man emerged in a bound from the trees, with twigs and leaves stuck in his hair, and his clothes filthy. "I heard about that Styopa, that he was killed. I couldn't think of a better place — "

"And I can't think of a worse place! I'm surprised you didn't remain up at — " The tsimbalist had been about to say, "up at Tatiana's place," but thought better of it. "In any case, they may search the cave again at any time. And we're little more than two *versts* from the Efimovski village!"

"Yes indeed, that's where I thought to go next, if you could help me get there safely. The villagers will hide me. But tell me, Reb Avrom, have you seen my mother? I'm worried about her."

"Your mother is all right, the only thing you have to worry about with her is that she's worried about you."

"And how is Koppel's condition?"

"Koppel? You ask about him?"

"Of course, his burn."

"Well ... as far as his *burn* goes, he's improving. But I take it back. Hermit's Cave is *not* the worst place I can think of for you to hide. What are you thinking of, Dovid? Styopa was from the Efimovski village. Everyone there must be one of his friends or relations."

"No, Reb Avrom, you don't understand. Arkady Olegovich was beloved in that village."

"And so?"

"Isn't it obvious? I was his friend. They'll take me in for his sake."

"Dovid, do you know that those villagers have burned down Shimmel Shenkman's tavern?"

"What?"

"And they came and almost burned down Koppel's place, too."

"What — what do you mean?"

"Yes, they failed only thanks to Deacon Achilles."

"Is Blume — did they — "

"Everyone is fine. Though not," Avrom gave Dovid a stern look, "in the best of spirits."

"Who was it?" Dovid clenched his fists.

"As I said, the peasants from the Efimovski village. Quite a number — "

"When?"

"The night before last."

"If I had been there — "

"But you weren't there, Dovid. You were most definitely somewhere else."

"I — "

"However, we mustn't squabble here, out in the open. Come, walk behind me — and *away* from the village. If you hear anyone coming, duck back into the woods. Now," Avrom mumbled, "let's think. Hide you with the deacon? ... no, it's too far. We'd have to go through town to get there ... farmer Kolbov is nearby ... if only I knew him better. I don't know that he would be ... in fact, he might be just as likely to ... ah but — "

He whirled round quite suddenly. "I've got it, Dovid, just the place — Dovid?"

No reply came, nor did the young man so much as meet his eye. He seemed, in fact, entirely lost in his own world, staring toward something, or somewhere, quite far away. Undoubtedly, that spot a few *versts* north of Balativke where Tatiana resided.

But then a second later Dovid lowered his eyes and opened his mouth. "Reb Avrom ... I think I'm in need of your advice. I've gotten myself into a sort of ... into a difficulty. That is to say ... Oh, Reb Avrom. Everything is completely impossible."

~

"Well ... at last," Avrom exhaled, becoming aware as he did that he'd been holding his breath since Dovid had appeared.

"Oh ..." Dovid's voice trembled. "Then, you've been expecting it? I suppose you think I'm a fool."

"I haven't known what to think, Dovid, other than that you've been doing Blume a very bad turn, keeping her in the dark. Of course, you may do with your own life whatever you wish ... But Dovid, what I can't understand at all is how you ever arrived at this point? How did it begin?"

"Oh ... That's difficult to say, Reb Avrom. It all took me by surprise, I had no intention ... I *planned* to marry Blume, until these other passions led me — I can't even describe to you the fierce struggle that's been raging between my heart and my mind! Or rather, it's that my heart has been at war with *itself*. Tell me, how is anyone to decide what among the many things dear to our hearts is the most important one? Which is the voice to which we ought to open our ears?"

"Your heart has certainly led you to some surprising places, Dovid. Far, far from Balativke, I should say, even if the distance in *versts* is not so great."

"Yes I see what you mean — quite far indeed! Because it all began when I first heard about the pogroms in Odessa. A wind from afar, so to say. Of course you know all about what happened in Odessa, the newspapers were full of it at the time. But I heard the worst from my friend Peretz, who was right there when it happened, in the city itself. Peretz said there was always trouble there, every year during Holy Week, between the Greeks and Jews. But what was different this time was that the Russians joined in ... The first he noticed things were bad was when a stone flew through the window where he was staying, at his aunt's. Then, he said, before you knew it, they were burning down everything in sight, in every street where Jews lived. He saw them murder a *bride* in her wedding gown ... with a knife ... A bride! And what happened, Reb Avrom? Not much, not to the ones who committed those crimes."

"No," Avrom sighed, "I don't suppose so ... Still, I can't quite see what that has to do with — "

"It's that for such a long time after, I couldn't stop thinking about that. The horror of it, the injustice — but especially, the fact that it had happened so easily. If it happened that easily once, I thought, why not again? And I wondered: what if the riot in Odessa, where at least they mostly limited themselves to looting and burning, and killed only six Jews — *only!* — what if that was just a foretaste, a preamble to a real massacre? What if another Chmielnitzki was — *is!* — just about to appear over the dark horizon? There wasn't — that is, there *isn't* anything at all to prevent such a massacre from taking place. It was when that became clear to me that I came to understand a few things in a new way ..."

"Yes?"

"Yes. The fact is, Reb Avrom, we Jews have sunk very low in Russia today. We've lost our self-respect as a people. Tell me, how long is it that we've been perfectly content to be treated as an inferior class, hiding in the study house, cringing before the nobles?"

Avrom didn't reply.

"The truth is that instead of demanding to be treated like human beings, we've learned to be overjoyed when we're merely tolerated — and ecstatic when, on occasion, the odd Russian deigns to befriend us. The real tragedy of it isn't the woe inflicted on us by our enemies. The real tragedy is that we invite such treatment, with our own inner weakness ... After a while, that weakness began to make me sick."

"Until, at a certain point, you had the idea that it might be better to become a Christian?"

Dovid gaped at him. "No, Reb Avrom, why in the world would you say that? What — no! It was just that … I talked it over many times with Arkady Olegovich, and we agreed. We've arrived at a watershed moment in history. Our — that is, *my* generation, since Arkady Olegovich is gone … we've been given a historic burden — but also an opportunity! It's up to all of us to take bold action, and that includes us Jews … the way Arkady Olegovich took bold action when he gave away his fortune to the peasants. It was his way of saying, look, we're all the same, aren't we, you and I and everyone?"

"And you, too, wish to erase distinctions? To say that the Jew and the Russian are no different? But Dovid, isn't this an exaggerated way of going about it, bringing marriage into the question?"

"I didn't intend to bring marriage into it, Reb Avrom! But anyway, half-measures will never do in a fight of this magnitude, a historical struggle of such significance. We must all work together and do our utmost. Think of our strength if we all unite! Just imagine, everyone, all whom life has trampled, all the worn-out women and starving children, all the alcoholics, the dying villages, and the cities' horrible poverty and diseases — all will disappear into one jubilant chorus of unknown, unprecedented, universal and boundless happiness! This is what Arkady Olegovich showed me."

"I see."

"Perhaps I've already told you about his ideas, but you can't imagine how convincing he was when he talked about them … it was simply impossible not to listen to him. It was impossible to want to do anything besides listen to him! And to take his ideas as your own, too. He made quite a few disciples out of us young folk hereabouts. He said to me, 'Dovid, the point isn't to defend yourself against the Jew-haters. The point is to take your two hands and make our Russia a place where there aren't any Jew-haters anymore.' 'And how do you do that?' I asked him.

'It's not as difficult as you might think,' he said. 'Tell me, what's the source of all strife? Money. What's wrong with money? Easy — too few people have too much of it. Well, now's the time to raise up the downtrodden. Wake up the peasants. And in the cities, wake up the workers. The tsar doesn't need so much, neither do I, and neither does your Mr. Brodsky the sugar magnate. Once they're awake, and everyone has their fair share, there won't be any of this strife between the Little Russian and the Great Russian, the Russian and the Tatar, the peasant and the gypsy and the Jew.' But he didn't just talk about it. I probably told you, Reb Avrom, that he went around to all the peasant villages. I asked him to take me with him, but he laughed and said they needed waking up first, before they'd like the sight of me."

"Indeed."

"But then — it was only two weeks ago — the two of us traveled to Chernigov, and I met some of his circle there — there were even Jews amongst them, Reb Avrom. And how lucky it was that I went, with him gone now. It's up to me to continue his work. But then I got into that fight with Styopa. There, I'm a bit confused. Because while there are still Styopas, don't we need to fight against them?"

"I don't know, Dovid. But — "

"In any case, on the way back from Chernigov, he finally did take me with him to a village, the one near here on General Kondratin's estate. Only, as luck would have it, the general himself arrived, not long after we did, and he pointed his rifle at Arkady Olegovich and warned him not to stir up his peasants, so we had to leave."

"General Kondratin pointed his rifle at Arkady Olegovich?"

"I saw it with my own eyes."

"Well, well. And why has no one heard about this? Only two weeks ago? I'm certain that Nikifor Kharitonovich doesn't know about it."

"Then you can tell him. But I mention it because maybe I could go hide with — "

"Hold, Dovid. Perhaps my head is so cluttered now that I can't understand anything, but pardon me: what does any of this have to do with Tatiana?"

"Who?"

"What do you mean, who? Tatiana."

"The ... merchant's daughter?"

"The girl you're in love with, you golem."

"The girl I'm in love with? Reb Avrom, the girl I'm in love with is Blume."

~

Avrom had been speechless before. But he'd never been quite so speechless as he was right now.

Dovid had something to say, though, or rather, to incredulously ask: "Reb Avrom, you thought I was in love with Tatiana, the merchant's daughter?"

Avrom tried to say yes, but could only nod.

"But why? Everyone knows I love Blume."

This time, Avrom could only shrug.

"So ... but ... Does this mean that you thought I was in love with Tatiana? And that I wanted your advice about *that*?"

Avrom nodded.

"Which means that you thought I *didn't* love *Blume* ... which means that you thought I was avoiding her because I didn't love her ... Reb Avrom — does she think that, too?"

Avrom nodded.

"Incredible! And yet ... In fact, maybe it's easier this way. Yes, I was confused when she came to see me after I was released from jail ... but isn't this, in fact, what I was already trying to accomplish? If she doesn't believe I love her, she won't wait around, she'll suffer a little now, instead of — "

"I'm afraid," the tsimbalist interrupted, "that there's no question of her suffering only a little."

"No?"

"No." Avrom looked at the young man with narrowed eyes. His own gesture put him in mind of Nikifor Kharitonovich — which ought to have made him laugh, only it didn't. "But Dovid, in that case, what was it you wanted my advice for?"

"About Blume. Because Nikifor Kharitonovich released me from jail."

"What do you mean? What does that have to do with Blume?"

"Isn't it obvious? You disappoint me, Reb Avrom. Tell me, why should the chief of police do such a thing? It doesn't make any sense at all. I did fight with Styopa. I was guilty of an offense. My release doesn't make any sense, unless we are able to perceive the great forces which are always at work behind the smallest events. Don't you see?"

"I'm afraid I don't."

"It's obvious that Nikifor Kharitonovich only released me because he was ordered to by the Third Section. They want to spy on me. Or have him spy on me. And through me, to find others who think as I do. Oh, mind you, Kharitonovich already tried to get information from me in the jail. But of course I said nothing. And so when he saw he wouldn't get anything from me, and when he told them, then they told *him* to release me. 'Make him think he's free,' they must have said. 'If he believes himself free, he'll be careless, and so lead us whither we desire.'"

"I see. This is what you think."

"No, Reb Avrom, this is what I know. And now, of course, you understand everything."

"I'm afraid I don't. You'll have to explain the rest."

"Reb Avrom, really. Wasn't it right by your house that Arkady Olegovich was found?"

"Of course."

"Ah, but he wasn't supposed to be found, was he? He was

supposed to vanish. It was only because Masha got into the water that we learned of his death. How long would he have remained there, undiscovered, if not for that?"

"A long time."

"Yes. He would have truly vanished. In a way, it's a sign of victory, a sign that we have already begun to win. The tsar fears men like Arkady Olegovich. No longer is it enough to send them into exile, from where their voices may still be loudly heard. Or to execute them, in which case they may become martyrs and inspirations. A dead man is powerful, and so is a living one, but the one whose existence lies somewhere in-between ... And this is why Arkady Olegovich was made to vanish."

"Hmm ... perhaps so. Only, Dovid, I don't believe it was the Third Section that killed Arkady Olegovich."

"Reb Avrom! I had no idea you were so naïve. No, believe me, what I say is an exact description of the truth. And that is why I have been at my wit's end. What if I am made to disappear, too?"

"For what? What have you done?"

"Those in power make no distinction between act and intent. And I have intended things — I still do. So that the moment they came and told me that I was to be released, I knew what they must have in mind. And my next thought was a terrible one: what will become of Blume?"

"Ah, now I begin to see."

"Yes. You have a neighbor, Reb Avrom, Rivke the *aguneh*. Blume has told me all about that unhappy woman — so unhappy that she can't even bear to be around happy people. For the rest of her life, thanks to our fine marriage laws, she'll live in a kind of prison of unhappiness, alone, unable to live in a way that could bring her any real satisfaction, unable to act in a way that would soothe her wounds. She's the subject of gossip, and malice, lies concocted by people more fortunate than her."

"Indeed."

"Now what do you think will happen if I marry Blume, and I'm made to disappear? If I died, she would only become a widow. But if I disappeared like Arkady Olegovich? Tell me, Reb Avrom, how can I marry Blume, and leave her to such a fate?"

"You believe you too will disappear."

"Of course."

"Because Arkady Olegovich did."

"Yes."

"And Blume will become an *aguneh*."

"*Would* become an *aguneh, if* we were to marry. So you see ..."

"I see. Yes Dovid, I see. Indeed, your logic is truly irreproachable."

"Of course."

"And this, this perfect chain of logic — this is why you've been hiding?"

"I hid to escape Nikifor Kharitonovich's notice. And to think what to do. The problem is ... Reb Avrom, the problem is that I want to marry her. I can't face telling her that we won't. I can't bear to say it myself."

Avrom sighed. Then he smiled.

"Indeed, it's quite a dilemma you've made for yourself. But Dovid, I believe there may be some hope for you. Of course I make no promises, but I have certain ideas ... what you told me about General Kondratin, or else my old idea that it was that tavern-keeper."

Dovid shook his head. "I don't know what you're talking about, but I'm afraid hope is too much to ask for. Things are hopeless — quite hopeless."

"Dovid, it's true that your release from jail was surprising. But it's my belief that Nikifor Kharitonovich doesn't like the Third Section any more than you do. Tell me: if we could finally discover Arkady Olegovich's murderer, and it was not who you thought it was — I don't know what dear Blume would do with such an excitable husband as you — but if we could prove these things, would it incline you to marry Blume?"

"I'm afraid that's idle speculation, Reb Avrom."

At that moment, the sound of hooves, and of a rickety wagon, came down the road from the direction of General Kondratin's estate.

"Quick, hide," said Avrom. Which Dovid, without any hesitation, did.

~

"Reb Avrom," said Dovid when the wagon had passed (it carried peasants from the Efimovski village, who gave Avrom a long look as they went by.) "Why in the world did you think I was in love with Tatiana, the merchant's daughter?"

"Ahem ... I'm a bit embarrassed to admit it ... the day you took a long walk through Balativke ..."

"Oh, yes, I saw you in your yard. I had been about to knock at Blume's door, to explain things, even though I still thought it might be best just to disappear. Only I didn't have the courage, and when I saw you ... But how did you know I walked all the way through the village?"

"Because I followed you."

"You did?"

"I'm afraid so, even as far as Bol'shaya Sosna."

"Is that what that place is called? I went in there because I didn't want to get any further from Balativke, that is, from home actually ... It would have been too far to go all the way around the lake, so I decided to wait until nightfall, and then sneak past Blume's house in the dark."

"So you didn't go up to the house, or meet Tatiana?"

"Of course not. I went along a bit, and then there was a sort of path, and then a clearing. There were rocks there, just made for lying on. So ... I just lay there for a long time, having it out with myself ... wondering if, purely out of selfishness, I should allow myself the happiness of marrying Blume."

"Well ... And so, you really snuck by while we were all in our beds?"

"No, you weren't in your beds. You almost ran into me when you came out of Koppel's house, and then it took me forever to get home, because Deacon Achilles came out too, and he was walking terribly slowly."

"Ah. I hadn't any idea."

"Oh, and while I was in that clearing, I came across something very odd."

"What was that?"

"There was a little metal box, sort of hidden among the wildflowers. I opened it up, and there was a note inside."

"A note?"

"In Russian. It looked like a girl wrote it — a woman I should say."

"Well? Tell me what it said. Can you remember?"

"I remember very well, even though I didn't understand a thing. I passed quite a bit of time looking at it. It said, 'I've had to come back up to write this, and if you're still not there when I return, I'll just have to leave it for you. The thing we've been fearing has come to pass. The time has come to do something. Please come to me soon!'

What do you think it means, Reb Avrom?"

~

"You took your time, Avrom Moisevich."

"I apologize."

"And you look all out of breath."

"It's nothing. But what has happened to *you*, Nikifor Kharitonovich?"

"To me? Nothing at all."

"I saw the petty-governor leaving just now."

"Well, yes ... He's quite persistent about your friend Dovid."

"But I can see that something else has happened too."

"In fact, yes ... Not much of a surprise, I suppose, but no less infuriating for that. I've had a little telegram from Irakli Tengizovich."

"The police chief in Pryluky?"

"Yes, indeed. Perhaps it will amuse you as much to hear about it, as it amused him to write it. He informs me that he has lost two roosters, which he simply can't locate, and wonders if I could keep an eye out for them here in Zav."

"Oh, no."

"It's intolerable! Roosters! I've become a laughingstock."

"It's my fault."

"If I could only lay hands on those three merchants."

"I'm certain you will, but — Nikifor Kharitonovich, meanwhile, have you looked in the mirror?"

"No, why?"

"Your skin is a most alarming shade."

"Too much blood, as I said."

"No, it's worse than that. I can see that you're on the verge of a collapse. The telegram must have been the last straw."

"Nonsense."

"Nikifor Kharitonovich, I see your face every day, and I've never seen it looking like this."

"It's that bad?"

"Haven't I just said so? You mustn't, under any circumstances, go to Chernigov."

"Not go to Chernigov? But I must."

"If you wish to expire on the road halfway there, then yes, you must."

"It's *that* ... all right, I can see from your face that it's that bad. But then, what must I do? What about letting a little blood?"

"Under no circumstances."

"A tonic then."

"I've told you, this is quite beyond the power of any tonic."

"Truly? Then what do you suggest?"

"You must do as I told you earlier. Find a distraction."

"You can't be serious."

"I'm quite serious."

"Well then ... what sort of distraction?"

"The sort that will restore your health in a matter of hours, and make someone else very happy: Go fishing with Deacon Achilles."

"Nonsense."

"Nikifor Kharitonovich, you rely upon me, don't you, to apprise you of the state of your health? Then listen when I say that you've pushed yourself too far, and do as I tell you. Both the deacon and the water will have a very calming influence. You'll be fixed right up. And then, you can set out for Chernigov, and still be there by evening."

"Preposterous. However, I'll think about it."

"No, you must do more than that."

"All right, then — really, Avrom Moisevich, I've never seen you so old-womanish. I'll go, I'll go."

"Will you swear it?"

～

"Moishe Shakhes, I need to borrow your wagon."

"What for?"

"Never mind what for, just lend it to me."

"When will you return it?"

"Later."

"Well, where are you going?"

"None of your business."

"Tell me, or I won't lend it to you."

"All right. I'm going to see someone who, lately, has been losing everything that they once held dear."

Chapter 19

A Return Visit

It was difficult to say just how the Efimovski mansion had changed in the days since Avrom's last visit. But there was no question that it had.

The changes in the *grounds* were not hard to spot. The bench near the avenue had lost its lanterns, though it still had its malva flowers. A dark, brown wound had opened in the earth amongst the scattered white gravestones, in contrast to which the family chapel managed to appear still more obsolescent than before. But why did the house itself look so different?

However, there was no time to find an answer to this frankly irrelevant question: almost instantly, purple malva, white chapel, brown earth disappeared from sight, Moishe Shakhes' wagon groaned past the last stripes of poplar shadow, Pasternak pulled to a stop in front of the mansion door, and then, the door itself opened. And Foka stepped through.

The old servant didn't notice Avrom's arrival at once. He shuffled outside, turned his back to the open door, and with effort, crimped himself into a deep bow. For a moment, Avrom thought Foka was bowing to him, in order to welcome him to the mansion. But of course, that wasn't the case. The next second, a man in official uniform followed the servant outside, a man with a most ill-favored countenance: the Collegiate Registrar, Pugovitsin.

Pointing his ugly face straight out and down, the bureaucrat studied the tsimbalist for three seconds, blinking three times as he did so. Then, as a kind of a greeting, he ducked his head and raised his narrow shoulder, before hurrying down the stairs and away, in the direction of the stables. Foka, meanwhile, failed to straighten up, remaining folded over while Avrom scurried up the steps and crossed the threshold — thus allowing the servant to get two bows out of one bend.

~

"What are *you* doing here?"

Avrom's eyes had not yet adjusted to the dim light in the entryway, but his ears recognized the voice of Madame Efimovskaya.

"A small matter ..." said his mouth.

"Of course — you want your pay. Foka, fetch Oleg Olegovich."

"*Cher maître*," said another voice, and then Aglaya Olegovna's outlines began to take shape. "How nice to see you again, and *merci* for yesterday. *Maman*, Avrom Moisevich was very kind to me when I had a little fit at market."

"Oh, there you are," replied her mother. "That dreadful *chinovnik* just came calling again. I'm sure he's working up his nerve to propose to you ... yet another suitor, and the worst yet. I fobbed him off on your brother as usual, and told him you weren't at home."

"*Maman*, quiet! There's no need to talk about that in front of *cher* — "

"Ah, Oleg Olegovich," Madame Efimovskaya interrupted. "The Jew is here about his pay. Take him away, will you?"

"*Maman*, really," said the dashing young man, who in the still dim light looked much like his sister, both of them appearing to be no more than masses of red-blonde ringlets bursting up from uniforms of black. "Avrom Moisevich, isn't it? Why don't you come with me?"

~

In the drawing room where, a few mornings earlier, Nikifor Kharitonovich had interviewed the Efimovski family, Oleg Olegovich turned toward his writing table. "Now, how much was it?" he asked, placing a hand on the key sticking out of the table's drawer.

"Hmm ... I don't quite remember," said Avrom.

"Ah, yes. It was not you, but the fiddler with whom I agreed on the amount. But since you're the one here, name your price. You've had to wait long enough for it."

"The truth is," said Avrom, "I didn't come for payment."

"Oh?"

"Your Illustriousness, I came because I have some information, which should be of the greatest interest to you."

"Oh?"

"It concerns your brother."

"My brother? What is it? Tell me!"

"It's ... that is ... the truth is, Your Illustriousness, it's something best told outside of this house. Nor is it something you are likely to believe, if I tell you only in words. It would be better if you let me show you."

"Best told outside of this house? What does that mean? Speak plainly."

"I beg that you will trust my discretion, and let me show

you instead. When you see it, you will know what to do. I haven't
even told Nikifor Kharitonovich yet."

The young nobleman looked down at the tsimbalist. Suspicion, puzzlement, doubt, took possession of his features in turn,
all in the course of a second or two. Then he grimaced, nodding
at the same time. "All right."

"Good," said the tsimbalist. "My wagon is at the ready."

～

Down the drive Pasternak raced, at a furious clip. Oleg Olegovich took the turn through the gate at full speed, blazed past the
orchards, plunged ahead into the forest — all without saying a
word. For his part, Avrom didn't so much as open his mouth.
The sun was at its highest point, forcing Avrom's gaze to his
knees. The rickety wagon shuddered, while branches snapped
beneath its wheels. Meanwhile, Oleg Olegovich stared straight
ahead, unblinking.

It was only after they'd come out of the woods that the
nobleman asked: "To Balativke, you say? Tell me now what we'll
find there."

"You must forgive me for trying your patience," said Avrom,
looking up. "But I assure you, it will be much better to wait." In
reply to which, Oleg Olegovich pressed his lips together, and
again nodded unhappily.

On the right, Zavlivoya appeared, and then the lake, brilliant and blue in the sunshine. The road was almost empty of
traffic. Oleg Olegovich lost his patience only once more, begging, as they passed Big Hand and came near to Balativke:
"Please, don't trifle with me."

"We are almost there," promised Avrom.

And then they *were* there, by the tsimbalist's house, pulling
the wagon in by the far side of his yard, away from Koppel's.

"Now," said Oleg Olegovich. "Show me."

~

"I suppose it won't surprise you to hear," Avrom said as they walked down from where the wagon was parked, "that we who live just here have spent a good deal of time speculating on how it all could have happened — always with the greatest respect and affection for your brother's memory, please believe me. That," he pointed out irrelevantly, as they descended further down the marshy yard, "is where I keep my tsimbls. You can see how close we are now to where your brother's body was found."

"May he rest in peace," Oleg Olegovich bowed his head. "Now where is it?"

"Oh," said Avrom, waving his hand in a circle which took in his house and yard, Koppel's house and yard, and the part of the water where Masha the cow had been stuck, and Arkady Olegovich's body had been found. "It is all of this ... the place where all the many strange and terrible events of the last few days took place, beginning with the robbery of my neighbor's house. You know, that was quite strange indeed. There were two things, especially, which stuck out at me — only it's been such an eventful week since, they nearly escaped my mind. I suppose you know, Your Illustriousness, that it was your former servant Styopa who sold my neighbor's things to the Pole."

"I heard as much," said Oleg Olegovich. "But enough, what does that have to do with my brother?"

"Oh, quite a bit, I assure you. It was Styopa who robbed my neighbor Koppel's house. But while he was there, he did two strange things. He snuffed out the candle in the back room — there. You can't see it from here, but just like at my house, the back has a window looking out on the lake. The candle was the first strange thing, and the second was, he failed to rob *my* house."

"I suppose you take some great meaning from that," said Oleg Olegovich, visibly impatient.

"I do," said Avrom, "though I didn't right away. Now, though, the meaning seems quite obvious to me. And then, later that night, when we were all here by the lakeside, there was a third strange thing that lodged itself in my head."

"And what was that?" This time, Oleg Olegovich made no attempt to hide his irritation.

"The fact that your brother was found in the lake without his shirt on."

The young nobleman nodded briskly. "I've changed my mind. I have no interest in seeing what you have to show me. Would you like to return me to my mansion, or shall I take the wagon myself?"

"Pardon me, please, pardon me," said Avrom, sounding contrite indeed. "I apologize most sincerely, Your Illustriousness, for treading far beyond what could be expected of anyone's patience. I'll come out with it now, no more beating around the bush. The thing I really brought you here to tell you is this: I know it was you who killed Styopa."

~

To Avrom's great surprise, a pleasant smile spread across Oleg Olegovich's handsome face. "That's quite amusing," he said. "But I really will go now."

"Why go?" said Avrom. "I'm only a lowly Jew. What could it hurt to *talk a little*?" He said these last words in a sing-song manner which made his Russian sound like Yiddish.

"*Talk a little?*" To Avrom's continued surprise, Efimovski replied in kind — except that he made the sing-song sound derisive. Then, his voice hardened: "All right, I won't deny I'm curious. I can't imagine what other absurdities might escape that filthy Yid mouth of yours."

"Very good," Avrom nodded, several times. "We understand

each other now. But I suppose what you'd like to know is how
I discovered it."

"Choose your own absurdities as you see fit."

"Yes ... well, to begin with ... I did see you, of course, you
and Styopa, when you went to get more ice for the party, whispering together. But that's no proof of anything. However, I also
know that Styopa came to your house on Saturday night, when
he was already on the run. Perhaps it was only to see his mother, but my guess is he also wanted to see you. He was trying to
blackmail you, of course ... But earlier, when Hezkel arrived ...
certain things Styopa said began coming back to me, once I
knew everything else ... I remember he said to you, *the truth
always comes out*. He called me 'Nikifor Kharitonovich's Jew,'
and said that Nikifor Kharitonovich would sometimes listen
to Jews — in fact, he would probably listen to anyone. I believe
the *anyone* he was referring to was actually himself."

"Preposterous."

"Not at all. Styopa may not have been educated, but he was
quite clever. Then there was another thing: after you knocked
Styopa to the ground, here by the lake — that was to impress
Tatiana Savelyevna, I think — he said you were going to pay for
that."

"And this is your proof that I killed him? I see I should have
left after all."

"Begging your pardon, Your Illustriousness, I hadn't quite
finished. I didn't mention why Styopa was blackmailing you."

"Oh, good."

"That was because he saw you put your brother in the
lake."

At this, Efimovski laughed. But his laugh didn't sound natural. It was too high in pitch, rather like one of his sister's.

"*Well*," he said. "That ups the stakes a bit, doesn't it? But it's
an obvious bluff. Or are you actually suggesting that Styopa

broke into your neighbor's house and stole his things, *then* came back in the middle of the night, to watch me murder my brother and throw him into the lake, all while your neighbor and his family slept peacefully on?"

"No, I'm not."

"Ah, just wanted to see how I would react? I must say, that's quite low, even for a Yid. Accusing me, while I'm still in mourning, of murdering my own brother — just for effect?"

"You misunderstand. What I meant was, I don't claim that Styopa came back to see you murder Arkady Olegovich. He didn't see you murder him, he only saw you dispose of the body. And he didn't come back for that. He saw you during the evening, while he was robbing Koppel's house. That's why he snuffed out the candle, and that's why he didn't go on to rob any more houses, as he'd surely planned to do. I remember, Saturday night, that you got very angry, when Styopa suggested your brother was murdered. Hezkel didn't say anything about murder, did he? He only said your brother was found in the lake. It was Styopa who kept talking about murder, and that made you angry."

"Aha," chortled Efimovski. "That's very, very good. Except for one little thing: that evening, my brother was alive and well, and for all we know, still on his way back from Chernigov."

"Come now," said Avrom. "You know as well as I that your brother never went to Chernigov."

⁓

"Of course he did," Efimovski replied, very quietly. "We had a telegram from him."

"A telegram? A telegram?" For some reason, the idea of a telegram seemed to enrage the tsimbalist. He drew closer to Efimovski, at the same time beginning to speak with such intensity that he was nearly shouting.

"Let's review," he sat at the top of his voice. "Supposedly, last Wednesday, you and your brother were about to play a game of chess. He clumsily dropped the board and broke it. Then, deciding to find you a special gift, he scribbled a note to your sister and left it in her room. Then he rode away for Chernigov — Foka and Marfa saw him go while they were replanting some flowers for your party. Is that about right?"

"How dare you shout at me, you filthy little Yid?"

"The fact is, however, that not one of those things happened. Do you remember, Your Illustriousness, it was when we were riding up here together on Saturday night that you told me your brother was beloved in the North Village? Well, I learned yesterday that he almost never went there. The problem must have been that I liked you too much, felt too sorry for you after your brother's death. I was so awfully slow to realize that it wasn't him that had lied to you. It was you that lied to me. I had just told you, as we came up here, that I often saw him riding by my house. And you made up that story about the North Village — probably because you'd already heard Styopa say I was 'Nikifor Kharitonovich's Jew,' and you wanted to spread around, through me, some explanation that would point away from the truth — that is, away from the precise reason you killed your brother."

"Which was?" sneered Efimovski.

"At your engagement party, it was obvious Tatiana Savelyevna wanted nothing to do with you. I gather there had been an informal agreement for some time between your families that the two of you would marry. But you were never interested — not until your mother devolved her fortune onto you. At that moment, your considerable gambling debt became collectible, and I suppose your creditors tried immediately to collect. You fled Kiev for here, and sought out Saveli Savelyevich right away, arranging your engagement to his daughter, and demanding a huge dowry. You were even followed. Pugovitsin — that's what he does, isn't it? He's a debt collector? And you've been paying him little bribes, so that he'd hold off on collecting from you until after you got your hands on the dowry. That's where he's been getting his gambling money."

"Nonsense — though it's true that I've been making him a few small loans."

"But Tatiana Savelyevna wasn't interested in marrying you, even if neither you nor her father knew that. She was in love with someone else — someone whose passions I believe she shared, or perhaps, whose passions she learned to take for her own. Your brother was very well-disposed toward my people, and so is she. It's not the usual thing. She even screamed, when she came to the road just above here, the other night, and saw him dead."

"That only proves she has a soft heart. A fine quality in a wife."

"No, I'm sure they were in love — she can tell us, in any case. They had been meeting in secret, because of the understanding between your families. They would meet at a little spot near her house — that was why he rode through Balativke so often, and that was why you made up that story about the North Village, to draw attention away from Bol'shaya Sosna. And when they couldn't meet, they would exchange notes. It was when I heard about one of those notes that everything became clear to me. Suddenly, it all lined up quite nicely."

"Oh yes? Why don't you tell me."

"I asked myself, who had she left a note for? Suddenly, the answer seemed obvious. Well, why had I been so slow, and not seen it before? Because of two false ideas: first, that your brother had been going to the North Village, and second, that Tatiana Savelyevna was in love with someone else, neither you nor your brother. The second idea, I was disabused of a little while ago. But who put the first idea into my head? You. And why? Because you didn't want anyone to know your brother had been going to Bol'shaya Sosna. And why not? Because that would make it clear that he was in love with Tatiana Savelyevna — and that, therefore, you had a reason for wanting him out of the way ... or at least, to fight with him ... After I understood that, all the other questions found answers, too."

"A positively ironclad case," sneered Efimovski. "Because I mistakenly believed my brother frequented the North Village, it's proof that I killed him? At a time when everyone knows he was still alive? If what you say is true, and they loved each other, I will simply have to do what I can to fill the empty place in Tatiana Savelyevna's heart."

"If what I say is true? Oh, that's very good. You know it quite well. The day you and her father Saveli Savelyevich made your agreement, Tatiana Savelyevna was supposed to meet your brother at their usual spot. But he never came. When he didn't, she wrote him a note, telling him the thing they had feared had come to pass, and that therefore, it was time for them to come out into the open. The thing they had feared was her engagement to you. He never saw her note, but he already knew about the engagement. At about the same time she must have learned about it from her father, he learned about it from you."

"Yes, I told him, and he congratulated me warmly. If they'd really been in love, why would he have done that?"

"He congratulated you? No. As soon as you told him, he determined to resolve matters. First he wrote Tatiana Savelyevna a note. I remember almost exactly what it said: *Well, my dear, my brother just told me he's engaged. I expect you knew even before I did to whom. I thus find that I have a piece of very important business to attend to. I know you were expecting me when you arrived — I hope you'll forgive me for leaving this note in my place. But you'll understand, won't you?* I suppose they were supposed to meet later in the day, but he couldn't wait there for her, he wanted to resolve everything at once. He didn't sound very worried, or maybe it was just bluster."

"You've got everything mixed up," laughed Efimovski. "That was the note that my brother left for Aglayushka."

"That's what everyone thought," replied Avrom. "You know, your sister told me that when you were children, the three of you would always be on the verge of getting into trouble, until you would make up some brilliant story on the spot to get out of it. But you never made up a better story than you did this time. Arkady Olegovich wrote that note for Tatiana Savelyevna, and he was going to leave it in the place where they always met. Only first, he decided to talk to you — or maybe you saw him writing it. He confessed to you that he was in love with Tatiana Savelyevna. You didn't care about her, but you did care about the dowry, your debt was a matter of the greatest urgency. The two of you fought, and when he had his back turned, you picked up the nearest object, a marble chess board — and you broke it over his head, killing him."

Avrom paused, to take a breath. Efimovski gazed at him with something like admiration, and said, "My father was never nearly so clever as that."

The first time Avrom had raised his voice, he'd been feigning anger. But seeing Efimovski marvel, at a moment like this, at a purely intellectual matter, he became sincerely enraged, and shouted anew: "I suppose Foka, who still, I must say, seems to admire and even love you, heard the noise and came running, along with Marfa. That was when you intercepted them, and ordered them to replant some flowers for the ball. Very quick thinking: the flowers were in front of the house, where you wanted the servants. While they were there, you carried, or I suppose dragged your brother's body to the icehouse. Was that a brilliant inspiration, or just a happy accident? Did you know it would disguise the time of his death, or was it just a convenient hiding place?"

"It didn't take me long to think of the possibilities," Efimovski smiled, steepling his hands in front of his chin.

"I believe you," said Avrom in disgust, turning briefly away toward the water.

"Although I didn't expect him to turn up so soon," added Efimovski. "That was a little bit of bad luck, since now we have to wait for the engagement."

"How inconvenient."

"Exactly," nodded the nobleman.

"In any case, your quick thinking wasn't done yet. You pulled your brother's shirt off his body and put it on yourself, and rode his horse Star through the gates at blazing speed. Foka and Marfa thought it was your brother riding away, and why not? The two of you looked quite alike, but on his horse, in his shirt, at that speed, you must have been his spitting image. I suppose you only rode a little way down the road, and then tied up Star in the woods — or maybe you already left him at Hermit's Cave that first time. And you returned home before they'd even finished their gardening. Ah yes, and either before that or just after, you had to deal with the note. You could have gotten rid of it, of course, but you had a better idea. You took it and put it in your sister's room, knowing she'd think it was meant for her, and put quite a different interpretation on it."

"Go on," said Efimovski, his hand clasped over his mouth. Somehow, there was a cigarette between his fingers — Avrom hadn't noticed him produce it — and he looked as though he were enjoying both the smoke and Avrom's conjectures very much.

"The next day," said Avrom, "you sent Foka and Marfa to market, all the way in Sosnitsa. You knew it would take them away from the house for hours, perhaps most of the day. You took advantage of their absence to ride to Chernigov — dressed like your brother again, to make sure you'd be noticed, a noble in peasant's clothing. And you sent a telegram, addressed to yourself."

"Come now, you'll admit that was clever."

"And then, you were almost done. You left Star at Hermit's Cave. You didn't know Styopa was using the cave, I think. But he saw Star there, next time he came. He didn't know how to sell a horse, so he decided to pass the information to one of the horse-traders. At the same time, *you* saw the wheel that he must have stolen from Kolbov's farm, and you came back to get it — the next day I suppose — in order to weigh down your brother's body in the lake. You couldn't have taken it right away, or Styopa would have noticed it was gone when he first saw the horse."

"Excellent," Efimovski laughed. "Did you have to write it down, or did you do it all in your head?"

"It was Friday when you fetched the wheel. That day, you sent Marfa and Foka away again, this time to pick cherries. You loaded your brother's body from the icehouse into your carriage — I suppose you first unloaded the champagne you'd bought that afternoon next to the icehouse, as a sort of disguise, in case anyone saw from a distance. And then, you just needed a place to deposit the body, although I don't know why you hadn't done it on the way to Chernigov."

"I was on horseback, and Foka had the carriage. And it was light out, of course. Anyway, there was no hurry."

"I see. Well, you knew from your conversation with my fiddler Moishe Shakhes that the Kelmer Maggid was giving sermons this weekend, and that all the Jews for *versts* around would be in attendance — that was how he pried another ruble from you when you were negotiating the fee for your ball. On your way to picking up your mother and sister in Bakhmatch, you stopped in Balativke, and deposited your brother's body in the lake. Isn't that so?"

"All due credit." Efimovski performed a swift bow. "It's as if you'd been sitting on my shoulder the whole time. Now, which do you suppose takes a higher degree of imagination? Planning it all out, on the spur of the moment, or reconstructing it, after the fact? I may be slightly biased, but I believe that, simply because of the quick thinking involved, planning it out is the more difficult ... in essence, it's the difference between creating a new world out of pieces of the real one, and imagining a new world that coincides with the real one ..."

Avrom's reply was completely incomprehensible: "Can you hear me?" And as soon as he said it, he turned his back on Efimovski.

It was a mistake. Almost at once, the noble delivered him a terrific clout on the back of the neck, and Avrom stumbled, his knees sinking into the muck. He whipped his head around. Efimovski was laughing.

"Don't worry, I won't hurt you any worse than that. It's as you said, you're only a lowly Jew, and you don't pose any real danger to me. But I had to get back at you a little, for getting me here under false pretenses. You'd agree though, wouldn't you, that it would be a mistake to kill you? Your neighbors might see."

"I may be biased," said Avrom, "but I believe you're right."

"In that case," said Efimovski, "I'll be going now."

"Now," repeated Avrom.

⁓

Oleg Olegovich was as puzzled by this reply, as he'd been a moment earlier by the other. This time, however, his puzzlement didn't last long. From behind him, he heard a noise — it sounded like music, a jangling of strings, and then a reverberation, a chord, he believed they called it, though a very unharmonious one. He began to turn, and as he did, his eye caught a moving shadow, something brushed him on the shoulder, and then there was a squeezing that pinned his arms to his sides.

In front of him, he saw a young Yid with a chocolate-brown beard and high forehead — it was that one who'd gotten into a scrape with Styopa the other night. The damned Yid must have been hiding in the little shack where the older Yid kept his instruments, in fact, he must have been crouched behind a tsimbl during their entire tête-à-tête. Now, he'd popped out like a jack-in-a-box, with one end of a rope in his hand. And by some kind of black magic, it was the rope's other end that was pinning his own shoulders!

Hmm ... Now was it better to give a great heave with his arms, to free himself? Or to throw himself to the ground with all his might, to pull the rope out of the Yid's hand?

Before he could decide, the older Yid had run over to grab onto the rope too, and then the younger one had, lickety-split, tied his end around one of the posts holding up the tsimbl shack. Oleg Olegovich ran toward the water to pull himself free. But the post held steady.

A most inconvenient situation in which to find himself! And an entirely stupid one. Glumly shaking his head, Oleg Olegovich addressed his captors in a highly reasonable tone.

"If I were you, I'd let me go. You'll have to eventually, and either way, I'll be whipping you both. We still have a *knout* lying around the homestead, and even if the police are only allowed birch whips now, I find the *knout* far more enjoyable. However, if you let me go right away, I won't be nearly so angry as I'm likely to get later on."

"I don't intend to hold you long," Avrom replied, in the same reasonable tone. "I only want to keep you until those fishermen can get to shore."

Oleg Olegovich turned as best he could to look out over the water, where a boat was approaching. "Fishermen? What do they have to do with anything?"

"Don't you know about the way sound travels on the lake here?" asked Avrom. "That's Nikifor Kharitonovich out there, with my good friend Deacon Achilles. And from the way he held his arm up just now when I asked — I'd guess he heard every word we've been saying."

Chapter 20

≈

Wrapping Up

Meanwhile, Blume and the rest of her family were waiting inside their house, bursting with curiosity and joy.

And why not? A few hours earlier, they'd been at home, minding their own business, when they'd heard a knock on their door. It was just the tsimbalist standing there — a welcome visitor, but not a surprising one. Except who did they see when they took a second look? None other than Dovid himself — who they'd never expected to lay eyes on again. A few words from Reb Avrom began to clear things up. But before they could quite begin to believe in their good fortune, the tsimbalist pulled the rug out from beneath their celebration: he shushed them, told them he was going away for a bit, and explained that while he was gone, he'd be hiding Dovid in his tsimbl shed. As for them, he warned that they must stay hidden, too, and under no circumstances come outside, or even make any noise.

That was quite a trial, when all they felt like doing was asking Dovid a million questions, and if things were really as they seemed, exclaiming and laughing, and hugging whoever was closest, and then letting go and hugging someone else.

But didn't that just make it all the more joyous, when Reb Avrom finally did come to fetch them out? Nikifor Kharitonovich was leading the criminal away at the same time, and between that and Dovid's return, nearly every trouble seemed to be at an end — excepting only the loss of the dowry-money. Every breath seemed sweeter, every word more delightful, every look more meaningful. If Koppel hadn't insisted that bride and bridegroom ought to be separated for at least a day or two before the wedding — which was to take place on Friday! — Dovid might have stayed well past midnight.

Thursday was devoted to baking, all sorts of things for the wedding dinner, and baking still more (to make up for the days lost to uncertainty over whether Blume would marry at all — thank goodness they'd be baking at Dovid's house too!), and giggling, and chatter, and sighing with happiness. Midway through the afternoon, Blume's friends Dvoira, Malka and Basheva from Zavlivoya arrived, to help with each of these activities, not least the sighing.

And then, just past sunset, a sudden commotion arose outside the door. It opened, and lo and behold! The red-haired fiddler, Moishe Shakhes, was standing there, fiddle beneath chin. Blume gasped. Was it really time already to go to the bathhouse for her ritual immersion, the first of the many ceremonies leading up to the joining of bride and groom under the *khupa* tomorrow evening? Was her wedding truly at hand?

"Just a moment," she cried, "I have to ready myself!"

But before the words had left her mouth, the whole band of musicians launched into song, and began walking north into the village.

"Come on, come on," urged her friends and sisters, ready to accompany her without delay to her immersion in the *mikveh*. What else could she do? Off she went, to the song's loping rhythm, walking down the road — only she was really walking on air.

~

As for Avrom … How many times now in his life had he played "Walking the Bride to the Bath"? And yet he'd never enjoyed playing it so much: no bride had ever worn a bigger smile to go to the *mikveh* — or was it really that no bride had ever been dearer to him?

Once they arrived, and the girls had disappeared inside, it was time for Moishe Shakhes to begin chanting out some of his rhymes, intended to impart moral instruction to the bride while she waited for the attendants to dunk her under. This was how things worked: for each of the ceremonies, which followed a fixed order, the musicians played a fixed set of pieces, and Shakhes recited a fixed set of verses, which were, however, tailored to the specific occasion.

The verses at the bathhouse were tailored less than most; Shakhes was just getting warmed up. For this reason, Avrom tended not to pay them much attention from one wedding to the next. But knowing it was all for Blume's benefit, the tsimbalist lent the fiddler-*badkhn* his ears, and found himself enjoying every word.

"*Tomorrow guests from far and near, and frankly mostly near, my dear,*" Shakhes began, "*will come to see you 'neath the khupa. Then we'll make a lot of hoopla. But when the Goodnight Song's been played, the guests sent home, and your klezmers paid, don't cry us a lake for your girl-hood, just be pious, modest and good.*"

A few more verses, and then, time for music: a series of songs which, like "Walking the Bride to the Bath," Avrom had played countless times, outside Balativke's bathhouse, and Zavlivoya's, and those of other towns, too. But this time he took special care with every note.

They played five songs in quick succession, then took a pause. Inside, the dunking must have finished: one of the girls was coming out with a plate of cake, half of it gone, eaten by the dunkers, for whom it had been brought according to custom. Shakhes' sons ate the rest in an instant. And a moment later, the girls came outside.

The tsimbalist went home. There, he slept soundly, without a single dream.

~

As soon as the sun rose Friday morn, it was back to work. Shakhes' wagon rattled into Balativke, the band jumped out, Avrom awoke his tsimbl in its shed with a few strokes of the sticks, and then they all played the "Good Morning Song" in front of Blume's door, before walking north into the village. This time, Blume and her sisters didn't follow. The Jewish Orchestra was on its way to invite guests to the wedding.

From one end of Balativke to the other they went, and wherever a guest lived, they came to a halt. Shakhes had a list of names (though Avrom told him where the houses were), and when they stopped, the fiddler would read out a name, embellishing it a little — for example: "Hezkel the Woodcutter, son of Nisson, open your door and give a listen. Be you, if the Almighty decrees it shall be, invited, with due humility, to help Blume and Dovid perform a good deed, namely, that of getting mar-ried."

This was followed by a kind of fanfare, during which the orchestra reached its loudest heights, the flute shrilling at the top of its range, Shakhes scraping with all his might, with his bow sliding every which way like a pike caught in a winter lake and set down on the ice. Meanwhile, the brash and precocious Itskele beat his little drum exactly the way his teacher Shmerl Melamed at Hebrew school beat *him* when he didn't learn his lessons — that is, as hard as possible. By the time the band reached the house of the second or third guest, Avrom's ears and his head were splitting.

When the fanfare was done, the band waited long enough to receive payment, in the form of a silver coin. Then they moved on to the next guest's house. And as the collection of coins clinking in Itskele's *tefillin* grew, so too did the crowd walking behind the band, which consisted both of wedding guests, dressed in their finest, and also of idle onlookers, there to enjoy the music and the spectacle.

It wasn't long before the promenade turned into a parade. Shakhes was marshall. The other musicians came next, then the guests and onlookers; and bringing up the rear, once they reached the southern end of the village, were two barouches hired for the occasion, carrying Koppel, three of his daughters (not including Blume), and a number of his relations (among whom were squeezed Shimmel Shenkman and his family.)

Southward this magnificent procession went, nearly as far as Deacon Achilles' house. There, they stopped to wait — but not for long. A rumbling was heard in the distance. Soon enough, a caravan of carriages appeared: a big *brichka* and two fine barouches, each of them drawn by horses with jingling bells attached to their harnesses; and at their head, an elegant two-wheeled calèche, in which Dovid himself rode, handsome as a prince.

A shout went up from the Balativkans: "The bridegroom! The bridegroom!"

A shout went up from Moishe Shakhes: "*Eyns, tsvey, drai!*"

The march which followed — named "Welcoming the Groom to Town", and played while Koppel and Dovid embraced, downed two glasses of brandy, and then climbed together into Koppel's carriage — could be heard all round the lake, and even as far as the little park on the shore in Zavlivoya where Nikifor Kharitonovich was, at that moment, smoking a cigar.

～

Speaking of Nikifor Kharitonovich: the chief had a dilemma. Early that morning, he'd traveled to the Efimovski mansion to wrap up a few final points. And upon returning to the courthouse, he was handed a telegram by Svistunov, the contents of which were both tantalizing and deeply frustrating.

It will be remembered that, on the day the false Maggid was apprehended, his three partners had managed to fly the coop; and that on Wednesday, Nikifor Kharitonovich had received a humiliating message from the police chief in Pryluky, concerning a supposed trio of missing roosters. To make matters worse, a similar missive arrived on Thursday, replacing roosters with goats, and sent by the police chief in Bakhmatch.

Today's telegram was of a different breed. Its sender, Igor Petrovich Bogdanovich, police chief for the great city of Kiev, was entirely too respectable for such tricks. Alas, in addition to being respectable, and also respectful, he was in this instance hopelessly vague. Three persons, he wrote, possibly matching the description of the merchant-thieves, but possibly not, might or might not have been spotted leaving Kiev. It was probable that they were headed for "parts west." That is, they, if it was they, had been seen traveling along a certain road. And that road, once it left the city, led towards the aforementioned "parts west."

Nikifor Kharitonovich read the telegram; and without hesitation, went straight to the park. There he had a friendly debate with himself, beginning with an examination of that most interesting phrase, "parts west."

"Parts west" ... in point of fact, a practically worthless term, indicating neither size nor shape, and covering everything from the suburbs of Kiev to the whole of Europe ... in metaphorical terms, not unlike the proverbial haystack, in which needles are always becoming lost.

The chief nodded his head realistically, and admitted it to himself: the presence of three needles in a haystack might make

it easier to turn up one or two of them. But it was still an unlikely proposition at best.

He took a puff on his cigar, the smoke of which was circling
his head like an icon's halo. Then he nodded again — but this
time, not so realistically.

Yes, he argued with himself, finding a needle in a haystack
might be difficult. But isn't it true that the greatest difficulties,
when overcome, also lead to the most spectacular successes?
And when is there greater need for a spectacular success, than
after a string of failures and humiliations?

Nikifor Kharitonovich nodded a third time, this time with
complete candor. "Avrom Moisevich, who is undoubtedly a med-
dler, is nonetheless generous when it comes to the apportioning
of glory," he said to himself. "Your reputation has recovered with
the arrest of Efimovski. But in your heart, Nikushenka, you
know the truth. Borrowed feathers don't sit well on that spartan
cap of yours. The fact is, Avrom Moisevich has been doing your
job better than you yourself, and you know it perfectly well."

It was a lonely and dispiriting thing to admit. The chief
sighed, stared out at the glittering lake, took another puff on the
cigar, and let the smoke out slowly through his teeth.

But what was that faint sound, drifting across the water?
Music ... the Jewish Orchestra ...

And who played in the Jewish Orchestra? Avrom Moisevich,
naturally ... Avrom Moisevich ...

The voice of reason whispered anew to the chief that he
had no chance of finding the three merchant thieves, that he
must suffer his failures, and perhaps one day, with a new case,
rise above them. But the voice of reason was drowned out by
the hushed echoes of the music, and by that name ... Avrom
Moisevich.

A moment later, the only trace left in the park of Zavlivoya's
police chief was a streak of grey, transparent against the blue
sky: cigar smoke, which was already vanishing into the morning

air. A breeze, wafting its way along the lakeshore, caught sight of the smoke and sported with it a moment, blowing it one way and the other. Then, kicking itself up to full speed, it gusted the smoke clean away, before executing a perfect somersault and racing off to play with a nearby telegraph wire.

Across that wire, a telegram was already shooting, having been dashed off in a trice by the efficient and energetic chief:

"Take no action. Will arrive Kiev in person this afternoon. NKT."

~

"Little Bride, Little Bride, weep, weep, weep," sang Moishe Shakhes. And Blume wept.

She was pale, almost as pale as her white dress and veil, almost white like them, but for a bit of red: sprigs of myrtle, crowning her head. Her chair was clothed in white, too, and reddened with myrtle, while its four legs all stood inside an enormous kneading bowl: to invite abundance, as they had explained to her.

To her left and right stood Zlata and Basheva, each of them holding, in one hand, a burning candle, and in the other, a fistful of raisins. About them were crowded other women: the bride's sisters and friends, Dovid's little mother, cousins, sisters-in-law, nieces, women of the village married and maids both, all of them adorned with diamonds and pearls.

The room in which they had come to gather was the largest in the house of Motl the Tinsmith — itself the largest house in Balativke, for which reason the tinsmith's wife had offered it for use as the "bride's house." That good woman stood nearly in front of Blume, next to the only two men allowed there: Shakhes, whose duty it was to make the bride and her companions weep at this ceremony known as the Seating of the Bride; and the tsimbalist, whose task was to punctuate each of

Shakhes' couplets with mournful fragments of music, to make the tsimbl's strings hiccup and groan so that they elicited and imitated the cries of the women around him.

Each time the tsimbl fell silent again, Shakhes raised his voice still louder:

"Like unto the solemnest of days,
  oh like unto the Day of Atonement
Shall be this day for you, O Blume,
  shall be your wedding day.
Never more shall your hair be seen,
  but hidden 'neath kerchief or wig,
Your friends have looked their last on it,
  according to the Law of Moses
Your hair is like a flock of goats,
  that must be put to barn
Else they might create some mischief —
  that's why you must wear a kerchief
No more you'll frolic as a young meydl,
  but every hour toil,
For the rest of your years, how hard your life,
  from this your wedding day
The pain of childbirth, again and again,
  shall wrack your slender bones
From Balativke straight to Zav
  they'll hear your cries and moans
And who shall see you marry, deary?
  Who shall see you wed?
Not your mother, olevasholem,
  buried in the ground.
Not her parents who died in the plague,
  nor your father's either.
Nor your sister who died as a babe,
  Blume too they called her."

After this last, the tsimbalist, instead of punctuating Shakhes' words, remained still. The surprise of silence drew forth the most wrenching sobs yet from the women — until Shakhes opened his mouth again, and changed the mood entirely:

"But why so glum? Enough regretting.
Look at the man to whom you're wedding.
A scholar, handsome, and a real whiz,
even if he's got some funny ideas.
And how 'bout your kiddies — you'll have a few.
When they're grown, how they'll worship you!
(Kina hora! No evil eye bring)
And now, of you I'd like to sing
A woman of valor, that's what you'll be
An example for all Balativke to see
Performing good deeds left and right
Keeping the commandments night after night.
A houseful of children, a good kosher kitchen
In short — that's why you and your Dovid are hitchin'."

Upon singing this last, silly line, Shakhes picked up his violin from the floor, where it had been precariously lying, and he and the tsimbalist broke into a *khorovod* dance. The women circled the crowded room, while Zlata and Basheva pelted Blume with raisins.

And after this sudden change of humor, it was time for the musicians to run over to the "groom's house," and invite Dovid to come for the Veiling of the Bride.

～

At Mendel the Butcher's, which served as "groom's house," the men were sitting around a few well-appointed tables, eating cake, drinking brandy and smoking cigarettes. The marriage contract had already been signed, and now, in addition to cigarette smoke, the room was filled with casual conversation, all of it concerning the recent remarkable events in town.

"It doesn't matter what ended up happening," Berl Melamed was saying. "We must still adhere to the Kelmer Maggid's teachings, and reform the way business is done around here."

"If anyone needs to reform his ways," rejoined Mendel the Butcher, "it's the Kelmer Maggid himself. What a crook!"

"But Reb Mendel," the groom himself protested, "that wasn't the Maggid, you know that. What the man pretending to be the Maggid did has nothing to do with the *real* Maggid's teachings."

"On the other hand, perhaps Reb Mendel has a point," said Berl Melamed, who seemed determined to feel enmity toward his onetime rival for Blume's hand, even at the cost of his principles.

"I hate to speak ill of the bridegroom on his wedding day," Motl the Tinsmith spoke up, "and Mazel Tov again, by the way. But the problem with you youngsters is that you're always talking about things you don't know anything about. Those words of the Maggid's were pretty. But we've seen enough proof now — haven't we? — that anyone can say pretty words. Why, I remember — "

"Quiet," interrupted Mendel the Butcher. "Look who's arrived."

A bevy of women filed in, half-dancing as they did, and behind them, the Jewish Orchestra. As usual, Moishe Shakhes was the first to open his mouth.

"Bridegroom, bridegroom,
Look who's come to your room
Here to take you away, but first
Give 'em some schnapps to slake their thirst
And some lekekh cake to slake
Their hunger, after that, they'll take
You to your bride, to see the veiling
Let's hope she's done with all her wailing."

As soon as Shakhes' instructions had been followed, and the women had been fed cake, the fiddler's oldest son raised up his flute and began playing "Walking the Bridegroom to the Veiling." Its familiar rhapsodic melody made the groom's heart beat faster as he realized that this time, it was being played for him. During his brief walk next door, the village children called out, once again, "The Bridegroom!"

When he arrived at the "bride's house," two rows of girls stood holding candles. Dovid walked between them, until he stood near the bride, still seated on her white chair. Glancing at her, he blushed; then remembered to look at Rabbi Bronshteyn, who had walked in behind him.

The rabbi pointed his bearded chin toward Dovid's mother, who was just approaching, a bowl in her hands, draped over with a silk kerchief. Dovid and the rabbi each grasped a corner of the kerchief and lifted it. There were seeds underneath, poppy seeds and *chernushkas*, by the look of it.

Suddenly, everyone shouted, so loud that it startled him: "Our sister, be the mother of thousands and tens of thousands!"

Along with the rabbi, Dovid lowered the kerchief over Blume's face, so that she was entirely covered, practically wrapped up like a mummy. And before Dovid could even straighten up, he felt something hitting his face, his head, the back of his neck: seeds, thrown from every direction. One of them hit him in the eye.

It made him laugh.

～

And on the ceremonies went, though the fateful meeting of bride and groom beneath the *khupa* was now fast approaching. Out went the men again, all except the musicians. The time had come for the Mazel Tov Dance.

Quietly, the Jewish Orchestra began to play the piece of

music which, at every Jewish wedding in that part of the country, always accompanied this dance, though the piece's composer was neither a Russian nor a Jew: the "Farewell Polonaise," written by a Polish count by the name of Oginski. It was a piece which never failed to transport Avrom, however briefly, to a different time and place: it reminded him of the little pieces by Chopin that he used to practice on the piano in his youth. For a moment, he thought of that music, of his father's house. Other related matters entered his head, too, which were normally kept safely buried deep in his soul. Then, his eyes saw what was transpiring in front of him, the bride being pulled up from her chair. And he returned to the here and now.

Blume's face was still hidden. But the tsimbalist could well imagine that it was even paler than before. She'd been fasting all day; it was now late afternoon. And she'd had quite a cry, too. Poor preparation for what was to happen next.

"Khana Lipkin, Dovid's mother," shouted Shakhes, "step right up or I'll call another!"

The little woman hurried forward, embraced her new daughter, and spun her around.

"Zlata, you're a *sheyne meydl*, spin your sister like a dreydl!"

Up stepped Zlata, embraced Blume, and spun her around a few more times.

Quickly, another guest was called and came forward. Another embrace, another spin; then another, and another. All the women twirled and whirled the bride, until without warning, but to no one's surprise, she fell to the floor in a faint.

～

At first, she wasn't sure if her eyes were open. Then, she perceived light, passing through the veil. Someone's hand was on her shoulder. She smelled onions, sweat. It was her father.

She heard his voice ... the afternoon prayers ... joined him, saying the Yom Kippur prayers too, on this, the solemnest day of her life. As soon as they finished, the klezmers began to play.

What next?

Her father's hand again, this time taking her own ... leading her outside, through the doorway, out onto the bumpy road. "Remember to take small steps," they had said. "You don't want to trip."

Now, they must be near the *shul*. The *khupa* would be set up by the *shul* door ... Dovid already standing beneath it, flanked by four young men holding its four poles. He'd be clad in white, like her, and wearing his new *tallis,* her gift to him.

Suddenly, the cantor's voice: "May He who understands the speech of the rose among thorns bless the bridegroom and the bride."

More circles — her father leading her, seven times, around Dovid. Seven, it must be, though she couldn't count now.

The sound of the *kiddush*, the blessing over the wine.

Her veil, lifted for just a moment. Dovid's eyes, looking frankly into hers, and lovingly. And then the veil dropping again.

A hand, lifting hers again, but this time, not her father's: Dovid's. The ring, placed on her finger. The sound of glass, breaking.

"Mazel Tov!"

~

A little while later, bride and groom were nowhere to be seen.

According to dictate, Blume and Dovid had gone inside for a short period of seclusion. But no one else had gone anywhere: all the guests were dancing. The musicians first played a *koyletch*, during which Khana Lipkin danced around with a braided *khallah* almost as big as she was; then a series of circle dances, faster and faster.

As he played, Avrom watched the dancers. For once, he was

jealous. He wanted to be dancing instead of playing. He wanted to celebrate. There were many things to be happy about: the union of a happy couple after so many travails, the light in Blume's eyes when the veil had come off her face, the end of the danger that Koppel would be arrested or that another tavern would be burned down. Of course, to play music was a celebration too. But this time, Avrom wanted to celebrate with his legs, to grasp the hands of the other revelers, to shout, instead of standing apart, condemned as always to spend the wedding with the Shakhes family.

Perhaps, he thought, he yearned to join the dancers in order to seize the moment, before it passed away like smoke on the breeze. How fragile, how fleeting a moment it was! Why, Dovid himself was proof that the days for weddings like this were numbered. The bridegroom was a living reminder that a whole way of life was on its way out.

Many times in the last few days, Avrom had talked with the young man — beginning on the wagon ride to Balativke, before they trapped Oleg Olegovich into confessing. And he'd gotten Dovid to see that, no matter what else, no matter what happened after, he ought to marry Blume. If only to make amends for all the suffering he'd caused her, he ought to allow her the happiness of the wedding she'd dreamed about. But once the festivities ended, who knew what Dovid would do? Where would his ideas, or the ideas of others — for he was quite impressionable — where would they take him? Without a doubt, Dovid would begin to abandon doing things as they had always been done. And after him, some other young firebrand would take things further, and another, still younger, would go still further ...

Avrom, not exactly a traditionalist himself, couldn't shed too many tears over this development. True, it might be inconvenient for him personally: it was well known that in parts further west and north, toward the border with Germany, Jews barely observed Jewish law anymore, and no longer went in for elaborate weddings like this one. Good luck to any klezmer try-ing to make a living in a place like that! And it was bound to be the same here sooner or later. Fewer prayers, shorter weddings — a broken glass, a few quick dances, and thank you very much. Not much use for musicians, when that happened.

But even if that was the case, there was a bright side: If a wedding was less important, marriage was less important, too. And if marriage was less important, then a woman like Rivke — who was conspicuously absent from this wedding celebra-tion — might have a chance at happiness, too.

Still, the fact that this wedding was not a link in an unbro-ken chain, but instead something at least somewhat autumnal, old, fading ... without a doubt, this added a certain poignance to the proceedings.

On the other hand, Avrom reconsidered, maybe the rea-son he felt like getting far away from the Shakhes family had nothing to do with any of these high-flown matters, but was something much simpler. The dinner, his least favorite part of any wedding, was coming up. And during this dinner Moishe Shakhes would insist on playing a few display pieces on his fid-dle, fantasies on tunes from famous operas, full of tricky little runs and high melodies. Avrom cringed at the thought of what it would sound like. A good thing no one in little Balativke had ever come within a hundred *versts* of a real opera house!

Avrom himself would probably be asked to play a fantasy on the tsimbl, too. He was always asked to, during the table music, and in fact, asked over and over. Unfortunately, Shakhes always became upset if Avrom was featured too much. Tonight, though, since it was Blume's wedding ... perhaps he would play a fantasy or two.

Come to think of it, it was nearly time now to move to where the tables had been set up. The wedding dinner had to end before sundown, when the Sabbath began. During the Sabbath, all wedding festivities would come to a twenty-four halt.

To Avrom's left, a movement caught his eye. It was Blume's brother, Yoysif. While everyone else was dancing, the little boy was sitting by himself, on the ground. He was playing with something, moving it in a circle. Avrom took a sharper look. Well, of all things: it was that wheel spoke again.

~

Evening came, and then morning. The Sabbath arrived and departed. And when it was done, Zavlivoya's Jewish orchestra, which had had a well-deserved rest, broke out their instruments again, to continue the festivities. As momentous and solemn as were yesterday's ceremonies, it was tonight that the real celebration would get underway. Now, the bride could smile.

Everyone who'd been at the wedding yesterday returned to the "bride's house." And one by one, they began requesting dances: *patshns* and *bulgars*, *sirbas* and *hongas*, *skotshnes* and *shers*.

"Here's where we make the real garnish," Shakhes reminded his sons; and it was true. Each dance was paid for separately, and in advance (which gave the buyer the right to call the tune.) The more dances, the more money they'd make. Tomorrow, all the dance money would be taken out of Itskele's money box, pooled with the invitation coins and the fee from the bride's father, and divvied up according to the usual formula: forty percent for Moishe Shakhes, twenty-five for Avrom, fifteen percent for Kuz'ma, ten each for Shakhes' older sons, and five percent for little Itskele. Moishe Shakhes didn't know that, on this occasion, the fee from the bride's father was actually being put up by Avrom: it was his wedding present to the destitute family.

Except that it turned out, a little while later, that the family wasn't so destitute after all. About an hour after the dancing started, a most unexpected guest arrived: Nikifor Kharitonovich. Shakhes, playing his fiddle, scratched to an awkward halt. The other musicians followed suit, while the energetic dancers, who'd been greedily gulping air in and puffing it back out, gulped it in and kept it right there, noses and mouths closed firm, and eyes a-goggle.

What terrible thing had happened, that Zavlivoya's police chief should be here?

"Good evening," Nikifor Kharitonovich called out. "Don't let me interrupt. I only came to deliver some lost property." He produced a silk bag. "The money that was stolen."

His words were greeted with a hundred gasps. Koppel and his daughters ran forward to where the chief stood, along with Dovid and Blume. "*Eyns, tsvey, drai,*" shouted Shakhes. And the music started up again.

As he played, Avrom could see Nikifor Kharitonovich being thanked many times, and finally, becoming embarrassed and making to leave. Instead of walking back to the road, however, the chief made his way over to Avrom.

The tsimbalist dropped out of the *freylekhs* the band was playing, and asked: "Well ... how did you do it?"

"Easy," replied Nikifor Kharitonovich. "I had a little chat with Styopa's mother Marfa. I suspected she might have the money. And I was right."

"I would have been most interested to hear that chat."

"It was nothing, really," said the chief, looking highly pleased with himself.

"I have the feeling, looking at you," said the tsimbalist, "that something else has happened."

"Indeed," the chief looked still more pleased with himself. "Something else has. I've arrested those three merchants."

"What? How?"

"I'll tell you the whole story," said Nikifor Kharitonovich, who'd clearly been dying to do just that. "Yesterday, I received word that the three of them might have been spotted leaving Kiev. Might, I repeat. It was no sure thing. But I decided to take the risk."

"And it paid off. Very well done."

"Now then, don't get ahead of the story ... I rode to Kiev. It was afternoon by the time I arrived. I spent only ten minutes with Igor Petrovich, the chief there — he had nothing to tell me that he hadn't already put in his telegram. Our trio had been spotted on a certain road. I found the road, and followed it out of town. However, it was still no sure thing."

"A gamble."

"Exactly ... I had no way of knowing whether I was on the right track. At first, I saw many travelers coming the opposite way, toward town, and I accosted a few who were in official dress. But they had nothing to tell me. I didn't want to bother with any Jews — now, now, don't stare that way, I had a good reason. You, Avrom Moisevich, know me, but those Jews there — they'd have had no reason to tell me anything, when I was looking for their co-religionists, unless I'd first taken the time to gain their trust. Do you agree?"

"I suppose I do, when you put it that way."

"And as it was already late in the day, I didn't have time to chat with them — though I did eventually take the time. However, that comes later. At first, my only help came from two peasants. The first, whom I met lolling by the side of the road a few *versts* outside of the city, confirmed that three Jews who sounded very much like my three had come that way earlier in the day. The second peasant, whom I met much later, told me even more. He'd seen them at a fork in the road I would soon come to. And he'd seen which direction they chose: toward the village of Boyarka. You've heard of it?"

"A sort of summer colony for millionaires and artists, isn't it? To escape the summer heat in Kiev?"

"Exactly so. Well, thought I. When I find those three impostors, they'll be dying to escape *my* heat. However, before I could arrive in Boyarka, I met with a nasty little surprise: a crossroads. The peasant hadn't mentioned that. The way straight ahead was supposed to lead to Boyarka, but all I could see in front of me was a woods. The road to the right disappeared over a hill. And to the left, I could see a village, but that couldn't have been Boyarka. On the other hand, how could I be sure that they had really gone to Boyarka?"

"A difficulty."

"Yes. Well, I thought, I'll try going straight, and if I don't find them soon, I'll come back, and go left. But I hadn't gone far into the woods when I met a wagon stopped in the road. There was a Jew sitting on its box, with a grey beard."

"Like me?" smiled Avrom.

"Not exactly ... He was whipping his horse, but it still refused to move, and he was pleading with it — in Yiddish, of course. I decided to take the opportunity to ask if he'd seen any strangers. I was afraid he'd be reticent, but he turned out to be a true expert at the art of talking, and highly amusing, too."

"Oh yes?"

"Yes. He said: 'Strangers, Officer? Who have I seen *but* strangers? *You*, for example.' I laughed at that, but then told him I wasn't thinking of myself. And *he* said: 'In that case, I've just come from Boyarka, a town inhabited entirely by strangers. And between you and me, when it comes to the artists there, it would be hard to find anyone stranger, even if you were to go to the ends of the earth, or even to China. Why, there's one who even — ' But I stopped him there, and told him it wasn't artists I was looking for. And *he* — I believe I remember exactly what he said. He said, 'As it happens, the Lord was at least kind enough not to make me deaf, dumb, and blind, not to mention that He didn't make you a policeman for no good reason either. In other words, I already suspected as much.' Isn't it amusing, Avrom Moisevich?"

"It is."

"Then he said, 'I can tell that when you say you're looking

for a stranger, what you're really looking for is a suspicious stranger. Well, I've got one of those for you too. I saw the man you want just yesterday: riding in a fine *brichka*, with a collection of girls around him who would have put King Solomon's wives to shame, if only any of them had actually been married to him — ' I stopped him again there."

"Did you?" asked Avrom, sounding very disappointed all of a sudden.

"Yes, and I finally said I was looking for *three* strangers ... three Jews. 'Oh? he said. 'And what good deeds have these Jews done, that you should do them the honor of asking about them?' I said, 'What good deeds? I'll tell you. They tricked every Jew in my town of Zavlivoya, and robbed three of them.' Then I told him the whole story — not excluding the role you played, Avrom Moisevich, as I thought it would help to convince him."

"And did it?"

"Indeed it did. First he said he'd like to meet you. And then he said he'd seen our trio only a little while before. I asked which way they'd been going, and he said, 'Which way should they have been going, when they were only coming?' It turned out they'd only arrived in Boyarka an hour before — they were entering the town tavern at the same time he was delivering a load of wood there. And that's where I found them."

"Well, *Mazel Tov* to you ... I mean, congratulations."

～

After the chief left, Avrom fell into a dark mood, even as the most joyous music continued to emerge from his tsimbl.

Nikifor Kharitonovich had covered himself in glory, no doubt about it. And when it came to Marfa, the chief had done a good deed for Blume and her family — both her old family and her new one. But he had overlooked something. Of course, the matter was of no real interest to him. And anyway, he couldn't have paid attention to it, when he had the three impostors to catch.

But that convoy of women? Avrom was nearly certain that Nikifor Kharitonovich's grey-bearded Jew had laid eyes on Mirele, not two days ago now. A stranger riding in a *brichka* ... with a collection of girls around him who would have put Solomon's wives to shame. It had to be the "recruiter" that Yudel Beck had described ... taking Mirele somewhere very far away ... and without a doubt, somewhere quite hopeless.

The tsimbalist scolded himself, while his hands moved quite on their own, to play tunes they'd played countless times before. If he were ever tempted to feel satisfied with any of his accomplishments ... well, he shouldn't. There he'd been, rejoicing for Blume ... and once again, he'd let Mirele slip out of his mind — Mirele, who was exactly Blume's age, and looked much like her. He'd let her slip away, nearly out of reach now. Nearly.

"Reb Avrom."

He looked up. It was Rivke. This was a surprise. He nodded a greeting, and went on playing.

"They seem happy," she said, looking back over one shoulder, and then turning again to face him. "Don't they?"

"Indeed."

"I'm sure they're grateful to you, Reb Avrom." She stared at him with that look that made him feel unquiet. "You did quite a lot for them."

Avrom shook his head. "Not so very much."

"Oh, you did, no need to be modest. It was good of you. You're very good to people ... most people, at least."

Avrom stopped playing. "It's difficult for me to talk now, Rivke. What is it that you wish?"

But she didn't answer at once. She looked at him, eyes burning darker than ever, and with a strange smile upon her lips. "I wasn't going to come. But of course, I could hear all the music you were playing. The same tunes as when I married. I still remember it all. You know, no matter what happened afterward — wherever he may be — the wedding itself was very nice."

"Rivke, I have to play music now."

"You're good at solving riddles, Reb Avrom. Who knew how clever you could be? Of course everyone always had an inkling, but now ..."

"Perhaps. I enjoy solving riddles. But what is it you wish?"

"But isn't it obvious?" Rivke raised her voice. "You've got good enough eyes to see it."

"Rivke, I — "

"I wish to be free, Reb Avrom. That's all. Free."

"I wish that for you too."

"Do you? Do you truly?"

"Of course."

Rivke stepped closer, and suddenly both her hands shot out and wrapped themselves around his. They were burning hot. "Go then. Go find out for me, what happened to my husband. Please, Reb Avrom. Please let me be free."

Avrom opened his mouth to speak. But at that same instant, he heard Moishe Shakhes call his name.

"Avrom, are you here to play or to chit-chat? I tell you! First you squawk for an hour with the *koyen-godl* and now it looks like you're ready to get hitched to the witch. *Eyns, tsvey, drai*, already, let's go!"

Avrom felt Rivke's hands release him. By the time he turned back to where she had been standing, she was gone.

After that, for a long while, no one came to interrupt the tsimbalist while he played. By light of torch and lantern, the wedding guests danced, trios and quartets of men or women only, joining hands and capering about, and around them, a circle of men and women both. Moishe Shakhes scraped away, the high flute shrilled, Kuz'ma grunted while sawing drunkenly at his bass, little Itskele punished his drum. And Avrom played, and for a little while, forgot the busy last few days, and any trials which might await.

Late into the night, he felt something behind him: a soft nudge, a caress against his shoulder. He turned. It was Pasternak the horse, who had been tied up behind the band.

"Pasternak," said the tsimbalist. "You've gotten loose, have you?"

No reply came from the horse.

"But you're not planning on going anywhere, are you?"

Still, Pasternak was silent.

"And so, things didn't turn out so badly, after all, did they?"

In answer to which, the horse looked up, gazing beyond the tsimbalist at something off in the distance.

Avrom twisted around, to see what the horse's great, shining eyes were seeing. There, at the far edge of the lake, the sun was just poking its head up, just dangling its fingers into the shallows to give the world a little color, a touch of innocent, rosy pink. Pasternak let out a quiet neigh. Morning had come.

A squawking rose up at Avrom's side: Moishe Shakhes, shushing the band, so that he could scrape out, with all his usual grace, the first notes of the "Good Morning Song."

As for the tsimbalist, he turned away from Shakhes, and away from the water, to give Pasternak's withers a good rub.

"Still, though," he said to the horse. "On the whole, life really is quite impossible. Don't you agree?"

Glossary and Notes

(note: though many Yiddish words derive from Hebrew, for simplicity, they are classified here solely as Yiddish.)

aleinu: (Yid.) the closing prayer of a Jewish service
alter: (Yid.) old man
apikores: (Yid.) heretic
arshin: (Rus.) measurement of twenty-eight inches
badkhn: (Yid.) entertainer and master of ceremonies at a wedding
balaveranik: (Yid.) sinner
barouche: a four-wheeled carriage with two double seats
besmedresh: (Yid.) house of study
bokher: Yeshiva student
borukh hashem: (Yid.) "Blessed be the Name"
brichka: (Rus.) long four-wheeled carriage
bristekh: (Yid.) a decorative band of material worn over a woman's bodice
calèche: (Fr.) light carriage
chernushka: seed also known as nigella, used as a spice
chibouk: long Turkish clay pipe
chinovnik: (Rus.) bureaucrat
Collegiate Registrar: in Imperial Russia, the lowest of the fourteen bureaucratic ranks

crown: in Russian Orthodoxy, a strip of paper placed upon the forehead of the deceased after death, upon which the hymn "Thrice Holy" is written

dreydl: (Yid.) spinning top

dyadka: (Rus.) "Uncle." Term used for manservant by children in his charge

ganev (pl. ganovim): (Yid.) thief

Gottenyu: (Yid.) "O God" or "Dear God"

Got zol ophitn!: (Yid., pronounced *op-hitn*) "God protect us"

Gusikov: Michal Gusikov (1806-37) famed nineteenth-century klezmer musician, player upon the tsimbl-like *shtroyfidl*

kahal: in Eastern Europe, local autonomous Jewish governing body. Abolished in Russia, 1844

Kelmer Maggid: Moses Isaac Darshan (1828-1900) famed Lithuanian Jewish preacher

kest: the obligation of a bride's parents to support a newlywed couple for a given period

khaper: (Yid.) "catcher"; a Jew who caught and turned over other Jews for military service in Tsarist Russia

khlat: (Yid.) also khalat. Man's casual garment

Kholmogory: locality in northern Russia, famous for carvings in walrus ivory

khupa: (Yid.) marriage canopy

kiddush: (Yid.) prayer over wine

Kina hora!: (Yid.) "No Evil Eye!"

klezmer-loshn: (Yid.) the private language of klezmer musicians in Eastern Europe

kmishbrot: (Yid.) twice-baked, sliced sweet almond bread; biscotti

knout: any of various fearsome Russian whips, incorporating one or more leather thongs, with the possible addition of wires, metal rings, and hardened leather hooks or points

koliva: (Rus.) boiled wheat dish, placed in front of memorial table following a death

koyen-godl: (Yid.) high priest (here used as slang for police chief)

kopek: (Rus.) small coin

kvetch: (Yid.) complain

leymener goylem: (Yid.) literally, clay golem; figuratively, idiot

malva: mallow flower

Maslenitsa: Russian holiday, celebrated during the week preceding Lent

Megillah: (Heb.) the Scroll of Esther, read on Purim, or any of various other scrolls

mentsh: (Yid.) good man

mieskait: (Yid.) ugliness

minyan: (Yid.) the quorum of ten Jews required for religious services

mishugas: (Yid.) craziness

Narodnik: member of a socially conscious movement in 1860s and 1870s Russia, devoted to raising up the peasants

Oginski: Michal Kleofas Oginski (1765-1833) Polish composer, diplomat, and politician

olevasholem: (Yid.) peace be on him/her

Osip Rabinovich: (1817-69) Russian-Jewish writer of literature in Russian

pakhitoska: (Rus.) thin cigarette

pasternak: (Rus., Yid.) parsnip

peyes: (Yid.) forelocks

pletzlekh: (Yid.) flat rolls

poretz: (Yid.) nobleman

préférence: (Fr.) a card game for three players, popular in nineteenth-century Russia

Salanter: Israel Salanter (1810-83) famed nineteenth-century rabbi, father of Musar movement

Salanter's Letter: Iggeres ha-Musar, or Ethical Letter, published 1858

sarafan: (Rus.) pinafore-style dress

shabbes mikra koydesh: (Yid.) idiot. The first letters of each word spell shmuck

sheyne meydl: (Yid.) pretty girl

shokhet: (Yid.) ritual slaughterer

shpanyer arbet: (Yid.) decorative work employing thread of cotton or linen that is woven into cord, then woven across with metal thread, and used for collars, cuffs, and caps

shterntikhl: (Yid.) headdress consisting of two bands sewn with pearls and precious stones

shul: (Yid.) synagogue

Spirit Monday: in Russia, the Monday after Pentecost

Sviatki: Christmastide

tefillin: (Yid.) phylacteries, that is, a pair of leather boxes containing parchment, attached to straps, and worn by Jewish men around the arm and on the forehead

Third Section: In Tsarist Russia from 1825-1880, the secret police

trakh tibidokh: (Rus.) magic words, similar to abracadabra

tukhes: (Yid.) rear end

verst: (Rus.) Russian measurement, slightly longer than a kilometer

"with a strong hand an outstretched arm": in the Passover Haggadah, a phrase which is interpreted to mean that the ten plagues were really fifty plagues

zhulik: (Rus.) cheat, swindler, thief

Acknowledgements

I had a great deal of help in the writing of this novel.

My mother, Melanie Margolis, shared with me her unerring
aesthetic judgment and book-sense, and my father,
Sanford Margolis, his unending wealth of knowledge
on an unending number of subjects. Together, they gave
an even greater gift: their unwavering support.

Many others offered valuable criticism, invaluable enthusiasm,
sharp eyes, psychological insight, and historical expertise:
thanks especially to Eliyana Adler, Faina Agranov, the late
beloved Chayim Barton, Dan Barton, Shimon Brand, Adam
Guth, Amy Mitsuda, Ari Pelto, Gretel Pelto, Wendy Pelto,
Pete Rushefsky, Amy Schechter, and Mark Timmerman, and
above all to Kathe Hannauer, Ellie Margolis, Marlene Rosen,
and Mari Yoshihara. Naturally, all mistakes are my own.

I am deeply grateful to three wonderful artists:
Dunja Pelto, for the gorgeous cover painting, Eli Rosenbloom,
for the stunning cover design, and David Moratto,
for the beautiful interior.

I am also indebted to the writers of the many books,
fiction and nonfiction, which served as sources
and inspiration for this novel.

About the Author

Sasha Margolis is a writer and performer, with a special focus on exploring the culture of Yiddish Europe. His dramatic work, *The Tale of Monish*, has been performed at the National Yiddish Book Center, and he is singer, talker, and fiddler for the klezmer band Big Galut(e). As a short story writer, he has earned a commendation from the Sean O'Faolain International Competition; his writings on music appear regularly in publications including *Opera America* Magazine. Mr. Margolis is also a professional classical violinist, and has appeared as an actor on stage and screen.

Websites where his work may be found include:
www.thetsimbalist.com
www.biggalute.com

Made in United States
North Haven, CT
14 September 2022

24098658R00203